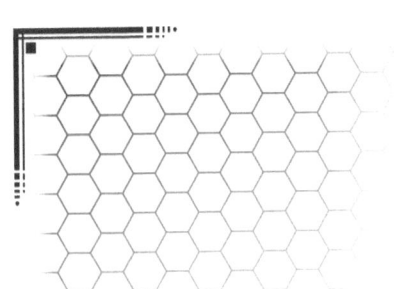

THE
EVARAN ORIGIN

THE EVARAN CHRONICLES

BOOK 5

ADAIR HART

Editing done by Laura Petrella
Cover done by Tom Edwards
Interior design done by Colleen Sheehan
Proofread done by Graham at Fading Street Publishing and Alexa

Published by Quantum Edge Publishing

ISBN: 978-0-9967172-4-3

www.AdairHart.com

To get updates on new books and other notifications, sign up for my mailing list at:

www.AdairHart.com/MailingList.aspx

THE
EVARAN ORIGIN

THE STORY SO FAR

Dr. Albert Snowden and his niece, Emily, were abducted by an alien race known as the Krotovore. They were rescued by a space- and time-traveling being known as Evaran, who dropped them back off on Earth.

When Evaran returned to check on them, they asked to travel with him, and Evaran accepted. Since then, they have helped the people of Fredoria, a planet of human ex-slaves, become a full trade partner with the Kreagan Star Empire, the local galactic superpower in Earth's region of the galaxy. They also fought the timeline invaders known as the Purifiers, a human-supremacist group that tried to change Earth's history. More recently, they tangled with a rogue time traveler while helping a time refugee who was pulled out of her timeline.

This book continues their adventures.

EVARAN'S TECHNOLOGY

Torvatta—his ship that can travel through time and space

Universal interface card (UIC)—a credit-card-sized device carried on his belt that allows access to any technological system

Augmented reality interface (ARI)—an interface that only he can see around him

Utility handle—a hilt-like device carried on his belt that can extend morphable matter in any shape, typically extended into a baton or staff; can also fire repulsion, grappling, heat, and stun beams

Illumination orbs—small orbs on his belt that provide lighting and can hover

Projection orb—an orb that allows projections to be sent to it from remote sources, such as Evaran's ring or the Torvatta

Ring—a ring that can provide holographic projection and also scan

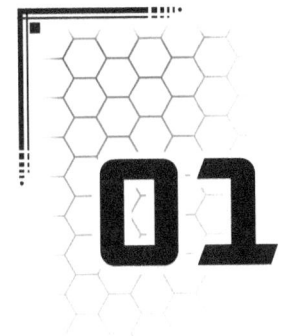

01

Only a half-inch transparent kinetic shield separated Dr. Albert Snowden from the crushing depths of the alien ocean. From what he understood, the more pressure exerted on the shield, the stronger it became. At the surface, he could walk through it, but several miles underwater, it was a steel wall. The shield possessed a slight reflective quality, which allowed him to see his brown twill pants, bow tie, jacket, and cotton vest that offset his white shirt and fair skin in the reflection.

He raised his eyebrows at the two four-hundred-ton gerus swimming outside the shield. At least they had each other. He thought about how close he had come to being with someone compatible a few months ago. It was clear that having any relationship would be difficult, if not impossible while traveling with Evaran, a powerful being who had rescued him and his niece, Emily, from an alien abduction a while back. After spending the last two months visiting several worlds and exploring various levels of technology, he enjoyed the nice change of pace from the hectic nature of some adventures.

Emily, V, and Evaran were his constant companions. V was Evaran's trusty mobile artificial intelligence that often took the form of an orb but could also fly into the chest of a humanoid robotic shell and operate in that mode.

Dr. Snowden recalled that during the abduction, V had been referred to as male sometimes, and other times gender neutral. V's male persona was cemented in Dr. Snowden's mind after V changed his voice due to his interaction with Jay Beerman, one of the other humans who was abducted alongside him and Emily. Even with V becoming one of Dr. Snowden's closest friends, it had been a challenge adjusting to traveling to any point in space or time, and even beyond the universe. With a sigh, he ran a hand through one of the gray tufts of hair that sat on the sides of his balding head while taking in the salty scent that seemed to permeate the area. He adjusted his glasses as he leaned back into the bench.

The underwater city around him was not quite as bustling as he had imagined it would be, and despite the shield humming, the silence invited a nap. As his eyes began to close, footsteps echoed out from behind him. His nanobots started to tingle. They had been injected against his will by the aliens who had abducted him long ago, but he had come to rely on them now. Their enhancement of his senses told him that the footsteps belonged to Emily.

"Uncle Albert?"

Dr. Snowden turned his head and watched as she sat next to him. In her early twenties, she stood out among the city's denizens with her muscular build, fair skin, and dirty-blond hair. He raised an eyebrow at her. "Yes . . ."

"You were about to take a nap, weren't cha?"

He snorted. "I thought about it. It's actually quite peaceful out here."

Emily shook her head with a small grin. "You could nap through a hurricane."

He studied her advanced, lightly armored power suit. She did not go anywhere without it. Compared to her, he looked like a tourist. She had been through some rough times since they had asked to travel with Evaran, and even though it was now in the past, the aftereffects were still visible in her. Still, seeing her crack a grin or a half smile here or there gave him hope. "Glad to see you're in a good mood. Where's Evaran?"

She pointed back the way she had come. "Him and V are at a plaza overlooking the city. The view is breathtaking."

"That doesn't surprise me. Maybe I should've stayed with the tour, but I wanted to be by myself for a bit."

"I can leave if you want to be alone," said Emily, lowering her head.

Dr. Snowden shook his head. "I might nap and you all could take off without me."

She swatted his arm. "Now you're being silly. Evaran said he would be there for a while. I was just making sure you were okay."

He knew she could have used her personal support device to contact him. The pen-shaped PSDs that Evaran had given them were like smartphones on steroids. They could extend morphable matter and shoot stun and repulsion beams, and they had dimensional mechanics and provided an augmented reality view that was useful when doing analysis. He figured she wanted to get away from the tour too. "Well, since you're here, you can enjoy watching these gerus with me."

She observed the gerus swimming outside the city shields. "Amazing they grow so big."

"Yeah . . . from what I read on them, they have a large, flexible backbone, with a strong skeletal structure. Two hearts, multiple organs . . . pretty advanced."

"You think they were created?" she asked.

"I didn't read that, but I'm thinking there was some genetic manipulation. Blue whales are half this size."

"Huh," she said, looking around. "Wow, it *is* quiet over here."

"It's why I like it," he said.

A whooshing sound emanated from a tube nearby. Inside it was a Dukashzeer, the natives of the city.

He initially thought she might have been repulsed by the bug-like nature of the Dukashzeer, but instead it had been he. Although he appreciated their city and technology, their appearance made his skin crawl. They stood about eight feet tall, with a segmented body and a pair of legs on each segment, except the last one, which was more of a tail. Their antennae and multiple-eyed faces were not something he would ever want to meet in the dark. They also had a strong smell that almost made him gag the first time he smelled it. He bobbed his head. "There were some Dukashzeer that slithered by earlier, but other than that, just me and the gerus."

She chuckled. "The Dukashzeer make you uncomfortable, don't they?"

"Well . . . I mean . . . I know they shouldn't . . . but they remind me of what a centipede would look like if it lived in water."

"I'm with you there. Come to think of it, we're probably the first humanoids they've ever seen. It seems all the other aliens here are insect-like."

Dr. Snowden drew his lips to the right. "And crab- and lobster-like. Evaran did say that the humanoid form was not quite as common outside of our galactic cluster."

The fact that they were in a galaxy on the edge of the Laniakea supercluster and that the date was September 9, 2012, relative to Earth, did not escape him. Of the one hundred thousand galaxies inside it, including the Milky Way, Evaran took them to a remote one and to the planet they were on: Bluizra. It was not a true water world, in that it had small islands with volcanic vents. The Dukashzeer had evolved around them and into quite a technological society both on the islands and in the water.

Emily eyed him. "You're thinking again."

He chuckled. "Yeah . . . guess I am." He cast a sidelong glance at her. "I thought you wanted to go on the tour."

"I did," she said. "However, it's moved on. Evaran and V stayed behind at the plaza, just like you stayed behind here."

He jerked his head back. "So they stayed back . . . and you came to check on me."

"Well . . . I get the feeling Evaran wants to talk to us. Given that you wanted to be alone, I think he wanted to give you some space. It's been two hours, so . . ."

"It's only a little past eleven, not even lunch time yet. And who does a tour at nine a.m. Bah," said Dr. Snowden, tossing his hand out. "Evaran must have sent you." He sighed. "All right. I think I've had enough of making eye contact with this geru."

Emily looked at the geru.

It paused as it stared back.

"Yeah . . . let's head back," she said.

Dr. Snowden chuckled as he stood and gestured out. "After you."

She nodded and took off down the metal walkway.

He surveyed the city architecture as he walked. The Dukashzeer zipped around in large tubes filled with ocean water. Although there were walkways like the one he was on, he got the feeling it was meant more for visitors in general. Their buildings reminded him of large upright pills with a pyramid-shaped base. Everything looked rounded to him.

The city was a patchwork of buildings, and the walkways linked everything together. Because the city itself was encased in a bubble shield, it seemed like every available space had a purpose.

After twenty minutes of walking, they reached the plaza that overlooked a large portion of the city. Evaran sat at a table out in the open area, with V in humanoid robot form next to him.

Dr. Snowden knew V wanted to be in flying orb mode, but the Dukashzeer were strict about flying machines, especially ones they did not build. Evaran, in his light-gray suit, with pads all over and segmenting, multicolored lines, stood out next to the tables filled with insectoid aliens. His dirty-blond hair with a wave out front never moved, even with the slight breeze that Dr. Snowden could feel brushing over him.

He squinted at the shimmering of Evaran's boots, utility belt, neck guard, and forearm guards. They always seemed to be squeaky clean. Hanging off his belt was a utility handle, which Dr. Snowden had learned could be extended and shaped as needed as well as shoot a variety of beams. Evaran's fair skin stood out compared to the darker hues on the surrounding aliens.

Evaran waved them over after spotting them. In a moment, they joined Evaran and V at their table.

"Is everything okay?" asked Evaran.

Dr. Snowden nodded. "I was just enjoying a bench and view out into the ocean."

"Understandable. Are you hungry?"

Dr. Snowden observed the aliens around him. Although he was not trying to stare at them, the various thoraxes, legs, and antennae turned his stomach. "I . . . think I'm okay."

"Very well," said Evaran. He half smiled at Emily. "Was he napping?"

Dr. Snowden harrumphed.

"I caught him right before he was about to," said Emily.

Dr. Snowden shook his head.

"Emily said you would be, and V gave it a ninety-six-percent chance," said Evaran.

Dr. Snowden raised an eyebrow at V.

"I apologize. I calculated that the serene environment you were in would lead you to nap."

"It's okay."

Evaran cleared his throat. "Well, now that you are here, I wanted to discuss our next journey."

Emily scooted to the edge of her chair.

Evaran wagged a finger at Dr. Snowden. "You were curious about my origin. I think we can explore that. However, there is a risk. We would move out of this timeline, out of this universe, and out of this plane. I am unsure how your form will react, given that your three-Ls are tied to this universe. Maybe I can record my trip and you can view it later, " said Evaran.

Dr. Snowden recalled that a three-L was a life link layer that sentient beings possessed, a link to a life layer that resided outside the universe. The concept that a universe was filled with nonintersecting timelines fascinated him. Their universe was one of many in a plane, which itself was part of a larger system. It boggled his mind how many layers of reality there were. "I think it's worth the risk." He glanced at Emily.

She nodded.

"Besides, I'm looking forward to seeing what's out there, and maybe even learning more about the Torvatta. After six months of traveling with you, we're ready," said Dr. Snowden. He extended a hand out. "Nothing against this lovely place, but I think I've seen enough of it."

"I figured as much. One thing to note. Although we are going to investigate where I came from, I also want to see if we can find out more on this female version of myself."

"Do you have any more information on her?"

Evaran shook his head. "I do not. However, there are some possibilities I have considered that would require extenuating circumstances. We shall find out."

Dr. Snowden nodded. He remembered fighting the timeline invader known as the overlord, who had tortured and killed a female Evaran in a pocket universe and then stuffed her life energy into a large rift stone. The look on Evaran's face when he realized that the rift stone had her energy was ingrained in Dr. Snowden's mind. "Another mystery we'll figure out."

Evaran eyed Dr. Snowden. "Your curiosity is refreshing. I too look forward to seeing what has changed since I arrived in this plane. We will check in with my main form."

"I thought that you came in to the plane and took on a form?" asked Emily.

"I did, but only a portion of me. The rest of me is still out there. I believe I have found the beginnings of what I was looking for in this plane, so I should probably update my main form."

Dr. Snowden shook his head. "I get the feeling this is going to be confusing."

"Keep an open mind, as I know you both will do. Whatever happens, know that I have been honored to have you travel with me."

Dr. Snowden gulped. "You make it sound so . . . final."

Evaran half smiled. "I did not mean to alarm you. However, I cannot predict what will happen once we leave this universe."

"Gotcha."

"Now, are you ready to expand your mind?"

"Let us do this," said V.

Emily chuckled.

"I think V speaks for all of us," said Dr. Snowden.

"Very well," said Evaran as he stood. "To the Torvatta."

Emily surveyed the command area of the Torvatta. With comfortable living quarters, matter replicators, and a holo room to train in, the Torvatta had become her home. It had six dimensional doorways that led to areas that did not take up any area in normal space. The back third of the ship contained the doorways along with the entrance and an elevator to the roof. She was in the front third of the ship, referred to as the command area.

The outside of the Torvatta reminded her of a hockey puck sitting on a wide-angled cone. She never considered it a large ship, as it sat approximately thirty feet wide by fifteen feet tall. The black mesh panels on the outside always seemed to shimmer a bit. She appreciated the shielding that resided about ten feet out, except on the roof. From her understanding of it, regular matter could not penetrate the shields, unless they were weakened for things like thrust.

To her right was Evaran in his large command chair, and even farther away was Dr. Snowden, sitting in a U-shaped seating area similar to where she was. Between the front and back of the ship was a walkway that had a guardrail on the command center side and side ramps leading to the back.

Her attention focused on V, in orb mode, as he hovered front and center in the command area, with a console that sat on two legs. His four extended segmented arms flew around the three-layered slanted holographic displays. V was her best friend, and even though he was still a young AI, she felt she could tell him anything.

"Analysis. We are within sufficient distance of Bluizra to travel," said V.

Emily knew that the Torvatta could only travel through space via a portal in outer space. This rule seemed to also apply to traveling through time without the portal. Given that they were now in space was no surprise to her.

Dr. Snowden gestured up. "Can we go to the roof for this?"

"Not this time. I do not know what might happen with your form," said Evaran.

Dr. Snowden sighed. "I wish we could see more than just the big screen in front of us."

"Perhaps . . . ," said Evaran, rubbing his chin, "a portion of the top and the sides could be merged into the front, making it all one screen. Then we could see out through the front and top and to the sides."

"Like a convertible," said Emily.

Evaran nodded.

"That works for me," said Dr. Snowden, "but I'm guessing that's something that'll take some time to do."

"I will add it to my list of Torvatta upgrades," said Evaran. He motioned at V. "Take us out of the timeline."

"Acknowledged."

Dr. Snowden gripped his chair arms.

A small grin crept onto Emily's face. This trip was just the change in scenery to get Dr. Snowden's mind off of Jane Trellis, the time refugee who almost ended up traveling with them but instead ended up living in a new timeline. Although he would rationalize it, she knew he was hurting still. She could see it in the what he ate, his listless shuffle in the mornings, and the long nights alone on the roof. A warm feeling spread out from her heart at seeing him excited about his true love, science, even if what she saw was beyond the science either he or she knew about.

She watched as the front screen showed everything outside fading away until there was nothing to see. From a previous adventure, she learned that this meant they were outside the timeline, but still in the same universe.

"Analysis. We are now in the timeline void."

Dr. Snowden raised his hand. "Is there any way to see the other timelines, or do they even have a structure?"

"They do, but it is more of a flow. V, highlight them," said Evaran.

"Acknowledged," said V as his claws flew around the front console.

Emily's eyes widened as the screen showed the outlines of cylindrical flows. It reminded her of wispy smoke on a dark night. Timelines did not intersect, but used the same space, from what she understood. Although one could be updated, they did not affect the others. Evaran had called it localization. She wrinkled her eyebrows. "There's so many . . . I can't even see how far a single one goes up or down."

Evaran raised a finger. "Remember, this is just a visualization by the Torvatta. To actually go to any other timeline, we would need a portal to it."

"Huh," she said. "So if we traveled in a straight line toward one, what would happen?"

"It would appear that we were moving for a bit, but once outside the small space around a timeline, there would be no movement. Space has a different meaning out here."

She shook her head. "Okay . . ."

"We are currently in the small space around the timeline, so we can form a portal here. However, outside of that, there is nothing to travel in."

Dr. Snowden snorted. "That just sounds crazy. Different physics, I'm guessing."

"Very different," said Evaran. "Now, are you ready to exit this universe?"

Dr. Snowden ran a hand down his pant leg. "Umm . . . sure." He glanced at Emily. "You ready for all of this?"

She met Dr. Snowden's concerned look. "Always."

"V, take us outside this universe," said Evaran.

"Acknowledged."

The Torvatta shot out a white beam that began to form a blue-bordered portal with a rippling dark-gray surface.

Emily remembered that the portal and the beam had colors to represent the different types of destinations. A gold beam with a silver-bordered portal and light-blue rippling surface was used inside the timeline. It was the one she was most familiar with. She had seen the colors change for going to a pocket universe.

"New colors," said Dr. Snowden. "I'm not too surprised about that. This portal seems to be taking a bit to form."

Evaran nodded. "It requires more energy. As powerful as the Torvatta is, and how quickly it can form a portal inside a timeline, this should give you an idea of how much is needed."

"Yeah, it does," said Dr. Snowden.

Emily could almost see the gears winding around in Dr. Snowden's head. This was definitely something he would be interested in. As of late, due to her physical and mental training, it was something that interested her now too. She understood why he liked science as much as he did. While she had been a history major in her sophomore year of college, she had never given much thought about studying the harder sciences. Traveling with Evaran and being stranded on a prison planet for nine months alone changed that.

The Torvatta flew through the portal once it was fully formed after a minute.

She gasped at the milky-white environment that the Torvatta emerged into. Her eyes were drawn to the semi-transparent walls that boxed in not only the Torvatta, but also what appeared to be a soap bubble. Changes in the striations of the environment made her think they were moving.

Evaran studied Dr. Snowden and Emily for a moment. "Interesting. Your three-Ls are not degrading."

"So if they were degrading, what would happen physically?" asked Dr. Snowden.

"Your subconsciousness would take over as your higher-level consciousness would fade away. However, it would take some time, more than enough to head back to our universe."

"That doesn't sound good," said Emily.

"It is not."

Dr. Snowden harrumphed. "Well, at least there's that then." He pointed to the screen. "What *exactly* . . . are we seeing?"

Evaran placed his hands together with the tips of his fingers on his lips. After a moment, he asked, "Are you familiar with the concept of cell walls?"

Dr. Snowden furrowed his eyebrows. "I've read about them."

"The semitransparent walls you are seeing are similar in concept."

"And that bubble thing . . . is that our universe?" asked Dr. Snowden.

"You are correct. It is one of many in the plane. We are in what is known as a universal cell."

Dr. Snowden licked his lips. "How . . . how many universal cells are there in this plane?"

"I do not know," said Evaran. He tilted his head. "I stopped counting after a hundred, but I suspect the true number is beyond comprehension."

Dr. Snowden gulped.

Emily narrowed her eyes. "What are we floating in? I feel like we're moving."

Evaran half smiled. "That is pure universal energy. It behaves much like a liquid in some regards."

Dr. Snowden pointed to multicolored strands that connected the outer walls to the universe bubble. "And those are . . ."

"Energy strands."

"Like . . . Daedrould?"

Evaran nodded. "They appear in our universe as exotic energy and are responsible for the unusual characteristics you would associate with exotic energy. I am still unclear as to why your planet has such an abundance of its manifestation. The parallel timelines I have seen have it as well, but none as powerful as the one you are from. The distribution of these exotic energies is an unknown process to me."

Dr. Snowden's eyes traced the energy strands for a moment. "There's so many of them."

Evaran half smiled. "I am still studying the various effects of each strand and its representation in the universe."

"So Earth could actually have more types of nonhumans then, outside of Daedrould, Wildborn, and Outsiders," said Dr. Snowden.

Evaran nodded.

Dr. Snowden gulped. "Absolutely fascinating. I'm guessing that the strand that is touching the Torvatta is from the life link layer."

"I believe so. Even through the Torvatta's shielding, it should be able to reach you."

"Have you been out here often?" asked Emily.

"I have, actually," said Evaran. "Seeing the strands gives me a good idea of what type of universe I will be entering. One of the reasons I chose this universe in particular is due to the amount and variety of strands. It gives the universe a signature, one that I was looking for. Once inside the universe, I searched for a timeline and planet where these energies would manifest in the population. The other requirements were that the denizens were of humanoid form and the dimensional walls were weakened."

Emily licked her lips as she pondered Evaran's words. After a moment, she faced him. "Why was that important to you?"

Evaran placed his hands in front of him, touching at the fingertips. "I was looking for the ancestral birthplace of some cosmic entities. The goal was to stabilize the timeline so that the event that allows them to escape the universe, and then the plane, occurs. It has taken me a while to find it, but I believe I have."

Emily raised her eyebrows.

Dr. Snowden cleared his throat. "So humans exist outside our universe?"

"If humans are what I think they are, they do, but they call themselves the Hoxscarus. They exist outside the plane. Obviously, I would like to verify that Earth is where their ancestral form started, and that is one of my goals," said Evaran.

Dr. Snowden's eyes searched the ground for a moment before looking at Evaran. "If we are the Hoxscarus' ancestral form . . . you really are going out of your way to help them."

"It is what I do."

Emily half smiled. "Well, will we get to meet these cosmic entities?"

Evaran nodded. "Our next step is to leave the plane. I will monitor your three-Ls, and you will hopefully have a chance to meet at least one of them and possibly one of my cosmic friends."

"Let's do it," she said.

"Very well," said Evaran. "V, take us outside the plane."

"Acknowledged."

Emily stared at the screen as a blue beam shot out, forming a black-bordered portal with a rippling white surface. She flexed her right hand several times while sneaking occasional looks at Dr. Snowden.

The portal took longer to form this time. Once the portal was formed, the Torvatta flew through it.

After examining the screen, she was not sure what she was seeing. Morphing shapes floated in pitch-black space and were connected by long rods. It was the absence of any starlike points that caught her attention.

"What is all this?" asked Dr. Snowden.

"The large shapes are the planes," said Evaran, observing them both. "The connecting rods, as the Torvatta is visualizing it, are direct connections between the planes. They are the scaffolding, if you will, of the plane system, which I call Synesia." He perused his augmented reality interface.

Emily wished she had an ARI she could access without having to use her PSD. Evaran's was natural, and he used it a lot. Maybe that was an eye enhancement she could ask about someday. "So we're in the plane system, I mean, Synesia, now, right?"

"Yes. It is one of many, but this one is the Core plane system that all others spawned from. It has many planes in it."

"Synesia is a cool name," said Emily, glancing at Dr. Snowden.

"Your three-Ls are still not degrading. Very interesting," said Evaran.

"That sounds good," said Emily.

"It is, although I am not sure I understand how that is possible. We are outside your universal cell, which is where your three-Ls are tied."

She found it refreshing at times to know that Evaran did not know everything.

"One worry down," said Dr. Snowden. "Going back to the planes . . . is each one similar to ours?"

Evaran shook his head. "Each has a different structure and set of rules. Some are sentient, others are not."

"Huh. So . . . the *space*," said Dr. Snowden, making air quotes, "is some type of void, I'm guessing, where you're from."

"It is the Cosmic Medium and, yes, where I am from. Everything in existence is formed from it, from living beings to dimensions," said Evaran. He rubbed his chin. "I see a problem."

Emily wrinkled her eyebrows. "And that is . . ."

"I am not here," said Evaran, rubbing his chin. "I will need to go find myself."

Emily and Dr. Snowden laughed.

Evaran tilted his head at them.

"We're not laughing at you. That just . . . sounds funny," said Emily, catching her breath.

Dr. Snowden exhaled. "Given all we've seen, though, I'm not too surprised. So what do we do then?"

Evaran paused for a moment. "I will need to leave the Torvatta and find out what is going on. You will be safe on the Torvatta while I do this."

A muted thumping bell sound echoed out.

"Analysis. A set of coordinates has been entered into the Torvatta. Activation is in thirty hours," said V.

"Where does it go?" asked Evaran.

"Unknown."

"Can you override it?"

"It is locked."

Evaran narrowed his eyes. "I see. The Torvatta wishes for us to go somewhere. I am guessing it was triggered upon exit from the plane. In that case, I will need to be back here before it activates."

Dr. Snowden snorted. "That spices things up a bit."

Emily bobbed her head. "If there is anything you need us to do, let us know. I'm gonna head to the roof and get a better view, assuming the roof is safe."

"It will be," said Evaran. "I will not be gone for long."

"I would like to join you on the roof," said V, looking at Emily.

"Me too," said Dr. Snowden.

Evaran chuckled. "I will exit from the roof then. Shall we go?"

Everyone nodded.

02

Dr. Snowden gazed around the roof. He had come to understand that the space between the shielding and the roof was a specialized holo room. Matter could be generated, such as consoles, chairs, benches, and the like, on demand, and there was always a waist-high light-blue guardrail on the edges.

Evaran stood next to V, in orb mode, who was interacting with a console in the middle of the roof. To the side was a bench where Emily sat.

Dr. Snowden spun around in a circle as his mind attempted to make sense of Synesia's structure. Something about it seemed familiar to him. He walked in front of Emily and Evaran and said, "Molecules."

"Huh?" asked Emily.

"Synesia. It reminds me of a molecular model. You know . . . like in chemistry labs. You have those little plastic spheres with connecting rods."

Emily peered around with an intent gaze, then focused on him. "Oh . . . I see it now. I guess it does kinda look like that. The planes aren't spheres, though. I'm not really sure what shapes they are. They seem to . . . change. Some have different colored regions too."

Evaran raised a finger. "A molecular model is a good analogy. As Emily has observed, the planes are not perfect spheres. Remember, what you are seeing is how the Torvatta is visualizing it. It is just a projection based on my input that is being displayed on the interior of the shields. If you were to step outside the shields, you would see nothing, since there is no light, or even the concept of it, out there."

Dr. Snowden took a seat next to Emily. "Amazing. I guess since we're out here, that means you will open more information in the Torvatta's database to us?"

"At this point, I will. You have knowledge that only a cosmic entity such as myself would have."

Dr. Snowden gulped and nodded.

Evaran eyed them for a moment, then strode to the guardrail. A portion of it disappeared, and a small walkway extended from the roof to the edge of the shielding. "I will not be gone for long, from your perspective."

Dr. Snowden slid to the edge of the bench and bounced his right knee.

"Do not worry, you are safe here," said Evaran.

"I know. It's just . . . you're just going to walk out into the Cosmic Medium?"

"I am. I will revert to my true form, but you will not be able to see it."

Dr. Snowden cleared his throat. "Because the Torvatta has no visualization of it, right?"

"Correct. Your vision is based on the concept of light hitting your retinas. With no light out there and no record of my true form, there is nothing to visualize," said Evaran.

"So you become a part of the Cosmic Medium?"

Evaran's ancient eyes glistened. "I exist as a separate entity within it."

Dr. Snowden shook his head. "Well, I guess all we can do is wait for you to get back at this point."

Evaran nodded. "I will be back." He walked to the edge of the shielding and stepped through it.

Dr. Snowden hustled over to the guardrail and peered out. Although Evaran had said there would be nothing to see, he half expected to see a gaseous cloud or energy form or something. It was pitch-black other than the Torvatta's visualization of the planes and their connecting rods. He sighed and tossed a hand in the air. "Well, we wanted to see his true form. Seems it is . . . darkness."

Emily shrugged.

"Analysis. I do not believe Evaran is darkness," said V.

Dr. Snowden chuckled as he walked over to V. "Has Evaran ever talked to you about any of this?"

"Not with my current incarnation, although there was some discussion of it in my predecessor's database. This is a new experience that I am processing, and I am privileged to share that with both of you."

"The feeling's mutual," said Dr. Snowden, raising a hand.

V paused for a moment. "High five. A physical expression of celebration or greeting." He extended one of his claws and tapped Dr. Snowden's hand.

"That'll do," Dr. Snowden said with a smile. He pivoted around. "This just makes me feel so small. I mean . . . we've seen a lot, but this . . . this is out there."

"Imagine having to explain this to your students," said Emily.

He snorted. "I'd have to fully understand it first. I wonder how long Evaran will be gone. V, can you scan anything outside the Torvatta?"

"Analysis. The Torvatta has cosmic scanners, but I am unsure how to interpret them."

"Oh," said Dr. Snowden. He bobbed his head as he wandered over to the guardrail. After a moment, he pointed out. "I think I see something. V, you picking that up?"

"The Torvatta says there are three objects headed our way."

"I only see one thing. I know it's just a visualization, but it looks like a glowing ball of . . . It's a great selector!" said Dr. Snowden. He recalled that they had run into a great selector before, in a previous adventure in deep space. It was a large luminous sphere, and Evaran had communicated with it. It seemed to know who they were and even said hello to him and Emily.

Emily joined him by the guardrail. "What's it doing out here?"

"No idea, but guess we're about to find out."

When the great selector reached the shielding, Evaran stepped back through and onto the walkway. He was followed by a medium-sized, dark-skinned humanoid male wearing a dark-blue exotic robe with golden inlays. A metallic band went around his ears and merged into a rhombus-shaped plate behind his head. His curly jet-black hair was short, and his eyes glowed a soft blue.

The great selector then passed through and assumed a human female form in a white robe with segmenting silver lines to match the human anatomy. She had fair skin, and her long blond hair cascaded over her robe. Various dark-gray straps crisscrossed her outfit, which stood in contrast to her slightly glowing yellow eyes.

Dr. Snowden's eyes widened. "Umm . . . I see you found more than one friend."

"Indeed I have," said Evaran. He pointed at the male. "This is Dian. His true name would not make sense to you, so he chose that one." He then pointed at the female. "I believe you know the great selectors already, but out here, they are known as the Hoxscarus. This one calls herself Pozarra. I have asked them to assume a humanoid form. They will stay up to the point that the unusual coordinates activate."

Dr. Snowden noticed Emily also had wide eyes. He gulped. "Uh . . . Hi."

Dian stepped forward and examined them. He gestured at Dr. Snowden. "You must be the great Dr. Albert Snowden." He examined Emily. "And you must be the heroic Emily Snowden. I'm privileged to stand before you."

"Umm . . . I guess that's us," said Emily with a half smile.

Pozarra knelt before them with a bowed head. "I'm . . . honored."

Emily shot a quizzical look at Dr. Snowden.

Evaran raised a finger. "Dian and Pozarra know who you are already."

"Oh," said Emily with raised eyebrows.

Dr. Snowden studied Dian and Pozarra. "How do you know us?"

Evaran shook his finger at Dian and Pozarra. "Remember, we do not discuss future events in personal time streams."

Pozarra stood, and both she and Dian nodded.

"Okay . . . so sometime in our personal future, we meet Dian or Pozarra, or maybe both of them. Out of sequence thing, right?" asked Dr. Snowden.

Pozarra gulped.

"Is that when we become known as great, heroic, and all that?"

Pozarra looked away.

Evaran monitored Pozarra. "I am not sure. However, out of sequence would be correct. I do not know when or what event transpires, and until that moment, it should be left that way."

"Well . . . I'm glad we got all that cleared up," said Dr. Snowden with a chuckle. His eyes swept over Dian and Pozarra. "So . . . do you two live out here in the Cosmic Medium?"

"I do," said Dian. "Most cosmic entities exist that way. The Hoxscarus are a bit different, though."

Pozarra nodded. "We exist in the Cosmic Medium, but at a different level, which means we don't have the insight into cosmic events like Evaran or Dian."

"Interesting," said Dr. Snowden.

"If we continue to evolve, though, we might move up an APR," said Pozarra with a smile.

Dr. Snowden rubbed his chin. "And APR is . . ."

"Arillian power rank." Pozarra shot Evaran a look. "You haven't told them about that?"

"I have not," said Evaran. "This is their first time outside their universe, and plane, for that matter. They wanted to know about my origin."

Dian laughed. "It's kinda hard if they don't know about the APR structure."

Evaran waved his hand in an arc. "Please proceed."

Dr. Snowden swallowed hard. It was not lost on him that he was speaking with beings far beyond anything he could imagine.

"Well," said Dian, flashing his hands out in front of him, "the APR structure is pretty simple. The structure, translated to what you would understand and using your metrics, goes from zero to one hundred, at least for those of us who are not Arillian."

"And the Arillians are . . . ," said Dr. Snowden.

Dian gestured at Evaran. "Creators of everything, even Evaran. No one really knows what they are, other than that there are those who are touched by them, such as Evaran, making him unique."

"Wow," said Dr. Snowden.

"Anyways, back to the APR. Every ten ranks is a new classification. Plane denizens are zero to ten. Evaran calls them mortals. Those who can travel or possess great power within the plane are known as ascended. They are eleven to twenty APR." He raised his eyebrows at Pozarra. "That's *usually* the cutoff for any entity in a plane."

Pozarra smiled. "Then you have us, quasi cosmic beings. We're twenty-one to thirty. We're one step removed from the plane but not at the same level as other cosmic entities. We can exist in the plane . . . but I cannot say why."

"For what reason?" asked Evaran.

"Your rules."

Evaran narrowed his eyes. "I see."

"It only goes up from there," said Dian. He tapped his chest. "I'm an ancient with an APR of seventy-three."

"Whoa," said Dr. Snowden. He had a difficult time processing how powerful that made Dian. After facing Evaran, he asked, "So . . . what's your APR?"

"I am a celestial, which would normally be around eighty-one to ninety," said Evaran. He raised a finger. "However, since I am Arillian-touched, my APR is around ninety-four, within the domain of the eternals."

Dr. Snowden paused as he chewed on Evaran's words. The idea that there were beings higher than Evaran in his main form was hard to fathom. The ranking system made sense and represented an ordered approach that he appreciated. He took a deep breath. "How do you know you're Arillian-touched if no one knows who they are?"

"There are others. We have spoken to them before."

"I take it you haven't shared your discussions with non-Arillian-touched. Otherwise Dian would know," said Dr. Snowden.

Dian smiled. "You're very observant. We just take Evaran's and the others' word for it. Not like we could prove it one way or the other. Given Evaran's abilities and personality, I trust him without hesitation."

Dr. Snowden nodded. "We do too."

Emily gestured at Dian. "So who're the eternals then?"

"The maintenance," said Dian. "Something has to clean up dead planes, help with the formation of new ones, and the like. There are several dozen of them, and they all have different functions, but they keep Synesia running. They are highly efficient at what they do, and only the Arillian-touched can say anything to them. If they decided I was to no longer exist for any reason, not much I could do, unless—"

"You have an Arillian-touched friend," said Emily.

Dian nodded. "Indeed. It's no coincidence that where Evaran is, you will find his own entourage of cosmic beings like me, Hoxscarus, and those with a lower APR."

Dr. Snowden glanced at Evaran while running a hand over his cheek. "Do you . . . have a listing of the APR structure?"

"I do," said Evaran. "And yes, I will make it available to you."

Dr. Snowden smiled. "You know me too well. I'm gonna guess then that when you enter a plane, your plane form APR is lower, right?"

"You are correct. My plane form is ascended, usually in the upper-teens APR-wise."

"At least that part of you that enters a plane," said Dian.

Dr. Snowden adjusted his glasses. "Yeah . . . Evaran mentioned a portion of him goes in. Not sure how that works."

Evaran half smiled. "Before we continue, we should head to the conference room. I have some questions of my own, and I suspect the ever-curious Dian and Pozarra would like to experience eating and drinking again."

Dian lit up. "Oh, yeah."

"Count me in. I wanted to see more of the Torvatta anyways," said Pozarra.

"Very well, let us head to the conference room then," said Evaran.

Dr. Snowden followed everyone as they headed to the elevator. Evaran was unique even in the power-ranking system, but the more puzzling piece was that the great selectors were the Hoxscarus. Dr. Snowden wondered about the one they had met in a previous adventure.

Emily tapped his arm. "Cool, huh?"

He nodded. "Let's go see what else is on this wild ride."

Dr. Snowden did not know what to make of Dian and Pozarra. Their speech patterns seemed unusual, but because they were cosmic beings, he figured it was the universal translator at work, or planar translator since they were not in a universe. He had noticed that Pozarra had been watching both him and Emily like a hawk. Maybe Pozarra had a lot of questions, something he had as well. He chuckled when Dian's eyes widened as he jabbed a pizza slice with his finger, then yanked it back.

"Huh. Heat. I forgot it can hurt this form," said Dian, rubbing his finger.

"Analysis. You were burned," said V.

"Let's see if we can fix that," said Dian. He focused on his finger, causing it to glow for a moment. "All better now."

Dr. Snowden wrinkled his eyebrows. It seemed even in the Torvatta Dian possessed some ability.

"It's good to see you again," said Pozarra, smiling at V.

"I do not believe we have met. I am a variable utility artificial intelligence. My shortened name is V, and I was created by Evaran."

Pozarra's eyes darted back and forth for a moment. "Right. My apologies." She cast a sidelong look at Dian.

Evaran rubbed his chin. "Your presence here was unexpected. Typically quasi cosmic beings travel away from the plane upon exit."

"The others did. Before your main form left, it asked me to stay behind and await your exit from the plane. Once you were here, I was to relay three messages," said Pozarra.

Evaran nodded. "What is the first one?"

"Multiple plane forms have been sent into the plane. These messages I am telling you now were given to me prior to the last plane form being sent."

Evaran narrowed his eyes. "There must be a good reason for me to send other plane forms. That would violate my one-plane-form-per-plane rule."

Emily raised her head a bit. "I bet that would also explain the female Evaran you sensed. She may be one of them."

"I concur," said Evaran. "However, I do not recall sending any other plane forms." He tilted his head at Pozarra. "Did any of the plane forms exit the plane already?"

Pozarra shook her head. "I haven't seen any."

Evaran narrowed his eyes. "I see."

"You don't know why they were sent?" asked Dr. Snowden, looking at Pozarra.

"I do," said Pozarra. "That leads me to the second message. There has been a breach in Synesia."

"Elaborate," said Evaran, sitting up in his chair.

Pozarra pointed at Dian. "I don't know too much about it, but he would."

"I would say so," said Dian, flashing his hands out and to the side. "The breach needs Arillian-touched help. I was actually on my way to help your main form when I noticed you and Pozarra."

Evaran drew his lips taut. "I encountered a Hadryn spawn known as the overlord earlier. He should not have been there. This must be related to that."

"I'm afraid so," said Dian. "The Hadryn, Immortal, and Elemental plane systems along with other minor ones have breached Synesia. It sounds like you've already met some of their foul creations."

Evaran placed his fingertips together and rested them on his lips. After a moment, he said, "So I would have left to investigate, while sending multiple forms to ensure that the Hoxscarus evolve and emerge. Normally I would wait for my plane form to exit, but a Synesian breach is a much higher priority. That is why my main form is not here then."

"Indeed," said Dian.

Dr. Snowden pursed his lips. "Not to barge in here, but . . . what's the difference between these plane systems?"

Dian smiled. "We're in what you would call the Core plane system, or Synesia, as you may already know. It has the highest concentration of what you refer to as energy and matter. Alaanirif is the Elemental plane system and is filled with elementals of all types. Druuzgortatares is the Immortal plane system and is similar to Synesia, except that each plane there is created and ruled by a being, or set of beings. Last but not least is Tollidrynhalla, the Hadryn plane system, and it houses the most ancient of beings, outside of the eternals."

"That's hard to fathom," said Dr. Snowden. "Are the APRs the same throughout?"

"Not quite," said Dian. "Hadryns go up to an APR of about eighty. Immortals to about sixty, and the elementals to about ninety. However, when inside a plane, everyone is about equal."

Dr. Snowden nodded. "The Hadryn we encountered said Evaran was his equal."

"In the plane, sure," said Dian. "But out here in the Cosmic Medium? They'd run away as fast as they could. Evaran would wipe them out of existence before they knew what hit them."

"Wow," said Dr. Snowden.

Evaran eased back into his chair. "I would not let any of those beings near this plane. It appears my absence has let some through." He tilted his head at Pozarra. "What was the third message?"

She nodded. "A set of coordinates should be activated in your Torvatta by now."

"They are," he said, rubbing his chin. "Where do they go?"

"To meet with Syrilus in a final event," she said, glancing at Dian. "She is who embedded the coordinates to the event when the Torvatta was created. You will also get the coordinates to meet with the last plane form that was sent in when you meet with her."

Evaran narrowed his eyes. "I see. I already went to an event when I entered the plane. She mentioned that it was her last moment before plane creation."

Pozarra licked her lips. "She may not have been accurate in that statement."

Evaran raised his head a bit.

"Back up," said Dr. Snowden with a hand out. "I'm playing catch-up here. Who's Syrilus?"

Dian cracked a smile. "I got this one. I must say, though, you are very curious. I like that." He gestured at Dr. Snowden and Emily. "I'll try to put it into a context you both would understand. Syrilus was Evaran's celestial wife, but she wasn't Arillian-touched. She traveled with Evaran in the Cosmic Medium and to other planes, then died and became a plane herself. This one that were outside of, actually. I knew her well, and . . . ," he said, swallowing hard, "was privileged to travel with both her and Evaran."

"She must have been a close friend," said Emily.

Dian nodded.

She motioned at Evaran. "And . . . you had a wife?"

"It is a bit more . . . involved," said Evaran. "Sometimes entities can become entwined with each other. It is analogous to your concept of marriage, except we do not have genders. However, when we took on plane forms and assumed a gender, she tended to adopt the traits you would attribute to the feminine form, while I adopted masculine ones."

"Oh," said Emily.

Evaran nodded at Pozarra. "I appreciate you bringing me these messages. Nonetheless, I now believe that Earth is one possible birthplace of your kind and that humanity could be the first ancestral form."

Dr. Snowden dipped his head as he faced Pozarra. "So . . . you're what we become."

Pozarra gulped as she looked to Evaran. "Possibly."

"I can shed some light on that," said Evaran, raising a finger. "The Hoxscarus escaped the universe by evolving into the great-selector form. When they appeared, they told my main form that I helped them evolve and escape. They also mentioned that I gave them instructions along with some rules to follow and abide by but could not tell me what they were due to timeline integrity."

Dr. Snowden chuckled. "So a future you will tell the Hoxscarus to not tell your main form everything."

"That is correct. I would have gone into the plane anyways, but their arrival added an additional purpose. I wanted to start by finding their ancestral form and go from there."

Dr. Snowden wagged a finger. "You know . . . this all sounds like . . . some type of planar reproduction or something."

Evaran tilted his head at Dr. Snowden. "Elaborate."

"Well . . . if Syrilus is a plane now and was someone or something that you were involved with and the Hoxscarus emerged from the plane due to you injecting yourself multiple times into the plane and interacting with them, that makes you the father, the plane the mother, and the Hoxscarus the children," said Dr. Snowden. He shrugged. "At least that's how it looks to me."

Emily chuckled. "I can see that."

Evaran pursed his lips as he examined Dr. Snowden. "That is an apt analogy."

Dr. Snowden noted that Pozarra's eyes had slightly widened, and Dian's eyes had narrowed. It made him think that he may have hit on something, but not something that either Dian or Pozarra would confirm. He focused on Evaran. "Given all that, how did you know to choose a human form? I mean . . . why not an insectoid form or a cloud of gas or something?"

Evaran gestured at Pozarra. "They showed me what the ancestral humanoid form was before I split off and entered the plane. Apparently, I told them what it was, and that was something my main form was supposed to know. I was surprised to know it was similar to the Hadryn form."

Dr. Snowden glanced at Pozarra. "You could have showed them Earth. It would have saved a lot of the hassle of searching for it."

Pozarra shook her head. "Evaran was explicit about that. He said he had to find it because that was how it happened."

"I got that. However . . . didn't the Hoxscarus guide the humanoid form?" asked Dr. Snowden.

Pozarra nodded. "We did. Before we left the plane, some of us traveled the rifts and seeded the form across the universes and timelines. The more chances that the form would arise, the higher the possibility of it evolving and escaping the plane. However, a majority of us left the plane."

Evaran narrowed his eyes. "My main form was against their involvement in their own creation, but they had already done some of it."

"Let me guess then . . . the future Evaran said you could and only up to a certain point, even though he knew his earlier main form would be against it. Timeline integrity again. Right?" asked Dr. Snowden.

Pozarra smiled. "That's correct. Evaran's rules."

"Out of sequence," said Dr. Snowden with a snort. "So in this future event that we're not supposed to know about, Evaran establishes some rules that you followed."

Dian laughed. "That's Evaran. Him and his rules."

"Those rules are in place for many good reasons," said Evaran.

Emily furrowed her eyebrows. "So at this moment, the Hoxscarus are in the plane and there are multiple versions of you in the plane too?"

Evaran nodded. "It would appear so, and now I am going to meet Syrilus again, although I am not sure how that is possible."

Dr. Snowden noticed Pozarra's eyes misting. If the Hoxscarus were the children of Evaran and Syrilus, then it would be the final meeting of their parents.

"I have to say, the Torvatta has an intriguing design," said Pozarra, looking away as she rubbed her eyes.

"It is appreciated . . . ," said Evaran, observing Pozarra.

Dr. Snowden chuckled. "You know . . . it just occurred to me that Evaran's plane forms are essentially quantified states of the main form's thoughts in time."

Dian narrowed his eyes. "Very perceptive. I can see even at this young age you have potential. You probably are the Hoxscarus ancestors."

"I believe they are," said Evaran, raising a finger, "and it is something I will verify."

A moment of silence passed.

"I need some to time to think this through, alone," said Evaran. "Dr. Snowden, Emily, I'm sure Dian and Pozarra would like to talk further with you." He wagged a finger at Dian and Pozarra. "Remember my rules."

Dian and Pozarra nodded.

Evaran stood and exited the conference room.

Emily watched as Evaran left. She figured the mention of Syrilus caused him some pause. Dian seemed to have an outgoing personality, but she wondered if that was the norm.

Pozarra appeared to have more intimate knowledge, but Emily could see that it took some effort to hold back information. She looked at Dian. "So . . . you've traveled with Evaran before?"

Dian nodded. "I've been to several planes that he can't enter but I can, due to planar APR restrictions. Sometimes I would travel with his plane forms."

"Planes rules," said Emily.

"Indeed. I just came from the Aztorian plane where Evaran had me deliver a message. Aztoria was . . . a close friend of Evaran. She died and her plane had a lot of humanoids there, but a very odd planar structure."

"As in . . . ," said Emily.

"It didn't have universal cells, just one," said Dian, circling his hand, "material structure, similar to a solar system with one planet, and there was no past or future, only the present. There also seemed to be an unusually high amount of dimensions there, and they formed a network where some connected to the main material structure. The exotic energy, as you know it, is much more pronounced there as well and has a great influence on the plane denizens."

"Like, what type of influence?" asked Emily.

Dian chuckled. "The plane denizens call it magic, but they would have no idea of exotic energies. Although I have traveled with his main form to other places, I can't split a copy of myself like Evaran can. If I went into a plane, that would be all of me."

"Fascinating," said Dr. Snowden. "It would be a risk too, I'm guessing, going from an ancient to an ascended."

Dian nodded. "Always is. However, you're traveling with an Evaran. I'd take that risk if asked every single time."

Emily could see the power in being able to put copies of yourself into a plane without compromising the main form.

Dr. Snowden motioned at Pozarra. "And you knew Evaran's main form too?"

Pozarra nodded.

"Was it like this Evaran? I mean . . . the one here?"

"He is the same to me regardless of main or plane form."

Emily eyed Pozarra. "That must be interesting."

Pozarra smiled as she peeked at Dian. "Oh, it is." She shook a hand out. "Have you met Max the matter mage yet?"

Emily and Dr. Snowden nodded.

"In that case, I can tell you since it is in your past. I kept him hostage on a rogue planet before exiting the plane."

"Oh," said Emily with widened eyes. She remembered helping the Fredorians achieve their destiny by finding and assembling the Arkaron. During that adventure, she recalled meeting Max, a matter mage who was capable of manipulating matter within a certain range. The Hoxscarus had been wiping matter mages out. "We met a great selector . . . I mean . . . Hoxscarus. Evaran said that it said hello and knew us. Guessing that was out of sequence. You had to know us before that event."

Pozarra half smiled. "I did."

"So Evaran knew you were Hoxscarus all along and never said anything," said Dr. Snowden.

Pozarra raised an eyebrow. "It would be unusual for a being of Evaran's APR, even in plane form, to share cosmic level knowledge with mortals. It's one of his rules. However . . . I'm not surprised he has brought you here. I suspect my acknowledgment of you both in that event intrigued him at that point in his personal time stream, at least enough to violate one of his own rules."

Emily narrowed her eyes. She was glad she was learning all this now, but it stung a bit that Evaran did not share as much as he could have in the past. Knowledge pollution as

Evaran called it. She understood the implications and was thankful that at least now they were getting some answers. "Back to the matter mages . . . Why were you fighting them? Max was a good guy."

"If any Hoxscarus saw a being, or group of beings, interfering with the seeding of the humanoid form, they would be stopped. The matter mages are ascended beings, but have a lower APR than us."

Dr. Snowden snorted. "They would be no match for you."

"They weren't."

He shook his head. "This is all . . . starting to come together. I didn't know Evaran was this complex. I do have an observation, though. Evaran says he is a traveler. It sounds more like he is an enforcer in some regards."

Dian smiled. "Well, he is a traveler, and a curious one at that. He has his own perspective on what's right, and what's not, and the ability to enforce his will on those who do not align with that. That's not going to change, main or plane form."

"To add to that," said Pozarra, with her hand out, "when a plane form returns to the main form and is reintegrated, all the plane form's knowledge accrued during their journey is assimilated."

Dr. Snowden pushed his glasses up. "Efficient way to learn about a plane, I suppose."

"You share Evaran's curiosity," said Dian. "From my perspective, this is all very interesting."

Dr. Snowden chuckled. "Yeah, definitely interesting."

"I can see why Evaran enjoys traveling with you," said Pozarra.

Emily shifted in her seat. "It hasn't all been good. The Hadryn spawn . . . I mean, the overlord we ran into had killed a female plane form. Her energy was stuffed into a main rift crystal. Evaran was horrified when he saw it. Well, as much as his plane form will allow an expression like that. The overlord had even taken some of Evaran's plane form. Now we know what happened to at least one of the plane forms."

Pozarra clenched her jaw for a moment. "Plane forms are vulnerable. If Evaran would let Hoxscarus travel with his plane form, we could help. He has forbade it, though, since we are no longer plane denizens and are at an APR level where we can retain an APR higher than a plane would normally allow. There could be . . . complications."

"We'll be there for him," said Emily.

Pozarra smiled. "I know you both will."

Emily chewed on Pozarra's words. To be able to speak with beings like Dian and Pozarra as a mere mortal made her feel small, but it was apparent that she and Dr. Snowden were important to someone of Evaran's caliber, and even to some future event that involved Pozarra.

Her thoughts drifted to Evaran. She hoped everything was all right, but Pozarra's body language suggested something negative was going to happen. Whatever it was, she and Dr. Snowden would work through it, like they always had.

03

Dr. Snowden's lips pulled to the right as he watched Dian and Pozarra exit the elevator onto the roof. They had stayed right up to the last ten minutes before the coordinates activated, and in that time, he felt like he really got to know them.

During their stay, they had gone to the holo room, and both Dr. Snowden and Emily immersed them in Earth culture. Dian and V's attempt at dancing solicited a deep belly laugh from Dr. Snowden. Dian and Pozarra were full of life, and they brightened the atmosphere during their stay.

What bothered him was that Evaran was scarce during their visit. He knew that Evaran was probably going through some emotions, even if his plane form never seemed to show it. Maybe it was too disconcerting for Evaran to learn that he was going to meet his cosmic soul mate again for the last time. Even now, standing at the guardrail, Evaran appeared to be someplace else in his head.

Dian stood next to the walkway leading out to the shield. "Well, it's been great. After all this is over, I'm coming back here."

"Me too," said Pozarra.

Emily half smiled. "It'd be awesome to see you two again."

"We can do that . . . dancing thing again, perhaps," said Dian, shaking his upper torso.

Dr. Snowden chuckled. "Anytime."

Dian faced Evaran and extended a hand, palm forward. "I will update your main form when I reach it."

Evaran placed his palm against Dian's palm. "It is appreciated. I apologize for my periodic absence during your stay."

"It's okay. I understand. When you see Syrilus and are sharing your experiences, show her this one, and let her know I miss her presence."

Evaran nodded.

Pozarra extended her hand out, palm forward.

Evaran met her palm with his. "I am glad you stayed behind. I chose well."

Pozarra smiled as her eyes watered. She placed her other hand on Evaran's shoulder. "You'll be fine."

"Thank you," said Evaran. "You can head to the breach now. If any of my other plane forms were going to emerge, they would have already. It appears I am the only one who has."

Pozarra nodded.

Dr. Snowden thought he could see the silhouette of a fire in Evaran's eyes. He had seen it before, but never understood what it was. Maybe it was Evaran's true plane form inside, and his eyes lit up during heavy emotional stress.

Pozarra slid over to Dr. Snowden and Emily. "Remember, you're all special. You travel with Evaran. Not many can claim that."

Dr. Snowden and Emily nodded.

Pozarra hugged them both. She faced V, who was in body mode.

V raised a hand, palm forward.

Pozarra wrinkled her eyebrows.

"High five."

"Oh," said Pozarra with a chuckle. She high-fived V.

Dian performed a slow dip of his head. He extended his hand, palm forward toward V.

V returned the high five.

"Watch over Evaran, he can be quite wily."

V nodded. "I will monitor his wiliness."

Dian laughed and, with Pozarra, walked to the edge of the shield. With one final look back, he said, "Don't forget us." They walked through the shield.

Dr. Snowden noticed that Dian just disappeared, but Pozarra turned back into the great-selector form.

Evaran watched as Pozarra flew away and then disappeared. "The coordinates are close to activation."

"Did you learn anymore about it?" asked Dr. Snowden.

Evaran shook his head. "Very little."

"Can we stay on the roof?" asked Emily.

Evaran nodded. "It is safe. I have monitored your three-Ls, and they appear to be intact. I am not sure how that is possible, unless the Torvatta has a relay system that is maintaining the link."

"Like a network router?" asked Dr. Snowden.

"Correct," said Evaran. "There are about five minutes before it activates."

After five minutes of light conversation, Dr. Snowden raised his arm over his eyes instinctively as a bright flash enveloped the Torvatta. After it passed, he surveyed the featureless white environment around them. "Uhh . . . what just happened?"

Evaran tossed a hand out to the side. "This is the plane event that Pozarra mentioned."

"There was no portal," said Emily.

Evaran nodded. "The Torvatta cannot open a portal to the coordinates that were listed. According to the Torvatta, they do not exist, yet here we are. Apparently, we were pulled in."

"I didn't know it could do that," said Emily.

"Me either," said Evaran.

Dr. Snowden wrinkled his eyebrows. "Will we need our suits?"

Evaran shook his head. "The shields are off already. This environment can sustain your forms."

"Oh . . . I didn't know that," said Dr. Snowden as his eyes darted around. He squinted, looking out. "Kinda empty out here . . ."

Emily reached for her PSD and put it into augmented reality scan mode. She pivoted in a full circle as she studied the small screen. "It says there's nothing out there. V, you reading anything?"

"Analysis. Cosmic scanners show nothing."

"There is . . . something here," said Evaran, surveying the surrounding environment. "This environment is like a loading stage."

"Is it like the first event you went to?" asked Emily.

"It is similar. In that event, I talked with Syrilus and the Torvatta was given to me as is. There is a lot about the Torvatta she did not tell me. Regardless, I was not expecting to come back here, or at least to something similar."

She scrunched her face. "I find it weird that she wouldn't tell you everything about the Torvatta."

"She said that the time would come when I would know, but that was not the time. There is probably a good reason for that, and maybe this is that time. We will find out soon. Come," said Evaran as he interacted with his ARI.

Dr. Snowden had an ARI in the formfitting survival suits that Evaran had created for him and Emily. It would show up on the inside of the helmet. His PSD also had an ARI mode, and had been very helpful in many situations.

His thoughts drifted briefly to the suits. It would have been prudent to have them on, but apparently, it was not needed. The suits had defensive capability in a shield they could project and offensive capability with a repulsing beam. Emily had a modified version that she had picked up on a previous adventure, and hers could camouflage itself and had more functionality. Maybe when this was all over, some of those enhancements could be transferred to the suit he used.

The walkway that usually extended out to the shield angled itself down.

Evaran waved forward as he began his descent.

Dr. Snowden focused his gaze on where the ramp ended. If there was a ground, he could not distinguish it from the rest of the environment. The Torvatta seemed to be resting on something solid. He gulped and, with one final look at Emily, followed Evaran down with the others in tow.

Once on the ground, he waved his hands in front of him. He was not sure how there was air, but he was breathing. With a quick tap of his foot, he verified they were on something solid, although the lack of any features made it seem like they were floating. He jumped when a sphere of pulsing yellow energy appeared in front of them.

The sphere shot a beam over everyone. It hovered for a minute, then transformed into a bronze-skinned male humanoid with glowing orange eyes and a bald head. His silver suit with black lines rippled as he bowed. "Welcome."

Evaran scanned the man with his ring. "You are a plane attendant."

"That's right. I've been expecting you, and you brought some friends," said the attendant.

"You were not here the first time I was here."

"Different event," said the attendant with a smile.

Evaran drew his head back a bit. "What is the intent of this event?"

The attendant nodded. "Two things. One. To meet Syrilus for the last time before she turns into the plane. Two. To verify your form is pure, and not corrupt. Thankfully, you are pure. Are you ready?"

Evaran's eyes softened.

Dr. Snowden was not sure what to make of the attendant. It was obvious he, like the environment, could be shaped as needed. A big holo room of sorts. He noted that the attendant also chose a male humanoid form, which made him wonder if that was a natural form or something also molded by his and Evaran's appearance. The corrupt comment made by the attendant caught his attention, but he figured he could ask about that if there was time.

Evaran looked down for a moment, then cast a sidelong glance at the others before facing the attendant. "I . . . am ready."

Dr. Snowden knew Evaran did not show emotion well, but he understood it was a limitation of this particular plane form. After traveling with Evaran for a while now, he understood the slightly imperceptible hints of Evaran's facial motions that indicated his emotional state. The hints were showing that Evaran was uncertain, something Dr. Snowden was not used to seeing.

"Very well. Dr. Snowden, Emily, and V will need to stay here," said the attendant.

"Of course," said Evaran.

Dr. Snowden leaned over toward Emily and whispered, "Surprised he knows who we are."

The attendant raised his head a bit. "I am everything you see around you. My initial probe told me all I needed."

Dr. Snowden jerked his head back. "Oh . . . uhh . . . that's interesting."

"Everything, that is, except for the actual event," said the attendant. He waved his hand in the air, and a large black cube appeared off to his side.

Dr. Snowden noted that the cube was massive relative to his position. It appeared to be several hundred feet wide by tall, but it was hard for him to judge the actual dimensions based on the environment. Inside the cube were floating specks of light.

The attendant gestured at the cube and bowed at Evaran. "You may enter when ready."

"I shall be back," said Evaran. He faced the attendant. "No harm will come to them while I am in there, correct?"

"Of course. In this environment, Syrilus is still active. The last thing she would do is harm anyone traveling with you, unless you were not pure."

Dr. Snowden narrowed his eyes. He was not sure what the attendant was referring to about being pure, but it made him glad to know Evaran was. Thoughts of what would happen if Evaran were not pure floated around in his mind.

Evaran closed his eyes and raised his head a bit. "I can feel her already." With a final glance at the others, he entered the black cube.

Dr. Snowden's eyes popped open when he saw Evaran transform as he stepped into the cube.

Evaran's suit and all his gadgets disappeared, and in their place was a glowing orange humanoid with black striations highlighting the muscle groups.

Dr. Snowden staggered over to the cube and took a deep breath. As everyone else assembled next to him, he said, "Is that his true plane form?"

"It is his raw essence, although it is still molded. Give it a moment," said the attendant.

"It's beautiful," said Emily, staring with intent into the cube.

"Analysis. It is pleasing," said V.

After a moment, a glowing silver woman with black striations appeared in the cube. She walked toward Evaran.

Dr. Snowden gasped as a flood of emotions surged through him. He saw what appeared to be tears flowing down Evaran's face. They stood out since they were darker in color than the rest of his face. Dr. Snowden's throat constricted. The death grip of Emily on his right arm confirmed she was feeling something to. It had been such a long time since she had done it. She was frowning, and a tear had landed on her cheek. V placed a hand on his left shoulder. Whatever was going on in the cube must be impacting them somehow.

"Empathy. Very interesting," said the attendant.

As Evaran and Syrilus approached each other, they dissipated into gaseous-like clouds with a lighter tone than their bodies. Darker streaks and lights appeared in the clouds. They swirled into each other when they touched.

"What just happened?" asked Emily.

"They are entwining themselves and enjoying their last moment together."

"That's so sad," she said, gulping. "How long can Evaran see her for?"

"Time is relative. From your perspective, it may seem like milliseconds, but it could be thousands of years for them."

"Whoa."

Dr. Snowden cleared his throat. "How do you know so much about all of this? Just something plane attendants know?"

The attendant smiled. "Not quite. Let me show you."

Emily wrinkled her eyebrows. It was becoming routine to meet others who had already met or knew of her. There was the lingering heroic title she had heard ascribed to her, and that was something she aimed to find out more about at some point.

The attendant shimmered for a moment and re-formed into a fair-skinned woman with short black hair and slightly glowing blue eyes. "I am a part of the plane, hence a part of Syrilus."

Emily pointed at the cube. "I thought . . . you were in there?"

"I am, and also here, although in a diminished plane form."

Dr. Snowden took a step back and gulped. "How . . . how could Evaran not detect you?"

"This is my domain, at least for this event. I know what awaits me afterward."

Emily narrowed her eyes. "So . . . inside the cube is your . . . essence?"

"Yes. I created two time-locked events before transforming into a plane, with each event containing the last vestiges of my being. Evaran only knew about the first one . . . until now. The first event was triggered by Evaran's plane form coming into the plane."

"Oh," said Emily with wide eyes.

"However . . . I did not expect that there would be seven other entries. From my perspective, they all happened at once. I had to split the first event eight ways to talk to them simultaneously. I did not give the others a Torvatta, but I did give them a capable ship that could travel inside a universe. In that regard, the first plane form is unique."

Dr. Snowden gestured at the Torvatta. "What makes it so special? I mean . . . we know it can travel anywhere."

Syrilus nodded. "The Torvatta is a plane unto itself. I allocated a portion of this plane to create the Torvatta. This is something that can happen during a celestial death-to-plane transformation, or if an eternal does it, which, although I know they can, I have never seen done. It is . . . extremely rare. It was my gift to him, my partner for as long as we have existed. You can imagine the danger of giving anyone other than Evaran the Torvatta. It would allow for plane invasions by powerful beings who could bypass the plane's defenses."

Dr. Snowden shook his head. "Yeah . . . that doesn't sound good."

"It is not," said Syrilus. "When Evaran's plane form dies and is being ejected from the plane, there is a brief moment where it has the abilities of a higher APR and can perform a few planar-wide actions if it chooses to do so. However, once ejected, the plane's outer defenses adjust and reentry with a new plane form is not possible."

"Unless there is a Torvatta," said Dr. Snowden.

Syrilus smiled. "Exactly. When I gave the first plane form the Torvatta, I locked down certain parts of it, such as the activation coordinates to come here. This event was created to ensure that no corruption existed in his plane form. The Torvatta would always come here upon exiting the plane, regardless of who was using it. If there was any corruption detected, then I would collapse this event, and it would be an extermination."

Emily jerked her head back. "It's a good thing he isn't corrupted then. What could possibly corrupt him?"

"Evaran's plane form has a lower Arillian power rank than his main form. As such, it is prone to attack by other cosmic entities that enter the plane, and those who have ascended to the highest rank possible in a plane," said Syrilus. "I needed to ensure that during his travels, he was not corrupted by such entities."

"So the other plane forms would never come to this second event, just this one, right?" asked Emily.

Syrilus nodded. "You are correct. The eighth and final plane form wishes to sync with the first plane form so that the first plane form is up to date with information only an Evaran would know."

"Did the other plane forms not want to sync?" asked Dr. Snowden.

Syrilus drew her lips taut. "Some did. However, only the last plane form should sync. I also saw . . . some disturbing things with some of the other plane forms. This plane form can deal with that if he chooses to do so."

"I guess then that we will meet with this last plane form after we leave here," said Dr. Snowden.

Syrilus nodded. "Since Evaran's main form is now gone, I have honored the last plane form's sync request and entered the coordinates in the Torvatta to a critical junction in the last plane form's personal time stream. The first plane form can make a judgment call on whether or not he wishes to help the last plane form. The last plane form has also requested that I withhold some information that only a sync between plane forms can provide."

"Why wouldn't Evaran help his last plane form?" asked Emily.

"That is not for me to say. It is his judgment."

Emily nodded. "So the plane . . . you . . . allow any cosmic entity in?"

"I do. However, other cosmic entities do not raise to a higher APR on their plane form's death. Evaran is unique in that regard. Also, if the plane is being flooded, it will trigger the defenses. However, Evaran is Arillian-touched. This allows him to send multiple versions of himself , as he did with the eight plane forms. Even if one of his plane forms caused the plane to reject his entry, the Torvatta is that safeguard that allows entry back in. As the first plane form is not corrupt, I am allowing this event to continue."

"Wow," said Emily with wide eyes. "I'm . . . glad it's continuing."

"Same here," said Dr. Snowden, nodding. "On another note, we met Dian the ancient, and Pozarra the Hoxscarus earlier when we were outside the plane."

Syrilus's eyes misted for a moment. "This plane form has shown me that visual." She swallowed hard. "I am not familiar with Pozarra, but I can see the Hoxscarus formation, at least one possibility of it." She stepped forward and ran a hand along V's face, then his arm. "You are beautiful. I did not know that . . ." She retracted her hand. "You will find out soon enough. I am just glad to see you."

V tilted his head. "Analysis. I do not understand."

"In time," said Syrilus as her blue eyes flared for a moment.

Emily half smiled. "You sound like Evaran."

"Or . . . he sounds like me," said Syrilus. She squeezed V's shoulder. "You sound like me too."

"Analysis. It is a function of the universal translator that came with the Torvatta."

Syrilus grinned. "Oh, I know."

"I feel like I've been saying this a lot lately, but we're honored to meet you," said Dr. Snowden, glancing at the others.

"It is I who am honored. Evaran brought you here. Do not take the weight of that lightly. He does not see what I see, but he will in time."

"We're just humans," said Emily. She glanced at V. "And he's an artificial intelligence."

Syrilus faced V. "Artificial? Not quite." She faced Emily. "Although I can see all of space and time at a plane level, there is every possibility. I do not know which will occur and which will not. All of you have a potential destiny. Whether or not it occurs, I do not know, but I do see a possibility of it."

Emily raised her eyebrows. "I suppose you aren't going to tell us. Timeline integrity, right?"

"It goes beyond that."

Emily's eyes widened.

Dr. Snowden gulped. "How long have you known Evaran?"

Syrilus eyed Dr. Snowden. "Imagine all the time he has spent involved with this plane. That is but a tiny fraction of how long we have been together. I was created after him, and although he is Arillian-touched, I am not."

Emily could not fathom that amount of time. It was incomprehensible to her, just like when Dr. Snowden tried to explain the number of galaxies and solar systems that must exist in all the universes. She peered into the cube, and a wave of sadness swept over her. A tear formed in her eye. "I feel . . . feel like I can sense how sad Evaran is."

"That is my doing," said Syrilus. "While I am outside the cube, what happens inside can leak out in small doses."

"Analysis. Evaran is in pain."

Syrilus gulped. "I know, but this event had to occur."

Emily swallowed hard. The emotion from Evaran in the cube was still impacting her and Dr. Snowden. Even V could sense it. It was like a spigot had been turned on and a torrential rain of emotions flooded out. She exhaled from her nose and wiped her eyes. "Evaran's emotions . . . so powerful."

Syrilus focused for a moment, then said, "I have dampened them as much as I can. You should feel yourself again."

Emily breathed a sigh of relief. "Much better, but is Evaran going to be okay? I mean . . . he's seeing you for the last time."

"He will be fine," said Syrilus. "Such is the way of cosmic beings."

Dr. Snowden smiled. "I wish we had the time to get to know you better. You're such a big part of his existence."

"Hmm, you do know me in a way. The matter that makes up your body is a part of me. In a sense, you are my children."

Dr. Snowden's eyes darted back and forth. "I guess so, come to think about it. I would say star matter, but planar matter might be more appropriate."

Syrilus nodded. "I suspect it is why Evaran hangs around, even if he cannot converse with me. He removes planar threats that might destabilize the plane with their very presence and also those who would prevent the Hoxscarus from forming."

"Well, we did remove one Hadryn spawn already," said Emily. "Sounds like there may be others like that in our future."

"Quite possibly. Whatever the threat, I have full trust that you can handle it," said Syrilus.

Dr. Snowden wagged a finger. "I do have a question about our three-Ls you might be able to answer. It's stumped even Evaran. If our three-Ls are universal, how can they function outside the plane?"

Syrilus eyed Dr. Snowden. "Evaran cannot detect planar three-Ls. They appear as universal to him. Your time aboard the Torvatta has changed your three-Ls from universal to planar. As the Torvatta is a plane itself, you are now bound to it."

Dr. Snowden's eyes widened. "So if we die . . ."

"Your three-Ls will dissipate and go into the dimension that powers the Torvatta."

Dr. Snowden raised his eyebrows. "Oh. I . . . didn't know the Torvatta was dimensionally powered."

"The last plane form has more on that."

Emily narrowed her eyes. "Being tied to the Torvatta would explain why we could travel outside the plane, but what about V?"

Syrilus smiled. "He already has a planar three-L."

V tilted his head. "Analysis. This must be due to my origin."

"You are correct, young one," said Syrilus. She raised her head a bit. "Evaran is coming out, and with that, my presence here comes to an end." She extended her arms out.

Dr. Snowden looked at Emily, and then they both approached Syrilus and hugged her, one on each side.

V joined them and placed his arms around Dr. Snowden and Emily. With a tap of his right hand on Syrilus's arm, he said, "There. There."

Syrilus laughed as they all stepped back. "You are funny too. An admirable trait. Nonetheless, it is time. Be at peace, my children." She transformed back into the attendant.

Emily swallowed hard. The sensation that coursed through her reminded her of love in its purest form. A great joy swept through her. Although she had only known Syrilus for this event, there was a deeper attachment. She enjoyed the conversation with Syrilus, and it dawned on her how unique this was. Having a planar life link layer had implications she was not sure she fully understood, but it sounded like they could go anywhere the Torvatta could. She tapped V's arm. "Did you feel that emotion at all?"

"It was a new sensation. I am still processing it."

Emily pointed at the cube. "Look!" She stood raptured as she watched the gaseous forms inside the cube separate.

They re-formed into their respective humanoid forms and hugged for a good while. After a deep kiss, they stepped apart. Syrilus faded away.

Emily frowned as she saw the pain on Evaran's face when he turned to head out of the cube. Her heart sank as he began his tortured walk toward the cube wall. She saw that Dr. Snowden was struggling to keep his emotions contained.

Evaran did a final look behind him, then stepped through the cube wall and back into the pure white environment.

She noted that when Evaran crossed the cube wall, he reverted back to the plane form that she knew. The only sign of emotion on Evaran's face was his lips drawn flat.

Evaran took stock of his surroundings and then joined the others. "I have spoken with Syrilus."

"We have too," said Dr. Snowden, rubbing his eyes.

"Elaborate."

The attendant chuckled. "That was me. Syrilus occupied this form temporarily while you were in there."

Evaran eyed the others. "Did you like Syrilus?"

Emily sniffled as she rushed over to give Evaran a bear hug.

Dr. Snowden wiped a tear off his face as he put one arm around Emily and the other around Evaran.

"Another hugging session," said V as he strode over and hugged them all.

"She can have that effect," said Evaran with a grin.

Everyone stepped back.

"She's amazing," said Dr. Snowden. "I can see why you traveled with her."

Evaran nodded. "Yes, and I miss her."

Emily smiled. "She said our three-Ls are planar too and tied to the Torvatta."

"She mentioned this to me when I was inside the event," said Evaran. He focused on the attendant and said, "According to Syrilus, I am to get the coordinates to my last plane form so that I may sync. That form has information for me."

"They're in the Torvatta already, along with the structural changes shown to her during your meeting."

Evaran studied the Torvatta for a moment, then nodded at the attendant. "Thank you. Do you know much about the Torvatta?"

"Actually, no, I don't, but your last plane form would, from what I understand."

Evaran wrinkled his eyebrows. "Syrilus said I would know at some point, so I am guessing I told her that I will tell myself. Before I go, is there anything I need to know about where my last plane form is?"

The attendant half smiled. "Only that the Torvatta has what you need to help your last plane form at the given coordinates."

"Noted," said Evaran. He swept his gaze across everyone. "I believe it is time to go."

Dr. Snowden adjusted his glasses and exhaled sharply. "I feel like I've been through an emotional ringer."

"Me too," said V.

Emily laughed. "I'm ready to go too." She smiled at Evaran. "We're with you."

Evaran paused for a moment as his eyes darted between them. "I am glad that you are. Let us go."

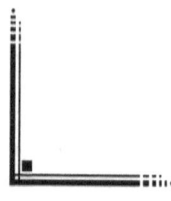

04

Dr. Snowden sat back in his usual chair in the Torvatta's command area. The only place he had spent more time was in the planar cartography lab. Syrilus's changes to the Torvatta were evident.

The left and right front screens had disappeared, and in its place was one screen that started at the midpoint of the ship and went all the way to the front. It was transparent, with various data windows, suggesting that there wasn't any structure behind it.

Looking around, he noted it was like the command center area jutted out from the rest of the Torvatta, leaving the front half open. The command center floor was not transparent like the rest of the front half, but it now had grid lines in it. He ran his hand over his mouth. "This is amazing."

Evaran, in his command chair, half smiled. "I showed her my experiences so far in this plane. She saw our conversation on this, and it appears it has been done. V, run a diagnostics analysis."

"Acknowledged," said V.

Emily gasped as the screen lit up with various pieces of data.

Dr. Snowden focused on one section that appeared to be a Torvatta status window. It had an external view along with a wireframe view and various labels and indicators around it. Another area had a large layout of the Torvatta, with colors, labels, and various metrics scattered throughout. He shook his head. "Breathtaking. There's no need to go to the roof with this setup."

"There is if you want the full three-sixty degrees, but this at least gives us a better view," said Evaran. "There are quite a few other changes. I think you will like this one. Prepare yourself."

Dr. Snowden scooted to the edge of his seat and gripped the arms.

Evaran pressed a button on his chair console.

The Torvatta interior changed to a wireframe view.

Dr. Snowden gulped as he surveyed the change. There were no walls or floor, just lines. Looking back, he noticed that the six dimensional doors seemed to be floating while glowing. It reminded him of a 3-D wireframe model. "What . . . what is all this?"

"Syrilus has given me the schematics for the Torvatta. It would seem the interior is now a functioning holo room. I can alter it as needed," said Evaran.

"Like the roof?" asked Emily.

"Yes," said Evaran. He gestured at Emily. "When you are in the holo room, you can access an options menu. Try that here."

Emily circled her finger in the air. An options menu appeared next to her. She jerked her head back. "Umm . . . okay . . . Guess we can do that in here now?"

Evaran nodded. "The dimensional areas are still the same, although one has changed. As you had to learn your PSDs, it looks like I will need to learn the Torvatta again." He pressed a button, and the Torvatta interior returned back to its normal state.

"We'll learn it with you," said Dr. Snowden. "So . . . which dimensional area changed?"

"The maintenance one."

Dr. Snowden rubbed his chin. "I've never been in there. What was the change?"

"I am . . . not fully sure yet. From what the Torvatta is reporting, it seems it has been added to. The schematics have the details on it, and I will need to research them. There were areas that had an unknown purpose, but now I will learn what they do or were meant to do."

"Syrilus was quite generous," said Dr. Snowden. He dipped his head. "Speaking of which . . . you okay after seeing her?"

Evaran nodded. "Syrilus and I are cosmic beings. We experience emotion different from what you would under-stand. This plane form translates it as best as it can, even though it is limited. I miss her, and wish I could spend more time with her, but that time has passed for now. All I can do is look forward."

Emily smiled. "We're with you there. She seemed like she would've been fun to travel with. I mean . . . if she was still around."

"I understand. Her transition to a plane is cyclical. She will be as you saw her at some point in the future, although she will not remember me," said Evaran. He clenched his jaw for a moment, then swept his eyes across everyone. "She chose to speak to you all. Do not dismiss that as something she would normally do. Something about you three has piqued her interest."

"She said it was because we traveled with you," said Emily.

Evaran shook his head. "At a high level, yes. There is more to it than that, I suspect."

V faced Evaran. "She mentioned my origin."

Evaran wrinkled his eyebrows. "What did she say?"

"She said I was beautiful, and was going to say more about my origin but then stopped. The last plane form has more information on it," said V.

"Interesting," said Evaran. "It is then something I wish to tell myself."

Dr. Snowden cleared his throat. "Yeah, apparently all the answers not already answered will be given by your last plane form."

Evaran studied his chair console. "A wise precaution. Plane forms are limited in terms of knowledge due to when they entered the plane. As I am the first plane form, I would not know what the last plane form knew. Two plane forms meeting can bypass that if they share knowledge. That assumes that the plane forms are actually plane forms and not something else impersonating them."

Dr. Snowden snorted. "Corrupted plane forms."

"Yes. I have never encountered that before, but anything is possible," said Evaran. He tapped at his chair console. "We will head to the coordinates given to us by Syrilus. I see that they are taking us to a parallel universe."

"And correct me if I'm wrong . . . ," said Dr. Snowden, wagging a finger, "but that would be . . . a universal cell with similar conditions to our universe."

Evaran eyed Dr. Snowden for a moment. "You are correct. However, although they may share similar signatures, they may be different internally. We shall find out. V, take us there."

"Acknowledged," said V, spinning back around and interacting with the console.

Dr. Snowden watched the white environment fade out and the familiar sight of space ease in. He walked over to the side and tapped the screen with his finger. "Remarkable. It feels like I could just walk outside. Where are we? I mean, relative to Earth and our time period?"

"Analysis. We are approximately one point eight hundred fifty-two million light-years away from where Earth would be and four hundred three million years in the past. It is eleven oh five in the morning Earth time."

Dr. Snowden chuckled. "Oh, well, at least the time of day is exact."

V tilted his head while Emily shook hers.

The screen showed a high-level map of galaxies. It had a red dot in the Milky Way galaxy and a green dot in the galaxy they were in.

"Woah," said Emily. She pointed at an orange swirly icon on the map. "What's that?"

V interacted with the console. "It is a rift."

"What type?" asked Evaran.

"Space-time. There is an object at the exit."

Evaran rubbed his chin. "I want to check that out after this. The planet in question is nearby. As a precaution, put the Torvatta into stealth mode."

"Acknowledged. Torvatta stealth mode engaged."

The Torvatta angled itself, and a planet highlighted with a green outline appeared.

Dr. Snowden studied the labels. "It's an ice world with what appears to be some type of rocky ring around it. What in the world would your last plane form be doing there?"

Evaran pointed at a red dot blinking on the planet. "We will head there and find out. V, take us in."

"Acknowledged."

Dr. Snowden took a step back as the Torvatta flew through the ring. The rocky portions of the ring whizzed by as he tried to study them.

Once through the ring, the Torvatta entered the atmosphere of the ice planet. It broke cloud cover and began a rapid descent.

He felt like he could just extend his hand out and feel the wind whipping by. With a quick turn of his head toward Evaran, he said, "It's gonna take a bit to get used to this new look, but I like it."

Evaran nodded.

"Me too," said Emily.

Dr. Snowden pointed at the screen area near her. "Check that out. It has everything within a ten-light-year radius." He hustled over and studied it.

"This is your dream setup," she said with a small grin.

He smiled. "Well . . . just look at this. There's not much detail farther out, it seems, but within a few light-years is a lot of detail." He cocked his head, then touched the screen. When he pulled his hand back, a copy of the screen followed his hand. "Woah . . . okay, now that is slick."

Emily stood up and walked around the free-floating window. "That is pretty cool. We can have our own version to play with or pull up."

Evaran nodded. "This will be a good opportunity to learn the Torvatta together."

"I'm on board with that," said Dr. Snowden. He tried to focus on the landscape, but the heavy snow obscured his vision. The Torvatta had outlined where the ground was, so at least he could see that.

After twenty minutes, they reached the coordinates.

Dr. Snowden noted that they had flown into a forested valley settled in a mountainous region.

"Analysis. Facility detected."

"Configuration?" asked Evaran.

"Time Warden."

Evaran clenched his jaw, and after a moment, he said, "That means the object we saw before outside the rift was a Time Warden rift anchor station. It is keeping the rift open by having an anchor outside each end. This is not good."

Dr. Snowden surveyed outside. "So . . . what do we do?"

"First things first. V, perform standard scans. Let us see what we are dealing with."

"Acknowledged."

The Torvatta angled down as it moved ahead.

Dr. Snowden could see the faint outline of four large black pillars, arranged in a square, that curved toward each other into a point above the facility, but did not converge. Shielding between the pillars kept out the snow and insulated an inner area. It reminded him of an elongated dome. Inside was a multilayered mound that had a composition of metal. Various entranceways dotted the rim. Outside the pillars were some smaller facilities that were covered with snow and ice. He gulped. "Looks pretty secure . . ."

"The Time Wardens are paranoid in general," said Evaran. "V, show them."

"Acknowledged."

Emily remembered Evaran had talked about the Time Wardens. From what she knew, they were not to be trusted. She studied the Time Warden that appeared as a holographic image in front of Evaran. Although bugs no longer bothered her, the metallic, horizontal, teardrop-shaped body that sprouted numerous segmented metallic tentacles made her skin crawl. It reminded her of a scaled-up robot version of a daddy longlegs.

The body had light-blue indented rings segmenting it horizontally, and numerous circular glowing yellow eyes extended out like short cylinders of various sizes. The tentacles probably had several purposes. Some held the body up, while others swirled around. Various attachments at the end of the tentacles suggested that it could form them as needed, similar to how her PSD worked.

Dr. Snowden drew his lips flat. "I'm glad I don't have trypophobia, because *those* eyes would trigger it."

"Yeah," said Emily. She furrowed her eyebrows. "So they're machines?"

Evaran shook his head. "What you are seeing is their suit. Although there may be variations of it, this is the most common one I have come across."

"So what do they look like underneath it?" she asked.

He tapped at his ARI, causing the holographic image to change to a blob of glowing yellow goo. "The Time Wardens are a species that exists in the timeline void. This is their natural form. They feed off the energy that a timeline creates. As they cannot exist in their natural form inside the timeline, or the small space around it, they use suits that are lined with timeline energy."

She wrinkled her eyebrows again. "How could they create suits out in the timeline void?"

Evaran nodded. "In our universe, they intercepted a rift that went between two timelines. As matter passed through, they interacted with it, molded it, and were then able to enter the timeline. They adopted the technology of the various civilizations they encountered."

"It sounds like they're pretty intelligent," said Dr. Snowden.

Evaran drew his lips flat. "Unfortunately, they are. They possess hideous intelligence and the ability to travel in rifts and keep them open using rift anchors. In each timeline, there is usually one entry point known as a timeplex that allows entry into it. It is a bit different than the anchor stations."

"Hmm," said Dr. Snowden, rubbing his chin. "Why are they called Time Wardens then? Goo in a can would be more appropriate."

"Analysis. Smart goo in a can."

Dr. Snowden pointed at V. "There you go."

Emily chuckled.

"My question still stands, though," said Dr. Snowden.

"And it is a good one," said Evaran. "The Time Wardens capture anything that comes through the rifts where they have an anchor station. Then they imprison it and slowly feed off the rift energy that all living organisms take on when going through the rift. They call themselves Time Wardens, but it is more of a rough translation on my part. It fits their mentality and what they do. If my plane form has been imprisoned, then they would be feeding for a very long time."

"They should be called Time Spiders," said Dr. Snowden.

"I initially called them something similar to that, but they corrected me," said Evaran.

"Oh. So . . . they're eating your form?" asked Emily. She imagined the Time Wardens at a dinner table, slicing off parts of Evaran with their tentacles.

Evaran drew his lips flat. "Not in the sense of physically eating. They siphon using their technology. The problem is, if they are doing it to my plane form, then they are also feeding off energy from the Cosmic Medium. I cannot allow that."

Dr. Snowden raised his eyebrows. "Then we need to get your last plane form off the dinner table."

Evaran nodded. "Of course. I believe we have some time, and I will need to go through the scan data. Take a break, and I will be back."

Dr. Snowden watched Evaran head off to the research lab. "Situation went from positive to negative pretty quickly."

"Yeah," said Emily. "Evaran mentioned the Time Wardens before. He said we should avoid them."

"That's not happening," he said.

She stood and gestured toward the conference room. "Care to join me for a snack?"

He stood and smiled. "Have you ever known me to turn down a chance to have a snack with the heroic Emily Snowden?"

She shook her head and swatted his arm as she headed to the conference room.

Dr. Snowden had taken a nap after enjoying a snack break with Emily. V had woken him up after several hours, and everyone had assembled in the conference room. Evaran sat at the head of the table, with Emily to his immediate left and Dr. Snowden to Emily's left. V hovered over a chair to Evaran's right.

Evaran interacted with his ARI, causing a holographic projection of an object to shoot up from the table. "This is a planar beam generator. It is a new pattern in the Torvatta database. It is powered by the dimension that sustains the Torvatta. It shoots out planar energy in any configuration. The downside is that it is a rather large device and requires a hookup to a specific internal port."

"Sounds like Syrilus didn't want you to make it a weapon," said Emily.

"I concur," said Evaran. "We can still move it due to its hovering ability. Placing it on the ramp will allow us to fire it at the Time Wardens' base shields."

"So . . . we're gonna fly around and shoot with it?"

Evaran shook his head. "Not quite. We are going to land in stealth mode, then open a small hole using a halo pattern that expands. V will fly in and scout the area. The scans did not reveal much about the interior, other than the top levels of what was visible on the surface. I suspect this base goes underground a bit. Once V has discovered where my last plane form is, I will do an assessment of the situation and figure out the next step."

"That sounds good to me," said Dr. Snowden.

Evaran stood. "V, take us to the coordinates I have put into the system."

"Acknowledged."

Evaran faced Dr. Snowden and Emily, who had stood. "Follow me."

After a minute, they were in a side room in the research lab.

Dr. Snowden noted that the room had a circular pad with three pillars evenly spaced around the edge. He had never seen it used but had seen Evaran in the room before.

Evaran went to a freestanding console on the side and tapped at it.

After a moment, a rectangular object with rounded edges and a firing extension materialized on the pad. It was roughly three feet long by six feet wide, stood three feet tall, and hovered off the ground. An exterior port on the top stood out with a digital screen next to it.

He gestured at the object. "This is the planar beam generator. I have to hook it up to a room in the maintenance lab, and once it is powered up, we can use it."

"It's kinda big relative to most of the devices we've used," said Dr. Snowden.

"That should give you some idea of how powerful it is," said Evaran. He got behind the generator and pushed it forward.

Dr. Snowden and Emily stepped out of the way.

Evaran guided the generator out to the Torvatta exit ramp. He pushed it up to the shielding and then interacted with the generator's console.

The generator lowered to the ramp.

"The generator cannot move while in use," said Evaran. "I need to hook it up while it is motionless." He took off toward the maintenance room.

Dr. Snowden and Emily caught up to Evaran just as he reached the maintenance entranceway.

Evaran paused and tilted his head. "You wish to see what is inside."

"Well . . . yeah," said Dr. Snowden. "We've been here all this time and never seen this door used."

"Very well," said Evaran. He interacted with his ARI, causing the normal white shielding over the doorway to dissipate.

Dr. Snowden peered in and noted that there was a feature-less hallway that led to a lit-up room at the end.

Evaran stood to the side and gestured forward. "Please proceed."

Dr. Snowden adjusted his glasses and, after a quick look at Emily, entered the hallway. When he reached the end, he stepped into an immense circular hub. His eyes widened at the hundreds of evenly spaced doors. There were multiple levels with ramps connecting it all. He pointed to a platform at the other end of the room. "What is that?"

"A control center of sorts. It is a . . . backup. If the Torvatta were ever lost, this dimension would still exist. It has some travel capability, it would seem, but I am unclear as to the rules of its operation. It is different from the Torvatta's approach."

"Huh. I guess if the Torvatta were ever immobilized, it would be like an escape hatch," said Dr. Snowden. He arched his head back to examine the ceiling. It was an arched dome, with transparent sections between the supports that allowed him to look out into space. A light strip ran along the ceiling edge and illuminated the room. "This is . . . amazing."

Evaran stepped into the room. "It is amazing, and also the maintenance hub, with power management and other rooms I have not yet identified. What we want is over here," he said, walking toward a circular port with a handle in the wall. He grabbed the handle and pulled it out slightly, then flipped it up, exposing a hole. After reaching in, he pulled out a device that was attached to the wall by a thick wire. He walked forward with the device and waved forward. "Back to the generator."

Emily looked around. "I'd sure love to see what all these other rooms are at some point."

"Same here," said Dr. Snowden.

"I will keep the dimensional doorway open. We can explore it together. For now, let us get my last plane form."

Dr. Snowden nodded. "Of course." He noted Emily's eyes had lit up at the prospect of learning about the Torvatta with

Evaran. The urgency in Evaran's actions did not escape Dr. Snowden's notice. Evaran wanted in that facility, and fast.

Once they were back at the generator, Evaran plugged in the device. The interface on top lit up with options as the generator began to hum.

Dr. Snowden examined the area outside the Torvatta's shielding. The Torvatta had landed and was only a few feet away from the facility shielding. He saw that V, in orb mode, had joined them and was hovering to the side of the generator.

Evaran raised his head at V. "The hole will only be open for a few moments. You will need to be in scouting mode. Are you ready?"

"I am," said V.

Evaran interacted with the generator console.

A small, circular purple beam shot out from the generator at downward angle and pierced both the Torvatta and facility's shielding. After a moment, the circular beam expanded its circumference, creating a small opening in the shields. The beam dissipated.

"V, go now," said Evaran.

"Acknowledged. Scouting mode engaged," said V. He shimmered and disappeared as he flew through the opening.

The facility and Torvatta shielding closed back up.

Evaran motioned back at the Torvatta entrance. "We can watch V in the holo room."

Dr. Snowden nodded. He remembered when they used it in their last adventure. Having a 360-degree view was extraordinary. He was impressed with the generator. Although he had not said anything, he had observed that the beam sliced through the Torvatta's and the facility's shielding like it was nothing.

When they got to the holo room, it had already adjusted itself to the view from V. Several chairs had been created that hovered in the air.

Everyone took their seats.

Dr. Snowden observed that as V flew toward the multi-layered mound, he could see V's analysis via his scan. Even the beam used to scan could be seen. The holo room gave a very deep look into how some technologies worked. The details being displayed about the mound were fairly high-tech. It had a built-in defense in the form of turrets that could be deployed. There were also small chutes that seemed to be filled with disc-shaped objects. Several of the discs had emerged and were scanning around where V had flown through.

V hovered in front of a wide doorway at the base of the multilayered mound.

Dr. Snowden thought it was interesting that although V's scan could not penetrate deep into the facility, it still showed what he could see a few feet in, and overlaid was what the Torvatta had scanned. This coverage provided a fairly detailed layout of the top part of the facility.

V flew up to the door and knocked.

After a moment, more of the disc-shaped objects flew out. The ones that had been scanning the shielding converged with the other drones. Their scanning range was shown in a light orange as they flew around the top of the facility. V had hovered out of range and hid near one of the pillars. The door that V hovered near earlier opened up.

Dr. Snowden held his breath as a Time Warden crawled out. It reminded him of a trapdoor spider coming to claim its prey. The Time Warden appeared to move efficiently using only four of its tentacles. Other tentacles waved around in the air. Their scanning beams were highlighted.

V dodged the beams as he moved inside the facility, past the Time Warden. Once inside, he began to scan the interior.

Dr. Snowden jumped when the door slid shut behind V. Emily touched his arm. He jumped again.

"Nervous?" asked Emily.

He licked his lips. "It's . . . so real in here. That Time Warden gave me the creeps."

"Yeah, me too."

V flew along a darkened corridor, with only a few spots of light along the walls.

Dr. Snowden did not like the low illumination. "Why is it so dark?"

"As timeline-void denizens, they are not used to light. The fact that we see any is mostly due to the systems that power the facility giving it off," said Evaran.

"Given their size, the corridors seem a bit large for them," said Dr. Snowden.

Evaran nodded. "The corridors are built to carry prisoners they can feed off of. Also, you have only seen the maintenance variety of Time Wardens."

Dr. Snowden gulped. "Right." He noticed that as V continued to fly through the facility, there were not many consoles or interfaces. The hallways were arched, with spaced pillars that had unusual designs etched on them, giving off a gothic feel. Between each pillar was a featureless paneled wall. He pointed at one of the circular ports he saw interspersed throughout the walls. "What're those?"

"Interface ports," said Evaran. "The Time Wardens can extend one of their tentacles into it in order to interface with the facility systems."

"I guess the UIC wouldn't work on that," said Emily. The universal interface card was a razor-thin credit-card-shaped device that could access any technological system. It did not work on mechanical systems or technological systems that had artificial intelligences.

"In its current form, you are correct. Also, my UIC would not work in this universe. I have a Time Warden extension that I modified that should work in those ports, though."

Emily nodded. "From your previous encounters with them in our universe, right?"

"Correct. I am not sure if it will work here, but I suspect it will. If this were the timeplex, I would be considerably less confident about that."

Dr. Snowden wrinkled his eyebrows. "Was it hard to get?"

"It was," said Evaran. "Time Wardens are tough, but if their form is exposed, they will simply cease to exist in the timeline and be tossed out."

"Oh," said Dr. Snowden. "So I guess puncturing their body would do that."

Evaran nodded.

Dr. Snowden sighed as he eased back into his chair. Over the next hour, he watched V fly around. The featureless hallways seemed to be the aesthetic choice for the facility. It made him wonder who built the facility. Maybe there were construction drones. He noticed that V had paused in front of a large metal door. According to a layout of the facility, it was several levels down from what was visible on the surface.

"Analysis. Coordinates are behind this door," said V. He flew out a bit from the door, then faded in while he shot at the door with a stun beam. After flying up a bit, he faded back out.

Dr. Snowden ran a hand along his arm as he observed Emily. She was standing and had her hands on her knees as she peered into the darkness. V had switched to infrared view.

After a few minutes, a Time Warden scanned around as it approached. Once it reached the door, it moved to the side and extended one of its tentacles into an open port on the wall. A clicking sound rang out, and the door began to rise. V flew in as soon as there was room to.

Dr. Snowden surveyed the large, empty, circular room. He noticed that the floor had round seals with several interior rings. They emitted a light that caused the room to be much brighter than he expected. He pointed at them. "What are those things?"

"Siphon tanks," said Evaran as his eyes flared.

The intensity of Evaran's eyes startled Dr. Snowden. He had seen that look before.

Evaran dipped his head. "V, head to where you detected the last plane form's signature."

"Acknowledged," said V. He flew across the room. Once he was hovering over the seal, he began scanning.

Dr. Snowden jumped as the holographic image of the Time Warden passed through him. "These Time Wardens . . ." He shook his head as he tried to focus his attention on the image that appeared above the seal V was scanning. He knew the Time Warden would not see V or the image and was thankful that V would not have to fight it.

The image showed a cylindrical tank filled with a mushy substance. Inside it was a humanoid form.

Dr. Snowden gestured forward. "Looks like that's it."

"Analysis. Life signs are weak."

Evaran clenched his jaw for a moment. "V, head back. It is time to retrieve myself."

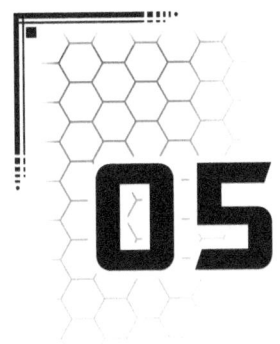

05

Emily followed Evaran and Dr. Snowden to the research lab. She knew Evaran was anxious to get in there and rescue his last plane form, but breaching the facility seemed like it was going to be tough. "So . . . what's the plan?"

Evaran paused at a panel on the wall and interacted with the console there. "I am going to go in and retrieve my last plane form."

"What's this *I* stuff?" she asked. "We're going with you."

Evaran shook his head. "It is too dangerous. Besides, I need someone to manage the planar beam generator."

She pointed at Dr. Snowden. "There's your someone. I'm going with you."

Evaran stepped back as the wall panel slid out. He extracted a Time Warden tentacle end that had a flat base with a rod extending from the middle. Several metallic fingers on the edge flailed around as he fidgeted with it in his hands. He eyed Emily. "I understand your concern. However, the Time Wardens are not to be taken lightly."

Dr. Snowden cleared his throat. "Emily might have a point, though. How are you going to fight them while carrying your last plane form? Be a good time to have that Krotovore shielded transport and someone to push it around."

Evaran's eyes darted between Dr. Snowden and Emily. "A good idea. I have the schematics for it." He shook a finger at Emily. "If you are determined to come, you can pilot it and cover my backside. V and I will cover the front and initiate combat if needed."

Emily nodded. "That's more like it. Will stun or repulsion beams work on them?"

"The repulsion might, but the stun will only anger them," said Evaran. "You have to puncture the body. Your PSD has a special pattern for a sharpened rod. That should be sufficient to puncture the sphere if need be. Hopefully, it will not come to that."

She pulled out her PSD and opened it up. It took her a moment to find the pattern, but when she did, she activated it. She had seen the pattern before but never understood its purpose. It seemed inefficient compared to the other patterns she had at her disposal. A three-foot-long metallic rod with a sharpened point extended with a light glow emanating from it. She furrowed her eyebrows. "What's the glow all about?"

"It is the same energy as the Torvatta's shield. While it may be harmless to denizens of this timeline, it is lethal to the Time Wardens. The more important function is that it can bypass their timeline energy internal shielding."

"Oh," she said.

Evaran walked over to the room where the plasma beam generator had been created. After a moment, he replicated a shielded transport.

She narrowed her eyes when she saw it. Evaran had used one to transport friends they had met during their alien abduction experience. It was heavily shielded and could transport up to two creatures. The one in front of her was smaller than what she remembered.

"It's a bit smaller, but we're not transporting a krall," said Dr. Snowden.

She remembered the grizzly-sized canine-like krall with plated armor that had saved her and Dr. Snowden's lives. It was injured again saving her from a Cepharus, an alien creature that reminded her of a large walnut with tentacles. She swallowed hard as she recalled holding the krall's head when it was injured. "It'll work." She slid behind it and accessed the interface, causing it to begin moving.

After they assembled on the ramp, Dr. Snowden took his position behind the plasma beam generator.

Evaran interacted with the console, then faced Dr. Snowden. "I have set the pattern to an opening wide enough for us to go through. As you saw from before, it will fire and leave an opening in the shield. That gives us approximately ten seconds before it closes back up. All you will need to do is press the activate button once for us to go through and once again when we get back. You can use your PSD to keep in contact."

Dr. Snowden nodded. "That seems pretty straightforward. I'm going to put on my survival suit then just in case."

"We'll be fine," said Emily.

V joined them in robot mode. "Defensive mode engaged." A semitransparent shield appeared around him.

She remembered seeing that for the first time in their last adventure. As powerful as V's humanoid robot form was, she knew he preferred being more mobile in his orb mode. Given what she knew of how U4, V's predecessor, had died, she figured this was Evaran's adjustment to that situation.

"I believe we are ready. Dr. Snowden," said Evaran.

Dr. Snowden adjusted his glasses and then pressed the activate button on the console.

The plasma beam generator shot out a pentagonal pattern large enough for them to go through. After a moment, the beam dissipated.

Evaran waved forward. "If we hurry to the entrance, we will be inside before the perimeter defense is activated. Let us go."

Emily pushed the shielded transport through the hole in the facility's shielding. Once they were on the other side, the hole behind them sealed up. Glancing back, she could not see the Torvatta or Dr. Snowden but knew they were there.

"V, take point," said Evaran.

"Acknowledged," said V. He strode to the front and headed toward the door he had flown in before.

Evaran pulled out his utility handle and extended it into a staff, with sharp points at both ends.

Several drones had launched toward them as they crossed the open area and were downed with a few stun shots.

When they got to the door, Evaran walked up to a small circular opening and placed the Time Warden tentacle end inside. With a few twists and motions, the door began to rise.

Emily narrowed her eyes. Her nanobots were tingling, and although it was pitch-dark looking in, she could detect movement. She had thought that since her helmet was up, she would not be able to sense anything, but it seemed she could. What surprised her more was the lack of a response when they walked across the open area. If they were in sleep mode before, they would not be now.

Once the door was open enough for them to enter, V strode forward into the darkness. A barrage of yellow lasers lit up his shielding.

Evaran tossed out two illumination orbs behind V.

Emily's eyes widened as she saw that a Time Warden had closed the gap to V and was trying to wrap its tentacles around him. The base was on alert, but the fact that there was only one Time Warden meant it was probably understaffed. The door behind them was closing, hopefully cutting off the drones she saw earlier from flying in.

Evaran moved behind V. "Hold it."

V reeled in the Time Warden by winding up the tentacles.

Evaran stepped to the side and jabbed the body, causing the Time Warden to emit high-pitched squealing noises. After a moment, it stopped moving, and a yellow goo oozed out where Evaran had punctured it.

The goo shimmered for a moment, then evaporated.

Emily gulped at the sound of evaporation. It was like a muted deep sigh with reverberation. The way it went limp reminded her a bit of the moment her father had passed while she held his hand. She exhaled and looked around. The architecture of the hallway they were in made her skin crawl. It had arched pillars with metallic panels between them. The pillars had unusual designs on them, giving her the impression of webs and bones. The dim illumination caused by the embedded lights made the facility creepier.

"We need to move," said Evaran. "The Time Wardens are networked together. I do not know how many are in this facility, but there is always one active. The death of the drones would have triggered the alert, but this one most likely raised the alert level."

"Lead on," said Emily, gesturing forward.

V untangled himself and continued ahead.

When they were halfway to the last plane form and in a large corridor, Evaran raised his hand. He narrowed his eyes as they scanned the ceiling. "We are not alone."

Emily could barely see the medium-sized holes above her, but they were large enough for a Time Warden to crawl through.

They proceeded with caution until they were near the end of the corridor.

Her nanobots kicked into overdrive as she spun around. She raised her shield as a yellow beam deflected off it. "They're behind us!"

Two Time Wardens crawled out of the holes in front of them and dropped to the ground. Another one ran along the ceiling behind them, with a second one on the ground, joining the attack.

Evaran pointed at the two Time Wardens in front of them. "V, hold them."

"Acknowledged."

Evaran raised his shield and joined Emily.

The Time Warden from the ceiling dove at them with tentacles extended.

Evaran dodged it as it landed. He finessed his staff between its tentacles, wrapping them up. He flicked to the left, causing the Time Warden to crash into the wall.

The other Time Warden rushed Emily, pushing her back.

Her eyes flared. Although her shield stopped the push, its tentacles were reaching around the shield. She pulled out her PSD and extended a morphable blade. It was the one she had become familiar with when she killed over sixty aliens on a prison planet. With a successive series of slashes, she cut off parts of the tentacles.

The Time Warden pulled back and tried to use Emily's shield to pull her off balance.

Emily dropped her shield arm. She switched to the special pattern that produced a pointed rod. With a lunge forward, she pierced the Time Warden's body. She stepped back as yellow goo oozed out. The Time Warden flailed around for a bit before it stopped moving. She headed over to Evaran, who had taken out the other Time Warden.

Evaran nodded. "To V."

They reached V, who had both Time Wardens entangled. They had lifted V sideways, with tentacles on both ends, as if trying to pull him apart.

"Analysis. I could use some assistance."

Evaran approached the right Time Warden and jabbed its body.

Emily got the other one.

When the Time Wardens stopped moving, V fell to the ground. After untangling himself from the tentacles, he stood. "Thank you."

"Sleeping on the job?" asked Emily.

"That was not my intent," said V.

Emily chuckled. "You did fine." She went back behind the shielded transport.

"That should be the last of the sentries," said Evaran. "I do not recall there being this many at a facility of this size. Usually just a few sentries and a defender."

"Umm . . . defender?" asked Emily.

Evaran nodded as he gestured forward. "They are bigger and much more powerful. Usually somewhere outside the base, although given the size of these hallways, there may be one inside. It is only activated at the highest alert level. I suspect we will encounter it on our way out. Let us get to my last plane form."

Emily pushed the shielded transport forward as she pondered the sense she felt earlier. She could feel the Time Wardens that had come up behind her. If she had not, they would have killed her. It was like she had a bubble around her where she could detect anything moving in it. She wondered if Dr. Snowden had seen or felt anything similar.

After thirty minutes without incident, they reached the room with Evaran's last plane form.

Emily struggled to keep up with Evaran as he hustled over to the seal V had marked earlier.

Evaran placed the Time Warden tentacle end into a circular port on the ground.

After a moment of twisting, a hissing sound spit out as the seal interior began to rise in the form of a cylinder.

Evaran closed his eyes. "Yes . . . I can sense it." When the cylinder was raised fully, he interacted with a console on the side. A flushing sound filled the air as a part of the cylinder slid back into itself, revealing a naked older man embedded in a green foam-like substance.

Emily noted that the fair-skinned bald man had a gray beard. His closed eyes and light breathing indicated he was in some sort of sleeping state. She jumped back when the man's eyes opened.

Evaran raised a hand out toward the man. "We are taking you from this place."

A tear ran down the old man's cheek.

Evaran interacted with the cylinder's console, causing the foam to soften. After a moment, he stepped forward and caught the old man as he collapsed forward. "Emily, bring the transport."

She pushed the shielded transport to align with Evaran and then dropped the shields. Once Evaran had secured the man inside the transport, she shielded it back up.

Evaran picked up his Time Warden tentacle end and put it back on his belt. "Let us leave this prison."

Dr. Snowden squinted and rubbed his eyes as he adjusted his glasses. His PSD lay next to the console on the planar beam generator. He had been watching the view from V's perspective. The way the Time Wardens moved made his skin itch. However, when they tangled V up, it was hard to see anything except a mess of tentacles.

He snorted as he caught glimpses of Emily. She was right in the thick of it and was probably loving it, given his recent observations of her. It had been forty-five minutes since Evaran's last plane form had been picked up, and now they were on their way back.

His eyes widened as the ground outside the front door rumbled, then exploded out. Metal flaps swung up and out as two large Time Wardens crawled out and approached the door. They were huge, at least four to five times larger than the ones inside the base. He tapped at his PSD and contacted Evaran. "Umm . . . there're some big Time Wardens outside."

Evaran narrowed his eyes. "How many?"

"Two."

Evaran nodded. "We will have to go through them. Prepare to fire the generator when we get outside."

"You're going to fight them?"

Evaran's eyes glowed for a moment. "Yes."

"Okay," said Dr. Snowden with a sigh. "I'm on standby."

Evaran nodded, and the screen closed.

Dr. Snowden monitored the Time Wardens. They were milling around and probing the front area with several tentacles. One of them was pivoting around every few seconds, as if looking for something. He noticed that the disc-shaped drones had been launched and were flying around. His heartbeat ramped up when two smaller Time Wardens crept out from holes in the pillars. There was no way Evaran and the others were going to get through that safely. He opened up communications with Evaran. "Looks like there are some smaller ones out, and now drones too."

Evaran's eyes flared. "So be it."

"Still going to go through them?"

"Yes."

Dr. Snowden exhaled from his nose. "Okay. Just wanted to update you."

"It is appreciated," said Evaran.

Dr. Snowden nodded as the screen closed. He inspected the console. It had an interface that was logically laid out. The pattern shaper was a window where a pattern could be drawn or a shape preselected. He peered back out at the Time Wardens and noticed they were beginning to cluster around the front door. Maybe they heard Evaran and the others approaching. Even as angry as he thought Evaran was, this was not going to be pleasant. There was no way he was going to stand around and let Evaran walk into that.

With his lips pulled in, he drew a series of concentric circles in the pattern shaper. He noticed that the window changed color briefly when he was drawing, then settled back in to what it was before. Probably an indication it was active.

Using the movement buttons, he repositioned the planar beam generator to aim at the closest large Time Warden. He pressed the activate button.

A concentric beam shot through the Torvatta's and facility's shields and ripped into the side of the large Time Warden, leaving a gaping hole. Yellow liquid oozed out. The drone's reaction was immediate as they flew over. Several of the smaller Time Wardens had pivoted and faced the Torvatta.

He gulped. The thought that maybe the drones could get through the hole in the ten seconds it would be open crossed his mind. He collapsed his PSD into pen mode and shot stun beams out at the drones.

Zzzt!

One of the drones dropped to the ground. Another fired an energy beam, hitting the generator. The generator's console flickered.

His eyes widened. He had not considered that they might be able to fire from that range.

Two drones flew closer as the smaller Time Wardens fired.

Dr. Snowden ran in front of the generator and put up his personal shield from his left forearm. He was glad he had put his suit on.

The hole in the Torvatta and facility shielding sealed up.

Dr. Snowden let out a measured breath. He watched as the front door opened and Evaran and V burst forward.

The drones and smaller Time Wardens pivoted around and headed back to the entrance.

Dr. Snowden could see Emily behind the shielded transport, shooting out at the drones. He realized he needed to change the pattern back. He tried pulling up the pattern shaper, but the fading in and out of the screen made it difficult. After a moment, he was able to draw a door shape.

He took a moment to assess the situation. V and Emily were headed over to the Torvatta while Evaran had engaged the remaining large Time Warden.

The two smaller Time Wardens approached V. The drones and Time Wardens fired, but they did not penetrate V's shielding.

V grabbed one of the Time Wardens, then dragged it along to the second one.

Emily took potshots at the drones while using the shielded transport as cover. She slid the transport up to V, then burst around the side and stabbed both Time Wardens in their bodies. After the smaller Time Wardens stopped moving and the drones were down, she got back behind the transport and began to push forward.

Dr. Snowden gulped.

V untangled himself and escorted Emily back up to the Torvatta.

Dr. Snowden waved them off to the side and fired the generator.

Emily pushed the transport through the shielding hole. V followed her in.

Dr. Snowden observed that Evaran was deflecting the large Time Warden's beams and they were circling each other. "What's Evaran doing?"

"Analysis. He asked me to tell the both of you to remain here."

"What?" asked Emily. "We need to help him!"

"This is personal," said V.

Dr. Snowden could see Emily simmering. He understood that Evaran did not want to endanger anyone else and knew Evaran could probably shield and run to the Torvatta. It was obvious Evaran had made another choice.

Evaran had extended his utility handle into a staff. One end had a circular blade; the other was pointed.

The Time Warden tried to pull Evaran off balance by controlling Evaran's shield.

Evaran angled his shield down, exposing its tentacles. With a swipe, he sliced through them.

The Time Warden reeled back for a moment.

Evaran ran forward and jumped onto its body. He spun his staff around several times, slicing off the tentacles where they were attached.

The Time Warden body fell to the ground.

He stabbed it several times with the pointed end.

Its body broke apart into several pieces.

He jabbed at the yellow liquid that oozed out.

The liquid evaporated.

He backed up and, with a running start, kicked the Time Warden across the open area, where it bounced off one of the pillars. After holstering his utility handle, he headed to the Torvatta.

"If I didn't know better . . . I'd say he's pissed off," said Dr. Snowden.

Emily nodded. "I would be too if I saw what they did to another version of me."

"Analysis. One of my predecessors, HA4, was killed by the Time Wardens."

"Oh . . . yeah . . . that and feeding off a plane form would do it," said Dr. Snowden.

V tilted his head. "We should make sure Evaran is pissed on, not off."

Dr. Snowden chortled as he tapped V's arm. "Yeah . . . Doesn't work like that." He eyed Emily. He remembered she had a nanobot duplicate. It gave its life to not only save a timeline, but also, he thought, to get back at the being that had imprisoned Emily on a prison planet for nine months. He knew that they had synced, and he wondered if Evaran could feel anything from the last plane form without a sync. Given everything that had happened in the last day or so, he could understand why Evaran was angry. His face might not show it, but his actions did.

When Evaran approached the Torvatta, he stepped to the side and signaled at Dr. Snowden, who tapped at the generator console.

When the hole opened and the beam dissipated, Evaran stepped through onto the ramp. He motioned forward. "V, take us out."

"Acknowledged," said V. He exited the ramp and flew inside.

Evaran motioned forward. "To the medical lab."

When they got to there, Evaran gestured for Emily to push the shielded transport alongside one of the slabs in the middle of the room. After she complied, he dropped the shielding and scanned the last plane form with his ring. His jaw clenched for a moment. "He is dying."

Emily gasped.

Dr. Snowden rubbed the back of his neck as he faced Evaran. "Is there anything we can do to help?"

Evaran shook his head. "Not that I am aware of. Typically when a plane form dies, it is either re-formed, absorbed by the plane, or ejected out of the plane. The plane form can also permanently disable the ability to re-form. If the plane form is damaged or severely weakened, it will not be powerful enough to re-form or leave the plane, and the plane will absorb it, or as I have learned, it will be integrated into the dimension that powers the Torvatta. Every plane is different, though. Some will expel it regardless of state into the Cosmic Medium, while others will absorb it. Some allow re-formation, others do not."

"Which is this one?" asked Emily.

"This plane allows re-formation and ejection."

The old man's eyes slowly opened.

"Can you hear us?" asked Evaran.

The old man cleared his throat. In a garbled voice, he said, "Yes, I can. It's good to hear another voice." He rolled his head to the side as his eyes scrutinized Evaran. "I sense . . . we are the same."

Evaran nodded. "I am the first plane form. You are the last, from what I understand."

The old man smiled, then swallowed hard. "I . . . wasn't sure if you would come before . . ." He coughed.

"Syrilus sent me here."

The old man's eyes misted. "I miss her."

"I do too."

The old man took a deep breath through his nose. "You've probably already detected that I'm dying." He struggled to prop himself up on his elbows. "We're in the Torvatta."

Evaran nodded.

"Good. You have a lot of questions . . . and I have answers," said the old man. He coughed and lay back down. "I sense you are not corrupted."

"And I sense the same about you," said Evaran.

The old man sighed. "I can barely hold this form anymore. If you allow me to re-form, I can sync with you and answer any and all questions you may have."

"Of course. Your plane form is greatly weakened. However, I am unsure of how to help you."

"Take me to the re-formation chamber."

Evaran narrowed his eyes. "I am not aware of any re-formation chamber."

The old man gestured outward. "It's in the maintenance area, fifth door to the right of the entrance to the main room."

"Are there any special instructions to operate it?"

The old man shook his head. "Just push me in there and close the door. We need to hurry. I . . . don't want to be absorbed."

"Understood." Evaran got behind the shielded transport and hustled out of the room, followed by Dr. Snowden and Emily. When he got to the re-formation chamber, he opened the door and pushed the shielded transport in to a pitch-black room. After a moment, he exited it and accessed the door console.

The re-formation chamber door closed as a part of the wall next to the door went transparent. A dim light appeared in the room. The outline of the shielded transport formed on the wall.

Evaran gestured toward the chamber. "He said it will take about an hour."

"I'm not going anywhere," said Dr. Snowden.

Emily bobbed her head. "Me either."

Evaran eyed both of them. "Very well." He tapped at his ARI, and several chairs appeared in front of the wall. "We can sit while we wait."

After everyone sat, Emily motioned at the room. "So he's going to re-form now?"

"Yes. A re-formation, if you will. As his plane form is greatly weakened, he would be absorbed. This chamber must give him a boost of planar and cosmic energy so he can re-form and protect him while doing so."

Dr. Snowden remembered that not only had the overlord from a previous adventure killed a female Evaran, but he had also siphoned off a part of Evaran. While they had tried to resolve another issue, the overlord came back to life with a new body. "So the overlord was able to change because he was not greatly weakened."

"That is correct. If anything, he was greatly enhanced. Being a Hadryn spawn was probably also a factor."

"Huh," said Dr. Snowden. He rubbed his chin. "So . . . a new form then. Does the old form get any input in what it will change into?"

Evaran shrugged. "Only aspects can be defined. I typically do not re-form but have on other planes before."

"So it's pretty rare then," said Emily.

"That is correct. Usually I go into a plane, and come out. One plane, one plane form. The plane also adjusts, so reentry is not an option. Most planes prohibit re-formation. The Torvatta has changed that, though."

Dr. Snowden and Emily nodded.

Evaran half smiled. "This re-formation chamber is new to me. In the rare cases I have re-formed, I did not need a chamber. I suspect this chamber is of the last plane form and Syrilus's design."

"Cool," said Emily.

Dr. Snowden focused on the shielded transport in the room. "I guess we wait then."

06

Over the next forty-five minutes, Dr. Snowden chatted with Emily and V, in body mode, who had joined them. He cast an occasional look at Evaran pacing around the room with his hands behind his back. There were many questions he wanted to ask, but Evaran seemed to want to be alone with his thoughts.

It reminded him of Dan's final moments, his deceased older brother and Emily's father. Dr. Snowden had paced around the room similarly to Evaran, while Emily held Dan's hand until the end. His chest tightened as the memory cascaded over him. He wiped his eyes as they watered.

"Hey, you okay?" asked Emily, tilting her head.

Dr. Snowden nodded. "Yeah . . . was just thinking of Dan is all."

"Oh," she said, looking down and away.

"Analysis," said V, looking at Emily. "Your heartbeat has increased."

She pulled her lips in. "It's . . . it's nothing."

V nodded. "I am here if you need me."

"We know," said Dr. Snowden, laying a hand on V's shoulder. His attention focused on a light inside the re-formation chamber. "Something's happening." He hustled over to the transparent wall, where the others joined him.

The old man began to tremble as a light-orange glow began to intensify around him. After a moment, the man yelled out as his skin dissipated, leaving a light-orange humanoid form with black striations. After another moment, the form collapsed into a swirling cloud with fast-moving objects in it.

Dr. Snowden remembered Evaran in both of these forms, but the cloud he was seeing was much smaller. Maybe the Time Wardens took so much that this was the end result. His eye caught streams of orange tendrils emanating from small holes in the ceiling. He pointed at them. "Look!"

The tendrils connected with the raw essence, boosting its size and intensity. When it had doubled in size several times, it exploded in a bright light.

Dr. Snowden raised his left arm and tucked his head, as the bright light seemed to persist for a few seconds. When it stopped, he checked around and shot Emily a look.

They both peeped out, and when it was safe to look again, they peered into the room. It had gone pitch-black again, and the silhouette had disappeared.

V stepped forward.

Evaran shook his head. "It is okay. Defensive mode is not needed."

"Acknowledged."

"What happened?" asked Emily.

The door to the room slid open. Out stepped a muscular six-foot female with a suit slightly different from Evaran's. Although she had fair skin like Evaran, her long black hair pulled back into a ponytail stood in stark contrast. On her face was a thin metal band that stretched across her forehead and extended down the sides. Two flat circular metallic pieces stood out near each shoulder and attached to a cape that flowed down her back to her calves. She strode forward. "I happened."

Evaran scanned the woman with his ring. "You are at full strength."

"Oh yeah, and it feels good," said the woman.

"Umm . . . hi," said Emily.

The woman snapped her head toward Emily.

Dr. Snowden gulped. "So . . . uhh . . . do we call you Evaran too?"

The woman eyed Dr. Snowden for a moment. "Since I'm the last plane form and an Evaran, and there is already an Evaran here, you can call me Levaran. Obviously, when it is just me, I will go by Evaran."

Emily stepped forward and extended a hand. "It's nice to meet you."

Levaran shook Emily's hand, then held it up. She ran her other hand over Emily's. After a few looks over Emily, she said, "Hoxscarus' ancestral form."

"I believe that they are, and they call themselves human," said Evaran.

Levaran smiled. "You actually found them, well, at least one possibility."

Evaran nodded.

Levaran walked over to Dr. Snowden and ran a hand across his cheek. "Amazing." She tilted her head at Evaran. "And they travel with you?"

"They do, and can be quite feisty."

She walked over to V and ran her hands across his upper chest. "You're beautiful."

"Analysis. Syrilus mentioned this as well. I believe it has to do with my origin."

She chuckled. "Of course it does. Your inner container was created alongside the Torvatta when the first plane form entered the plane, and it houses both planar and cosmic energy. The outer container is the plane form, and would be built. I don't know, though, if your current plane form was the first."

Evaran examined V. "He was not. The first one introduced itself as D."

Levaran nodded.

V tilted his head. "Analysis. This means I possess a combination of energy similar to Evaran and Syrilus."

Emily's eyes widened. "So . . . V is Evaran and Syrilus's child?"

"In a sense," said Levaran. "He is a raw essence that is unique."

Evaran eyed V. "I did not know that your essence was mixed. My scans indicated your inner container was just planar energy."

V swiveled his head toward Evaran, then Levaran.

Levaran nodded. "Syrilus kept some things from you. From all of us actually, at least until I met her."

"For what purpose?" asked Evaran.

She grimaced. "As you're here, then you know she met all plane forms initially, splitting that event eight ways. You got the Torvatta, the rest of us got a ship that could travel within the universe. She sensed that there were . . . abominations in some of the futures she saw. Part Evaran, part . . . something else. As I was the last plane form, I decided to have you sync with me after your second meeting, assuming your plane form was pure. The other plane forms agreed, or at least that is what Syrilus told me. It appears you have had your second meeting already and met Pozarra, the Hoxscarus I asked to stay behind and relay my messages before I entered the plane."

Evaran narrowed his eyes. "Pozarra has relayed your messages. What was the something else?"

"Syrilus said some were corrupted by various energies. Some were extra planar in origin."

Evaran rubbed his chin. "I see. She saw that I was not corrupted, and directed me to you so we could sync. I suspect she would have exterminated me if I were corrupted."

Levaran pulled her lips in for a moment. "That's right." She stood back and swung her head around. Then she ran her hands over her suit and body parts. With a yank of her ponytail, she chuckled. "It appears I'm female."

Dr. Snowden adjusted his glasses while looking at Levaran. "Were you able to choose what you wanted to become?"

Levaran shook her head. "It doesn't work like that. However, I was able to signify elements I wanted."

"Oh," said Dr. Snowden. "Well, I have noticed you speak differently."

"Every plane form can choose how they speak when created," said Levaran. She waved her hand out in an arc. "Before we go any further, I wanted to say . . . thank you for my second chance."

Evaran nodded.

"The Time Wardens . . ."

Dr. Snowden chuckled. "Evaran took care of them, and then some."

Evaran met Levaran's gaze, and then they nodded in sync.

Dr. Snowden cleared his throat. "So to be sure that I'm understanding this . . . you're both Evaran, just different plane forms."

"You got it," said Levaran. "Although we're the same in the Cosmic Medium and would merge into our main form, our plane forms take on a unique identity, shaped by the form we take. The plane forms are, in essence, sentient suits made up of planar matter that has its own life link layer. Our raw essence is a dimensional overlay on the body. That allows each plane form to have its own take on things, while still being an Evaran. Our plane forms are quite resilient."

"We've seen it," said Emily.

Dr. Snowden chuckled. "We don't mean to rapid fire questions off of you, it's just . . . we've traveled with Evaran for so long and are just now learning all of this."

"It's okay," said Levaran. She tilted her head. "Your curiosity is refreshing. I can already see why he travels with you."

Emily half smiled. "Speaking of which . . . do you remember anything from your old plane form, the old man?"

Levaran nodded. "I do. My previous form was unique, as is this one, but the memories are the same. However, new memories from this plane form will take precedence." She took a deep breath. "I'd been preparing to no longer exist."

"So . . . how'd you end up with the Time Wardens?" asked Emily.

Levaran clenched her jaw for a moment. "I had been on a planet with a civilization that was technologically primitive. The Time Wardens found it, and the civilization tried to protect me. The Time Wardens rained destruction upon them, and although I was able to stop a few, it was clear I had to leave."

"In your universal ship," said Emily.

Levaran nodded. "Its shielding was subpar to the Torvatta's, but still powerful. When I tried to leave the planet, the Time Wardens were able to grapple my ship. Although they could not breach my shielding, they dragged my ship to the edge of a black hole."

"Whoa," said Dr. Snowden.

Levaran chuckled. "Whoa is right. I had a choice. I could either go into the black hole, which would crush my ship or surrender and have some time to formulate a plan. They accepted my surrender and . . . ," she said, with eyes flaring, "ended up where you rescued me. I was there for approximately one thousand three hundred ten of your years."

"Oh, wow," said Emily. "That must have been torturous."

"It was, and they slowly fed off me the whole time," said Levaran. She glanced at Evaran. "How'd you get inside their base?"

Evaran nodded. "Syrilus gave us a pattern for a planar beam generator to breach their shields. I also used the end of one of their tentacles to access their doors."

"You've fought them before . . ."

"I have, and they no longer possess a timeplex in the timeline that I inhabit."

"I was not strong enough and underestimated the Time Wardens," said Levaran. She clenched her jaw. "I won't make that mistake again."

Evaran nodded. "I suspect that will have some influence on your new plane form. The Time Wardens most likely have a timeplex in this timeline. I will help you shut it down. However, before we do that, I need to update my UIC for this universe, and you will need one as well. It would also be helpful for you to travel with this timeline's version of Dr. Snowden and Emily."

"Say what?" asked Dr. Snowden.

"Huh?" asked Emily.

Evaran half smiled. "I have found that travel with you both has broadened my perspective. I value your insight and am glad you are with me. I believe Levaran could benefit from this as well."

Dr. Snowden bobbed his head. "So we're going to meet our parallel-universe duplicates?"

"To them, you would be the duplicates," said Evaran.

Emily shook her head and exhaled. "Can't be any crazier than meeting a nanobot duplicate." She nodded at V. "Don't forget him."

"I have not," said Evaran.

"I can work with that," said Levaran. She nodded her head back at the re-formation chamber. "There are two containers in there. They were filled during my re-formation. One is for a new Torvatta, mainly the Torvatta's dimensional doors, access to shielding, and the planar dimension that powers the Torvatta. The other is for V, or my version of it. Assuming you have no issues with another Torvatta, I will need a shell to work from. That could take a while to replicate."

Evaran raised a finger. "There are no concerns here. As for the shell, I may know a few friends who can help with that."

"Excellent," said Levaran.

Dr. Snowden wagged a finger. "So that's an additional benefit of the chamber. Not just to boost you, but create containers of re-formation energy to be used as needed."

Levaran nodded. "The boost was my design, but the containers were Syrilus's. The re-formation chamber would only exist if the first plane form was not corrupted. I am thankful he was not."

"Did you have a V?" asked Emily.

Levaran's eyes lit up. "A2 was killed trying to save me when I was forced to leave my ship by the Time Wardens."

Evaran's eyes glowed for a moment. "They will be dealt with. This, I promise you."

Evaran and Levaran synced gazes, and then nodded.

"Levaran and I have some things to discuss," said Evaran. "It is almost six p.m. Earth time. Let us meet tomorrow morning at ten a.m. in the conference room."

"Going to do that sync thing?" asked Dr. Snowden.

Evaran nodded.

"All right," said Dr. Snowden. He inhaled as he dipped his head. It was apparent the Time Wardens had all but destroyed Levaran. Now with two plane forms, and a bigger group, he knew they would be in for a fight, but he suspected it would not go in the Time Wardens' favor this time. Being on the opposite side of one determined Evaran was bad enough, but two was suicidal. Although Evaran showed little emotion, the anger and determination on Levaran's face was all too easy to read.

The prospect of meeting this universe's version of him and Emily intrigued him. Although he remembered Nanobot Emily was a duplicate of Emily, he was not sure what he would make of meeting his duplicate. He understood the Torvatta's origin now but would have a chance to see one built. His nerves pulsed at the thought of everything he was learning. He would even get to see Levaran's version of V created. The friends that Evaran mentioned did not ring any bells for him, but he suspected they would be powerful. As he left the maintenance room, Emily half smiled at him. Given everything they had seen, he was glad she could share in this experience with her.

Emily eyed the blank holo room. She was up early at 7:00 a.m. and figured she would get a workout in. The previous night, she and Dr. Snowden had gotten dinner and then gone their separate ways. After that, she had a training session with V, which tuckered her out. The night ended with her adding notes to her virtual workspace with information she had learned. There was a lot to add. It was not long before she had fallen asleep.

Before she had gone to the holo room, she had searched around. Both Evaran and Levaran were nowhere to be seen. She figured they probably went somewhere private to do the syncing thing for the rest of the night and maybe were still at it. What would be synced or how long it would take was a mystery. She wondered if they would tell her. With a smirk on her face, she stretched around. The border of the holo room doorway lit up, catching her attention. She wrinkled her eyebrows as Levaran entered the room.

"I figured you might be here," said Levaran as she strode over to Emily.

"How'd you figure that?"

"I synced with Evaran last night. He showed me the major parts of his journey from his entry to the plane to now. Quite a journey."

Emily half smiled. "Yeah."

"I'm aware of what you went through, and sad that you had to go through it."

Emily searched the ground for a moment. "At least I learned from it, and I feel like I'm overall stronger."

Levaran nodded. "You are. I saw your fight with the Time Wardens. Very impressive."

"What about you? I assume Evaran got to see parts of your journey as well."

"He did. My journey was . . . not quite as extensive as his, although it's apparent we made different decisions based on the circumstances. I find that interesting."

"So plane forms can make different decisions," said Emily.

"Of course. Where I would jump in and fight, he sometimes left."

Emily jerked her head back. "You sure about that? The Evaran I know has jumped in every time."

"As of late he has. His first five thousand years, not so much."

Emily's eyes widened. "First five thousand years!" She shook her head. "He always avoids discussing his age."

"There's a good reason for that."

"I knew Evaran was old . . . well . . . the plane form we travel with anyways, but not that old."

"Indeed. We are ancient relative to a human lifespan," said Levaran.

"Yeah," said Emily. She snorted. "It's so weird to talk with you. I know you're the same as Evaran in the plane system void and different in plane forms, but you seem a lot like him."

Levaran smiled. "Our essence is the same. The first . . . your plane form . . . is more resilient than the others. I suspect that is due to being more cautious in general. That is unusual in a plane form. He also travels with others."

Emily swatted a strand of hair out of her face. "I'm just happy he lets us. You didn't have any traveling companions?"

"I didn't," said Levaran. "Other than A, A1, and A2, it was just me, and whatever civilization I visited, and I wasn't shy to showcase my physical prowess if needed."

"Huh," said Emily. "Care to join me?"

"Sure. The Kreagan colony ship? V says that's your favorite."

Emily smiled. "Sounds good to me. Speaking of which, where is V?"

Levaran crooked her thumb back. "He is observing the creation of my version of V."

"What're you gonna name it?"

"To honor you all, I am going to call it Edev. An acronym of you, Dr. Snowden, Evaran, and V."

Emily chuckled. "I like it. Will Edev have the same personality as V?"

Levaran shook her head. "I don't know, but I suspect since the inner container merge with the outer container requires some of our raw essence, it will be different."

"I look forward to meeting Edev."

"As do I. Now, transformed?"

Emily nodded. "What level do you want?"

"Your highest to date, and set it to triple."

Emily's eyes widened. "You sure?"

"I am. I want to see what this new form is capable of."

"Okay . . . ," said Emily. She pulled up the options menu and set the holo room to the Kreagan colony ship. Tripling the amount of transformed—mutated humans covered in leathery skin with appendages poking through—made the total amount around sixty. She extended her utility handle into a staff with one end glowing blue and the other glowing white. "What weapon are you going to use?"

Levaran pointed to her plated forearm that had her utility handle attached to it. "My utility handle will cover ranged fighting, and I have shielded gauntlets for close-quarter combat. I can create a shield on my left and right forearms as needed."

Emily bobbed her head. "Interesting setup. All right. Let's do this." She started the simulation.

A swarm of transformed rushed toward them.

Emily adopted a defensive stance. She drew her head back when Levaran surged forward into the transformed.

A light-orange shielding appeared that wrapped around Levaran's fists.

Emily noted that Levaran did not move as fast as Evaran.

Levaran swung to the left and right as she charged into the middle of the transformed, who went flying in every direction. One of them jumped on her back. Levaran calmly grabbed it and threw it into the air, then punched it when it came down. It went tumbling like a bowling ball through the others.

Over the next couple of minutes, Emily dodged the few transformed that got past Levaran and used her staff to deal with them. Levaran had all but dismantled the rest of them. There were transformed on the ground that had their heads knocked off. Emily swung her gaze from side to side, examining all the transformed as she approached Levaran. "Those shielded gauntlets are pretty tough, but so are you. Do all plane forms have the same abilities?"

Levaran shook her head. "It varies. Plane forms can take on many different abilities, but it is informed by how the previous plane form died."

"Ohh," said Emily. "I guess spending a thousand years in a Time Warden siphon tank gave you super strength."

Levaran sighed. "I think you're right. I noticed I don't move as fast as I used to."

Emily eyed Levaran. "If you had this strength when the Time Wardens took you initially, would it have helped?"

"It would've. The Time Wardens would've been torn to shreds."

Emily nodded.

Levaran swayed her head back and forth. "That was a good workout. I want to talk with your uncle alone before we all meet up again as well, but I'm up for another run at this if you are."

"You want to talk to Uncle Albert alone?"

"As I did you. I wanted you to feel comfortable with me while I'm a guest aboard your plane form's Torvatta. I didn't get a chance to really introduce myself to you yesterday. Since I've never traveled with companions before, this is new to me."

Emily chuckled. "Well, you seem just like Evaran so far, although you speak and look different."

"I look better, though," said Levaran.

Emily laughed. "All right then, round two!"

Levaran nodded.

Over the next forty-five minutes, Emily and Levaran went through several rounds.

Emily enjoyed her time with Levaran. She was easy to get along with and had a similar, yet distinct, demeanor to the Evaran Emily knew. Bonding with Levaran would be easier since Emily already knew Evaran, and it felt like she was talking to a different side of Evaran. She knew the plane forms were different, but Levaran seemed to have more in common with Evaran than not.

As she watched Levaran leave the holo room, she reflected on the pain that Levaran had to endure in the siphon tank for over a thousand years. She wondered what impact it had on Levaran's views now. Although she did not see anything outright, she was looking forward to having Levaran aboard for a while.

07

Dr. Snowden sat down in a hover chair in the middle of the planar cartography lab. It was 9:00 a.m., and his sleep had been uneventful. After dinner with Emily yesterday, he had spent the rest of the night in the lab. Evaran had loosened the restrictions on the cartography lab, and he could see other universes, timelines, and the like. Being back at the lab in the morning was business as usual for him.

The amount of unlocked information had been over-whelming. The one facet he appreciated was that every place Evaran visited had an information marker. Going through some of them was surprising. He remembered Evaran mentioning something about an Earth where Neanderthals had evolved. Although the information label on it was a simple title, expanding it opened up reams of information, more than he would have been able to digest in a few hours. He shook his head. All he needed was a sleeping bag. His attention turned to the entrance of the room as Levaran arrived.

"Hope I'm not disturbing you," said Levaran with a bow.

"Not at all. Come on in," he said. He noticed that Levaran, like Evaran, always seemed alert and wide awake.

She strolled in and observed the holographic model that he had been looking at. "Studying your plane form's journey I see."

"Oh, yeah. All this information. I don't see how he keeps it all in his head. Maybe I do now."

She nodded. "He has a link to the ship, at least in terms of knowledge."

His eyes narrowed as he wagged a finger at her. "You know . . . when my nanobots acted up on our last adventure, I thought I saw tendrils from him reaching out to the shield. I guess that was his connection to the Torvatta."

"It was. Even when a plane form leaves the ship, it still has a connection to the Torvatta. The issue is when the Torvatta is no longer available."

Dr. Snowden adjusted his glasses. "Or if you don't have one."

Levaran sighed. "Unfortunately, yes. Without a Torvatta to keep me sustained, I withered in that siphon tank." She clenched her jaw for a moment. "Never again will that happen."

"I hear ya," he said. "On a positive note, how did your sync thing go last night?"

"It went well. The plane form you travel with has been through a lot. He is very happy to travel with you and Emily."

He cleared his throat. "As we are with him. It's hard to see any emotional aspect with him, but we have become accustomed to his semiemotionless state."

She smiled. "Oh, he has emotions . . . it's just that his plane form has more in common with our main form than mine or others. Our main form doesn't really have emotions, more like . . . to use something you may be familiar with . . . actions based on a predictive analysis."

He wrinkled his eyebrows. "Really . . ."

"As an example, we know a plane should have certain characteristics. We also have a baseline of what we consider to be good. After observing the plane and gathering new data, an action would be performed when compared against the baseline. That's a simplistic overview, but the plane form you travel with has that mentality more than the others. His speech is even closer to it, although what would pass as speech in our main form would be very different. Think . . . fluctuations in the interaction of cosmic energy, planes, and other things."

He chuckled. "I'm glad his baseline turns out to be good then. I guess seeing the Hoxscarus was considered good."

"The Hoxscarus appearing outside the plane upon formation was considered an unintended effect of plane creation, but one which I . . . well, we, in this situation, appreciated since it was something created from Syrilus indirectly."

Dr. Snowden furrowed his eyebrows. "I notice you keep referring to our Evaran as 'our plane form.' I guess it would be odd for you to call him Evaran, considering you call yourself that."

Levaran bobbed her head. "It's . . . unusual, as our raw essence is the same. There isn't a protocol on plane forms meeting, much less sending more than one to a plane. Then again, a Synesian breach has created an unusual situation."

"I bet that the plane being Syrilus was also a big factor."

She nodded. "I miss her so much. She was . . . a steady hand that was always there." She looked off into the distance for a moment, then back at Dr. Snowden. "I see why Evaran enjoys traveling with you. Good conversations."

"I feel like I'm talking to Evaran . . . I mean . . . our Evaran," he said with a smirk.

She smiled. "I will go by Levaran, and you can call him Evaran. I'm okay with that. Whatever makes it easier for you to understand. I didn't want to interrupt your studies, but I did want to make the effort to meet you personally."

"It's okay, and I appreciate that," he said. "If anything, it gives me more of an insight into Evaran, since your plane form seems to show emotion more."

"You're a wise being," she said as she studied the holographic models. "What were you researching?"

He swiveled in his chair to face the models. "Oh . . . just something Evaran mentioned during our abduction. He said he saw a parallel Earth that was run by Neanderthals."

Levaran nodded. "Evaran showed me that. There was quite a distinction between them and your species."

"I bet," he said. He rubbed his chin. "Speaking of Earth, maybe you can answer something for me . . . How much time had Evaran spent on Earth before our abduction?"

"He arrived several years before meeting you and Emily. However, between that event and your introduction, he has spent roughly forty-five of your years exploring your planet and humanity's timescape, at least up to a certain point."

"Wow . . . that's a lot of . . . exploring," he said.

"In the grand scheme of things, not so much."

He nodded. "I suppose . . . you don't know his age . . ."

"I do, but that is something he should tell you if he feels the need to. Emily also asked about it," she said.

He snorted. "He's pretty secretive about that."

"There's a good reason. I suppose I can tell you, and you can tell Emily. In another plane, I ran into an energy that can form a beam that can destroy not only the plane form, but also the raw essence. In that instance, I was lucky. That plane form was able to leave before being utterly destroyed. To produce the beam requires a specific variable in order to modulate it. Age. Since then, age is not discussed. Some hints may be given for parts of it, but that is the extent of it."

He raised his eyebrows. "Oh . . . I didn't know that. He could've just told us that."

"He could've . . . but if your mind was ever probed, then those who didn't know about it before would then know. If not of the energy, at least that variable."

"Isn't telling me this dangerous then?" he asked.

"Normally, yes. However, you have a planar link now and have seen more than any mortal was meant to see. Syrilus allowed you into a plane event. That is highly abnormal. If I had companions and they wanted to know my origin, they would not have gone as far as you have. Evaran and Syrilus have decided that it is worth the risk."

Dr. Snowden gulped. "I appreciate you telling me this. I . . . realize how special this is."

"Perhaps if I had companions, I would have changed my view as well."

He chuckled. "Watch out for us humans. We can be feisty."

"Of that I'm sure," she said with a smile.

He shook his head. "You know, I really enjoy talking to you, in any form."

"The feeling is mutual," she said, looking around. "I'll let you get back to it. I just wanted to stop in and say hello."

"I'm glad you did. We still have about an hour before the meeting."

"Yes, but I wanted to talk with V alone," she said.

"Gotcha. Okay, well, looking forward to having you on board."

She bowed slightly, then exited the room.

He rubbed his cheek. Questions he had been hoping to have answered were now being discussed. Evaran's age. His plane form. His previous time on Earth. Dr. Snowden shook his head. All this recent knowledge just opened up more questions to explore. Maybe now that they had broken past the planar part, there would be more answers to some of the questions pertaining to their previous adventures. He smiled and went back to the holographic models.

V studied the outer container being created in the research lab. It was being fitted with the inner container that had been made when Levaran had re-formed. His scanners picked up the approach of Levaran. Her profile, of what he had stored on her, pulled up in his mind. A few milliseconds later, he turned to face Levaran as she neared. "It is good to see you again."

"And you too," she said. "Anxious to see the process that created you?"

He nodded. "I am. Have you given it a name yet?"

"Edev. Based on Emily, Dr. Snowden, Evaran, and you."

"An acronym. It is pleasing," he said.

She chuckled. "I figured you would like it."

"It is unusual to hear you laugh."

"I bet it is," she said with a half smile, "but you now know that I am Evaran, just in a different plane form."

"I do. I think Edev will be of great value to you."

She put her hand on his shoulder. "Just as you have been for the Evaran you have traveled with. I was able to sync and saw your various outer-container forms. Although I know that each form is unique, I think your current one has a special bond with Evaran, and I think you're an excellent friend."

His chest lights glowed a bit. Subroutines that caused pleasure were executed when around Evaran in either form. Although each Evaran had a different organic marker to him, Evaran and Levaran registered almost identically. Other than the physical features, he had calculated that there was less than a two-percent deviation in behavior that he had analyzed so far.

"I like this outer-container design. It's been modified slightly, but the base idea is the same. On the ones I used, it was just a thick layer. A2 was not just my creation, she was also my friend," said Levaran, looking down. "Although Edev will not have the memories of his predecessors, I'm sure he will be just fine."

V tilted his head. "You have given Edev a male persona."

"I believe that is how Edev is forming. As you know, you can choose the persona you want, and based on my scans, Edev will probably have a male persona."

He ran a calculation in his head. "There is a high probability Edev is taking input from the environment and has detected me. Perhaps this is a contributing factor."

"It could be," she said. "I don't know the decision-making process that goes into that. Why did you take on a male persona?"

He pulled up memory files of Jay Beerman. "I enjoyed the company of a human who showed me Earth culture. He said I was his 'metal brother from another mother.'"

She laughed. "Earth slang. I got to see some of that during the sync. They have some unusual phrases, but they make me laugh, given their context. I can see why you chose the way you did. These humans are intriguing, and if they are indeed the Hoxscarus' ancestral form, even better."

He nodded. "Dr. Snowden, Emily, and Jay are my friends. Sanjay was too, but he is no longer active."

"They're good ones to have," she said, eyeing V. "When Edev has finished connecting to the outer sphere, I bet he would appreciate some help adjusting to this new environment. I will of course be there for him, but it may be very helpful if you could give him a hand."

"I will give both hands."

Levaran chuckled. "Excellent. You should be able to communicate wirelessly with him. I think the holo room will also help in his training."

"He will be my metal brother from the same mother."

She laughed. "That he will be. What do you think of your origin now that you know it?"

"I have stored it in my database, and it brings me pleasure to know that I am unique and of value to Evaran."

She nodded. "You know that when Syrilus saw you, she knew you were the creation of her and our main form's essences."

V pulled up a list of probabilities that he had stored when assessing that situation over the last day. He took a statistical average. "Analysis. I calculated a ninety-six-percent chance of that possibility after our first meeting with Syrilus." He tilted his head. "Query. My outer container is analogous to a plane form. If my inner container was crushed, what would happen to my essence?"

"It would be absorbed into the planar dimension that powers the Torvatta, and any previous knowledge would be lost," she said. "The only way to re-form for you is in an Evaran plane form re-formation. You are linked to the plane form and have as much of the plane form in you as I will have with Edev."

"I hope the probability of my demise is low."

She half smiled. "Me too, my friend." She perused her ARI. "It's about time to meet up. Are you ready to go?"

His chest lit up. "Let us do this."

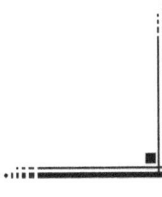

08

Dr. Snowden swept his gaze around the conference room. It was intriguing to see Evaran and Levaran together, especially since he knew how rare that was. He sat to Evaran's left with Emily, while V in body mode sat next to Levaran on the other side. His attention focused on the holographic planet that shot up from the table.

"We are going here," said Evaran. "It is where I first encountered the matter mages and Hoxscarus fighting and where I got my UIC. Levaran will get hers, and I will update mine to work in this universe."

"The matter mage colony we visited when helping the Fredorians?" asked Dr. Snowden.

"You are correct. I suspect the same situation is occurring in this parallel universe," said Evaran.

Dr. Snowden wrinkled his eyebrows. "You think they'll help?"

"I do, and I will ask them to create a shell. We can then hook up the re-formation energy container to it in order to create Levaran's Torvatta."

Levaran raised a finger. "We'll have to mark the areas we want as dimensional areas, and then we can hook it up. One thing to note is that this must be done in a universe cell so that the dimensions are not bound."

Emily chuckled. "Huh. So get a UIC and a Torvatta shell, exit the universe, and then apply a re-formation container with planar energy to the shell. Simple."

"Only if you have another Torvatta," said Dr. Snowden with a smirk. He glanced at Evaran. "These matter mages could be crazy or something."

"We shall find out," said Evaran. "I suspect they will be in line with what I know from our universe." He drew his lips taut for a moment. "When we arrive, Levaran and I will go out. It will be safer for the rest of you to stay here for this. We can ask the Hoxscarus to assume humanoid form, and after they stop fighting, we can talk to the matter mages. I will need to use a translation orb."

"For the matter mages?" asked Emily.

Evaran nodded. "They would not be able to understand the Hoxscarus or us without it. Fortunately, I know the names of the matter mages, and if they are similar to our timeline, it should be a bit easier."

Dr. Snowden nodded. "Don't worry. With this new setup, we'll be able to look outside with no problems anyways."

"Excellent. Are you going to have breakfast before we leave?"

Dr. Snowden shook his head. "Just gonna get a cup of coffee."

"Orange juice for me," said Emily.

"Very well," said Evaran. "Let us head to the command center."

After getting a cup of coffee, Dr. Snowden headed to the command area. When he got there, he saw Levaran sitting next to his usual spot. He paused for a moment, then took his seat and cast a sidelong glance at Levaran.

Levaran tilted her head at Dr. Snowden. "I can scoot over if I'm crowding you."

"Oh . . . uhh . . . no, it's fine," said Dr. Snowden. "I just figured you might want a section to yourself."

Levaran smiled. "Not at all. Besides, it's an honor to sit next to the great Dr. Snowden."

Dr. Snowden raised an eyebrow as Levaran chuckled. Being teased by Evaran was not new, and Levaran doing it seemed to be par the course. He turned his attention to the front of the ship.

Evaran pointed forward. "V, take us there."

"Acknowledged."

A portal opened, and the Torvatta flew through.

Dr. Snowden noted that even though they were in a parallel universe, the familiar silver beam had shot out, forming a portal with a gold border and light-blue rippling surface. This meant they were traveling inside a timeline and over a long distance.

After the Torvatta exited through the portal, the outside faded out, then back in.

Dr. Snowden understood this to mean that they had traveled in time. Taking the portal to a location, then going through time was something he had seen several times now.

"Analysis. We have arrived. As Dr. Snowden will ask, we are roughly three point six billion light-years from Earth and seven point eight million years in the future."

Emily grinned.

Dr. Snowden snorted. "Well, it doesn't hurt to be curious. I'm not surprised at the distances both in space and time anymore for some of these events."

"Curiosity is a good trait to have," said Levaran.

Dr. Snowden nodded.

"The planet we need to go to is nearby. V, take us in," said Evaran.

"Acknowledged."

The Torvatta angled itself and flew for ten minutes before reaching a brown planet.

Dr. Snowden stood and walked up to the front of the ship to see the planet's details. He pointed at one of the information labels. "This is a dry world, it looks like. I'm not sure what to make of all those light flashes, though."

"Those are points where the Hoxscarus and matter mages are engaging in battle, assuming this is similar to our universe," said Evaran. He tapped at his chair console. "Time to introduce ourselves."

After thirty minutes of flying, the Torvatta landed on a flat patch of a crusted dirt plain. Plumes of dust swelled up from the impact.

Dr. Snowden's eyes peered through the cloud. After it settled a bit, he focused on the sight of Hoxscarus chasing lights around. "Yeah . . . looks like a big game of tag out there. I'm just glad we're not it."

"You have nothing to fear while you are in here," said Levaran.

"I know . . . I was being silly."

Levaran stood and placed a hand on Dr. Snowden's shoulder. "Humor. It's a trait the Hoxscarus use, even in the Cosmic Medium. It was refreshing to me."

Dr. Snowden shot a look over at Emily, who shook her head.

"Let us go," said Evaran as he stood.

Levaran nodded and exited the Torvatta with Evaran.

"Kinda crazy, huh?" asked Dr. Snowden.

"Yeah, but also kinda cool. Wonder if Levaran would consider traveling with us. Probably not, given that she's getting her own Torvatta and UIC."

Dr. Snowden nodded. "What do you think of all this, V?"

"Analysis. It is, to use Emily's phrase, cool."

Emily chuckled, then pointed out. "Looks like whatever they're gonna do is starting. V, can you boost the audio and zoom in a bit?"

V nodded as his hands flew over the interface.

Dr. Snowden noted that Evaran and Levaran stood directly in front of the Torvatta. The Hoxscarus had paused in midair, and the smaller lights had stopped as well.

Levaran tossed out a translation orb.

"Hoxscarus, heed our call," said Evaran, with his hand raised.

The Hoxscarus floated down toward Evaran.

"Assume humanoid form," said Evaran.

Dr. Snowden raised his eyebrows as the three Hoxscarus in great-selector form landed to the left of Evaran and assumed a humanoid form. They resembled beings of light, unlike what he had seen with Pozarra. "Amazing."

Evaran turned his head toward the matter mages. "Please stand by. The Hoxscarus, or deathlights, as you know them, will not attack you in our presence."

The twenty or so matter mages in their spherical light forms clustered off to the right.

One of the Hoxscarus approached both Evaran and Levaran and kneeled.

"Rise," said Evaran.

Dr. Snowden noted that the matter mages were zooming in, then back out. He figured they were nervous.

"These matter mages are to be left alone," said Evaran.

"As you wish," said the Hoxscarus.

Levaran extended a hand out, palm forward. "You are needed in the Cosmic Medium. Sync with me, and all will be revealed."

The Hoxscarus reached out and touched Levaran's hand. The Hoxscarus turned its head, and a light shot out to the other Hoxscarus. After a moment, they said in unison. "We obey." They changed back into their great-selector form and began to fly into the sky, then paused.

One of the Hoxscarus flew back down and assumed humanoid form. "A ship approaches." It extended a hand, causing an area with a wriggly border to appear in midair. Inside the area was an image of a T-shaped ship moving through space. The long part of the ship had spheres all along its side.

Evaran rubbed his chin. "That is a Time Warden ship. Intriguing. There must be a rift nearby, and the Torvatta caught its attention." He extended a hand toward the Hoxscarus. "Stay until it lands."

The other Hoxscarus landed and assumed humanoid form.

Evaran walked over to the matter mage lights and extended his hand. A projection shot up of a human in several slices. Each slice was more complex than the other, but showed the nervous system, skeletal structure, clothing choices, and other pieces of data.

The matter mage lights flew over the projection, and after a moment, twenty or so humanoid matter mages shimmered into view. They were covered in a swatch of elegant robes.

Dr. Snowden noted there was an even split between males and females. Some had long hair, some short, but they all seemed to have similar builds for each gender. They also had a variety of skin tones.

"Can you understand me?" asked Evaran.

One of the female matter mages stepped forward. She ran her hand over her neck, then said, "I believe so. Sound waves for communication. Interesting."

Evaran gestured at Levaran, who stepped forward.

"I am Levaran, and with me is Evaran. Are you Kaxirillotensicatus?"

Kaxirillotensicatus wrinkled her eyebrows. "That is how my name would sound translated to sound waves."

"I'll call you Kax for short, is this agreeable?"

Kax nodded.

Dr. Snowden chuckled. Matter mages loved long names.

"Good. You have nothing to fear anymore," said Levaran. "The Hoxscarus are being sent away. Do you understand this?"

Kax peered back at the other matter mages, then faced forward. "We do, but why are you doing this?"

Levaran gestured at Evaran.

Evaran stepped forward and showed Kax his UIC. "I am from a parallel universe where this card allowed me access to nonsentient technological systems as well as biological systems. It was a gift to me from the matter mages there. It does not work in this universe. I wanted to have it upgraded, and one created for Levaran. In addition to that, I also need the shell of a ship to be built and placed on top of our existing ship."

Kax motioned at the UIC.

Evaran handed it to her.

Kax took the UIC to the other matter mages. They talked among themselves for a moment, then Kax came back. "We do this for you, and the deathlights stop killing us?"

"Yes," said Levaran. "They will not . . . exist in this universe after they leave, at least these three."

"And if we encounter others?"

"I will check in periodically. You are long-lived, as are we. If there are any concerns or issues, I can address them."

Kax handed Evaran back his UIC. She twisted her hand, and another UIC appeared. With a smile, she handed it to Levaran. "The cards are done. What ship did you need?"

Evaran showed a projection from his ring of the Torvatta shell. "This is the schematic of the ship we need built. It can be placed on top of our current ship."

Kax ran her hand through the projection, then waved at the top of the Torvatta.

Dr. Snowden raised his head back and saw the bottom of another Torvatta. His eyes widened. "Wow, that was quick."

Kax pointed at the Hoxscarus. "Why do they attack us?"

Levaran raised her head a bit. "They were seeding the universe with the humanoid form. You stood in their way. It wasn't malicious in nature, but you were seen as a threat. They'll no longer bother you."

"You can guarantee this?" asked Kax.

Levaran gestured at one of the Hoxscarus.

"It has been decreed. We abide by the will of Evaran."

Kax peered back at the others, then at Levaran. "It's appreciated."

Levaran raised a finger. "If I run into any other matter mages in trouble, they will be brought here. Is that acceptable?"

"Of course," said Kax.

"You're a true leader of your kind," said Levaran.

Kax nodded. "What is this ship that is coming? We cannot sense it."

"It is a race of creatures called the Time Wardens. They possess an energy that you cannot detect. While it is not lethal to you, they possess other means by which they can hurt you. The Hoxscarus will deal with them later. For your safety, I would not engage them."

The matter mages nodded.

Dr. Snowden gulped as he remembered the first time he met a matter mage. The mage had called himself Max, and he had been rescued and moved to a matter mage colony. This would be that colony in his universe, and the joy the matter mages expressed when seeing Evaran made sense to Dr. Snowden now. His attention focused on a boom from the sky as the Time Warden ship approached, then landed a bit away.

The steel bubbles on the side of the ship peeled back, and four large Time Wardens crawled out.

Dr. Snowden rubbed his arms. He knew those to be defenders. Time Wardens had a sinister factor about them that made him uneasy. Maybe it was because of what they did to Levaran.

Eight smaller Time Wardens crawled out in addition to one that was a little larger than the eight. It was colored blue unlike the others.

Dr. Snowden turned his head toward Emily. "What do you make of all that?"

"They make my bug thing flare up."

He nodded as the blue Time Warden approached with the four defenders at its side and the smaller ones scuttling about, waving their tentacles in the air.

Levaran stepped forward and raised her hand. "Hear me, Time Wardens."

The Time Wardens all paused. The blue Time Warden took the lead position. "You are time transgressors and must come with us."

"I did that once. Never again," said Levaran. "I was imprisoned by others of your kind for over a thousand years. My ship was destroyed. My closest friend was killed."

The blue Time Warden waved a tentacle in the air. "Irrelevant."

"Not at all. I just wanted you to know that an Evaran is now active in this timeline," said Levaran.

Evaran raised his head a bit.

Both Evaran's and Levaran's eyes glowed a bit.

Levaran's pointed toward the Time Wardens. "Hoxscarus, remove these Time Wardens, except the blue one, from the timeline."

The Time Wardens reared up and began to shoot orange beams.

The Hoxscarus raised their right arms, causing the beams to halt in midair.

The hairs on Dr. Snowden's neck shot up when he saw the Hoxscarus assume the great-selector form, but with hundreds of tentacles writhing around.

The three Hoxscarus flew through the Time Wardens, leaving a trail of yellow goo oozing everywhere. The Hoxscarus tentacles sliced through the Time Wardens like a hot knife through butter. When only the blue Time Warden was left, they flew back to their starting point.

It was not lost on Dr. Snowden that in under five seconds, the Hoxscarus had utterly destroyed the Time Wardens. From his understanding of APR, he knew the Time Wardens would be much lower. If the power differential between them was this great, he couldn't even fathom someone like Dian or Evaran's main form.

The three Hoxscarus transformed back into humanoid form. The lead one said, "It is done."

"Why did you do that?" asked the blue Time Warden.

"To send a message," said Levaran. "Your activities will not be tolerated. I know you can communicate with others via rifts. Do so, and let them know they have been warned. Now crawl back to your ship."

The blue Time Warden emitted a hissing sound, then crawled back to its ship. After a minute, the ship took off.

Levaran faced the Hoxscarus. "Your effort was appreciated. I await you at the end of the directions I have given you."

The three Hoxscarus kneeled with bowed heads, then rose and transformed into their great-selector form. They shot up into the sky.

Dr. Snowden noticed that the matter mages had taken a few steps back from Levaran.

Levaran extended a hand out to the matter mages. "I apologize that you had to see that. They imprisoned me for over a thousand years while they fed on my energy. They would do the same to you. Although your energy is not time sensitive, it is ascended, which they can feed on."

Kax wrinkled her eyebrows. "It's understandable. What is . . . ascended?"

Levaran half smiled. "Not important. What is important is that the Hoxscarus and the Time Wardens will not be a threat to you."

Kax bowed. "We are . . . indebted to you."

Levaran shook her head. "You have helped me, so we are even. I will stop in periodically to see how you're doing."

Kax's face lit up as she returned to the other matter mages.

Evaran's and Levaran's gazes met as they nodded in sync, then headed back to the Torvatta.

Dr. Snowden rubbed the goose bumps on his arm. Seeing such powerful beings interact reminded him of the first time he saw Evaran with Max and Pozarra in great-selector form when helping the Fredorians. The matter mages were powerful, but next to the Hoxscarus, they seemed powerless.

It intrigued him that the Time Wardens could pose a threat to the matter mages. Maybe the Time Wardens had some type of antimatter technology. That would definitely be lethal to the matter mages. The Time Wardens could also attack from space. While the mages could control the environment, that might not be as useful in that situation. His guess was that the Time Wardens had a higher APR. He shook his head at the realization that his thoughts would have been unimaginable to him just six months ago.

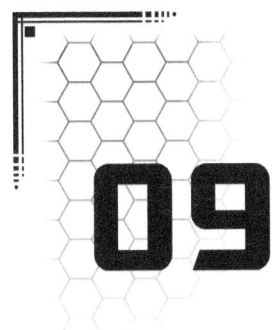

09

r. Snowden gazed around the Torvatta's roof and out into the universe cell. He was trying to figure out how the dimensional areas of Levaran's Torvatta would be built. The others were at the base of a ramp that led up to a cut-out hole in the second Torvatta. He gestured upward. "How's it being held in place?"

"Analysis. The shields have been extended, and the shell rests on a secondary shielding that has been erected," said V.

"Oh," said Dr. Snowden. He could not see the secondary shielding but figured it was probably transparent.

Levaran gestured up the ramp. "Let's check it out. V, can you get the second container?"

"Acknowledged," said V as he headed to the roof elevator.

Dr. Snowden bobbed his head as he ascended the ramp with the others. Once he was inside the second Torvatta, he took a look around. The dimensional doorways were just empty spaces. The flooring, minus the hole they used to enter, was the same shape as the Torvatta's, as was the ceiling and the walls. He wrinkled his eyebrows. "Where are the outside panels . . . ?"

Evaran motioned toward the dimensional doors. "Like the dimensional doors, the panels will be created on the outside. They are directly connected to the dimension that powers the Torvatta. A regulator does exist that allows control not only of the flow, but also of what goes out. It could be a morphable item, such as the utility rods, or raw planar energy."

"Huh," said Dr. Snowden. He raised an eyebrow at Emily. "Catching all this?"

Emily nodded. "I remember the smaller dimensional panels extending rods and lights from before. I figured they were using some type of dimensional mechanics since there is no way they came from inside the ship." She swiveled her head toward Levaran. "Are you going to add any weapons or anything?"

Levaran shook her head. "The Torvatta will not allow that. That would go against the very essence of what it is."

Emily chuckled. "I understand. It's just that given the situations we've been in, it could've resolved things a lot quicker."

Levaran laid a hand on Emily's shoulder. "Violence should be the exception, not the norm. By enforcing this design limitation, Syrilus is reminding us of this. It requires a different approach to situations. The Torvatta can still be used in an aggressive manner with its shields."

Dr. Snowden snorted. "Kinda ironic that the best offense the Torvatta has is something meant for defense."

"Even then, those situations should be rare," said Evaran, raising a finger.

Dr. Snowden furrowed his eyebrows. "I just realized the Torvatta creation is new to you too."

"It is," said Evaran. "However, Levaran showed me how it would be done in our sync."

Emily focused on Levaran. "So Syrilus showed you how it was to be built, but not Evaran."

Levaran nodded.

Dr. Snowden laughed. "I still find it odd that Syrilus talked to eight different plane forms simultaneously."

Levaran grinned as her eyes darted between Evaran and Dr. Snowden. "Imagine it from Syrilus's perspective."

Dr. Snowden gulped. "It's hard for me to fathom seeing time like that, or even dealing with it in that manner."

"Yeah, me too," said Emily.

"Understandable," said Levaran.

Dr. Snowden's attention focused on V coming up the ramp with a hover slab supporting a rectangular container on top. The container was pitch-black with lights swirling around inside it. It looked like someone had taken a chunk out of space, like cutting a cake. He figured the darkness was much more than it appeared to be. He ran a hand back and forth over his mouth. "So leftover energy from Levaran's re-formation is inside that?"

Evaran motioned at the container. "You are correct. It is bounded by the constraints the Torvatta has put on it. The re-formation energy is a mix of raw planar energy from the plane and cosmic energy from the Cosmic Medium."

"Oh, wow," said Dr. Snowden. "If I touched it, what would happen?"

Evaran half smiled. "You would cease to exist, except in the memories of ascended or higher. If it makes you feel better, I would remember you fondly."

Emily snickered.

Dr. Snowden pulled his lips to the right. "Very funny. But seriously, what would happen?"

"As I mentioned before, you would cease to exist everywhere. However, the Torvatta has it contained, so it is not possible for you to touch it directly."

"Well then . . . what's up first?" asked Dr. Snowden.

Levaran interacted with the hover slab, causing square dots to appear in various places inside the Torvatta. "We need to hook the container up to the dots. Like this." She touched the container and walked toward the door that would house the maintenance area. As she walked, a flexible white strand, anchored on the container, extended, with her finger as the end point. When she got to the door, she moved her finger up to the dot, and the flexible strand turned light blue as it splayed out and began to fill the doorway.

Dr. Snowden raised his eyebrows. "And . . . what was all that?"

Levaran nodded. "It is directing the raw re-formation energy to specific points. The configuration is already known, so it's a matter of making sure the power is available."

"Like wiring a house," said Dr. Snowden.

"Or stringing up Christmas lights," said Emily.

"Both good analogies," said Levaran. She pointed at the container. "Dig in."

Over the next several hours, Dr. Snowden helped set up the connections between the container and the dots. He was hesitant on the first one, but after that, it was routine. The number of connections surprised him, and some even required the strands to be connected to each other. He tripped a few times on the lower ones, but so did Emily.

Emily had asked V to play some music, and the overall atmosphere was cheery. V even replayed Dian trying to dance, making everyone laugh.

Dr. Snowden enjoyed these moments. A break from the sometimes chaotic situations they found themselves in. It was not lost on him that he was helping to build a ship that could travel through space and time, while sitting outside the universe. Once everything was hooked up, he stood at the top of the ramp leading back to the Torvatta. "Looks like a spider went wild with webs in here."

Levaran chuckled. "It does, doesn't it." She bobbed her head. "It will take about thirty hours, relative to the Torvatta."

"Looking forward to seeing the finished product," said Dr. Snowden.

Levaran nodded.

Evaran raised a finger. "Edev should be coming online in about three hours. We can reconvene then in the research lab."

"You two gonna sync some more?" asked Emily.

Levaran shook her head. "Not this time. However, there are some things I need to discuss with Evaran."

"Oh, all right," said Dr. Snowden. "In that case, I think I'm gonna get a nap in before then."

"I will as well," said V.

Dr. Snowden snorted. "Since when do you nap?"

"I go into low-power mode and analyze data. It is my form of napping."

"Come to think of it, I have seen you do that before."

Emily shook her head. "I'll be in the holo room while you two sleep the day away."

Dr. Snowden raised an eyebrow as Emily swatted his arm and passed by. He nodded at both Evaran and Levaran and shot a two-finger salute at V. "See you then."

Three hours later, Emily studied Edev's new outer container along with everyone else assembled around it. It had similar ports like V's, but the container was octagonal shaped with more outward-facing ports. Each smooth side had a small mesh of smaller hexagons covering it. Multiple indented grooves ringed the container, with the top one having several vertical lines that crossed the horizontal ones. Four of the sides had a segmented arm like V that ended in a six-pronged claw. She walked around it. "This is an interesting design. Why isn't it like V's?"

Levaran gestured at V. "I created it based on a mix of V and A2. I like the extended arms on V, so I added that."

V's orb lights glowed a bit brighter.

"Oh," said Emily, running her hand along Edev's surface. "I like it."

Dr. Snowden wrinkled his eyebrows. "So . . . does Edev just . . . turn on or something?"

"Something like that," said Levaran. She nodded at Evaran.

Evaran interacted with his ARI.

The pedestal that Edev sat on began to hum. The indented grooves emitted a light-blue glow. After a few seconds, they glowed bright orange for a moment.

"Systems online. Initial allocation of resources commencing," said Edev in a neutral monotone voice with a digital rasp.

"It will take a few moments to get up and going. This is the pure outer-container aspect running right now," said Levaran.

"Databases online. Sensor array online. Defense systems online. Communication systems online. Initiating . . . ," said Edev.

Emily wondered if this was how V started but suspected that it was probably different. They had never discussed it beyond V's offhand comments about existing. It was a topic she marked to ask V about.

After a few minutes, Levaran interacted with her ARI. "Opening the inner connection . . . now."

Edev glowed bright for a moment, then hovered off the pedestal. In a female voice, she said, "Hello."

Levaran jerked her head back. "Welcome. You chose a female persona. That was unexpected."

"My input matrix was influenced by my creator," said Edev.

"Interesting," said Levaran, rubbing her chin. "Have you integrated fully with your outer container yet."

"It's ongoing," said Edev as she flew over to Levaran and scanned her. "You're Evaran, and my creator."

Levaran nodded.

Emily raised her eyebrows. Edev spoke like Levaran. Emily wondered if that was also a personal choice by Edev.

Edev flew over to Evaran. "You're also Evaran."

"That is correct," said Evaran.

"You're the first plane form."

Evaran nodded. "I see you are up to date on the current situation."

"It's still processing," said Edev. She flew over to V. "You're like me."

"Analysis. We have the same origin with different input variables," said V.

Edev hovered around V for a bit, then said, "Communication protocol accepted. We have a lot to sync."

"Acknowledged," said V.

Edev flew over to Dr. Snowden and Emily and scanned them both. "Humans. Possibly Hoxscarus' ancestral form."

"That's us," said Emily with a half smile.

Edev extended a segmented arm and raised it toward Emily.

Emily drew her head back.

"High five," said Edev. "V has communicated to me that this is how humans greet each other in moments of joy. My existence is a moment of joy."

Emily chuckled and high-fived Edev.

Edev flew over to Dr. Snowden and repeated the same action with him.

Dr. Snowden wrinkled his eyebrows. "It's good to meet you, Edev. I think we'll get along just fine."

"Me too," said Edev. "I like your bow tie. Perhaps I can get an equivalent one."

Dr. Snowden laughed. "Oh . . . Now *that* was unexpected."

Levaran grinned. "I can see Edev is going to be full of surprises. It appears she has taken on some traits of V's impressions." She waved a finger between Edev to V. "V is going to help you get accustomed to your new form in the holo room. I'll be available to you, as I'm sure the others will be, should you want to interact with us."

"On it," said Edev.

Evaran tilted his head. "Intriguing. It would appear my sync with Levaran has also had an impact."

Emily remembered Evaran talking about his first time coming to Earth. He had helped Jake Melkins, who often said, "On it." The fact that Edev was pulling from all these impressions made her think Edev was going to be more lively than V. It occurred to her that Levaran and Edev seemed to share the same zeal for being alive. She enjoyed the upbeat atmosphere that their presences provided.

V walked over to the room exit. "Follow me."

"You got it," said Edev as she zipped behind V.

Dr. Snowden and Emily chuckled.

After they went to the holo room, V and Edev flew to the center of the room. V began to pull up various simulations, showing Edev how to shoot, stealth, and use holograms.

Everyone else stood just inside the entrance of the room and observed.

Emily's eyes widened when she saw Edev assume a humanoid female holo form. She had seen that technology before and knew V could project it out in a beam, but to see it used as a way of creating a form around Edev intrigued her. She pointed at Edev. "Now that's cool."

Evaran nodded. "I concur. Adding holo emitters on the outer container would be a good enhancement for V, and I suspect he is already adding it to his enhancement upgrade list."

"It would be great for deception," said Dr. Snowden. He wrinkled his eyebrows. "Speaking of which, what type of body will Edev have?"

Levaran narrowed her eyes. "I'm not sure yet. I'll have to build one, and discuss it with Edev. She may not even want one. Although, after seeing V's, I think it would be a good idea."

Dr. Snowden nodded.

Emily focused her attention on Edev and V's interaction. They were running the transformed simulation she trained on. Edev had shed the holographic form and assumed her natural form. While V would engage the transformed up front, Edev flew around with her arms extended and spinning at a high velocity. It reminded Emily of a buzz saw. One thing she was sure of, it was effective.

Edev flew through the transformed and mowed down group after group.

Dr. Snowden snorted. "That's pretty powerful."

Evaran drew his lips flat. "Yes, for transformed." He inter-acted with his ARI. V and Edev paused as the simulation changed to an environment with hallways.

Emily remembered it as the facility known as Malacruuz, owned by the Voss Imperium, a jackal-like race they encoun-tered previously. She narrowed her eyes as she wondered how Edev would handle reconnaissance.

V set himself as a noninteractive entity, while Edev shim-mered out of view.

Emily noted that although Edev was in stealth mode, the holo room had tagged her so that she could still be seen.

Edev flew into a room with three Voss. After angling three of her arms, she fired a stun beam from each of them simultaneously. All the Voss crumpled to the ground.

"Wow," said Emily. "The stun beam is in the arms."

Evaran nodded. "I suspect V is going to want that too."

"It would make him more versatile, even if the beam is weaker," said Dr. Snowden. He ran a hand down his throat as he observed Levaran. "Did A2 have all these enhancements?"

Levaran shook her head. "He had some, but this is a mix of design approaches. After seeing what V has had to deal with, I think these enhancements will work well."

Dr. Snowden nodded. "So you have your Torvatta being built, a UIC, and now Edev. What's next on the plate?"

Levaran turned her head toward Evaran for a moment, then toward Dr. Snowden. "Evaran has suggested I travel with your counterparts here."

"I remember that being mentioned. So you're really going to do it?" asked Dr. Snowden.

"I think I am," said Levaran. "It will require visiting the Krotovore ship, as that is the last point where you can be retrieved before dying, assuming events are the same. Evaran has offered to help with that and dealing with the Time Wardens afterward."

"Wouldn't it be easier to go to a point earlier in the time stream of our duplicates?" asked Dr. Snowden.

"It would. However, retrieving your duplicates from the Krotovore ship has the least impact since without intervention, they would die there given what we know of what happened in your universe."

Dr. Snowden gulped. "Ahh . . ."

"Well, you can count us in," said Emily.

Levaran nodded. "It's appreciated. Given what I know of both of your abilities now, versus what I was shown during Evaran's initial encounter, I suspect things will be a bit easier."

Evaran half smiled. "It should be. However, based on Earth time, we should do it tomorrow. It is five twenty p.m. now."

Emily narrowed her eyes. "That sounds good to me. At least this time I have my suit."

Dr. Snowden raised his PSD. "And don't forget this. I do wonder if we will see Jerzan, and if the creatures will be the same."

"The draug," said Emily with her lips pulled taut. "Maybe . . . we could check on the krall too."

Evaran nodded. "We can do that. I thought about bringing a shielded transport along. However, with this group, I think we will be okay."

Dr. Snowden snorted. "*Okay* is putting it mildly."

Evaran faced both Dr. Snowden and Emily. "I would suggest you use the rest of the day to consider what you will say to your counterparts. You know what they will be experiencing and feeling better than I."

Emily sighed. "It'll be like meeting Nanobot Emily again." She fondly remembered the nanobot duplicate from a previous adventure. Although Nanobot Emily died to save them, she was a snapshot of Emily's outlook on life prior to her prison-planet experience.

"Yeah . . . and I'll need to deal with my skepticism," said Dr. Snowden. He scrunched his face. "We could even see Jay and Sanjay, but . . . what if it's a completely different group of people?"

"It is a possibility," said Evaran. "We will deal with it when we get there."

Emily took a breath. "Okay, well, I'm gonna sit here for a bit and watch V and Edev, then do that after a while."

"Same here," said Dr. Snowden. "I'm enjoying watching Edev learn."

Levaran smiled. "I'm anxious to meet my new traveling companions, assuming they want to travel with me."

Dr. Snowden harrumphed. "I'm sure they will. I mean . . . who would pass up an opportunity to travel through space, time, and beyond and watch V and maybe Edev dance?"

Everyone laughed as V and Edev paused to focus on them.

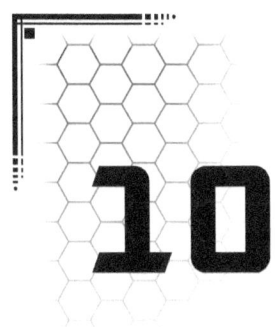

10

Dr. Snowden yawned as he stared at the ceiling. It was 9:00 a.m. the next day, and after a night filled with observing and interacting with Levaran and Edev, he enjoyed the silence in his room. Edev learned quickly, and with V at her side, she would be a formidable adversary to anyone who challenged her. Her holo form ability was something he noticed V admiring, given that V mentioned it no more than five times throughout the night. In their former situations, that ability would have been useful.

He snorted as he climbed out of bed and checked his PSD. Emily had sent him an invitation to join her in the holo room an hour ago. He sighed as he ran a hand over his mouth. At some point, he would join her. Her combat ability and situational awareness were way above his, and she knew how to use the PSD in ways he had never thought of before. He had joined her in studying, and that was perhaps his favorite part of the day. Her eagerness to learn was infectious, and she absorbed everything put in front of her.

She was no longer the young, innocent niece he had known. Taking some of the advice he had learned from Evaran and others, he was adjusting to it, and it was not as difficult as he thought it would be. There were still glimmers of that innocence that shone through, and he enjoyed seeing it every time.

After a quick stretch, he jumped out of bed. When he was cleaned up and dressed, he headed out to the conference room. It was empty, as he suspected it would be. The others were probably in the command area. He got his cup of coffee and took a seat at the conference table. Movement at the door caught his eye.

"I was wondering when you would get up," said Emily.

He nodded. "Good morning to you too."

"You get my message?"

"Yeah . . . I was just . . . tired. You know."

Emily shook her head while chuckling. After getting an orange drink from the replicators, she took a seat opposite him. "So . . . you ready to meet ourselves?"

Dr. Snowden smiled. "I think I am. I mean . . . I thought about what to say to myself, but every time, I felt like I would just piss myself off."

"You?" she asked after jerking her head back.

He waved a hand in the air. "I know I can be stubborn, and I'm not even sure I can convince myself. It took draug falling from the ceiling and attacking us to snap me into reality."

She shrugged. "Then maybe that's what you need to do."

He chuckled. "Drop from the ceiling and attack myself?"

"You know what I mean," she said, drawing her lips to the right.

"What about you? Have you figured out what you're going to say?"

She nodded. "I have, actually. I'm just gonna lay it all out, describe some of the things I've been through and the decisions I've made, and it should be all good."

"What if the other you is wild or something?" he said, taking another sip of his coffee.

"Then she will see what constrained wild can look like," she said with a twinkle in her eyes.

He grinned. After some more light discussion and finishing his coffee, he stood. "We may not even have to do any of this if it's someone else. Anyways, command center time." He exited the room, with Emily in tow.

Once he got to the command area, he noticed that Evaran was in his command chair like he always was. V was showing Edev how to operate the front console, and Levaran was in her seat next to Dr. Snowden's usual spot.

Levaran waved at them. "Hey, you two. Ready to head out?"

Dr. Snowden took his seat. "Ready as I'll ever be. What's our first stop?"

Evaran tapped at his chair console. "We are going to the Krotovore ship in the Andromeda galaxy at the moment when I would have appeared out there."

"Oh . . . fun times ahead. This is going to be interesting to see everything from your perspective," said Dr. Snowden. He smiled at Levaran. "I guess you've already seen it."

Levaran nodded. "I have, and it was an interesting experience."

"I bet," said Dr. Snowden with a chuckle.

Evaran interacted with his chair console. "V, take us there."

"Acknowledged."

A white beam shot out from the Torvatta. After a few minutes, a blue-bordered portal with a dark-gray rippling surface appeared. The Torvatta flew through it.

Dr. Snowden thought that they would enter into space, but based on what he knew, they were now in the timeline void. Since they were in the universal cell with Levaran's Torvatta, it seemed the progression was to go to the timeline void inside the universe, then into the timeline.

The Torvatta shot out a silver beam, and after the green bordered portal with a red rippling surface appeared, it flew through.

The familiar feeling of deep space comforted Dr. Snowden. Although he was glad to have seen what was outside the timeline, universe, and beyond, it was the stars that he felt most at home with. A planet loomed under the Torvatta, with a small moon in the distance. He swung his head around as he surveyed the screen. "So . . . there should be a Krotovore ship here, right?"

Evaran nodded. "V, perform long-range scans."

"Acknowledged."

An overhead view of the solar system and surrounding ones appeared to hover on the front screen. A wave pulsed from a dot outward in concentric circles. Items popped up as they were detected.

Dr. Snowden had seen it before and recognized some of the objects. The swirly spiral object he knew was a rift, probably the one the Krotovore ship was supposed to come through. It was the gray icon near the rift that caught his eye. "What's . . . that?"

Evaran drew his lips taut. "A Time Warden anchor station."

"Were they there before in our universe?"

"They were not," said Evaran. "It would seem they are more active in this universe. This could imply that things are very different here. V, take us to Jupiter and to February 5, 2012, at three p.m. Engage stealth mode prior to flying through."

"Acknowledged," said V as his segmented arms flew around the front console.

"I thought we were abducted on the fourth?" asked Dr. Snowden.

"You were. However, it took them a day to get to Jupiter."

"Oh, I guess that makes sense," said Dr. Snowden, nodding.

The outside of the Torvatta shimmered from view, then eased back in. The Torvatta then shot out a portal.

"Torvatta stealth mode engaged," said V.

Dr. Snowden noted that in the past, he could never tell if the Torvatta was in stealth mode, but with the new screens, he could see the outline of it on the Torvatta layout display. The outline was light blue and the text "Stealth" sat under the display. It occurred to him that he would now be able to see a lot more of what the Torvatta actually did. One of the actions he remembered was that the Torvatta extended utility rods. His understanding of it was that they extended from the sides and past the shields and allowed interaction for things like communication or scanning. Looking at the display, he could see that the rods were extended.

The Torvatta flew through the portal and exited outside Jupiter.

Dr. Snowden's eyes widened. It never got old to him to see the planets up close. From where they were, Jupiter covered up a significant part of the view.

"V, perform long-range scans," said Evaran.

"Acknowledged."

Emily narrowed her eyes. "Are you looking for the ship that took us?"

"I am," said Evaran. "We will know momentarily if the Krotovore ship even came here."

"Cool."

"Analysis. Krotovore main ship detected. Two Krotovore scout ships en route to the main ship."

Evaran gestured forward. "Track and follow them."

"Acknowledged."

"Two of them? It was one in our abduction," said Dr. Snowden.

Evaran nodded. "I suspect then that whoever or whatever was abducted will be different."

Dr. Snowden gulped. "Seems like everything is . . . slightly off over here."

"I concur," said Evaran.

Levaran laid a hand on Dr. Snowden's shoulder. "Whatever the situation is, we'll handle it."

A warm glow washed over him. Levaran, like Evaran, was a calming presence. He wondered if she could detect his uneasiness. Part of it was seeing or doing anything in relation to the Krotovore; the other was now knowing that the situation was not happening as expected. His experiences so far had led him to believe that when things were not as they should be, then something bad was happening.

For the next several hours, the Torvatta followed the Krotovore scout ships.

He knew that the Krotovore would not be able to detect the Torvatta. The outline of the ships on the screen with various details showed that they were hauling it out of the solar system. The Torvatta was able to match the speed of the ships with ease. The speed at which the ships could move still astounded him. The Oort cloud was not a trivial distance away.

When the Krotovore ship appeared, his skin crawled. He had never seen it fully from the outside, but the insect-like appendages on the slim body seemed Krotovore in design. The immense size surprised him, and the scout ships were but tiny dots as they approached the main ship.

"V, perform standard scans," said Evaran.

"Acknowledged."

The Torvatta scanned as it flew around the Krotovore ship.

Dr. Snowden sat mesmerized by the detail labels popping all around the outline. It had everything from shield type and strength to engine type and hull material.

After twenty minutes, Evaran interacted with his chair console. "V, move us away a bit, then open a portal to where the Krotovore ship will leave this galaxy. After that, take us to February 25 at twelve oh five in the afternoon and engage stealth mode."

"Acknowledged."

Dr. Snowden remembered that the Krotovore ship would fly for three more weeks, run into a Kreagan Star Empire fleet, get damaged, and then escape through a space-time rift. At least that is how Evaran described it when he had rescued them from the Krotovore ship long ago.

The Torvatta moved away until the Krotovore ship was but a blip in the distance. After opening a portal, it flew through.

Emily fidgeted in her seat. The sight of the Krotovore ship caused her nanobots to pulse a bit. Memories flooded her mind, from the death of Sanjay, another human whom Evaran tried to save, to the krall that defended them at the expense of its own health.

This situation appeared to be slightly different, and she was unsure of how that would impact things, but going back into the Krotovore ship would be therapeutic for her in a way. This time, instead of being unprepared and scared, she had a suit, weapons, appropriate training, and experience.

She watched as the Torvatta exited the portal. The outside of the Torvatta shimmered away, then eased back in. A quick survey showed that there was nothing but deep space.

"Torvatta stealth mode engaged."

"V, perform long-range scans," said Evaran.

"Acknowledged."

Emily scanned the screen as the familiar overhead view of various star systems appeared. She had studied the icons with Dr. Snowden and had become familiar with them from other systems. The orange swirly icon of a rift appeared, with a massing of other dots. "Well, at least the rift is there."

"Indeed," said Evaran. "V, take us there."

"Acknowledged."

The Torvatta opened a portal and flew through. It exited it into a firefight.

Emily's eyes widened as she saw the Krotovore ship being hammered by a fleet of other ships. The space-time rift also had a structure hovering out in front of it, firing at both the fleet of ships and the Krotovore ship.

Evaran narrowed his eyes. "V, place us between the Krotovore ship and the Time Warden rift anchor station."

"Acknowledged."

As the Torvatta moved to place itself, Emily eased back into her chair while clasping her hands. "You think the reason there was no Krotovore ship is because it was destroyed before making it to the rift?"

Evaran nodded. "It would appear that way. The Torvatta should be able to disable the Time Warden anchor station. From past experience, we know that the Krotovore ship can handle the sustained Kreagan fleet assault."

"So we're going to cause a timeline change then, right?" she asked.

"We are."

"Umm . . . ," said Dr. Snowden, raising a finger. "How is the Torvatta going to disable the Time Warden station?"

Evaran gestured at Levaran.

Levaran half smiled. "We're going to ram it."

Dr. Snowden raised his eyebrows as he scanned the screen. "Well, I guess that would do it."

"It should. Without the station's support, the Time Wardens on board will be flushed out to space and torn apart by the rift," said Levaran.

"What if it has shields?" asked Dr. Snowden. "The facility had shields, and it required the planar beam generator. I would guess they would have shielding on anything near a rift."

Evaran clenched his jaw for a moment, then unclenched it. "The anchor station has a different type of shield. It is more of a kinetic shield meant to deflect, mixed with a timeline energy shield meant to protect from the rift. It is much weaker than the facility's shields, but it allows them to use stealth without being detected. If they had the same shielding as the facility, it would light up on every sensor around. The Torvatta is capable of penetrating the station's shields." He raised a finger. "However, the connection between both anchor stations must be disrupted first. Once it is destroyed, we will head through the rift and destroy the station on the other end."

"Then everything should be normal, relatively speaking," said Dr. Snowden.

Evaran nodded. "In our universe, it was a bit less complicated. I suspect, like this encounter, that when we board the Krotovore ship, what we encounter will be very different. I expect Jerzan will appear as expected. However, he most likely will not be the only mercenary group that arrives."

"Hopefully they're as incompetent as Jerzan," said Emily.

"If it is the groups I am thinking of, we will need to be extra cautious. I took care of those groups in our universe. That is not the case here."

Dr. Snowden nodded. "I'm sure we can handle it. I mean . . . c'mon . . . two Evarans . . . V . . . Edev . . ." He pointed at Emily. "And if that's not enough, we have her."

Emily snorted.

"We will deal with it when we get there. However, first, we need to get the Krotovore ship through the space-time rift," said Evaran.

Dr. Snowden nodded.

After ten minutes, the Torvatta had flown around the Krotovore ship and was angling in toward the Time Warden anchor station.

Emily noted that there was a visible beam emitting from the station into the rift. She gestured at it. "The anchor line that keeps the rift open."

"You are correct," said Evaran. "It tethers the two stations together and is partially made of pure timeline energy, which keeps the rift open. The Torvatta's shields can disrupt it. Once down, there is a small window of time before the rift collapses."

"Gotcha," said Emily, bobbing her head. She remembered that the Torvatta had used its shields to disrupt space-time rifts before to deal with a troublesome time traveler. "Like the space-time rifts with Billozein."

Evaran nodded. "It is similar in concept." He gestured at V. "Disrupt that beam."

"Acknowledged."

The Torvatta moved between the Time Warden anchor station and the rift. After some positioning, it intercepted the beam. The Torvatta's shields pulsed for a moment, expanding out for a bit in a spherical fashion, causing the beam to dissipate as it washed over the Torvatta's shields.

The unwavering antagonism shown by both Evaran and Levaran toward the Time Wardens intrigued Emily. She understood Levaran's issue with them, but even Evaran was irritated by them. They crossed his line long ago.

Evaran interacted with his chair console. "I have modulated the shields to the Time Warden shield frequency. V, take us full speed into the Time Warden anchor station."

"Acknowledged."

Emily gripped her chair's arms. One of the more interesting aspects she had noticed about the Torvatta was that even if it was shaken, hit, or held, it always seemed to be calm inside. She had asked Dr. Snowden about it, and he had said something about inertia dampeners, but he was not sure. Now that the Torvatta schematics were available, she was looking forward to finding that out. She chuckled as she realized this was how Dr. Snowden must think.

Dr. Snowden raised his eyebrows at Emily.

Emily half smiled. "I was just remembering our discussion on the dampeners."

"Oh," said Dr. Snowden. He circled a finger in the air. "I guess even if we hit the station at full speed, we won't feel the effects in here."

"The Torvatta is stabilized inside the shield," said Evaran. "Forces outside the Torvatta do not carry through the shields unless the force is crafted to do so. That is extremely rare, and I have only encountered it a few times."

Dr. Snowden chuckled. "I would say buckle up, but no need to, it seems."

The Torvatta flew in a straight line toward the Time Warden anchor station. When it reached the shielding, the Torvatta punched through it, leaving behind a display of bright lights around the edges of the hole. As the Torvatta accelerated, Time Warden ships began to launch from the station. Station turrets and defense systems locked on to the Torvatta and began to fire. The Torvatta closed the distance quickly, and hit the station on its side.

Emily studied the interior of the station as it zoomed by. It reminded her of looking at a cutout of a building, except up close and personal.

The Torvatta exited the station, which began to fall apart. The screen showed a rearview shot of Time Wardens being sucked out into space as parts of the station began to crumple. When the Torvatta was a bit away, the station exploded.

"The Krotovore ship is more damaged than expected due to taking fire from two sources. We need to distract the Kreagan fleet until it flies through the rift. V, provide cover for the Krotovore ship from the Kreagan fleet until it reaches the rift, then head in," said Evaran.

"Acknowledged."

The Torvatta spent the next twenty minutes intercepting the large Kreagan beams that were focused on the Krotovore ship's shielding.

Emily observed the beams hitting the Torvatta and pushing it back a bit, but then reflecting off at an angle. The Torvatta's presence seemed to draw additional fire from other ships. She recognized the Kreagan Dreadnoughts. They were massive, with huge swarms of smaller ships around them. She knew the Kreagans referred to this as the Durnass incident.

Dr. Snowden gulped. "That's a lot of firepower."

Evaran nodded. "At least we know the Kreagan Star Empire is where it should be."

"Good point," said Dr. Snowden.

"The Krotovore ship is entering the rift," said V.

"Follow it in and head to the other Time Warden anchor station," said Evaran.

"Acknowledged."

The Torvatta broke off from the Kreagan ships and headed into the rift behind the Krotovore ship. It overtook the Krotovore ship and exited the rift, barreling toward the other Time Warden anchor station. After a few minutes, it had a hole in it and exploded shortly thereafter. The Krotovore ship had exited the rift as well and drifted toward the nearby planet.

Dr. Snowden exhaled sharply. "That was intense."

"Your first station ramming?" asked Levaran with a half smile.

"Well, it's my first time seeing the Torvatta being used as a battering ram anyways."

"Understandable. I suspect now that you have the schematics, there will be other ways to utilize the Torvatta."

Dr. Snowden rubbed his chin. "Okay, now you got me curious. What ways are we talking?"

Levaran shot a look at Evaran for a moment, then back at Dr. Snowden. "There's a tractor beam, a repulsing beam, and even shield enhancements that allow the Torvatta to control its temperature."

"That sounds . . . interesting," said Dr. Snowden. "At least there will be more options anyways."

Emily bobbed her head. "Yeah, I'd like to check those out, but I think we have another issue to attend to first."

"Right, right," said Dr. Snowden. "I'm guessing the plan now is to board the ship, retrieve ourselves, reset the ship's trajectory, turn on the main engines, then get off it, right?"

"That is the plan," said Evaran. "I expect that the Time Wardens will send a ship to investigate, but hopefully we can achieve our objectives and be gone by then. The rift is beginning to close. It appears the Kreagans decided not to fly into it."

"Thankfully for us. Okay. In that case, I'll go get my survival suit," said Dr. Snowden.

"Perhaps you and Emily should stay on board. Levaran, V, Edev, and myself should be more than enough."

Emily shook her head. "No way. We're going."

Evaran half smiled at Levaran. "As you can see, humans can be stubborn. Even when presented with the safer choice, they can sometimes choose the riskier one."

Levaran smiled. "I like it."

"Well, we won't be a hindrance this time," said Emily, raising her head a bit. "Besides, if it's our duplicates in there, who better to talk to them?"

Evaran half smiled. "You both are, of course. I would be remiss if I did not offer the chance for you to stay behind where it is safe, but I should know better."

"Yeah, you can't leave half of Evaran and the gang behind—well, a quarter this time around," said Dr. Snowden.

"Thank you for including me in the gang," said Edev as her lights glowed a bit brighter.

Dr. Snowden chuckled. "No problem."

Evaran gestured at V. "Very well. Take us in."

"Acknowledged," said V. He interacted with the console, then pivoted toward Edev. "In situations like this, it is appropriate to say, 'Let us do this.'"

Edev's lights blinked for a moment. "Let's do this!"

Everyone chuckled as the Torvatta approached the Krotovore ship.

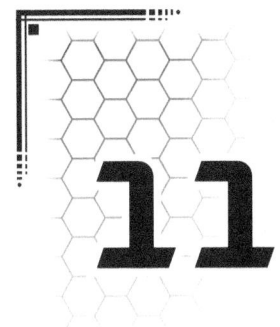

11

Dr. Snowden surveyed the docking bay that the Torvatta had landed in. Memories of the alien abduction rushed through his mind. The last time he saw this room, at least in his universe, was when V led him and Emily along with the krall and Jay to the Torvatta.

He was glad to have his survival suit on and helmet up, as the internal temperature was helping to cool him down. The inside of his helmet faceplate showed a view from Edev, who was flying around and scanning everything in sight. She acted like a kid in a candy store.

Looking to his left, he saw that V was in body mode. Considering what they might face, that seemed like a good decision. Evaran and Levaran were standing next to V and examining their ARIs. They had each placed their UIC on a wall console. Dr. Snowden jumped when Emily touched his arm.

"Thinking again?" asked Emily.

"Yeah . . . I was . . . remembering is all. I know we're in good company, but this place . . . it just . . ."

"I know," she said, tilting her head. "Just remember, this time we're prepared."

He could see the look of defiance in her eyes through her transparent faceplate. With his lips drawn flat, he said, "Let's hope it isn't too different."

She nodded and they both joined the others.

Evaran surveyed the group. "Per Edev's and V's scanning, this room and the adjacent room appear to be identical to the one from the other universe. That is a good sign. However, the power levels suggest that they are more intact."

Dr. Snowden furrowed his eyebrows. "What does that imply?"

"A good question," said Evaran. "The biggest concern is that some of the Krotovore AIs are active. Our UICs ran into several of them. That was not an issue before. The global security system appears to be partially active. This means that the engine room may be challenging. There are also some active Krotovore life signs."

Dr. Snowden jerked his head back. "I'd like to give them a piece of my mind."

"Perhaps you can, assuming they stay alive. One of the life signs is on the bridge."

"Should we split up?" asked Emily. "Maybe one group go to get ourselves, and the other go to the bridge?"

Evaran shook his head. "I think we should all stick together. I understand your confidence. However, there is no need to take chances, and we have a buffer of time to work with."

Emily shrugged. "Okay."

Dr. Snowden narrowed his eyes. It almost seemed like Emily wanted to split up so there would be more of an opportunity to fight. He knew that the Krotovore ship was one of the more frequently simulated environments that she had practiced with in the holo room.

She pivoted her head toward him.

He dipped his chin as his eyes searched the ground.

"We'll be fine," said Levaran. "With V in body mode, that gives us a walking shield."

V tilted his head.

Levaran smiled. "A smart and handsome walking shield."

"Acknowledged."

Levaran raised a finger. "However, we should still deploy our shields and have our weapons ready." She pulled off her utility handle and lodged it into a groove on her right arm.

Dr. Snowden stepped forward. "Interesting design. You're not going to use a staff?"

"I could, but this can still extend into a baton as needed, and I would mainly use it for stun, repulsion, grappling, or heat. I prefer to use shielded gauntlets."

"They're awesome," said Emily.

"Huh," said Dr. Snowden. He gestured at Evaran. "You going to get something like that?"

Evaran shook his head. "We have different approaches to combat."

Dr. Snowden rubbed his chin.

Levaran chuckled. "I mentioned this to Emily already, but plane forms are created with unique abilities, relative to a human." She gestured at Evaran. "He has above-average strength and speed. I am physically much stronger, but not as fast. Some plane forms can manipulate a field or morphable orbs, while others have mental abilities. The abilities are influenced by the plane to some degree. I have been to many planes and seen a great variety of these."

"You said . . . orbs?" asked Emily.

Levaran nodded. "It was an ability I had on a plane I visited long ago." She gestured at Evaran.

Evaran smiled. "I had just taken on a plane form and then knocked myself down because I did not know how to control them. They were powerful, though. I could make them into flattened discs that allowed me to fly or form shields."

"Wow," said Emily. "It sounds like how the Wildborn are, the same energy but different abilities."

"There are similarities there, except our abilities are born from a mix of planar and cosmic energy, while theirs is wild energy," said Levaran.

Dr. Snowden shook his head while he chuckled.

Evaran and Levaran tilted their heads at him.

He shook a hand out. "I'm not laughing at you. It's just that it . . . it dawned on me that your orb experience was one that occurred before coming to this plane. You both have the same memory of it and talk of it from a personal point of view."

"Of course," said Evaran.

Levaran smiled. "We still do have some differences that influence our approaches to situations, such as combat. The utility handle was built to manage all these different approaches. For me, it is mostly used for ranged combat. As I mentioned before, I prefer close-quarter combat with a morphable energy gauntlet."

V's chest lit up. "I like close-quarter combat in body mode as well."

"Hopefully we can avoid combat," said Dr. Snowden. "Not much hope there, but worth a shot."

Evaran gestured toward a hallway on the side. "We will try to avoid it if we can. Let us head to docking bay 3. The exit to this room is collapsed as it was in our universe."

Dr. Snowden nodded and followed Evaran and the others into the hallway. When they were about a third of the way, he examined the ground. The memory of one of Jerzan's mercenaries being mutilated there sprung into his mind. He took a deep breath and continued on.

When they reached docking bay 3, they took a right along the wall. They paused as they hit the corner.

Evaran tossed an orb up into the air. It hovered for a moment, then flew to the ceiling where it positioned itself. "The remote viewing orb will let us know if anyone else comes."

"Like Jerzan?" asked Dr. Snowden with a smirk.

"Correct. However, I suspect if there are any Time Wardens around, they will investigate not only their destroyed station, but also this ship. This is our early warning system."

Dr. Snowden nodded. As he followed Evaran along the wall toward the room entrance, he stopped to study a container. He waved Emily over. "Same one."

Emily shook her head. "I don't miss that at all."

Evaran paused, causing the others to hold position. He faced the container. "It served its purpose. I am curious about its contents." He placed his UIC on the container's console. After a moment, the hatch door flipped up.

Dr. Snowden peered in. As expected, the arrangement of containers was as he remembered it. He recalled that Evaran had placed him and Emily inside it when the docking bay was depressurized during their abduction. "Hopefully I don't need to move those inner containers out again."

Evaran laid a hand on Dr. Snowden's shoulder. "I do not think it will come to that. Let us go."

Dr. Snowden exhaled, then followed Evaran's lead out of the room. They had come straight into docking bay 3 during his abduction, but this time, they went to the right.

He gestured forward as they walked down the hallway. "New route?"

Evaran nodded. "This is a faster route to where your duplicates would be. Edev, scouting mode. V, defensive mode."

"Acknowledged. Defensive mode engaged," said V as a semitransparent shield went up around him.

"You got it!" said Edev as she shimmered, then disappeared.

Emily chuckled. "Edev seems like she's so happy."

Levaran nodded. "Everything is new to her. Hopefully that exuberance will not diminish."

"Analysis. I am happy as well."

Emily slapped V's back shielding. "We know."

V's lights glowed a bit brighter.

Evaran snapped his head forward. "A creature is approaching."

Dr. Snowden could see, via the view from Edev, a large, extremely muscled, scaled raptor-like creature with a crocodile-like snout. It sat on two powerful legs that ended in razor-sharp talons, and its four large arms had hands with sharp claws. The creature reminded him of a dinosaur somewhat, but this one only stood around seven feet or so, and it resonated power and speed from its profile. He rubbed the goose bumps that formed on his arm. "What is that?"

"It is a Terrox," said Evaran. "Per the Krotovore system, it does not rely on intelligence."

As the creature came into view, V stepped forward.

Evaran extended a hand out toward V. "Levaran and I will handle this. Everyone, wait here."

Dr. Snowden held his breath as Evaran and Levaran approached the now-startled Terrox.

Evaran extended a hand. "We are not your enemy."

The Terrox emitted a low growl followed by a high-pitched whining noise. It stomped the metallic floor and snorted.

"No, we're not food," said Levaran.

The Terrox uttered a deep growl.

"I would not suggest that," said Evaran. He peered behind him, then back at the Terrox. "It would not go well for you."

The Terrox took a few steps forward while swaying its head.

"You will be harmed if you try. We are stronger," said Evaran.

The Terrox paused for a moment as it studied the others behind Evaran and Levaran. It then charged forward.

Levaran extended a hand out toward Evaran. "I got this one." She ran forward with her left arm shield in front of her. When she and the Terrox met, it went flying back a good distance. It righted itself and, with an indignant shake of its head, took off in another direction.

Dr. Snowden gulped. He knew Evaran was strong, but Levaran seemed like she was on another level. If it had been Evaran who had hit the Terrox, he would have expected some pushback, or even just a halting, but not a complete blow back like he had just seen.

Evaran waved for the others to come forward.

When Dr. Snowden reached them, he raised his eyebrows at Levaran and said, "You're . . . quite strong."

Levaran smiled. "There's some residual re-formation energy that resides in me. It's boosting my natural abilities and should fade away after a while, maybe a few weeks from your perspective."

Dr. Snowden harrumphed. "That made this encounter a lot easier."

"We should not get complacent," said Evaran. "The research labs are a bit away. Let us go."

Dr. Snowden nodded as the rest of the group moved forward. Although his muscles were still a little tight, the encounter with the Terrox made them relax some. He remembered Evaran's confidence the first time he had met him. It was unshakable, and Levaran shared that trait. This encounter just bolstered his impression of that. An apex predator that could probably tear apart anything ran off after just one moment with Levaran. It must have sensed it was outclassed. Probably a foreign concept to it, but it recognized raw power. He wondered how often that occurred. With a deep breath, he soldiered on.

After an hour of traversing various rooms of different sizes, they came to a stop near a four-way intersection.

Dr. Snowden expected there to be more creatures roaming around, but the only ones they saw had scattered at their approach. The sounds were consistent with what he remembered, and the Krotovore architecture was as he expected.

They had dipped into several smaller rooms along the way, and dead Krotovore were everywhere. Evaran had said there were a few alive, but Dr. Snowden was not banking on that being true for too long. The delay in the Krotovore ship meant that the times would not align with the abduction experience he knew.

He never asked before how long it took Evaran to get from the Torvatta to the research labs that held them, but he guessed it was about two hours, and that was probably with Evaran moving much faster. At the pace they were going now, it would probably be another hour and a half.

Dr. Snowden swiveled his head around at everyone. "Why are we stopping?"

Evaran raised a hand. "It appears we have a visitor. Edev, show docking bay 3."

"You bet," said Edev. She flew between everyone, then shot down a projection of a small ship in docking bay 3.

Exiting the ship was a lightly armored humanoid in a power suit with an array of weapons and gadgets. The humanoid then shimmered out of view.

Dr. Snowden's skin crawled as the glowing blue eyes on the helmet were the last thing he saw. The humanoid walked with confidence.

Evaran's eyes narrowed as he gestured at the screen. "That is Tolkus Gare. I recognize his ship, and the readings and technology align with what I know of him. He is a Dalrun Wildborn, which is exceptionally rare. He can extend a camouflaging shield around himself without the need for technology. In my previous encounter with him, he was the number-one most wanted in this region. He was very difficult to track down and capture."

Dr. Snowden raised his eyebrows. "You hunted him?"

Evaran nodded. "Tolkus had a bad habit of attacking underdeveloped worlds that had not reached the technological threshold for space travel."

"How'd you catch him?" asked Emily.

Evaran inspected the floor for a moment. "U4 . . . ," he said, meeting Emily's gaze, "baited him out of the mountainside where he was sniping people. When he popped out of the cave he was hiding in, I jumped from the Torvatta and subdued him. He is a lethal bounty hunter and mercenary, and one of the best. He has an array of gadgets and is proficient in multiple weapons. On top of that, his power suit gives him exceptional strength, almost on par with mine.

However, even in my diminished physical capacity, I would still be a bit stronger, and faster."

"He better not cross paths with us then," said Emily.

Dr. Snowden shook his head. "So we know Jerzan is coming, and now we have this psychopath roaming around."

"He will head to the bridge after determining where it is. Although he may not be able to decipher the information there, he carries a tool that can pull it for later analysis. We will need to get to the research lab and then to the bridge, hopefully before he does. We have a head start."

Emily snorted. "He isn't the only one with camouflage technology."

Evaran nodded. "He is trackable by his thermal signature, and with Edev, it will be difficult for him to sneak up on us. However, we have stopped for another reason."

"Oh, no," said Dr. Snowden.

Levaran laid a hand on Dr. Snowden's shoulder. "It isn't anything bad."

Dr. Snowden sighed. "Probably not. I'm just used to things going sideways a lot."

Levaran smiled. "The route ahead is blocked by a Jankra Hull Shen, as the Krotovore call it. Its mass is substantial. We're going to go around it. Edev has already calculated a new route."

Evaran raised a finger. "This Jankra was not there during your abduction, so this is new to me."

"We can do it," said Emily. "Bring it on."

Dr. Snowden jerked his head back. "What do you mean by substantial? Can we see it?"

Evaran gestured at Edev.

Dr. Snowden shuddered at the projection Edev cast. The creature appeared to have internal organs stitched together by hairy limbs. He inspected closer, and revulsion swept over him. The creatures that it had killed became a part of its fleshy mass. He shook his head. "That's . . . absolutely disgusting."

Evaran nodded. "More importantly, it occupies the full height of the hallways and extends back a bit. According to the internal scans from Edev and what the Krotovore report, it appears it can shoot out a fleshy appendage that pulls in prey."

"Like a frog," said Emily. She harrumphed. "It tries that with me, I'll slice it off."

"There will be no need for that," said Evaran as he furrowed his eyebrows at Emily. "The Jankra is ahead, but we can take the passageway to the right and go around it. The alternative is we cut through it, and even then, we would be fighting it at the same time."

Emily shrugged. "Okay."

Evaran waved off to the right. "Let us go."

As they continued on, Dr. Snowden thought he heard mushy sounds broken up by a crackling noise. He rubbed the goose bumps on his arm. While the situation kept him on edge, Emily seemed to be relishing it. She was ready to fight. He knew that was her father's side in her. Since they were in a group that would be able to hold its own, she seemed more confident than she would normally be. He shook his head and focused on moving forward.

After thirty minutes, they reached a large storage room.

Dr. Snowden's skin crawled at the flashing lights, muted alarm sound, and mist that rolled across the ground. Although he had seen the mist and heard the muted alarm before, the flashing lights seemed to cast moving shadows off a container in the room.

Evaran motioned for Edev to go forward.

Edev flew ahead and scanned the room.

Dr. Snowden could see that thermal signatures were registering. The odd thing was that the shape of the thermal signatures reminded him of a large capsule. The material it was made of was organic.

Evaran narrowed his eyes. "Interesting. This must be some type of egg chamber."

"Draug?" asked Dr. Snowden.

"They are too big for draug."

Dr. Snowden gulped. Although he knew he was with a tough group, the unknown element of the room bothered him.

"Edev, distraction hologram," said Levaran.

"On it," said Edev. She flew to the center of the room and shot down a hologram of a grizzly bear. A chittering sound along with crackles and pops emitted from a hallway that was perpendicular to them.

Levaran glanced at Evaran. "It appears whatever birthed these things is nearby but isn't fooled by the projection. We should be able to cross."

"I concur, but we should not spend more time in the room than needed," said Evaran. "V, take point."

"Acknowledged."

"Everyone else, shields out."

Dr. Snowden activated his shield and pulled out his PSD. Emily had her shield out, and her baton was already active. He realized she had done it before Evaran had asked.

They crept through the room with a watchful gaze on the hallway that the sounds came from. As they neared the opposite side of the room, a large brown creature with an armored, segmented, centipede-like body emerged from the hallway. Each segment had a short leg attached to a sharp claw that was connected like a knee joint. Half the body was on the ground, while the other half was raised. The appendages on each upper body segment were larger and more muscled, with a long talon at the end of them.

Its head reminded Dr. Snowden of a dragon's, except this one had four eyes. It was like a mega version of the Dukashzeer, except on steroids.

"Go!" said Levaran, pointing forward.

Dr. Snowden and Emily hustled along with Evaran toward the hallway opposite from where they had entered the room.

Levaran fired a few repulsion and stun beams at the creature, but that just made it more active. As she and V walked backward toward where the others were, the creature picked up its pace.

Evaran placed his UIC on the wall console outside the room and interacted with his ARI. "Hurry!"

Levaran and V turned and ran.

The creature exhibited unusual speed and slammed a claw into V, sending him sprawling to the side.

Levaran pointed at V. "Get him!" She turned around and rushed headlong into the creature.

Evaran pulled out his utility handle. He extended a baton with a light-yellow glowing end and aimed at V.

A beam shot out and attached to V's shielding.

V righted himself as Evaran pulled him in.

Levaran had reached the creature and, with several hits, knocked it back a bit. The creature roared as Levaran hit it in the chest, sending it another few feet back. It spit a green substance at her that she blocked with her shield.

Dr. Snowden's eyes raised. This creature must be very strong.

Evaran shot out a grappling beam to Levaran, who grabbed it and, with a flip kick off the creature's chest, propelled herself toward the others. Once she was safely behind Evaran, he interacted with his ARI, causing the door to close.

Levaran stood and shook her head. "That was an angry mother."

"Strong one too," said Emily.

Levaran nodded. "More so than I expected. I suspect it could have even pierced V's shielding with that amount of force given enough time. According to the Krotovore, that was a Sarzarak. Without my shield, that acidic spit would have gone through me."

"One thing's for sure. We aren't going back that way. At least not easily," said Dr. Snowden.

Evaran pursed his lips. "There will be no need to. We are about an hour away from the research lab where your duplicates should be. From there, the bridge and engine room are on the way back on a different route."

Dr. Snowden exhaled from his nose as he followed the others. Although it had only been two encounters, he could see that there were creatures that would give even Levaran and Evaran a handful. Not to mention they now knew there was an elite hunter on board. He sighed. It could never be easy, but then again, if he had to do this with anyone, he was glad it was with this group.

Memories and sensations flooded Emily's mind as she walked through various corridors for the next hour. The black strip near the ceilings, the low lights, and the mist did not bother her as much as she thought it would. Going into the situation prepared was a much different experience from trying to come to grips with the fact that aliens and nonhumans existed, they were in another galaxy, and nanobots coursed through them.

Several sharp noises had rung out as they walked.

From what she could tell, it sounded like something had become prey to something else. Even with the power somewhat on, it seemed the door shieldings were still powering down across the ship. When they crossed a large, open plaza-like room, several creatures had flown at them, but with Edev flying around and repulsing them and everyone else firing, the creatures flew away in haste.

As they approached the corridor that led to the research labs where Dr. Snowden and Emily's duplicates were held, Emily tapped Dr. Snowden's arm. "Remember all this?"

Dr. Snowden clenched his jaw for a moment. "I'd rather not, but here we are."

She pulled her lips in as she recalled how scared she had been back then. Now the apex predators and whatever else got in their way had something to fear. As they stood outside the lab, she observed how the light from everyone's shielding lit up the environment. It gave a slight glow to the mist, but it comforted her.

Evaran placed his UIC on the console, and after a moment, the light-blue shielding that covered the door dissipated. He turned toward Dr. Snowden and Emily. "Are you ready for this?"

Dr. Snowden gulped. "I think so."

Emily nodded. "Let's do this."

V swatted Dr. Snowden's arm.

Dr. Snowden chuckled nervously while shaking his head. "You don't need to do that every time someone says that."

"Acknowledged."

Levaran gestured back the way they had come. "Edev, patrol this area and alert us if anything approaches."

"On it," said Edev. She shimmered and disappeared as she flew away.

Evaran pointed at the door. "V, hold this position."

"Acknowledged."

With a final look around, Evaran entered the room, followed by the others.

Emily wanted to rush over to the slabs, but they had a clouded barrier surrounding them, preventing visibility.

Evaran and Levaran had moved to the freestanding console off to the side.

While they interacted with it, Emily walked over to the slabs with Dr. Snowden. "Well, guess it's almost time."

"We'll be okay," he said.

There were only three of the six slabs with a barrier. It occurred to her that she never saw the shielding around each slab. During her abduction, they must have fallen when Evaran entered the virtual simulation. She turned toward Evaran. "Umm . . . there's only three shielded slabs here . . ."

Evaran gestured for Dr. Snowden and Emily to head over to the freestanding console. "That is correct, and there is a reason there are three. That selection is not coincidental."

Emily wrinkled her eyebrows. "So . . . who's missing then?"

"You both are," said Evaran. "Sanjay and Jay are not in there either."

Dr. Snowden cleared his throat. "Okay . . ."

Evaran cast a sidelong glance at Levaran for a moment, then pulled his lips taut as he faced Dr. Snowden. "Your brother, Dan, and his wife, Sarah, along with Dr. Bryson are in there."

"What!" said Dr. Snowden with widened eyes.

Emily gasped as she trembled. "Dad and Mom . . . are in there? Alive?"

Evaran nodded. "This universe's version of them is. They will go through an awakening, and we will need to guide them out."

Dr. Snowden swallowed hard as he circled a finger out. "Wait a minute. Dr. Bryson was nowhere near where Dan lived, unless things are really different."

Evaran raised a finger. "They are from different locations. I suspect that is why there were two ships. However, I believe I know why they are here, and it answers a question I had during your abduction experience."

Dr. Snowden stepped forward as Emily latched on to his right arm.

"Their presence here means that the Krotovore emergency beacon was on something near them. It would have been placed prior to this point in time and space, and I believe the person who will do that is Levaran."

"How do you figure that?" asked Dr. Snowden.

"The beacons would have to be precisely placed. This means there was intent. The only person who would know of these three individuals in this universe is Levaran due to the syncing we did earlier. This also implies that," said Evaran, waving a finger between them, "you two do not exist here."

Dr. Snowden narrowed his eyes. "Does this mean . . . you placed the emergency beacon on our car in our universe? And that's why the Krotovore came after us?"

Evaran ran a hand across the back of his neck. "It would appear that I do, sometime in my future."

Dr. Snowden gritted his teeth. "Oh . . . well . . . that's just great."

"It's part of a time loop, it would seem," said Levaran. "One that stretches across the plane."

Emily lightly squeezed Dr. Snowden's arm. "It's hard to be angry at something he hasn't done yet."

Dr. Snowden shook his head and sighed. "I know. It seems we were destined to be a part of this time loop. It just . . . sometimes feels like I have no control over my own life."

Evaran bowed his head. "I apologize for my future actions, but as Levaran mentioned, it is now part of a time loop. When this is over, we shall attend to it."

"When are we going to place it?" asked Emily, swallowing hard.

"The beacon was placed half an hour prior to the abduction," said Evaran.

Emily sighed. "We were still at Dad's grave site . . ."

Dr. Snowden adjusted his glasses. "This is nuts but, relative to everything else, I guess, pretty routine."

"It's about to get nuttier," said Levaran.

Dr. Snowden eyed Levaran. "Oh, no . . . what now?"

"I'll be going into the virtual simulation to meet with Dan and Sarah. If they're to travel with me, it has to be me. Dr. Bryson on the other hand . . ."

Dr. Snowden sighed. "I guess that's me . . ."

Levaran nodded. "There are several open slabs, and your nanobots can hook into the virtual simulation."

"Deeper and deeper," said Dr. Snowden.

Levaran raised a finger. "You will have an advantage—an administrative console."

Dr. Snowden perked up. "You mean I can, like . . . control things or something?"

"That's one facet," said Levaran. "You can pull it up and teleport using a map or move things or interact with objects from afar."

Emily could see the gears turning in Dr. Snowden's head. "What if I went instead?"

Dr. Snowden shook his head. "You might not have even existed, and if I had, he would know me. It has to be me."

"Maybe I could go with Levaran?"

Levaran eyed Emily. "Do you think you would be able to control your emotional state upon seeing your father's duplicate? It might make things confusing for them."

Emily sighed. "You're probably right. Can I at least see what's going on in there?"

Evaran gestured at the large screen on the opposite side of the room. "We can watch it together from there."

"I guess that's better than nothing," said Emily. She noticed Dr. Snowden had lowered his helmet and was rubbing his temples. "You'll be fine."

"I guess. Let's just get this part over with. I'm not even sure what to say to James."

Evaran walked over to the open slab. "Come. We can hook you up. All you need to do is let Dr. Bryson know that the virtual simulation is ending and that when he awakes, he will be in the real world. If anyone can convince him of that, it is you."

Dr. Snowden sighed as he trudged over to the slab. All the preparation he had done to converse with himself was now useless. Dr. Bryson might be someone completely different. He hopped up onto the slab and lay back. "Just like old times. Great."

Emily hustled over and laid a hand on his shoulder. "I'll be right here. Besides, you'll have an administrative console to play with."

He snorted, then bobbed his head. "Yeah, you're right." He rolled his head to the side to face Levaran. "Speaking of which, how do I turn it on?"

"When you enter, the console will be to your right," said Levaran. "It will appear as a floating screen with a keyboard. I've modified it to an input system you are familiar with. The interface will make sense once you're inside."

Dr. Snowden gulped. "I hope so." He took a deep breath and stared at the ceiling.

Emily wanted to go with him, but she knew it would probably only exacerbate the situation. Seeing her dad and mom would probably make things even worse for them and Levaran, even if it was just the parallel version of them. She sighed as she stood back.

He flashed Emily a thumbs-up as Evaran hooked him up.

She smiled at him. Despite everything going on, he was able to maintain control. She knew he had a short temper, and if this had been a few adventures ago, he would be flipping out. Traveling with Evaran allowed him to be in greater control, although she knew it was more the nanobots.

Levaran gestured at the three shielded slabs while facing Emily. "I'm going to lower the shielding and then interface with the system. If you were curious as to what they look like, this would be a good time to see them."

Emily nodded and followed Levaran.

Dr. Snowden harrumphed. "Oh, wait until I'm hooked up to do that. I see how it is."

"It's a matter of efficiency," said Levaran. "These shields will take about thirty seconds to lower, and that is time you can be helping Dr. Bryson."

Dr. Snowden sighed. "I figured. Ahh well. So . . . when do I—" His body went limp as a light glow formed around the nodes attached to his head.

Evaran pointed at the screen. "He is in."

Levaran nodded and interacted with her ARI. After thirty seconds, the shielding around the slabs dropped.

Emily's heartbeat ramped up as she studied both Dan and Sarah. Dan was just as she remembered him, maybe a bit older. Sarah caught her by surprise. She was a spitting image of Emily, except maybe a little slimmer in the face. Emily's breathing went haphazard.

Levaran laid a hand on Emily's shoulder. "You're definitely their child. Just remember, in this universe, they may not have had a child, so while they may look the part, they're not your parents. However . . . their three-Ls are close, which means your knowledge of how to interact with them is probably still relevant, at least for your father."

Emily struggled to breathe as her eyes watered. In a weak voice, she said, "Looks just like him."

Levaran extended her arms out.

Emily trembled as she hugged Levaran.

After Emily stepped back, Levaran placed her UIC on a console on the wall. Once it had connected, she faced into the room and nodded at Emily. "It's time."

Emily wiped her eyes and then joined Evaran by the screen, which was split into two feeds, with the top feed showing the view from Dr. Snowden and the bottom one from Levaran.

"Do not worry," said Evaran, placing an arm around her. "Hopefully this will go smoothly and we can talk to them when they come out."

V walked into the room and stood next to Emily. "Analysis. Your heartbeat has increased."

Emily half smiled. "I'm good. I just didn't expect to see . . . my parents."

V tilted his head. "That would be unexpected. Perhaps a hug will make you feel better."

She laughed as she hugged V. "Thanks. Now I guess we just watch and see what happens."

Evaran raised a finger. "Be aware that the feed will be sped up a bit since there is a time-dilation effect, but your nanobots should be able to compensate."

She nodded. "Here we go, I guess."

12

Dr. Snowden closed his eyes and braced himself as the familiar pulse of the nodes cascaded over his head. The last time he felt it was when they came off of him during his awakening. He jumped as the sound of cars driving by rang out.

After opening his eyes, he realized he was standing on a sidewalk outside the college where he taught. It made sense to him that if he was looking for Dr. Bryson, it would be near there. Looking down to his right, he saw the floating black screen with several menu options on it. The screen was semitransparent and had a small text box to type in with a keyboard extending from the bottom. Levaran knew exactly how to conform the console.

He flinched when a woman bustled past him. Reaching out to grab the console was an instinctive move on his part, but it caused the woman to pause and give him a look of confusion. He waved a hand in the air. "Sorry, was just deep in thought."

The woman snorted and continued walking.

This was not going to be as easy as he thought if he could not focus. With a look both ways before crossing the street, he headed into the open court area that had a statue of the college's founder. The temperature was warm with the sun shining, and the sound of undergraduate students filled the air. He took in a deep breath. A part of him missed the academic experience. However, he knew that his knowledge was now way beyond anything that could be taught without running afoul of knowledge pollution.

He examined the administrative console and, after perusing the options, pressed the map option. It pulled up an overhead view with a grid overlaid on it. A blinking green indicator showed his current location, while a yellow one showed where Dr. Bryson was. He smirked at the thought that Evaran probably used this to get to him and Emily. He ran his finger over the console and tapped the yellow dot.

A bright flash erupted around him.

His eyes had closed instinctively before he had time to think about it. When he opened them, the door to Dr. Bryson's office stared at him. It took a moment for him to realize he had been teleported to the hallway in the science department. That was something he would need to be careful about. He did a quick survey of the hall and noted that no one had been around to witness the teleportation. With a look of determination in his eyes, he knocked on Dr. Bryson's door.

"Office hours start in an hour," said Dr. Bryson.

Dr. Snowden pushed the door slightly open and peeked his head in. "Hey, James."

Dr. Bryson studied Dr. Snowden for a moment before scrambling out of his chair. With widened eyes he said, "A . . . Albert?"

"That's me," said Dr. Snowden with a smile.

Dr. Bryson trembled as he stared at Dr. Snowden. "How . . . how is this possible?"

Dr. Snowden wrinkled his eyebrows. "What do you mean?"

"You died five years ago."

"Oh," said Dr. Snowden. He remembered that Evaran had said he and Emily might not exist, but it had not dawned on him that he could exist, but be dead. "Yeah . . . about that. Got a moment to talk?"

Dr. Bryson's breathing staggered.

"Okay . . . look . . . I'm not a zombie or a ghost. Maybe this isn't the place to talk. Can we talk at your house later tonight?"

Dr. Bryson gulped.

"Oh, c'mon. The last time I saw you like this was in our undergrad years when we roomed together and you woke up with Hannah next to you in bed."

A small grin crept up on Dr. Bryson's face. "Well, she was *your* girlfriend."

Dr. Snowden smiled. Hannah was just a friend in his universe, but that memory seemed to unarm Dr. Bryson some. "Will you at least give me a chance? How about eight tonight? I'll even bring the pizza. Pepperoni, extra cheese, and light sauce."

Dr. Bryson wrinkled his eyebrows. He studied Dr. Snowden for a moment, then said, "Okay . . ."

"You still live at 4300 Aspen Street, right?"

Dr. Bryson nodded.

"Okay, I'll see you then, and . . . just to give you something to think about. You remember all those discussions, well, arguments we had about parallel universes?"

Dr. Bryson nodded.

"Buckle up," said Dr. Snowden. He walked out of the office and, after verifying no one was around, went back to where he had entered the virtual simulation. At least he now knew that the parallel-universe topics he used to argue with Dr. Bryson about had occurred in this universe. He navigated his way to a bench and sat. Scrutinizing the interface, he saw that he could set a time in addition to moving by clicking. He was a mini Torvatta.

After going back one level to the top menu options, he pressed on the objects button. It took him a bit to navigate, but he found the pizza icon, which had several options under it. He shook his head. How did Levaran know how to do all of this? She was an Evaran, so maybe this was trivial to her, but to him, he could see the many hours, if not months, it would take to build an interface like this.

He went back to the map option and set the time to 7:55 p.m., then scrolled the map using his finger without tapping. Once he found Dr. Bryson's house, he tapped just in front of it. A bright light flashed around him, and when it dissipated, he verified he was where he needed to be. Flipping back to the pizza option, he created a pizza in a box, which appeared on the ground in front of him. After picking it up, he headed to the front door and pressed the doorbell.

The sound of footsteps thumping down a stairway echoed out. After a moment, the door swung open. Dr. Bryson had on jeans and a short-sleeve buttoned-up shirt. He wagged a finger at Dr. Snowden. "I . . . I think you're from a parallel universe."

Dr. Snowden smiled. "I figured if I gave you some time to chew on it, you would come to that conclusion."

"I knew it!" said Dr. Bryson. He exhaled sharply and then stepped back from the door while gesturing for Dr. Snowden to come in.

Dr. Snowden entered and took his usual spot on Dr. Bryson's couch. He laid the pizza box on the living room table. "Just how you like your pizza."

Dr. Bryson took a seat in a chair perpendicular to Dr. Snowden. He sighed. "A parallel universe. That's the only logical answer, but it doesn't make sense. Those were just hypothetical arguments. Why . . . why are you here?"

"There's a good reason for that, I assure you. In my universe, we were the best of friends, as it appears we were here as well. Now . . . this is going to sound wild, so bear with me. Emily and I were abducted by aliens and taken to another galaxy through a space-time rift."

Dr. Bryson studied Dr. Snowden for a moment. "Emily?"

"My niece. I'm guessing she doesn't exist here."

Dr. Bryson shook his head. "Sarah couldn't have kids."

"Oh . . . ," said Dr. Snowden. "That's going to be interesting."

Dr. Bryson cleared his throat. "Okay, so alien abduction, travel through a space-time rift, and another galaxy. You sure you didn't just write a science-fiction novel?"

Dr. Snowden chuckled. "I'm being serious, and here is how it relates to this situation. In this universe, apparently I'm dead, and Emily doesn't exist. The abduction still occurs, though, except . . . it's the people who were nearest to me and Emily."

"You mean . . . Dan and Sarah?"

Dr. Snowden chewed on his upper lip for a moment. "And you."

Dr. Bryson furrowed his eyebrows. "Don't you think I would have noticed if I was abducted?"

Dr. Snowden shook his head. "You wouldn't have. They pumped you full of nanobots, then altered your memory so that the transition was seamless."

"Nanobots . . . right. Okay . . . but . . . I'm here. In my house."

"Not really. You're in a virtual simulation and have been for the last year, well, three weeks, due to time dilation. It's why you couldn't sleep at times and, at other times, you could barely keep your eyes open. I'm here to tell you all this because in . . . ," said Dr. Snowden, looking down at the administrative console, "ten minutes, this all goes away."

Dr. Bryson gulped. "And you just popped in to tell me all this?"

Dr. Snowden sighed. "The guy who rescued us, his name is Evaran. He walked me and Emily through it and called it our awakening. Once we were out, we were ready for it. There were two other people, and they didn't get that treatment. They were in shock and went crazy."

"Mental conditioning," said Dr. Bryson with a smirk. "Well, I guess we'll find out when all of this disappears, assuming that *is* how it ends."

Dr. Snowden half smiled. "If your Albert was like me, then you had a C programming class in college."

"Yeah . . ."

"Then I bet you remember where we learned about memory management?"

"Of course, it was one of my favorite classes."

"Well, you'll get to see a live deallocation."

Dr. Bryson jerked his head back. "And . . . how does that look?"

"Let's go to your backyard. We can see it from there."

"I'd offer you a beer, but assuming this is all true, it's probably not real."

Dr. Snowden nodded as he stood. After a few minutes, he was outside with Dr. Bryson, he pointed to the sky in the west. "It'll come from there. Blocks of the environment will begin to deallocate. There will be a wind, and a weird noise."

Dr. Bryson surveyed the sky. "Don't see anything yet."

Dr. Snowden examined the administrative console. "We have . . . seven minutes left."

Dr. Bryson looked at where the console would have been relative to Dr. Snowden. "What exactly are you looking at when you say the time?"

"You're going to love this. It's an administrative console."

"No kidding. Like . . . what can you do with it?"

Dr. Snowden pressed the pizza option he had before, causing a pizza in a box to appear on the ground in front of them.

Dr. Bryson took a step back. "That's . . . that's pretty impressive. What else can you do?"

"Teleport, for one thing. I did that earlier to your office. Essentially, anything you can think of."

Dr. Bryson shook his head. "It would make learning about the stuff we study a lot easier with something like that. I guess there is some merit that our universe is a simulation."

"Not . . . quite. It's a bit more extensive than that. You'll meet your universe's version of Evaran. We call her Levaran so as to not be confusing. If we get off the ship that abducted you without issues, she might offer you the chance to travel through space, time, and everywhere else, even outside the universe."

"Have you . . ."

Dr. Snowden nodded. "Oh, yeah, and reality is *much* stranger than you might believe."

Dr. Bryson looked down for a moment as his eyes misted. "You know . . . I miss this so much, just hanging out, discussing theories and the impossible. I'll never forget that asshole that hit you and took you away from us."

"Oh . . . sounds like this universe version of me died in a car accident."

Dr. Bryson wiped his eyes. "Yeah. Drunk truck driver named Jay Beerman. You were on your way back from a conference on I-70. It was such a senseless death."

Dr. Snowden jerked his head back. "Jay Beerman? He was one of the others Evaran rescued alongside me and Emily. We're actually good friends."

Dr. Bryson laughed. "Then this universe is a cruel joker."

When the deallocation came, a booming sound followed by static radio noise washed over them.

Dr. Bryson shook his head. "You were right. Holy shit."

Dr. Snowden raised his voice over the noise as it grew louder the closer the deallocation came. "Just close your eyes and focus on waking up." He walked over to Dr. Bryson and put his arm around him. "We will do this together."

"This is crazy!"

"Focus!"

Dr. Snowden peeped out and saw that Dr. Bryson had positioned himself as if expecting a tidal wave. When the familiar feeling of the deallocation passed them, he relaxed, and the sound of Evaran and the others caressed his ears.

Dan Snowden took a break from mowing his lawn. The sun was beating down, and the heat was tiring him out faster than he expected. Mowing four acres on his riding lawn mower made things a bit easier, but not by much. It was around 1:00 p.m., so he figured he may as well check the mail.

As he rode up to his mailbox, his attention was drawn to a middle-aged woman in a skirt suit. He narrowed his eyes as he killed the mower.

The woman altered her path and walked up to him. She bowed with her left arm across her stomach and said, "My name is Levaran, and I'm here to save you."

He sighed. His brother, Albert, used to prank him by sending Jehovah's Witnesses to his house. He shook his head. "Oh, really? And how's that?"

"The world around you is an illusion. It's a virtual simulation, and I'm here to guide you through your awakening."

He laughed. "A what?"

Levaran half smiled. "I realize this may sound odd, but there isn't much time." She tapped the air to her right, and a timer showing fifteen minutes appeared above the mailbox. As it decremented, she pointed at it. "When that hits zero, the world as you know it will disappear, and you will emerge into the real world."

Dan examined the timer. There was no way that could be there. The hairs on the back of his neck rose. "Look, lady, Levaran, or whatever . . . I don't know how you're doing that, but I think it's you who needs to join the real world."

She chuckled. "You have similar qualities to Dr. Snowden."

His eyes widened. "How do you know Albert?"

"He's in the real world, waiting for you to wake up. Let me ask you this. Have you had dreams of a medical room, unlike any you've seen, with unusual symbols and a free-standing console that you know was not meant for humans?"

He gulped. "Yeah . . ."

"And you find that sometimes you just can't sleep, and other times you can barely keep your eyes open. Instead of a day or two, these spells can go on for weeks."

He did not think it was possible to sweat more than he already was. "That's . . . that's uncanny. How could you possibly know any of this?"

"Because I'm standing between you and Sarah in the real world. Let me demonstrate."

He watched her freeze, and then almost fell out of his mower due to the sensation of something squeezing his shoulder. After getting off the mower, he rubbed his shoulder as his breathing staggered.

"I don't mean to alarm you, but I'm telling you this because when the world disappears, you will awaken. Your mind needs to be prepared for this. You should call Sarah."

"Uhh . . . okay . . . ," said Dan. He ran up to the house and shouted for Sarah.

Sarah ran to the door. "Dan? What is it?"

He pointed at Levaran and gestured toward her. "Just . . . follow me."

"Dan?"

"It's . . . hard to explain. C'mon."

After they returned, he nodded at Levaran. "This is Levaran. She says she knows Albert, and that we're living in a"—he motioned at Levaran—"what'd you call it?"

"A virtual simulation," said Levaran. She eyed Sarah. "You cannot have children, correct?"

Sarah's lips parted as she stared at Dan, then back at Levaran. "How could you know that?"

Levaran pointed at the timer, which now showed five minutes. "All will be explained when this world deallocates. I need you both to understand that the last year has not been real, and in five minutes, you will be back in the real world. There . . . will need to be some explanation about what you will see in the real world, but we can cover that once you're there."

Sarah grimaced as she latched on to Dan's arm. "Is she for real?"

He sighed. "I don't know, but the timer, her knowledge of our dreams, sleep patterns, and . . . she went into the real world, assuming that's true, and squeezed my shoulder. I don't know how any of that is possible, but everything points to it being real."

Sarah began to breathe heavier. "What's gonna happen to us?"

Levaran nodded. "When the world ends, you will feel no pain. You will awaken in the medical lab you saw in your dreams. I will be there, along with Albert and . . . some others that will need an explanation."

"Albert?" asked Sarah.

Dan exhaled from his nose. "She mentioned that he is waiting on us to *awaken*. I guess . . . I guess we'll know when the timer hits zero, right?"

"You're correct. If I didn't come, you would just wake up without any warning, in that medical room, and things would be very complicated."

He nodded as a look of defiance crossed his eyes. "Well . . . hell. If you're lying, we'll know here shortly."

"I understand. We have a few minutes, so I wanted to cover some things," said Levaran. She waved a finger at the both of them. "You were both abducted by an alien race known as the Krotovore. They put you into these virtual simulations for research. To keep your body functioning, they injected nanobots. Due to the time difference, you've been in this virtual simulation for three weeks, although from your perspective, a year has passed. The ship you're on is badly damaged, and the system powering the virtual simulation is powering down."

Dan snorted. "If that ain't the craziest thing I've ever heard . . . but given these last few minutes . . ." He exhaled from his mouth. "I'm gonna have a hell of a lot of questions if we go back to the real world."

"Of course, and my friend and I will be there to help you," said Levaran. She checked the timer. "Do you have any questions before the deallocation occurs?"

He gulped. "If this is true, why are you helping us?"

"It's what I do, and who I am, in any form."

"So . . . what should we expect?" asked Sarah.

Levaran pointed to the sky in the west. "It will begin there. A wind will develop, and you'll hear static noise. When it happens, stand by me, and we'll leave this world together."

Sarah sighed as she squeezed Dan's arm. "Is this really happening?"

Dan shrugged. "We'll find out."

When the timer hit zero, a booming sound shot out from the west.

Levaran pointed at the sky. "It begins. Come."

His eyes widened as he watched chunks of the sky turn semitransparent, then disappear. "What the hell!"

"Come!" said Levaran.

Dan and Sarah scooted over to Levaran.

Levaran placed an arm around each of them. "Just focus. I promise when this is over, I'll be there to help you."

He swallowed hard as the deallocation crept toward them. Watching football this afternoon was out. Now he had to deal with an awakening that he knew very little about. Half the stuff Levaran said to him sounded like gibberish. He shook his head.

When the deallocation was ten feet away, everyone closed their eyes.

The noise was irritating his ears, but after a moment, everything went quiet. He flailed around as the sensation of falling swept over him. Opening his eyes, he saw darkness, and a small light in the distance. The light grew exponentially until it was all around him. Pain shot up and down his body as he tried to breathe. His vision was blurred and his throat dry. Trying to cough did not help things.

A prickling sensation swarmed around his heart region. He tried to put his hand over his chest, but his arms were not responding.

The familiar sound of Levaran echoed out. "Give your body a moment to adjust."

Although fear had been his first reaction, Levaran's voice calmed him down. The sound of Dr. Snowden's voice in the background excited him. Maybe Levaran was telling the truth. He could feel his senses returning at a rapid pace. It was time to find some answers.

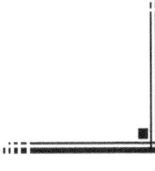

13

Emily had watched the split-screen interaction in both virtual simulations. Although they were sped up due to the time-dilation effects, she was able to follow them. Dr. Bryson was similar to the man she knew in her universe. Apparently in this universe, he and Dr. Snowden were also close friends. It seemed Dr. Bryson had accepted Dr. Snowden's word at face value. It probably helped that they had a theoretical discussion like this in the past.

Watching her dad and mom had been rough. She now knew that she had never been born in this universe, so they would have no idea who she was unless told. They were not her parents, but being duplicates of them tore at her emotions. Although it had only been a little over one minute from her perspective, it was about twenty in the virtual simulation.

She shot Evaran a look. "That was quick."

"It was," he said. "Levaran used a different approach than me, but now, with everyone awakening, we will need to bring them all to the same level of understanding." He eyed her. "Are you ready for this?"

She swallowed hard. "As ready as I'll ever be, I guess."

He smiled. "Let us do this?"

She shook her head as she swatted Evaran's arm. "Let's."

Levaran and Dr. Snowden had disconnected from the virtual simulation and joined them at a spot in front of the slabs.

"I kinda like that administrative console," said Dr. Snowden.

Levaran waved her thumb between herself and Evaran. "We figured you would."

"That teleport aspect was pretty nifty. And the control . . . I guess I could replicate that in the holo room, but it feels different with a real person in there not knowing."

Emily bumped Dr. Snowden. "Don't let it go to your head." Her attention focused on Dan, Sarah, and Dr. Bryson propping themselves up on the slabs. "Looks like they're about to become fully aware."

Evaran nodded. "This time everyone was guided." He gestured at Levaran. "I think it is best for Levaran to be the spokesperson until they are dressed."

"No problem," said Emily, eying her parallel-universe parents. Dan's personality in the virtual simulation was every bit the father she knew. Sarah much less so, but she did not have much to go on. She sighed as she latched on to the left arm of a startled Dr. Snowden. Although she was trying to put up a brave front, the emotions swirling around inside her were fighting for control.

After a moment, Levaran gestured outward to the others. "Please, come forward."

Sarah gripped Dan's arm as he inched his way forward.

Dr. Bryson swung his head around in confusion, then focused on Dr. Snowden.

When Dan passed Dr. Bryson, he paused. "James?"

Dr. Bryson shook his head. "Looks like I'm in the same boat as you."

"I guess we're about to find out what the hell is going on."

Dr. Bryson nodded and followed Dan and Sarah up to the first slab. They stood just in front of it.

Emily and Sarah locked eyes. It was easy for Emily to see where she got her looks. She could see a hint of recognition in Sarah's eyes. When she checked Dan, she saw the same hint. It was their intense focus on Dr. Snowden that did not surprise her. They would have known him, regardless of her status.

Levaran raised her hand and positioned it palm down in front of her. "When I have my hand here, breathe in. When I lower it, breathe out. It will only take a few minutes."

After Levaran raised and lowered her hand several times, she said, "You should all be feeling a bit more relaxed."

Dr. Bryson exhaled from his mouth. "Yeah. I am, at least. Feel like someone tossed me in a washing machine."

Emily chuckled. Dr. Bryson had the same humor she had known growing up.

Dr. Bryson half smiled as his eyes searched Emily over for a moment. "I think I know who you are."

Levaran raised a finger. "I'll explain that. First things first. I have covered some of this already with Dan and Sarah, but I want to make sure we are all on the same level of understanding. You're here because you were abducted by an alien race known as the Krotovore. You've been here three weeks inside a virtual simulation. Nanobots were placed inside you to help maintain your bodies during this time. The ship we're on jumped through a space-time rift and is now badly damaged in the Andromeda galaxy, one year into the future. Do you all understand this?"

Dr. Bryson nodded. "Albert covered it with me, but I have to say, it sounds outlandish. However . . . it's hard to argue with reality slapping you in the face."

Dan exhaled from his nose. "So this is the *real* world you spoke of."

Levaran nodded.

"And these . . . nanobots. What are they exactly?"

"They are nanometer-sized machines that will maintain your body," said Levaran. "They do have some side effects such as increased strength, speed, the ability to comprehend things faster, the ability to breathe in harsher environments, and . . . other aspects. Your well-being is their goal, and you have nothing to fear from them."

Sarah wrinkled her eyebrows as she ran a hand over her arm. "That's . . . kinda creepy. So do we know who or what these Krotovore are like?"

Levaran interacted with her ARI.

V walked into the room.

Dr. Bryson and the others jumped back. He exhaled sharply. "Holy moly! Is that . . . an android?"

V gazed at Dr. Bryson. "I am a variable utility artificial intelligence. My shortened name is V. I have two modes, orb and body. I am currently in body mode."

"Absolutely fascinating," said Dr. Bryson, running a hand across his mouth.

"You're adapting pretty quick to this," said Dan.

"I . . . might dabble in science fiction a bit," said Dr. Bryson with a grin.

Levaran gestured at V. "Display the Krotovore species."

"Acknowledged," said V. He shot a holographic display of a three-foot-tall creature from the top of his head. It had six eyes on a bulbous head; two were larger than the four surrounding them. Where a mouth would be, a short proboscis protruded. Small antennae extended from the head, which had little bumpy ridges around the top. The kidney-shaped body was covered in short hairs, and the back had segmented armor plates. Four legs supported the body while two arms on each side of the body hung to the side. Each arm had a hand section with three slim fingers, one of which was opposable.

Dan peered at the projection, and after a moment, he said, "That is one *ugly* alien."

Sarah shook her head. "Reminds me of a large flea, kinda."

Emily smiled. "Did to me too."

Sarah half smiled at Emily.

Dan put a hand over his mouth for a moment, then pointed at Dr. Snowden. "I'm very curious to hear how Albert is here. I buried him five years ago."

Levaran nodded. "This will sound strange." She waved a hand between Evaran, Dr. Snowden, Emily, and V. "They are from a parallel universe. In their universe," she said, pointing at Evaran, "he rescued them from the Krotovore. He is that parallel universe's version of me."

Dr. Bryson waved a finger. "And in this one, since Albert is dead, we were chosen." He gestured at Emily. "I'm going to guess that is Dan and Sarah's kid."

Emily felt a wave of emotion sweep over her.

Levaran nodded. "You are correct. I can see why you and Dr. Snowden were friends. In their universe," she said, motioning at Sarah, "she died giving birth to Emily." She pointed at Dan. "You died in her sophomore year of college. Dr. Snowden took her in so she could finish college."

Emily's eyes watered as she saw the realization sweep over Dan and Sarah. They were staring at her with intent, and it was becoming increasingly hard for her to maintain control.

Dan choked up a bit as he dipped his head toward Emily. "Not sure I fully understand what a parallel universe is, but guessing it's some sort of duplicate, and . . . that's our parallel-universe little girl?"

"Yes," said Levaran.

Emily smiled as she wiped her eyes.

Dan smiled at Sarah. "She has your looks."

"Yeah, but she has your defiance," said Dr. Snowden.

Dan swallowed hard. "This is . . . unexpected."

Emily wanted to hug them, but figured it might be odd.

Levaran cleared her throat. "Before we continue, why don't you three get your clothes on." She tapped a panel on the bottom of the nearest slab. "Your clothes are in the lower panel on your slabs, and there are changing rooms in the back. Once you're finished, you can talk among yourselves. Evaran and I have some things to go over."

Dan nodded. "Right. Sure. No problem." He turned and tapped Sarah's arms. "C'mon."

Dr. Bryson examined his robe and chuckled. "White robes with dots. How original." He smiled at Dr. Snowden. "I think I'm going to enjoy hearing more about all of this."

Dr. Snowden chuckled. "I knew you would, and for the record, I was right about the parallel-universe argument we had at that convention in St. Louis."

Dr. Bryson eyed Dr. Snowden for a moment. "You were, as hard as that is to admit. Ahh, well. At least I hope they abducted me in decent clothes."

Emily chuckled.

Dr. Bryson half smiled at Emily and then went to his slab.

Once they were all in the changing rooms, Dr. Snowden said, "Well, that didn't go too bad."

"Yeah. It's a bit easier when you don't have two people going crazy," said Emily. She sighed. "This . . . version of Dad is dead-on."

Dr. Snowden nodded. "He definitely is. So is James. Sarah is too, but she is a bit older. I guess we'll get to know them."

Emily nodded. She studied the others when they came back from the changing rooms. Dan had on work boots, jeans, and a green flannel. Sarah wore jeans and a large shirt. Dr. Bryson was wearing sneakers with jeans and a short-sleeve patterned shirt. The clothes fit the image she had in her head.

Dr. Bryson stretched his neck. "Well, at least the clothing situation worked out."

Dan tugged on his flannel. "Feels a little lighter than I remember."

"You're probably just realizing the increased strength from the nanobots," said Dr. Snowden.

Dan exhaled as his eyes misted. He swallowed hard. "Sorry . . . I . . . I just wasn't expecting you."

"Take your time," said Dr. Snowden.

Dan wiped his eyes as he bobbed his head. "Right. About these nanobots . . . what if we don't want them in us?"

"Evaran can take them out, well, I mean, our Evaran," said Emily. "I wasn't sure if I wanted them in either, but now . . . I couldn't do without them."

Dan nodded as he approached Emily. "So . . . in this . . . other universe, me and Sarah are dead, and you and Albert are still alive, is that right?"

Emily's throat constricted as she nodded.

Sarah peered at Emily. "You're beautiful."

"Thanks," said Emily in a soft voice.

Sarah moved her hand close to Emily's face. "May I . . ."

Emily nodded.

Sarah touched Emily's hair, then ran a hand along her face.

A tear dropped onto Emily's cheek as she leaned her head into Sarah's hand.

"Oh, I didn't mean to make you sad," said Sarah. She opened her arms, and Emily hugged her. "You may not be our daughter here, but somewhere, you are."

Dan sniffled as he placed both arms around Emily and Sarah.

Dr. Bryson raised an eyebrow at Dr. Snowden. "If you think you're getting hugs out of me, forget it."

Dr. Snowden chuckled as he wiped his eyes. He joined the others in hugging.

After a moment, V tilted his head. "Is this an open hugging session?"

Emily laughed as she stepped back. She went over and hugged V. "How's that?"

V's lights brightened.

Levaran and Evaran joined the group.

Evaran raised a finger. "I do not mean to break up this discussion, but it appears we have visitors."

Dr. Snowden swallowed hard. He had an idea of who it would be, and with a sigh, he said, "Let me guess . . . Jerzan?"

Evaran drew his lips flat as he pointed at the large screen on the wall. After interacting with his ARI, the screen showed docking bay 3. Jerzan's ship stood prominently inside. Evaran pointed at it as Jerzan and his crew disembarked and headed over to investigate Tolkus Gare's ship. "You are correct. That is Jerzan and the Bloodbore mercenary group."

Dr. Snowden recalled that during their abduction, he saw Jerzan's arrival when they were at the bridge. Seeing Jerzan now was not surprising, given that the Krotovore ship had been delayed in coming through. "Great. I was going to suggest we split up and get Dan and the others to the Torvatta, but I guess not now."

Evaran raised a finger. "It would be too dangerous. We are going to head to the bridge as we had initially planned, then the engine room, then to the Torvatta."

Dan chuckled.

Dr. Snowden shot a look at Dan.

Dan shook a hand out. "You're a carbon copy of the Albert I know. If there's something crazy going on, you're *right* in the thick of it."

Evaran nodded. "An apt description."

Dr. Snowden jerked his head back. "What . . ."

"I take it this Jerzan guy is bad news," said Dan.

Evaran drew his lips flat. "Jerzan is a ruthless mercenary, and so are the Bloodbores. If they were to capture us, we would go to the slave markets."

"Oh," said Dan, moving his head back.

"Levaran and V will take point. Dan, Sarah, and Dr. Bryson will be in the middle, with Dr. Snowden and Emily on either side. I will take the rear while Edev scouts out front," said Evaran.

Dr. Bryson narrowed his eyes. "Edev?"

"You have not met her yet," said Evaran. "She is like V, except in orb mode."

"Oh," said Dr. Bryson. He waved a finger between Evaran and Levaran. "You never told us what you two are . . ."

Dan and Sarah perked up.

"We are . . . complicated," said Evaran with a small smile.

"You're aliens, right?" asked Dr. Bryson.

"Something like that," said Evaran.

Dr. Bryson raised an eyebrow at Dr. Snowden.

"They're . . . different," said Dr. Snowden.

Dr. Bryson snorted.

Evaran waved forward. "Come, we should go."

They exited the room and headed toward the bridge.

Memories of the large silo-like room, the elevators that resembled columns, and the dim light and mist ran through Dr. Snowden's mind. He could tell Dan was trying hard to keep it together. The constant looking around and Sarah clasping his arm showed they were in distress, but Dan would never admit it. It just was not his way.

As they headed to the elevator that would take them up to floor that the bridge was on, Edev flew in and scanned Dan and the others. "Hello, I'm Edev!"

Dr. Bryson moved his head around as he examined Edev. "Well . . . hello back."

Dan and Sarah nodded at Edev.

"You're in safe hands," said Edev.

"I hope so," said Dr. Bryson. He squinted as he studied Edev. "So you're like V, just in orb mode?"

"I am," said Edev. "V is much older than me, though."

"Analysis. Edev is one day old," said V.

Dr. Bryson jerked his head back. "Oh, wow. Okay."

Dr. Snowden chuckled. He figured Dr. Bryson and the others would get along well with Edev on their adventures, assuming they agreed to travel with Levaran. His suspicion was that Dr. Bryson and Edev would form a close bond, similar to Emily and V.

As they exited the elevator on level 555, from level 546, Dan shook his head. "This is a pretty big ship."

Dr. Snowden nodded. "You should see it from the outside."

Sarah gulped. "It's kinda eerie."

Emily nodded. "That sensation, regardless if you've been here before, never goes away."

A shrieking sound in the distance caused a wide-eyed Sarah to jump.

"You'll get used to that," said Emily.

Sarah closed her eyes for a moment as she nodded.

Dr. Bryson adjusted his glasses. He tapped Dr. Snowden's arm with one hand and pointed at the segmented arch they were approaching with the other. "So in your universe, while I was teaching class, you were on an alien starship and getting to study things like that?"

"I hadn't quite . . . believed . . . we were on a ship at that point," said Dr. Snowden.

"Oh," said Dr. Bryson. "What changed your mind?"

Dr. Snowden furrowed his eyebrows. "Draug. Insect-like hive-minded creatures. They swarmed the large room we're about to enter."

Dr. Bryson's eyes widened.

"Don't worry. If they come, they're gonna be in for a surprise," said Dr. Snowden with a chuckle.

As everyone reached the arch, Dan walked up to one of the segments and studied it. "Huh. I . . . can read this . . . somehow."

Levaran raised a finger. "It's the universal translator. Although I don't have my own ship yet," she said, gesturing at Evaran, "his has the same functionality. Your nanobots have interfaced with it, and you can now understand different languages and writing."

Dr. Bryson joined Dan in examining the segment. "No kidding. That's awesome. You mean I can now understand . . . say, German . . . or Russian?"

Dr. Snowden chuckled. "You're just excited to be able to read research papers in their native language."

"Well . . . yeah," said Dr. Bryson. He shook his head. "Having a hard time distinguishing you from the Albert I know."

Dan nodded. "Same here."

Sarah half smiled.

Dr. Snowden took a moment to look them over. "Yeah, and vice versa."

Evaran motioned forward. "Let us head to the bridge. It is approximately a mile ahead."

"A mile?" asked Dan.

Emily grinned. "That was me and Uncle Albert's same expression when we first learned these distances."

Dan nodded at Emily. "Well . . . hell. Let's get a move on then before any of those draug things come."

Emily smiled.

Dr. Snowden had thought Emily would be all over the place, and maybe she was, but she seemed to be holding it together. Perhaps the knowledge that this was not her real father helped, but it was hard to see much to distinguish that.

Emily swiveled her head at Dr. Snowden.

He grinned.

When they reached the center of the main bridge concourse, Evaran and Levaran paused to scan around.

The sound of weapon fire punctuated the silence they had been enjoying.

Edev flew back toward the entrance. After a few minutes, she came back and said, "Tolkus Gare signature detected."

"Shields out. Now!" said Evaran as he extended his utility handle into a baton.

Levaran gestured at V. "Take Dan and the others to the bridge."

"Acknowledged," said V. He motioned forward. "Dan, Sarah, and Dr. Bryson, please follow me."

Dan pivoted his head toward Dr. Snowden.

"I'll go with them," said Dr. Snowden.

Evaran nodded as he motioned back toward the entrance. Levaran and Emily followed him.

Dan watched as the distance increased between the two groups. "They're going to fight, aren't they?"

Dr. Snowden nodded. "They should be able to handle it. V, show a projection from Edev's perspective."

"Acknowledged," said V. A projection shot out above his head, showing an isometric view of Evaran, Levaran, and Emily approaching the entrance.

A thermal signature of a humanoid appeared near the entrance and then moved to the side. Labels showed that Tolkus was using a camouflage effect. Following behind him were the vanguard of a draug brood.

Dr. Bryson's eyes widened. "Woah. I can see why you began to believe. Those are the draug?"

"Yeah. Nasty creatures," said Dr. Snowden. "They fell from the ceiling in a surprise attack on us. This Tolkus Gare, though, is going to make this more difficult."

Dr. Bryson shot Dan a look. "This is pretty crazy."

"Tell me about it," said Dan. He gestured at the projection. "Emily's going to fight?"

Dr. Snowden put two hands out and shook them. "Trust me, she's more than qualified. She used to be more . . . innocent, then got trapped on a prison planet, alone, for over nine months. She is much tougher now. A lot like you, actually."

"That sounds horrible," said Sarah.

Dan raised his eyebrows.

"The prison-planet thing," she said, swatting Dan's arm.

Dr. Snowden's eyes misted a bit. "I'm . . . I'm still trying to adjust to the new her." He forced a smile as he cast a sidelong glance at them.

"Looks like you're doing a damn fine job picking up where my duplicate left off," said Dan.

Dr. Snowden nodded.

The projection showed Tolkus Gare creeping along the wall. Tolkus paused for a moment and held still.

Dr. Snowden realized that Tolkus did not know he could be seen.

Evaran and the others opened fire on the draug pouring into the concourse entrance.

The draug had more numbers than Dr. Snowden remembered. There were the armored pill-bug-like ones, the ant-like soldiers, and the spiderlike ones. There were two large ones that reminded him of a cross between a praying mantis and a spider. It was like the whole brood was agitated.

"That Tolkus guy trained them here," said Dr. Bryson.

"Trained?" asked Dan.

"Ohh . . . umm . . . lured them. Sorry, that's an old gaming term."

"Definitely looks that way," said Dr. Snowden.

Evaran went to the left and began firing repulsion beams.

Levaran stepped forward a bit and angled her repulsion blasts at the ground of the incoming swarm.

Emily, to Levaran's right, swept the ceiling and walls.

The coordinated effort was keeping the swarm at bay. However, there were too many. When the large ones got to the front of the swarm, the repulsion beams' effectiveness ended.

Evaran transformed his utility handle into a staff, and Emily did the same with her PSD.

Levaran activated an energy shield in the shape of a gauntlet around her right hand.

Together, they charged into the swarm.

Sarah gulped. "I can't believe they're going into that!"

"They'll be okay," said Dr. Snowden.

Evaran and Emily danced inside the swarm, ducking jabs by the soldiers, and knocking the smaller draug back.

Levaran charged head-on into the first large one.

It grabbed her with one of its claws, and when it tried to lift her, it struggled.

She seized it by the arm and raised it off the ground.

The arm snapped, and the large draug emitted a high shriek that caused others to swarm onto her.

She disentangled herself from the claw and swung the large draug in a circle to push the other draug away. When a space opened up, she launched it.

Evaran and Emily cleared the immediate area near Levaran with a combination of melee strikes and repulsion and stun beams.

Levaran used the moment to charge the second big one.

The large draug snapped at her as she drew near.

She dodged the attack and punched the draug in its chest, sending it hurtling back and clearing a path.

Evaran and Emily used the distraction to funnel the remaining draug into the void and were able to push the swarm back.

Dan pointed at Tolkus in the projection. "He looks like he's about to take a shot."

Dr. Snowden nodded. "If you saw it, you can be sure they know it too."

As if on cue, Evaran positioned himself to block Tolkus's shot. Evaran leaned his head slightly to the side. "Take care of the swarm. I'm going after Tolkus." He shot a repulsion beam at Tolkus, causing him to sprawl back. A stun beam made the camouflage shimmer for a moment, then dissipate.

Tolkus shook his head and tried to orientate himself. He tossed an object in front of Evaran.

A smoke-filled explosion sent Evaran sliding back as he raised his shield to deflect it.

Levaran and Emily had turned to face the explosion, allowing the draug behind the ones that were knocked down to swarm ahead of and around them.

Tolkus shot a grapple at the entrance, where an opening had occurred, and pulled himself toward it. As he landed, the large draug that Levaran had punched surged forward and grabbed him. It held him in place, and he screamed as smaller draug tore him to shreds.

"Holy shit," said Dan.

Sarah dry heaved as she turned away.

"That is . . . brutal," said Dr. Bryson with wide eyes and a hand on his chin.

Evaran rejoined Levaran and Emily, and with some focus, they were able to cause the draug to retreat.

Dr. Snowden and the others reached the bridge door as Evaran, Levaran, and Emily began to come back.

Dan exhaled. "I'm tense, and I wasn't even in the fight."

"It takes some getting used to," said Dr. Snowden. "Since Emily and I have been traveling, danger is just part of the routine."

Dan shook his head. "Wish I could help, but it seems I'm way out of my league here."

"Not as much as you might think. Give it time. Remember, you have nanobots. You're a lot stronger and faster now," said Dr. Snowden.

Dan harrumphed. He looked down the concourse. "Just glad you guys were here. Waking up with no one around and having to deal with that would be a nightmare."

Dr. Snowden nodded.

Emily surveyed the entrance area strewn with dead draug. Others were scurrying out of the room. Her nanobots were pulsing. After lowering her helmet and wiping the sweat off her face, she beamed a big smile. "Yeah! How about that!"

Evaran tilted his head toward Emily.

She pretended to study something on her forearm. Although she knew that Evaran did not want her to sensationalize violence, sometimes the heat of the moment overtook her. The draug got payback, even if they were a parallel-universe version. It was proof that her training in the draug simulation had payed off.

Levaran walked up to Emily and raised her hand. "You did well. High five for a good fight."

Emily laughed as she complied. She saw Evaran narrow his eyes in the background. It was the first time she saw a difference in Evaran's and Levaran's attitudes toward violence. Levaran seemed to almost relish fighting, whereas Evaran avoided it if possible. She avoided Evaran's gaze as they headed back.

"V said that the others are at the bridge door now," said Evaran. "Edev, take my UIC to the panel." He pulled his UIC off his belt and held it in the air.

"On it," said Edev. She flew by Evaran and, with one of her segmented arms, grabbed the UIC and headed off into the distance.

"I can work on getting the door open as we go," said Evaran.

"Efficient," said Emily. She fidgeted with her fingers. "Tolkus Gare . . . I guess you won't need to capture him now."

Evaran nodded. "It will not be a great loss. I would have liked to have given him over to an old friend."

"Warden Borox," said Levaran, gesturing at Emily.

Emily wrinkled her eyebrows. "You knew the warden by name?"

Evaran half smiled. "I did. Tolkus Gare was not the only one causing mayhem in this region of space and time."

"Huh," said Emily. "With it being just Jerzan now, things should be a bit easier."

"We shall see," said Evaran. "The slight differences here have so far been anything but small."

Emily nodded.

When they were halfway back, a clanking sound rang out. The group paused.

Emily's eyes widened. "I know that sound. Security drones, right?"

"It appears someone activated them. We need to move," said Evaran. As they ran, he interacted with his ARI. "There is someone on the bridge, fighting me for control of the door."

Emily surveyed the ceiling. As she expected, the hatch doors that lined the top of the side walls were opening, and metallic spiderlike drones were emerging. She remembered what they could do, and being on the opposite end of them was not a good place to be.

As Dr. Snowden and the others came into view, she saw that the door was moving up and down. There was enough space to go under, but energy blasts were hitting the area just under the door. She was thankful that Dr. Snowden had moved the others off to the side. When she neared the door, she activated her shield, then slid under the door while reflecting the beams.

Once inside, she saw an armored Krotovore near the front of the room using the workstations as cover. She gritted her teeth. "We're not here to hurt you! Stop firing!"

The Krotovore continued to fire.

Levaran had joined Emily, and the both of them charged up and around a workstation. Their shields reflected the Krotovore's beams.

The Krotovore pulled out a small, jagged knife with a blue glow.

Emily knocked it out of the Krotovore's hands with her staff while Levaran grabbed the Krotovore and pushed it to the ground.

Emily peered back and saw that Evaran had gotten the door raised, and everyone was rushing in.

"Please. Don't hurt me," said the Krotovore.

Levaran pointed a finger. "Sit."

The Krotovore's multiple eyes blinked rapidly as it complied.

Emily saw that the bridge door was closing, and just in time.

The narrowing gap between the door and the floor revealed a swarm of security drones racing toward the bridge. Once the door was closed, the others joined Levaran and Emily around the Krotovore.

"Who are you?" asked Levaran.

"I'm Second Commander Kri'tokhaar. How can you speak our tongue?"

"It's not important. What is important is that your ship is in disarray. We need to adjust the thrusters so that the ship will not crash into the planet," said Levaran.

"And then what . . . ?"

"We're going to activate the main engines so that this ship flies into the sun," said Levaran.

Kri'tokhaar fidgeted around. "You want to destroy the ship?"

"Yes. It's not supposed to be here. Jumping through space and time via the rifts and abducting apex predators has consequences."

Kri'tokhaar sighed. "I . . . I didn't agree with the first commander on the abducting part. How . . . how do you know that?"

"We know many things," said Levaran as her eyes sparkled. She placed her UIC on one of the workstations.

"What is that?" asked Kri'tokhaar.

"Something that gives me access to the controls and information from here," said Levaran. She interacted with her ARI, and after a moment, she said, "The security drones have been recalled, and data transfer is in progress."

"Why do you want this information?"

"You are a very curious Krotovore. It's for our own knowledge and also for your Matriarch De'zokaar," said Levaran.

Kri'tokhaar trembled. "So you know our matriarch."

"We do."

"How do you know where she is? We've been lost for a long time now."

Levaran nodded. "From when you launched, you're six hundred thousand years in the past, in what you call the Wuus'riken galaxy, or Andromeda as it's known to us."

Kri'tokhaar shuddered. "Time travel . . . we speculated that the rifts had a temporal component. However this . . . so far away . . ." He emitted a low guzzling sound. "What will become of me? Am I your prisoner now?"

Levaran glanced at Evaran, who nodded. She cocked her head back. "You're not our prisoner. We can take you home. I don't know what'll happen to you when you go back, though."

"You can time travel . . . and go that distance?" asked Kri'tokhaar.

"Yes. The choice is yours."

Kri'tokhaar stood. "I'll take it. Anything is better than here."

"Okay," said Levaran.

Emily narrowed her eyes as she watched Levaran introduce the rest of the crew to Kri'tokhaar. It struck her that she was not angry with Kri'tokhaar, or really any Krotovore. They were unsuspecting players in a time loop. Looking at Dan and Sarah, it was evident there was disgust in their eyes. They would not understand, at least not yet. Dr. Bryson did not surprise her either in his reaction. He was like Dr. Snowden in many ways, and his curiosity could override almost any emotion.

Levaran cleared her throat. "I would not expect a warm welcome from those you have captured and tortured in your virtual simulation."

Kri'tokhaar dipped his head and moved off to the side. He slumped against the wall and searched the ground.

Emily walked over to him. "You'll get through this."

Kri'tokhaar inspected her. "You were one of the captured?"

"Not in this universe," she said with a half smile.

Kri'tokhaar sighed. "I'm not sure I understand, but . . . you're not angry with me? I would understand if you are."

She shrugged. "I might have been initially. However, this is life. When it gets rough, you learn, adapt, and evolve."

"You're empathetic, and wise," said Kri'tokhaar. He made a slight hissing sound. "If I had tried to stop the first commander, he would have killed me and someone else would have taken my place. It's the way of the Krotovore. Obedience is absolute."

She pulled her lips to the right. "The first commander should have stuck to the original mission then, yeah?"

Kri'tokhaar nodded. "Your friends . . . I suspect they do not share your sentiment."

She observed Dan eying Kri'tokhaar. "They'll get over it. What's important now is that we need to get off this ship, and we may need your help."

"You shall have it," said Kri'tokhaar. "If this is my chance at some redemption, then so be it."

She laid a hand on Kri'tokhaar's armored shoulder, then headed over to Dan and the others. "I know you may be angry with Kri'tokhaar, but what happened has happened. We need to focus on the next step."

Dan gritted his teeth and shot her a defiant look. "My tolerance has limits."

"It's best to channel that energy into something positive," she said, returning a defiant look.

Dan's eyes widened as he glanced at Sarah, then back at Emily. "That's what Sarah always tells me."

"And what my dad taught me," said Emily with softened eyes.

Dan studied her for a moment as his face relaxed. "Well . . . hell. You're like the best of me and Sarah, but a hell of a lot tougher."

Emily smiled. "I had a good teacher."

"I helped train her in combat," said Dr. Snowden, shaking his fists in a boxing manner.

"Analysis. I do not think that is correct," said V.

Everyone shared a moment of light laughter.

Evaran raised a finger. "It appears we have more visitors. Transferring to the main screen."

Dr. Snowden shook his head. "It's a like a party that just won't stop."

The screen lit up and showed another ship dock and land next to Jerzan's. Once it stopped, a crew of seven-foot-tall humanoids with blue skin, bald heads, and facial tattoos emerged. Their heavy armor and weaponry were no surprise to Emily since she had seen Bilaxians like that before.

"Now who're these guys?" asked Dan.

"Dolgus Kree and the Zhama mercenary group," said Evaran. "He is even more brutal than Jerzan. Sadly, he was the heir to a powerful clan inside the Bilaxian Empire but has wasted his talents doing what he does. He prefers over-whelming force as a tactic."

Dan sighed. "Is there anything not deadly on this ship?"

Levaran shut off the screen display and grabbed her UIC. "Not that I'm aware of. We have the information we need, and the adjustment thrusters have been fired. This ship is now headed to the sun. We just need to make it go faster."

"Engine room time," said Emily. "I wonder if the krall will be there."

"If she is, we're gonna have a sizable group," said Dr. Snowden.

Evaran nodded. "We will need to be careful."

Kri'tokhaar stepped forward. "Where is your ship docked?"

"Docking bay 4," said Evaran.

Kri'tokhaar went to a workstation and tweaked a few controls. "There is a docking bay near the engine room that is much closer. If you can get your ship to that one, the trip from the engine room to the docking bay would be halved. There's also a set of service tunnels between the engine room and the docking bay that are secure and make the trip safer from that point on."

Evaran and Levaran perused their ARIs.

Levaran focused on Evaran. "He's right."

"Edev can stealth and go get the Torvatta, right?" asked Emily.

Levaran shook her head. "V could since he is bound to it. Edev is not. However, Edev will be bound to mine, but that's not an option now."

Evaran's eyes darted around the group for a moment. "I will go."

"Analysis. I will join you," said V.

Evaran shook his head. "Not this time. It would be better if you stayed with the group. Your shielding would be more valuable as a tactical asset."

V's lights dimmed. "Acknowledged."

Emily snorted. "Well, I'm going with you then. No way you're doing this alone, and yes, I *can* keep up. I did on the Dyson bubble."

Dr. Bryson's eyes widened. "Dyson bubble?"

"Uncle Albert can catch you up on that," she said, gesturing at Dr. Snowden. "However, me and Evaran can get the Torvatta, while Levaran takes everyone else to the engine room, flips it on, then heads to the other docking bay."

Levaran nodded.

"Very well," said Evaran. "We can come back if needed, but I suspect that will not be required." He gestured at Emily. "Let us go."

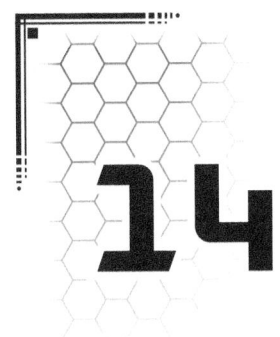

14

Emily reflected on the situation as she followed Evaran. Her mind was a jumble of thoughts, and although she knew she needed to focus, she was not too worried with Evaran around. She bumped into Evaran, who had paused at the main bridge concourse entrance.

"You are deep in thought," said Evaran.

She half smiled. "Yeah. There's just a lot going is all."

"I understand. I did not want you to step on the draug body in front of you."

She examined the ground, then scooted back. "Oh! I didn't even see it."

"You will need to remain focused. With Dolgus Kree, Jerzan, and apex predators, this could get dangerous very quickly," he said.

She nodded. "I'm with you."

He laid a hand on her arm and lightly squeezed. "I know. Come."

She smiled as he took a left out of the concourse. The scattered remains of Tolkus Gare's armor and equipment made her grimace. It reminded her of when she had seen a large draug tear up one of Jerzan's crew. She shook her head. "What a way to go."

He pivoted and examined the remains. "He caused a lot of pain to people. On one of the planets I visited, he had poisoned the local water supply. Hundreds died, and painfully. What bothered me about the situation was that what he wanted, he could have taken. Instead, he chose to play a game with a lesser-developed society, and purposely decided to harm others."

"What did he want?"

He nodded. "To be treated as royalty during his stay. He seemed to enjoy having others bow to him. Removing any competition was a game to him."

Emily shook her head. "Maybe he didn't want to deal with the fallout if he took it by force."

"It is possible. However, he will no longer be able to do that to anyone," said Evaran.

She wrinkled her nose as she closed up her helmet. The smell of rotting flesh was making her stomach turn. As they continued on down a large corridor, she turned toward him. "I guess we're not going back the way we came. What's the route?"

He flipped his hand out, and a projection shot up from his ring. It showed a map with a dot indicating where they were, a dot for the Torvatta, and a green line showing the path. "We are going to go through the living quarters on this level, then take an elevator near there down to the storage bays. From there, we only need to cross a few large rooms, but they will lead to an intersection that ends at the docking bays. Although it took us two and a half hours to get from the docking bay to the medical lab, we should be able to do this in about an hour and a half."

"Seems reasonable," she said.

"Keep your shield out and your PSD ready to fight. Are you ready?"

She nodded. "Let's do this."

He dipped his head and wheeled around.

They took off at a light sprint.

She focused on the environment as they hustled through it. The sounds were as she expected, and she was thankful she did not have to endure the smells. The light mist and dim lighting no longer bothered her, and the heads-up display inside her helmet highlighted everything.

It hit her how much she missed having V show things from his view inside her HUD. One aspect she found interesting was that she could hear the heartbeats of creatures a bit away. It was like a distant thumping of a drum, but noticeable enough to catch her attention at times.

The carcasses of creatures and Krotovore were everywhere. A bloodbath had taken place. Emily understood that this was a new path on the ship that she had never seen before. Memories of when she was on the prison planet flashed through her mind. If she could handle that, she could handle this. Traveling with Evaran, anything could be overcome.

When they reached the living quarters fifteen minutes later, they paused.

Evaran raised a hand and slipped to the side of a slightly cracked door. In a low voice, he said, "It appears the living quarters are not empty."

She dipped her head and listened. Several heartbeats came into focus, in addition to the sound of footsteps and grunting noises. "What's the plan?"

He pointed at himself, then at the door.

She nodded.

He crept up to the door and peeked in. After a moment, he retreated back to his initial position. "It appears Carrus Kilns are in there."

She narrowed her eyes as he shot up a projection from his ring. The Carrus Kilns resembled orangutans with some sort of chitin-like armor on their bodies. Large fangs extended from their mouths, and their hands had powerful claws. It was the scorpion-like stinger tails that surprised her. Maybe they were poisonous.

"I believe our stun beams will work on them. They are too heavy for our repulsion beams," he said.

She nodded.

"I'll lead," he said as he positioned himself opposite the door. With a kick, the door crumpled, and he entered the room.

Emily followed him in and took aim at the first Carrus Kiln. It went down quickly along with the one beside it, which Evaran hit. The third one jumped back, then scattered out of the room. She began to chase after it.

"Hold on," said Evaran, raising a hand.

She paused near the two stunned Carrus Kilns.

Evaran scanned them. "The third one needs to stay alive to protect these two. I do not believe the third one will be a threat. Although they will die with the ship, they should at least have the chance to live out their lives to that point. However, there are others scattered about. We will need to remain vigilant."

She sighed as she inspected the dead Krotovore bodies the Carrus Kilns had been feeding on. The Krotovore did not have any armor on, and from the looks of things, this had been their last stand. She wondered how many Krotovore were like Kri'tokhaar, hating what was being done but powerless to stop it.

They exited the room into a large hallway that had multiple rooms hanging off it like the one they were just in.

Evaran gestured down the hallway, and after a moment of surveying the area, they continued on.

After ten minutes of relative peace, they came to halt outside a four-way intersection.

Emily strained to hear the distant sounds, and the weapon fire stood out. "Dolgus or Jerzan?"

"I do not know. The weapons used by both are the same," he said. He crept to the corner and peeked around. After a moment, he shook his head. "It is Jerzan's crew. Hulldar is standing guard. Whatever they are firing at inside the room has their attention for the moment."

Emily gulped as she remembered Hulldar. He had wanted to put shackles on her and use her as a sex slave. "Can we go around them?"

"Possibly, but I see an opportunity. If we can seal that room and put Hulldar in an adjacent room, we should be clear. However, it requires my UIC to be placed on the console."

She narrowed her eyes. "How are we gonna do that?"

Evaran half smiled. "You have camouflage ability. If you can place my UIC on the console, then shield it inside your cloak, I can lock the door."

"And Hulldar?"

"Your choice on how to take him down."

She grinned. "Sounds like a plan."

He handed her his UIC. "Go now while they are occupied."

She nodded and activated her camouflage. After shimmering out of view, she turned the corner and crept in silence toward Hulldar. Her resolve strengthened with each step. Hulldar looking around listlessly made her think he was not at peak focus. When she reached the door console, she peeked into the room.

What she saw was no surprise. It was a security storage center of some type. The panels on the wall could be pulled out and had holes on the front. She eased back and placed Evaran's UIC on the door console. Leaning against the wall with her back toward Hulldar, she covered the UIC's light.

The UIC connected, and the door slammed shut a moment later.

Hulldar stood straight and reached for his weapon. He pounded on the door. "What the hell are you idiots doing?"

Emily pulled off the UIC and then crept behind him while angling her PSD. When she was in position, she said, "Probably something they shouldn't."

Hulldar spun around as her stun beam enveloped him. He trembled for a moment, then collapsed to the ground.

Evaran joined her as she began to pull Hulldar across the hall.

The sounds of Jerzan's crew pounding on the door echoed out.

"You did well," said Evaran.

Emily paused to hand him his UIC and then continued dragging Hulldar into a side room. Once Hulldar was inside and Evaran had sealed the door, she smiled. "I don't think they'll be going anywhere."

"Perhaps not. However, I only sense five heartbeats."

She concentrated for a moment and verified his claim. "This means . . . there are three more somewhere. I saw the Rybox brothers in there with Galkett and not sure who the other one was. Maybe Simas or Rondall."

"It could be someone we are unaware of as well," said Evaran. "Nonetheless, good job. We are not too far away from—" He raised a hand and tilted his head.

Emily could feel it too. "My nanobots are tingling like they did when I was able to detect time anomalies." She recalled feeling this way in their last adventure when they crossed paths with a rogue time traveler.

He sighed. "Yes. This time signature is well-known to me. The Time Wardens have arrived."

"That's not good."

"It is not. I do not know where they are specifically, but every apex predator on this ship that crosses their path will know what a true apex predator looks like."

Emily cracked her back as she stretched from side to side. "Well, we'll deal with it if we have to. Maybe we'll get lucky and not run into them."

"It is possible," said Evaran with a smile. "Your optimism is refreshing. They will be able to sense us as well and will destroy anything in their path."

She grinned. "Let them come then."

He nodded as they continued on.

Dr. Snowden had watched as Evaran and Emily left the bridge. It was not a surprise that she went with Evaran. Although he suspected she wanted to stay and learn more about her parents, at least the parallel-universe versions, she probably understood now was not the time to do that. Assuming everyone got off the ship, there would be time.

Dan tapped his arm and then gestured at the entrance. "They're pretty close."

"Yeah, they are," said Dr. Snowden, looking down. "No one could replace her dad, and I was more of a close friend to her. Evaran sort of fulfills the father role to her, I think, in some way." He noticed Levaran casting a sidelong glance.

Dan shook his head. "Well, she's incredible." He lightly squeezed Sarah's shoulder. "We at least have an idea of what our kids could look like."

Sarah sighed. "If I could have kids . . ."

"You'll be able to soon," said Levaran. "The nanobots inside you will resolve that."

Sarah's eyes widened. "Are you serious?"

"Analysis. She is serious."

Sarah's lips parted as she swiveled her head toward V, then Dan.

Levaran smiled. "We should head out to the engine room. Let's go."

Dr. Snowden noticed Sarah almost bouncing out of her skin as they walked the length of the concourse. Looking behind him, he saw that Kri'tokhaar hung back with V and kept his distance from Dan. Kri'tokhaar was probably still a bit unsure about the situation. Dr. Snowden tapped Dr. Bryson's arm and nodded back at Kri'tokhaar. They slowed a bit to walk alongside him.

Dr. Bryson angled his head toward Kri'tokhaar. "I don't want you to think I'm angry with you. I may have been at first, but at this point, what's done is done. I'm looking forward to learning more about your culture if I get the chance."

"I don't believe that is the consensus with the other abductees," said Kri'tokhaar.

Dr. Bryson waved a hand forward. "Give it time."

"You are a member of a curious race."

Dr. Snowden chuckled. "We're scientists." He pointed at Dr. Bryson. "My duplicate used to work with him."

"Your duplicate?" asked Kri'tokhaar.

"I know it will sound crazy, but some of us are from a parallel universe."

"That's not crazy at all. The Krotovore have postulated its existence for some time now. We actually thought that the rifts we were going through would possibly take us there," said Kri'tokhaar. "I'm curious as to how you achieved inter-universal travel."

Dr. Snowden gestured at Levaran. "I'll leave that up to her to tell you if she wants, but in this universe, my duplicate is dead."

"Very interesting," said Kri'tokhaar, glancing at Dr. Bryson. "And the duplicate of Dr. Snowden was a scientist in this universe as well?"

Dr. Bryson nodded. "I was more on the cutting edge, but yeah."

"Then it's the reverse in my universe," said Dr. Snowden with a chuckle.

"Pfft," said Dr. Bryson.

"I'm ashamed at what my species has done to the both of you," said Kri'tokhaar. "I'm not even sure what type of tests they were going for."

Dr. Bryson shrugged. "It's water under the bridge."

Kri'tokhaar's large eyes narrowed.

"Oh . . . umm . . . just an idiom for what's been done is done."

"I see," said Kri'tokhaar. His eyes blinked rapidly as he surveyed the dead Krotovore strewn about.

Dr. Snowden shook his head. "So much death."

Kri'tokhaar nodded. "It is . . . water under the bridge."

Dr. Bryson smiled. "Now you're getting it."

When they reached the concourse entrance, Levaran took a right.

Dr. Snowden activated his shield and hustled up to Dan and Sarah. He motioned at V. "This is when Sanjay died."

"Acknowledged," said V. "I have transmitted the coordinates from where we saw Simas and Rondall from Jerzan's crew in our universe to Edev, and she is checking it out."

Dan wrinkled his eyebrows. "Sanjay?"

Dr. Snowden bobbed his head. "He was one of the other two that were abducted with me and Emily. He died taking a hit in the head."

"Oh," said Dan.

Dr. Bryson snorted. "You'll never guess who the fourth was."

Dan narrowed his eyes.

"Jay Beerman."

Sarah gasped.

Dan's face turned red. "What?"

Dr. Snowden sighed. "From what James tells me, Jay killed me in an accident. In my universe, we're good friends."

"In this universe, he's rotting in a cell," said Dan. He swallowed hard. "He took our Albert away from us."

Dr. Snowden met Dan's gaze. "I wish it didn't go down like that."

Dan shook his head. "Unbelievable."

"The focus here, now, is to make sure what happened to Sanjay doesn't happen to anyone else," said Dr. Snowden.

"Right," said Dan. "Don't mind me. Just . . . that name." He snorted.

Dr. Snowden placed a hand on Dan's shoulder and then hustled to the outside of the group and walked backward with his shield at the ready.

"Edev is not showing anyone there," said Levaran. "She has also scanned for the krall but has not seen her yet."

Dan narrowed his eyes. "Krall?"

Dr. Snowden half smiled. "The krall is not a threat, well, wasn't in our universe. She's like a big dog, with armored plates, and the size of a grizzly. More importantly, she saved my and Emily's lives."

"Oh," said Dan. He shook his head. "I don't want to imagine what it must have been like going through this without having you and the others to help."

Dr. Snowden cast a sidelong glance at Levaran. "It was . . . trying."

Levaran smiled. "You and Emily did well, though."

He nodded.

When they got to the large engine room, they assembled just inside the entrance.

Dr. Snowden noted that it was just like he remembered it. A large black orb surrounded by metallic rings, with three curved metallic pillars shooting a red beam at the rings. There were three hallways leading off to other parts of the engine area. One was opposite of where they were, and the other two were on the sides.

Dr. Bryson's eyes widened as he pointed at the orb. "What . . . is that?"

"Our antimatter drive," said Kri'tokhaar.

Dr. Bryson exhaled from his mouth. "Absolutely incredible."

Levaran placed her UIC on a wall console and then cleared her throat. "As incredible as it is, we need to disable those red beams. Three people are required for this." She pointed at the hallway opposite them. "Kri'tokhaar, are you familiar with the beam shutdown process?"

Kri'tokhaar nodded.

"Okay, you can take that one. Edev will go with you in case we need to communicate," said Levaran. She pointed at the right hallway. "V, you take that one." She pointed at the left one. "Dr. Snowden, you can take that one. I'm going to stay here and make sure nothing comes in."

"Albert, is what you're going to do safe?" asked Dan. "I mean . . . could me and Sarah go with you?"

"I think so," said Dr. Snowden, tossing Levaran a look.

She nodded. "It should be safe. The bio scans are operational here, unlike your universe. There is nothing in this room or the control rooms. From your encounter, the Grynge came after everyone left. If they do this time, they will deal with me."

"These Grynge don't sound friendly," said Dan.

Dr. Snowden bobbed his head. "They weren't."

Dr. Bryson's eyes darted between Dan and Sarah. "Well, if you two are going with Albert, I'd like to go with V." He extended a hand out toward V. "If that's okay with you, that is."

"Your presence would be appreciated," said V.

Dr. Bryson puffed his chest out a bit. "Awesome."

"Very well," said Levaran. "Dr. Snowden and V already know what to do. Contact me if need be."

15

Dr. Bryson surveyed the dimly lit corridor as he walked alongside V. The raw smell of something rotting made him gag. He could not see what was causing it but wished he had a helmet to raise like he saw on Dr. Snowden and Emily. The distant shrieking sounds reminded him of a pig squealing. He gulped at the thought that maybe something was being murdered at that very moment. He jumped when V swiveled his head.

"Are you okay?"

"Me? Oh, yeah. Pfft. I'm great," said Dr. Bryson, tossing a hand out.

"Analysis. Your heartbeat and breathing have intensified."

Dr. Bryson sighed. "I can't hide anything from you, can I?"

"You can if you wish."

Dr. Bryson stared at V for a moment, then burst out laughing. "Sorry. I didn't mean literally." He shook his head.

"I'm amazed at the technology that must have gone into you. You mentioned you were an AI or something?"

"I am what Dr. Snowden has classified as a strong AI, but it is more complicated than that."

"Oh," said Dr. Bryson. He bobbed his head. "I bet you've had a lot of interesting discussions."

"We have. Dr. Snowden is very curious."

"Oh, I know. The version I know couldn't sleep unless he knew the answer to something, and in our field, that meant a lot of sleepless nights."

V tilted his head. "In the virtual simulation Dr. Snowden was in, your name was mentioned."

"Really? And . . . what was it in relation to?"

V shot out a projection above his head, showing the scene where Evaran had just met Dr. Snowden and was standing outside Dr. Snowden's house.

Dr. Bryson's eyes were glued to the projection.

It showed Dr. Snowden ask Evaran if he was a Jehovah's Witness and if he had been sent by Dr. Bryson.

After it finished, Dr. Bryson said, "So . . . you had footage of what happened in the virtual simulation. Amazing. And Albert woulda been right. I woulda sent Jehovah Witnesses and others to his place."

"Query. For what purpose?"

"You know," said Dr. Bryson, shrugging. "Just messing around."

V's lights flickered for a moment. "I see. You were mentioned again when Evaran met with Dr. Snowden and Emily three months after they had returned to Earth. It was in relation to your wife, Karen, in their universe."

Dr. Bryson raised his eyebrows. "Karen . . . Osgood?"

"You are correct. In the virtual simulation, you had a baby boy. However, in reality, there were conception issues. When

Dr. Snowden tried to congratulate you on the baby boy in reality, you began to ignore him."

"That's . . . kinda weird," said Dr. Bryson. He harrumphed. "In this universe, Karen was his wife."

V nodded. "Previous records in Dr. Snowden's universe indicated that it was Dr. Snowden who introduced you to Karen."

Dr. Bryson snorted. "He really liked her, well, at least here he did. I bet he did over there too." His eyes searched the ground for a moment. "I bet he knew I liked her and set us up, even though he was interested."

"It is a plausible conclusion and fits with the personality profile of Dr. Snowden," said V.

Dr. Bryson took a moment to scan the surrounding environment as they walked up a ramp. He enjoyed talking with V and could see why Dr. Snowden would too. When they got to the top of the ramp and continued, he said, "So Albert and Emily travel around with you and Evaran all across space and time? I mean . . . I picked up on the time travel thing when Levaran was talking to Kri'tokhaar."

V nodded. "I was created by Evaran, and together with Dr. Snowden and Emily, we travel where we are needed, and also to satisfy curiosity."

Dr. Bryson swallowed hard. "That's a once-in-a-lifetime opportunity. I'm guessing Evaran asked them to join him when he came back three months after dropping them off."

"It was Dr. Snowden and Emily who asked to join Evaran. I had calculated an eighty-six-percent chance they would ask given Dr. Snowden's profession and general personality profile."

Dr. Bryson chuckled. "Yeah . . . well . . . I mean, who the hell would pass that up?"

"I do not know."

Dr. Bryson slapped V on the back. "If I get the chance to travel with Levaran, and Edev is like you, I would take it in a heartbeat."

V nodded. "I assign a high probability to that, and it would be beneficial for Levaran."

"Why do you say that?"

"Levaran has never traveled with companions before. It would help modify her perspective if humans provided input."

"I see," said Dr. Bryson. He bobbed his head. "Maybe Dan and Sarah could come. We'd be Levaran and the gang!"

V paused as he stared at Dr. Bryson.

"I didn't mean any offense . . ."

"No offense has been taken. I was calculating the possibility that you would say that."

"About Dan and Sarah?"

"About Levaran and the gang. Intriguing."

They continued forward.

Dr. Bryson narrowed his eyes. "Let me guess. Albert probably said 'Evaran and the gang' before, right?"

"You are correct."

Dr. Bryson smirked. "Ol' Albert. Maybe we're more alike than either of us knows."

"I would agree," said V.

After fifteen more minutes of light conversation, they reached the control room.

Dr. Bryson followed V into the room and observed as V headed over to a panel on the wall with a red dot above. The clutterless room surprised him.

After a moment, the dot turned green, and V interacted with an object that slid out.

Dr. Bryson was not fully sure what the object's purpose was, but he understood at a high level that it needed to be configured in order to shut down the beams that prevented the ship's antimatter drive from running.

The idea of sending all this advanced technology into the sun without the opportunity to study it saddened him, but getting out alive was a higher priority. Just from his interaction with V and his observations of the others, he could see they were a potent group. His eyes lit up at the thought that he might be able to experience traveling with Levaran.

"It is done," said V. "We can head back now."

Dr. Bryson nodded. "Sounds good. That was pretty simple. Was it this easy in Albert's universe?"

"It was not. They had to fight various creatures, and Dr. Snowden almost died."

"Oh . . . ," said Dr. Bryson. "That's terrible."

V nodded. "Dr. Snowden had gone with Emily, and I went with Jay Beerman."

Dr. Bryson clenched his jaw. Jay may have been friends with Dr. Snowden in their universe, but in this one, he was dead to him. He swallowed hard and then let out a measured breath. He swept a hand toward the door. "After you."

"Acknowledged."

Kri'tokhaar observed Edev fly ahead to scan. His multiple stomachs were upset, and his set of black eyes blinked continuously. What his race had done to these humans and the other species was wrong, and as the only representative of his race around, the guilt tore at him. He emitted a low hissing noise from his proboscis.

When Edev came back, Kri'tokhaar had reached the halfway mark to the control room. He motioned a claw at Edev. "Your friends are quite powerful."

Edev's lights blinked. "They're very powerful. Does this trouble you?"

He sighed. "It doesn't, but the fact that such powerful beings are here because of my species does not escape me."

"You believe what you did was wrong?"

Kri'tokhaar gestured with one of his clawed hands out. "Of course I do. I was the second commander. I . . . I should have done something."

"It's in the past," said Edev. "What's done is done."

"Perhaps," he said. "It's still a stain. One which pervades my very being."

"I'm detecting elevated pressure in your biological system."

He slowly blinked his big set of eyes. "That's the shame of my race bearing down on me."

"You will be home soon with your own kind."

He sighed. "And then what? Display my shame to the rest of my species? Let my brood cluster live on in shame knowing what I failed to prevent? This is unbearable."

Her lights dimmed. "I have not had time to analyze your species."

He cocked his armored head back. "You're an unusual machine."

"I'm more than that. Part machine, part . . . something else."

He clacked two of his claws together. "I see. How long have you been in existence?"

"One day."

He gazed intently at her as they rounded a corner. "And . . . how were you created?"

"Levaran created me. I travel with her."

He emitted a guzzling noise. "Strange traveling partners. From what I've been told, Dr. Snowden, Emily, Evaran, and

V are from a parallel universe. The others, including you, are from this one."

"That's correct," she said. "In Evaran's universe, this encounter is in their past."

His six eyes scanned ahead. "I'm guessing there was a version of me then."

"There was. Would you care to see him?"

"You have visual?"

Edev's lights glowed a little brighter as she flew ahead a bit. She shot down a projection that showed a video feed of his parallel-universe counterpart.

Kri'tokhaar stood mesmerized as the conditions of the ship were described. Hearing how his assistant Ghaa'kiPruut died made his eyes blink slower. Ghaa'kiPruut was loyal and obedient to him, and probably sacrificed himself. At least Ghaa'kiPruut's death was better in the parallel universe than this one. Ghaa'kiPruut had been swarmed by small humanoid creatures with large knives, and had sacrificed himself to give Kri'tokhaar some time to get away.

She paused the projection. "I'm sorry if this bothers you."

"It's . . . it's okay," he said. "Continue." He listened to the report of the attack on the ship prior to going through the rift. The casual description of capturing a sentient species made his antennae flicker. It appeared there was a difference between that version and himself. Maybe over there, it was he, and not the first commander, who ordered the capture of sentient species. That could have happened only if the first commander was dead and Kri'tokhaar had assumed control. It struck him that Dr. Snowden and Emily should have been furious with him, yet they were not.

The projection ended as Edev's lights glowed. "An interesting perspective, don't you think?"

Kri'tokhaar's voice slowed. "Sure." He swayed his head around for a moment as if to clear it. "These . . . humans are resilient. They have empathy, even after what was done to them. They exhibit traits of nobility and compassion and handle adversity with finesse. It appears we did not live up to the same standards, although we were the more technologically advanced species."

"Humans are an interesting species. I'm looking forward to traveling with and learning about them."

"Dan, Sarah, and Dr. Bryson will travel with you and Levaran?"

Edev lit up. "Most assuredly. We will drop them off for three months, then come back. I calculate a ninety-point-two-percent chance they will ask to travel with us."

Kri'tokhaar emitted a guzzling sound. "At least they have a future."

"You do to. Matriarch De'zokaar will surely grant you a pardon, given the situation."

"You know the matriarch as well?"

"Only from visual records. Do you wish to see her?"

He wiggled his proboscis for a moment. "If you don't mind."

She flew out again and shot down a projection of Matriarch De'zokaar apologizing on behalf of all the Krotovore for what transpired.

He clenched his four smaller eyes shut for a moment. For a matriarch to apologize was not trivial. It meant great shame had been brought onto the species. The difference this time was that if he were to reach his home world, they would have someone to pin it on.

When the projection finished, he gestured ahead. "We need to hurry. The others are probably waiting on us."

"You have no comment on seeing your matriarch," said Edev.

He emitted a wheezing noise. "I . . . need to think on this."

"As you wish."

When they got to the control room, he was a blur in getting the panel to open and the console configured. Dr. Snowden and V would be able to get their consoles set, and the engines would fire. The thought that the ship deserved to be burned by the sun no longer bothered him. After what his species had done, he felt it was needed.

"You have been quiet for some time now. Is everything okay?"

He motioned toward the door. "I wish it were. I really do. Let's head back."

"You got it."

Dr. Snowden had lowered his helmet as he walked with Dan and Sarah toward their control room. The smells brought back a sense of déjà vu for him. He definitely did not miss the pitter-patter sound of footsteps echoing throughout. The mist that hugged the floor obscured it somewhat, but from what he had seen so far, the path was the same as the one from his universe.

The thought briefly crossed his mind that maybe the Grynge were already here, but he would know of their presence before they would know of his, and if it came to it, the Grynge would learn what a PSD could do. The dimly lit corridor gave him flashbacks of walking through it with Emily at his side. He wondered how she was doing.

"Hmm," said Dan. He waved a hand around in the air. "This place is right out of a horror movie."

"I don't like it," said Sarah. Her eyes scanned Dr. Snowden. "You seem to be at ease with all of this."

Dr. Snowden shrugged. "I've already been through this one. It's a lot easier when you're not being tracked by headhunters."

Dan wrinkled his eyebrows. "I'm guessing this time around . . . they'll run into Levaran first."

Dr. Snowden nodded. "I doubt they will be getting past that."

"So you had to fight these headhunters?" asked Sarah.

Dr. Snowden smirked. "Yeah. They're called Grynge. They stand about two to three feet, have red skin and wild hair, a large mouth with razor-sharp teeth, and they carry a lot of bone armor and weapons. Three of them cornered me and Emily in the control room. Once inside, they attacked me while Emily got the console going."

"You took on three?" asked Dan.

"Unfortunately. They stabbed me in the leg several times. Apparently their knives were coated in poison. I didn't think I was going to make it," said Dr. Snowden. He exhaled from his nose. "I tried to draw them to me so Emily could get out, but she decided to fight instead, and we both got out."

"Unbelievable," said Dan. "Emily's tough as nails from what I saw."

"That's from our version of you," said Dr. Snowden. "She was more like Sarah until a certain point. Now she's more like you."

Sarah contemplated his words as they went up a ramp. "She sounds like she's had a lot of rough moments."

Dr. Snowden drew his lips flat. "She never got to know our version of you since our version died at childbirth. With our Dan dying while Emily was in college, I was the only one left she could turn to. I will say the holidays have never been the same."

Sarah sighed. "So she grew up without a mother."

Dr. Snowden bobbed his head. "There were . . . girl-friends, but none really stuck around."

Sarah swatted Dan's arm.

Dan jerked his head back. "What? That's their version, not me."

"I could see you doing that," said Sarah.

Dan shook his head and chuckled. "I'm getting blamed for what my parallel-universe version did."

"At least she has you. Does she have a boyfriend?" asked Sarah.

"She doesn't," said Dr. Snowden. He raised a finger. "However, she has had several girlfriends, and also met someone on our adventures that she had a relationship with. An older woman."

Sarah's eyes widened. "Oh. Okay. So she . . . likes women."

"Both men and women. She's more attracted to a type of personality and outlook, regardless what gender it is."

Sarah wrinkled her eyebrows. "I could see that."

Dan turned his head toward Sarah. "Really?"

"I know what you're thinking," said Sarah with a half smile. "What's important is that she's happy."

"She was," said Dr. Snowden as they turned a corner. "She's starting to be more like the Emily I grew up with, but she's now a lot more aware of what's going on around her. She trains four to five hours a day, studies like there is no tomorrow, and in general seems more comfortable with the situation overall."

"She's adapted," said Dan.

Dr. Snowden met Dan's gaze, and in unison, they said, "Learn. Adapt. Evolve." They enjoyed a laugh.

Dan shook his head. "Sounds like regardless of the universe, the philosophy is still the same."

"Yeah," said Dr. Snowden. "You used to put me in a headlock when you taught me that. Well, my version."

"I did the same to our version," said Dan with a cracked voice. "This . . . situation is so messed up. Not only do we have to deal with the fact that aliens exist and we were abducted, but also that there are parallel universes, and I can interact with versions of my dead brother and a daughter I never knew."

Dr. Snowden wagged a finger at Dan. "Don't forget the nanobots."

Sarah rubbed her hands together. "About that . . . have you seen any side effects?"

Dr. Snowden gazed off into the distance for a moment as the myriad of issues he had with them cropped up in his mind. He bobbed his head. "I think the big thing is that you age five weeks every year. On top of the enhanced strength, speed, and general senses, you'll also be able to raise them to a higher activity level, with a corresponding increase in effectiveness of your abilities."

"What do you mean?" asked Dan.

"Like . . . if you get lost in emotion, you can reach a state that calms you. Or if you're in a fight, they can . . . sorta tingle, and you become stronger, or faster. Also any damage heals faster. I can't imagine my life without them. They cured my prostate cancer even."

"Huh," said Dan. "Something to consider then."

"You want to keep them?" asked Sarah.

Dan motioned a hand out. "It . . . deserves some thought. If it means we can have a kid . . ."

Sarah smiled. "I'd like that."

Dr. Snowden swallowed hard. He missed Dan, and being with a parallel-universe version just reminded him of how much he did. Sarah was close with him too, and the three of them spent many a night hanging out. Since Dr. Bryson was his college roommate, he would join in the group at times.

When they reached the control room, he entered and headed over to the panel. It did not take long for the red dot above it to turn green, and when it did, he activated the console and pulled out the switch he needed to flip. Once it was done, he turned to the others. "That's it. We can head back now."

Dan stood next to the table in the small room and swept a hand between the wall and the table. "Is this where you fought those three Grynge?"

Dr. Snowden eyed the area and nodded.

"Albert . . . that's not a lot of room to maneuver in."

"I was on my back."

Dan shook a hand out in front of him as he slowly raised his head at Dr. Snowden. "You were giving your life to save Emily's . . ."

The memory of the fight in the room came roaring back. Dr. Snowden averted his eyes as he struggled to breathe. He had been stabbed three times, and he knew that he would not win that fight. The sudden onslaught of emotions caught him off guard. "I . . . wanted to buy her time to escape."

Sarah rushed over and hugged Dr. Snowden. "Parallel universe or not, you're a great person."

Dr. Snowden exhaled as his eyes reddened.

Dan laid a hand on Dr. Snowden's arm. "I suspect if we had a daughter and it was a similar situation, our Albert woulda done the same thing." He shook his head as his voice cracked. "We'll get through this. Once this is all over, you and Emily should stick around for a bit. Maybe we can get to know each other better."

Dr. Snowden nodded as Sarah stepped back. "I'd love that and think Emily would too."

"It's settled then," said Dan, clearing his throat. "We'll have a cookout with burgers and hot dogs."

"My favorite," said Dr. Snowden. With a final sweep of the room, he said, "Let's get outta here."

16

Emily surveyed the large empty room that she and Evaran had just entered. They had traveled without much resistance for the last hour and were nearing the Torvatta. Some creatures postured as if they were going to do something, but all it took was Evaran communicating to them that they would not fare well. Others just ran. Some appeared to be sentient but took off before any communication could be done. Her nanobots began to tingle.

Evaran raised a hand. "A Time Warden is near."

She activated her shield, pulled out her PSD, and extended it into a staff. "Should I camouflage?"

"No, they can see through that."

She surveyed the room and counted four doorways into smaller rooms, with a large hallway opposite them and one to their right. The room seemed like a junction room whose purpose was connecting other areas, but it had conveniences scattered about. Broken tables, chairs, and machines were strewn on the ground. The screens on the wall were cracked, and some emitted electrical sparks.

Despite all that, she knew the Time Warden was near. Her heartbeat increased as she picked up the faint sound of something tapping on metal. It reminded her of a clock.

Evaran extended his utility handle into a staff and activated his shield. "It is a Time Warden predator."

Emily wrinkled her eyebrows. "A different type?"

He drew his lips flat. "Yes. These have heavier shielding and armor and can paralyze their victims. They are larger than the ones we fought inside the facility where my last plane form was."

"Predator or not, we got this."

He eyed her for a moment. "I appreciate your confidence, but these are not to be taken lightly. My last run-in with them in our universe was almost fatal. To be fair, I fought six at once, including a Time Warden commander. And I was full strength at the time."

Emily sighed. "I'm not underestimating them. It's just that we make a good fighting unit."

"We do," said Evaran. "I will serve as the main distraction. When an opening to its body appears, take the opportunity to jab it."

She nodded. "You can count on me." She gulped as her attention focused on the sound of the predator in the opposite hallway. Trying to peer in was difficult due to the lack of lighting. Her breath staggered as the first segmented tentacle snaked into the room along the right wall. Another went on the other side, and the predator pulled itself into full view.

She noted that it was similar in design to the smaller ones, but this one was colored black and gold. Its multiple eye sockets ended with a red outline. Four tentacles were attached on the underside, with four more on top. The elliptical body seemed heavier to her as well.

The predator paused and homed in on them. It crawled forward, flicking debris out of its way as it moved.

Evaran stepped forward and raised a hand. "Hear me, Time Warden."

The predator paused, then raised itself. In a deep, synthetic-sounding voice, it said, "You are the time transgressor. Submit to the will of the Time Wardens."

"I cannot do that," said Evaran. "I have already defeated some of your brethren. This is your chance to turn around and crawl away."

"Time Wardens do not crawl away," said the predator.

"They do when facing a superior opponent."

The predator vibrated a bit. "Are you responsible for the destruction of our anchor station?"

"I am."

"Then you will suffer the consequences." It raised its top tentacles in a backward arcing manner and fired orange energy beams at Evaran.

Evaran raised his shield and braced himself as the beams hit.

Emily angled her shield in front of her and made her way toward the back of the predator.

The predator pivoted its tentacles to fire on Emily.

She gritted her teeth as the beams pushed her back. Her nanobots began to pulse.

Evaran charged forward, and when he was within striking distance, he jumped into the air and sliced off two of the top tentacles on the right side.

The Time Warden fumbled back. It pivoted and used the other two tentacles to knock Evaran away. It then wheeled around and crawled toward Emily.

She rushed up to it and dodged the first tentacle. With a downward motion, she cut the end off the second tentacle.

The first tentacle grabbed the top of her shield and tried to pull it away.

She went flying forward.

The predator released its grip on her shield and stabbed her in the back of the leg.

She screamed as the predator tossed her to the ground. Her body fought her as she tried to get back up. A fire ran up her leg and began to spread. Sweat seeped into her eyes, and every motion was a struggle. Although her nanobots were at full tilt, whatever the predator injected into her was more effective. She pushed against the ground, but the effort was futile.

Evaran was a tornado of strikes as he rushed forward into the predator. It slid back with each attack.

Once he severed the two remaining top tentacles, he jumped on top of the predator. He changed the staff into a rod capable of puncturing the body.

The predator rolled to the side and used three of its underside tentacles to grab Evaran and began to squeeze. The other tentacle grabbed the staff and pulled it away. Once the staff was on the ground, the four tentacles had Evaran wrapped up.

Emily clenched her jaw as she crawled toward the Time Warden. The fire had become an inferno, and the war fought between her nanobots and the toxin made it hard for her to breathe. Each movement took everything she had.

The unusual face Evaran was making pushed her even harder. She had to do something. With no free tentacles, the predator was a sitting duck. She raised her PSD and changed it into the rod that could pierce the shielding and body. With all her strength, she pulled herself to within striking distance. She yelled as she plunged it deep into the predator's body.

The predator emitted a loud shrieking noise as it shuddered. A yellow goo oozed out of the wound. It evaporated while making an unearthly sound, and Emily collapsed to the ground.

Evaran untangled himself when the tentacles lost their tension. He picked up his utility handle and rushed over to Emily. After scanning her, he knelt and said, "You have been paralyzed. Thankfully, the dose is not fatal, at least for you. I need to get you to the Torvatta immediately. The effects usually last about six hours, but it may be faster for you due to your nanobots. I have something in the medical lab that will shorten it even more and help deaden the pain some. I need to update Levaran." He interacted with his ARI.

After a few minutes, he picked her up and slung her over his shoulder. "Levaran has been updated. They are nearing docking bay 6."

Emily tried to move but nothing responded. She bet Dr. Snowden was probably ready to charge across the ship. The thought made her laugh in her mind, as nothing else reacted physically. The only thing that seemed to be working was breathing. The feeling of helplessness washed over her and brought back a memory of being caged on the prison planet. Her breathing intensified.

"Try to stay calm," said Evaran. "I know this is difficult, but I will keep you safe until we can get to the Torvatta."

She did not doubt his words. It was the shame of having fallen so easily. Despite all her training, all it took was one jab and she was down. She understood that the predator was a challenge even for someone like Evaran. Even so, she vowed to look at ways to make her body armor tougher. If Evaran had been laid out, they both could be going to the Time Warden ship now instead of what was happening.

When Evaran had traveled for about ten minutes, he paused in a long corridor and laid Emily down.

Lying on her side, she watched as he approached three men.

It was Jerzan and two others. All three had on a patchwork of brown-and-gray light armor with weapons in their hands.

Emily recognized Jahl, Jerzan's right-hand man, but not the other one. Maybe it was Hosk, although she never saw him during her and Dr. Snowden's abduction. Their greased-up hair and pockmarked fair skin did them no favors. Although she was paralyzed, she could still smell the foul odor of weeks aboard a cramped ship on them.

Jerzan strutted forward. "Well, well, well. What have we here?" He gestured at Emily. "Looks like I'll be first for a change."

The other two men laughed.

Evaran extended his utility handle into a baton with a glowing blue end. He aimed forward and shot the two men with a stun beam, causing Jerzan to stumble back in surprise.

Jerzan took out his weapon and fired. The energy beam reflected back a bit over his head.

"Jerzan. I would advise you not do that again," said Evaran.

Jerzan's eyes widened as he relaxed and moved his weapon to the side. "Who are you?"

"Someone who has already dealt with you. However, I do not have time for your foolishness this time. Jahl and Hosk are stunned. The rest of your crew," he said, pointing back the way that he and Emily had come, "are back there, locked in a room."

"So *you* locked them in . . . ," said Jerzan.

"I did," said Evaran. He walked backward and scooped up Emily with one arm while keeping an eye on Jerzan. He held her around the waist as he approached Jerzan. "I would suggest you get your men and get off this ship. It is headed toward the sun."

"What!"

Evaran stared Jerzan in the face. "I am giving you a chance. Take it. I am not in the mood to deal with you. If you wish to test that, I will stun you and leave you and your friends at the mercy of the first creature that passes by."

Jerzan's face turned white. "Um . . . O . . . okay. No need to get crazy. We're all friends here, right?"

Evaran narrowed his eyes and continued on. He slung Emily back over his shoulder.

She could no longer see what Jerzan was doing, but she suspected he was trying to figure out how to move two stunned members and get the others out. Evaran's demeanor surprised her somewhat. It was like he showed a bit more emotion than normal. She wondered if it was due to syncing with Levaran and seeing things through her eyes. Whatever it was, he was not happy. She wanted to shake her head, but could not. At least it would be a straight shot to the Torvatta, hopefully.

When they reached docking bay 3 thirty minutes later, Evaran paused just outside the entrance. "There is another Time Warden predator inside."

A sense of dread welled up inside Emily. She was now a liability, something she had vowed never to be. Her mind had been working in overdrive to try to move, and she thought she could almost wiggle her fingers.

"I have an idea," he said. He laid her up against the wall and gazed into her eyes. "We are going to use your camouflage shielding. I'll keep my left arm toward the predator just in case. However, I will need to hold you close, so I apologize ahead of time if it makes you uncomfortable."

She had no issues with being used as a shield, but she thought it was funny that he felt the need to apologize.

He accessed her forearm control. After the camouflage activated, he picked her up and wrapped his right arm around her waist.

She could see why he would think she might be uncomfortable. At her height, her head fell onto his shoulder, and her body was held close. The situation was dire with the predator lurking inside, but his reaction would have made her laugh if she could.

Evaran slipped inside the docking bay doorway and hugged the wall.

All she could see was the wall, but at the pace they were moving, it was not long before they hit the corner. There were a few stops where he held perfectly still behind the containers. She guessed maybe the predator was close by at those times.

When they got to the hallway leading to docking bay 4, he rushed down it.

From her vantage point, she could see the predator. It had been much closer than she had thought, just one container away.

The predator had waved a tentacle into the hallway behind them, as if checking for something. A light beam filled the corridor. After a moment, it jerked away and disappeared from her view.

Evaran increased his pace. "It has detected us, but it has no way of fitting in here. It will try to bore its way through the docking bay 4 entrance."

Emily's heartbeat ramped up. Given how strong she knew the predator was, she figured it would have no problem clearing a path. Maybe it would even shoot through it. It dawned on her that they could have done that too, but maybe there was a structural reason for not doing so.

A wave of relief swept through her when she saw that they had exited the hallway. It was not much longer before she could see they were inside the Torvatta's shielding. The sound of something being pummeled against the wall filled the docking bay.

A few moments later, she was lying on her stomach on a medical slab. Her face was turned to the right.

Evaran bent over and met her dull gaze. "I am afraid I have to apologize again. I need to remove your lower body armor to access the wound. I have a gel that will neutralize the paralyzing toxin. The nanobots I inject will help disseminate the gel across your body with the help of your own nanobots."

Emily's mind raced as she watched Evaran head off to get the gel. She was not wearing underwear since her suit had a formfitting replacement for it. The problem was that it was part of the suit.

He returned and began to work on her armor.

She could feel the lower part of her suit slip down her legs. The next sensation was a cloth material that landed on her buttocks. It seemed Evaran had anticipated this already. When he began to rub the gel into her wound, she wanted to jump off the table. Although she was paralyzed, she could still feel the burning sensation the gel caused.

After a prick in her leg, he bent over near her head and said, "You should be able to move in about an hour. I am going to shield the slab so no one can see inside. When you can move, you can remove the shielding by tapping on the button at the top of the slab. I need to get the ship over to docking bay 6." He placed a hand on her head, smiled, and then exited the room.

The dispersion pattern that the nanobots took was easy to visualize. It felt like they were pummeling her muscles, but the initial pain had subsided, and a numbness had settled in. Evaran had said the paralyzing effect normally lasted six hours, so she was happy with an hour.

Her mind turned to the fight with the predator. She suspected that if Evaran had been at full strength, he would have knocked the predator all over the place. The memory of him tossing around heavily armored humanoid Purifiers in another adventure crossed her mind. He had moved them like they were nothing. Maybe that was why he was now more hesitant to engage in physical encounters.

Her eyelids began to sag. Maybe she would just take a cue from Dr. Snowden and nap. There was nothing she could do at the moment anyways. With that thought, she pushed for her eyes to close and, with some effort, was able to do so.

17

When Dr. Snowden got back to the engine room's main entrance area, he noticed that the red beams that had been keeping the engine from firing were now gone.

The metal rings swirled around the black orb, with occasional blue arcs of light streaking between it and the rings.

From what Kri'tokhaar had said, the black orb was some type of antimatter. How it was not decimating everything around them was a mystery to him. Maybe the metal pillars created a magnetic shield of some type around the antimatter. He suspected that what he saw was just the tip of a much larger engine. His attention turned toward Dan, who had stopped.

Dan pointed at the krall lying next to Levaran. "Is that . . . the krall thing you talked about earlier?"

Dr. Snowden smiled. "It sure is." Looking across the room, he saw that V and Dr. Bryson had returned. Kri'tokhaar and Edev had come back as well and were headed toward Levaran.

The krall rose up and growled.

Levaran balled up her fist and placed it on her chest. She then pointed in sequence at everyone. "Extend your arm, palm up."

Dan nudged Dr. Snowden. "Umm . . . what's this all about?"

"It's the way the krall communicates. When she nuzzles your hand, you'll be her friend."

"Oh. And it's female? Huh," said Dan. He jumped a bit when the krall used her large head to nuzzle his hand.

After a minute, the krall had nuzzled everyone's hand except for Kri'tokhaar's. She stood and snarled, causing Kri'tokhaar to step back.

"I don't think she likes me," said Kri'tokhaar. He emitted a low guzzling sound. "I don't blame her."

Levaran stooped in front of the krall and made another attempt at getting the krall to acknowledge Kri'tokhaar. The krall dipped her head toward Kri'tokhaar, then headed over to Dr. Snowden.

"I'm sorry," said Levaran. "She's acknowledged you, and won't attack, but she doesn't consider you a friend."

Kri'tokhaar clacked his claws. "I understand."

Dr. Snowden extended his right arm toward Sarah with his palm down.

The krall moved to Sarah's side.

Sarah's eyes widened.

Dr. Snowden chuckled. "Don't worry. I just told her that she should focus on protecting you. She likes head rubs and scratches behind the ears."

Sarah met the krall's gaze. She reached down and patted the krall and then scratched her behind her ears. The krall slowly blinked.

"The slow blink means she likes it," said Dr. Snowden. He wondered if the krall could understand Evaran and Levaran without hand signals. The memory of Evaran kneeling and saying goodbye to the krall in his universe made him think so. Evaran had said that communication with animals was often a rough translation. Hand signals would be clear about their intent.

"Look at you," said Dr. Bryson. "The alien whisperer."

Dr. Snowden snorted. "She . . . is my friend, regardless of universe."

Levaran nodded. "She was under attack by a large pack of Grynge when she fled into the room. I drove them back, and she will now travel with us. We need to go. Edev has point with me. V has the rear, and Dr. Snowden and the krall will take each side. Let's move."

Dr. Snowden took his position as they exited the engine room.

They walked without incident for the next thirty minutes.

Although he saw some creatures, they scattered at the sight of the group. Looking around, he could see how they might appear threatening. Levaran exuded confidence in her walk, and V and the krall showed physical strength. Edev flying around served as a distraction, and if it came down to it, he could defend as well. He imagined for a moment how much easier his and Emily's abduction would have been with the suits and PSDs.

Levaran raised her hand and paused when they were halfway down a massive corridor.

Dr. Snowden focused and could hear heartbeats. There were about ten of them ahead. "I hear them."

Levaran nodded. "Edev is scanning. It appears we have found Dolgus Kree's crew." She faced Kri'tokhaar. "Is there a way around this hallway?"

Kri'tokhaar shook his buggy head. "There is, but it's the long way around. Going forward is the quickest path."

"Very well," said Levaran. She extended a hand at the krall, then focused on Dr. Snowden. "You and the krall wait here with the others. V, Edev, and I are going to talk with Dolgus."

Dan snorted. "Why can't we just go past them? We could take them."

"I don't want to endanger you needlessly," said Levaran, eying Dan. "All it takes is one stray shot and you're dead."

Dr. Snowden sighed. "She's right. I've . . . seen it before."

Dan nodded as he cast a sidelong glance at Dr. Snowden.

Levaran held her palm up to the krall and then flipped it around.

The krall stepped forward and shook her head, causing a curved shield to appear in front of her.

Dr. Bryson's eyes widened. "Whoa. What type of shield is that?"

Dr. Snowden smiled. "It's meant for ranged combat."

"Looks like it could also be used to bulldoze," said Dr. Bryson, running his hands along the front of the shield.

The krall eyed Dr. Bryson, causing him to scamper back.

Levaran tossed out an orb. It shot up a projection from Edev's perspective. "This will show you what's going on. Wait here." She nodded at V and then headed toward Dolgus Kree's group.

Dan chuckled. "Man, I'm glad she's here."

"Me too," said Sarah.

Dr. Snowden could see that Dan and Sarah were beginning to look to Levaran as a leader. He wondered if they all could have traveled as one group instead of splitting off and if the split was more for Dan and the others to bond with Levaran.

Dr. Bryson walked around the projection. "3-D holographic projection. Man . . ." He shook his head at Dr.

Snowden. "I can't even imagine what you know. Your conversations with my duplicate must make me seem foolish."

"Not really," said Dr. Snowden. "Come to think of it, I haven't talked to our version since a bit after our abduction. I sorta mixed up memories and . . . it caused an issue between us." He rubbed his chin. "I'll make a point of fixing that after all this, though."

Dr. Bryson nodded and pointed at the projection. "Look, there's those guys."

Dr. Snowden studied Dolgus's group. They were dressed similarly to how he remembered Jerzan's crew. Light armor, a variety of weapons, and a general appearance that indicated hygiene was not too important. The two things that stood out to him were that one of them was robotic in appearance and the rest were Bilaxians. Dolgus was easy to spot. He stood in front of the assembled group. Some had been checking out the side rooms but had gathered behind Dolgus.

"That's a mean-looking group," said Dan.

Dr. Snowden nodded. "And if they caught us, it wouldn't be good."

"Yeah . . . I'm getting that sense."

Dr. Snowden focused on the projection as Dolgus sneered at Levaran.

"Damn," said Dolgus, his eyes ravaging Levaran. "Looks like maybe there is something of value on this ship. You lost, sweet thing?"

"One, I'm not your sweet thing, Dolgus Kree. Two, you're in my way. Head back to your ship, and forget about this encounter," said Levaran.

Dolgus's crew laughed.

Dolgus smiled. "So you know me . . . and got quite a mouth. Something I'm sure we can find a good use for." He inspected V and Edev and then turned his head toward the robotic humanoid in the group. "Hey, Saza, looks like we found you some spare parts."

Saza emitted a digital chuckle. "Looks weak to me, but I'll take it."

"Analysis. My parts are not available for retrieval," said V.

"Just try!" said Edev.

Dolgus's group smirked and sneered.

"Well, this'll be quick," said Dolgus. He nodded at his group, and they all raised their weapons. With gritted teeth, he said, "Get down on your knees and put your hands above your head."

Levaran clenched her jaw for a moment. "I'll do no such thing. This ship is headed toward the sun. This is my last offer. Leave while you can."

"Listen here, bitch," said Dolgus. "I give the orders around here. Not you or your robot friends. You just encountered the wrong clan in the wrong place."

"I see," said Levaran. She extended her left arm and activated her shield. As Dolgus's crew began to fire, she knelt and aimed at the group with her right arm. They went tumbling back from her repulsion wave beam.

Edev followed up with a second repulsion blast.

Levaran tapped at her utility handle and fired a grappling beam at the nearest group member. When he was pulled forward, she clotheslined him, sending him sprawling to the ground.

Saza was the first to get up, and he charged toward Levaran. V tackled him, and they grappled off to the side.

Levaran hurtled into the group as they attempted to get up. One group member was crushed against the wall. She grabbed another and slung him like a bowling ball through the others.

Edev angled her four arms and shot a stun beam out, hitting four more.

One of them shot at Levaran but fell when his beam reflected back at him.

Dolgus lowered his weapon and pulled out a large knife. With a shake, it began to glow. "Surround her! And take out that damn orb!"

Dolgus and one of the remaining two members who could function flanked Levaran. The other member tried to fire at Edev but could not get a bead on her.

One reached in to grab Levaran and was batted away. She stepped back and kicked Dolgus in the chest, sending him flying across the hallway.

Edev spun with extended arms as she flew into the last member, knocking him down.

Levaran went over to where Saza and V were locked in a grappling match. She grabbed Saza and untangled him from V. Once V was clear, she fired a stun beam point-blank. Saza crumpled to the ground. She pointed at the group. "V, Edev, collect their weapons."

"Acknowledged," said V.

"On it," said Edev.

After a few minutes, all of the crew's weapons were assembled on the side.

Dolgus and the remaining members of his group who could stand gathered opposite them.

"What the hell are you?" asked Dolgus, rubbing his chest and spitting blood.

"Someone in a hurry, and you were in my way. My offer still stands. You can gather your wounded and leave this ship or die with it. I'll give you back your weapons after my friends have passed. If you wish to challenge me further, I won't be as lenient in a second altercation. Do you understand?"

Dolgus nodded vigorously.

Levaran faced down the hallway. "Dr. Snowden, bring the others."

Dr. Snowden nodded at the projection he had been watching. He tapped the krall and then waved forward. "You heard boss lady. Let's go."

Dan hustled up next to Dr. Snowden. "That was incredible. She can fight."

Dr. Bryson shook his head. "She literally wrecked them. I'm glad she's on our side. V is tough too, and Edev is a little spitfire."

"Is that something we could learn?" asked Sarah.

Dr. Snowden half smiled. "The Levaran stuff sure, not so much the V and Edev part. Levaran's ship, well, when it's ready, has a room that can project hard holograms. We call it the holo room. It has some great training programs. Emily uses it a lot."

"I'd like to check that out," said Sarah.

Dr. Snowden nodded.

"Levaran is impressive. Her commitment to your species is admirable," said Kri'tokhaar. "I suspect she has a dim view of mine."

"Maybe," said Dr. Snowden. "There are positives to look at, though. Yeah, I hated you guys for a while, but now, I understand that . . . it's better to focus on the positives and not dwell on the negatives. Levaran knows you were against the abductions."

"But I did nothing to stop it."

Dr. Snowden bobbed his head. "That's due to your culture, though. Correct me if I'm wrong, but from what I studied about your species, you have a hive-minded approach, and obedience is the law of the land."

"Yes. Even so, for events that break our cultural norms such as this, that should be enough to take action, yet I did not," said Kri'tokhaar.

Dr. Snowden observed Kri'tokhaar as they continued toward Levaran. It was obvious that guilt was tearing him apart. From what he understood of Krotovore, that would be a problem, at least one to deal with afterward.

When they got to Levaran, she waved them through the hallway entrance.

Dolgus and his crew jumped a bit when the krall growled at them as she passed.

Once they all had crossed into another hallway, Levaran placed her UIC on the door console. She faced Dolgus and his group. "You have your weapons again. Do as I say and leave this ship. To do otherwise is suicide."

The door closed, and Dr. Snowden watched as Dolgus's crew scrambled across the hallway to get their weapons. Maybe they had learned a lesson and would heed Levaran's word. He did not think they would, but at least she had given them a chance. There were differences between Levaran and Evaran, but at their core, their actions were similar. He shook his head as he and the others followed Levaran.

As they continued on for the next fifteen minutes, Dr. Snowden observed the interaction between the members of the group. Dr. Bryson and V seemed to have hit it off right away. That was not too surprising since in his universe, Dr. Bryson was a fanatic about artificial intelligence. Edev had joined in the conversations when she was in range. Despite all that was going on, he thought Dr. Bryson was going to be okay.

Dan and Sarah were beginning to relax some. He noted that they were now talking to Kri'tokhaar. Something about the way Kri'tokhaar spoke and moved seemed off to him. Maybe it was because he had studied them in his off time while traveling with Evaran. He had learned a great deal about their culture and norms and wanted to visit their empire at some point. It reinforced his observation that Kri'tokhaar probably felt the full weight of what his species had done.

Nonetheless, he thought it was good for Dan and Sarah to be able to talk with Kri'tokhaar. He observed that Kri'tokhaar was thoughtful and humbled by their desire to talk with him. Maybe at some point, Dan and Sarah could visit Kri'tokhaar after he got home.

Levaran kept to herself. That was not unusual to Dr. Snowden. He realized her full attention was on the environment around them, and as they progressed, she was the frontline defense. He wondered how Levaran being female would affect future confrontations. The look on Dolgus Kree's face when he saw her was one of lust. He understood at least that since Levaran was very attractive. That could be the aura she exuded as well. Others had also said he and Emily had a glow about them.

When they reached a large room that reminded him of a cafeteria, Levaran raised her hand.

"I am being contacted by Evaran. One moment," said Levaran.

As Levaran perused her ARI, Dr. Snowden examined the room. It reminded him of the encounter with Hulldar and Galkett from Jerzan's crew during their abduction. Hulldar had been killed by a slime creature called a Slivyn that could melt flesh with just a touch. He did a focused sweep but saw no sign of its presence. It was a different part of the ship, but the rooms were like duplicates. His attention was disrupted by Levaran.

"Evaran and Emily have fought a Time Warden predator. He has forwarded the details to me, V, and Edev. Emily was paralyzed, and they are on their way to the Torvatta," said Levaran.

"Paralyzed?" asked Dr. Snowden with raised eyebrows. "Is she okay?"

"For the moment. Evaran said it did not look fatal, and he is carrying her."

He swallowed hard. "How far away are they now?"

Levaran eyed him. "I know what you're thinking, but they're too far away at this point. It would take us some time to get to them and would expose the others to risk."

"I know," he said. "What is this . . . Time Warden predator?"

Edev flew over and shot down a projection in front of the group.

His eyes narrowed as he studied the black-and-gold predator. It was larger, had eight tentacles, and seemed like it would be tougher than the smaller ones, but not as tough as the defenders. He gestured at it. "Ever fought one of them before?"

Levaran nodded. "Several times. They were no match for me then, and now with this form, they're out of their league."

Dr. Bryson shuddered while looking at the projection. "They look like . . . large mechanical spiders."

"An apt analogy," said Levaran. "Time Wardens in general like to swarm, although the predators prefer to hunt alone. If they're here, then we should expect that there will be a Time Warden commander somewhere."

Dan shook his head. "I wish I had a weapon or something. I feel useless not being able to contribute."

"I like your spirit," said Levaran. "However, we should—" She tilted her head and faced the other side of the room. "We're not alone."

Dr. Snowden swiveled his head around. "I don't sense anything."

"It's the Time Wardens. They are too far away for you to sense, but I can. As I was saying, we should take a moment to refresh ourselves. This room has replicators."

Kri'tokhaar pointed over at a series of replicator stations embedded into the wall a bit away from them. "Some of those look like they still have power."

Dr. Bryson rubbed his throat. "Yeah, I could use some water, come to think about it." He gestured at Kri'tokhaar. "Lead on."

Kri'tokhaar swept his head across everyone for a moment and then headed over to the replicators.

Dr. Snowden noted that although Dan, Sarah, and Dr. Bryson followed him and Kri'tokhaar, Levaran, V, and Edev had begun to move around the room, scanning.

When they got to the replicators, Dr. Bryson said, "So these replicators just . . . what? Create matter based on a pattern?"

Dr. Snowden gestured at Kri'tokhaar. "Based on what I saw from the future, I'm going to guess it has an element storage tank of some type, with a matter converter unit that feeds it. It can then make those patterns based on what's available element-wise."

Kri'tokhaar faced Dr. Snowden. "That's very close to how we designed it. We don't use tanks so much as streams. Every replicator is tied into a pipe that has a stream of elements. It can pull out what's needed."

Dr. Bryson narrowed his eyes. "So these . . . pipes . . . contain all elements needed for replication?"

Kri'tokhaar nodded.

"How does it keep them separated?"

Kri'tokhaar drew in the air with his claws. "Imagine this pattern. Draw a circle. At two points on the top, draw two parallel lines up. The gap between the points on the circle is open."

"Like a keyhole?" asked Dr. Bryson.

"I'm . . . unfamiliar with that term. Nonetheless, each element area has that shape and is buffered by shielding. The size of the shape depends on the rarity of the element."

Dr. Bryson rubbed his chin. "A layered pipe. Fascinating. Then the replicators would have specialized extractors that interact with the pipe."

"Yes. You learn quickly."

Dan shook his head and crooked a thumb at Dr. Bryson. "He might. That all sounds like mush to me."

Dr. Snowden smirked. "The funny thing is, with your nanobots, these types of things will be easy to learn in time."

Sarah swatted Dan's arm. "That I would like to see."

Dan smirked.

Everyone except Kri'tokhaar got a container of water and settled down at a nearby table.

"I've heard you mention the nanobots before," said Kri'tokhaar, facing Dr. Snowden. "They were meant for short-term use. How long have you had yours?"

"About six months now. Matriarch De'zokaar gave us a device that can extract them, but Emily and I kept them. It's saved our bacon several times."

"Bacon?" asked Kri'tokhaar.

Everyone chuckled.

Dr. Snowden gestured outward. "I mean that it's helped us tremendously. We're stronger, faster, smarter, live longer, and there are other effects that more recently materialized, like controlling our emotional state."

"They should have left your body on their own after a month," said Kri'tokhaar, narrowing his smaller eyes.

"Huh," said Dr. Snowden. "Then it sounds like humans are unique to the nanobots. Like a symbiotic relationship."

Kri'tokhaar's eyes blinked slowly. "You humans are truly unique. It sounds like the nanobots have evolved, and they did it with your species. Very unexpected."

Dr. Bryson smiled. "I don't want them out. It sounds like it's the next step in our evolution."

Dr. Snowden bobbed his head. "Augments are, actually, but I suspect nanobots at some point."

Dan chuckled. "Well, if these nanobots are supposed to make us smarter, mine haven't kicked in yet."

"Give it time," said Dr. Snowden. "It's not like a switch is flipped, but over time, things will make sense to you that would have been *mush* before."

"I'd like to learn to fight like Emily," said Sarah.

"Me too," said Dr. Snowden. He noticed V looking over at them as everyone laughed.

Dr. Bryson followed Dr. Snowden's gaze. "I like V. It's so cool that you get to travel with him."

Dr. Snowden nodded. "He's one of my closest friends now. Had a situation a while back where if he hadn't stepped in to help me, I wouldn't be here."

"Well, if Levaran lets me travel with her and Edev, maybe I can get to know Edev like that," said Dr. Bryson.

Dr. Snowden nodded. "It's possible."

"Levaran and Evaran are very powerful. It's good to see them using their abilities to help others," said Kri'tokhaar. He lowered his buggy head. "Even if it is an abduction."

"Hey, man," said Dan. "Shit happens. How you respond to it is what's important."

"I . . . I wish you did not have to test that approach like this," said Kri'tokhaar.

Sarah smiled. "At least we get nanobots and to meet a parallel-universe version of Albert and our daughter."

Dr. Bryson nodded. "Yeah, I mean . . . there are positive things that can come from this. Just have to look at the bright side and not dwell too much on the past."

"I wish I could have met your species under different circumstances. It is . . . water under the bridge, though," said Kri'tokhaar.

Dr. Bryson grinned. "There you go."

Levaran walked up to the group. "I've had Edev scout around. She has detected two predators, but they are a bit away. We can go when you're ready."

Dr. Bryson slapped Kri'tokhaar's back shell as he stood. "I think we're good."

Levaran tilted her head at Kri'tokhaar as he rose. "Very well." She circled a finger at V, who joined them on the way to the hallway entrance on the other side of the room.

Dr. Snowden enjoyed talking with Kri'tokhaar and saw that the others did too. The thought crossed his mind that Kri'tokhaar could even travel with Levaran. How that would work when visiting Earth would be interesting. Maybe a camouflage suit or holographic overlay or something.

He was surprised at how quickly Dan and the others adjusted to where they were. It could be that his presence helped to stabilize things. He knew that if he and Emily had come out of the virtual simulation and Dan and Sarah had been there for them, it would have been much easier.

Dan slapped him on the back. "Thinking, aren't you?"

"Always," said Dr. Snowden as he half smiled.

18

Over the next thirty minutes, Dr. Snowden observed the environment and the corpses of various creatures. In the first fifteen minutes, creatures ran away from them. The group did get challenged by a humpbacked humanoid with an elongated neck and unusually large arms, but Edev's repulsion beam hit the ground before it and sent it packing. The temperature had gone down some, and judging by Dan and the others rubbing their arms, he knew they would need to get off the ship soon, before it got too cold.

In the second fifteen minutes, he began to see a pattern in the few dead creatures they saw. They had halted at one of them to investigate. It had been stabbed several times and had energy-beam marks across its body. Initially he thought it might be the Time Wardens, but the wounds indicated that multiple small creatures had done it. Levaran mentioned that there were several possibilities, but nothing to confirm with.

He was glad to see that Kri'tokhaar was looking a bit more relaxed. Dr. Snowden was unable to decipher Kri'tokhaar's feelings based on his waving antennae, his clacking claws, or the variety of noises he made, but he got a sense of Kri'tokhaar's emotions in the way he walked and talked. And mostly, it was his eyes. Always his eyes.

It seemed almost universal that slow blinking indicated calm and rapid meant nervousness. It made him proud that Dan and the others were accepting of Kri'tokhaar. It showed the best of humanity, that, in his opinion, they could adapt and evolve and even change their views. He suspected Kri'tokhaar noted this too.

The krall and Sarah seemed to have formed a bond. As they walked, Sarah would scratch the krall behind the ears, or pat it on the side. The krall seemed to enjoy the attention and had even been less antagonistic toward Kri'tokhaar. He suspected that if it came down to it, the krall would help Kri'tokhaar in a pinch.

He had spent most of the time since the cafeteria with V, and he got the sense that V felt a little left out. Based on the looks V had been giving, it seemed he was curious and wanted to interact. This situation must have intrigued him, and although Edev was his counterpart, Dr. Snowden figured interacting with people who were parallel versions of important people in his and Emily's lives was a priority for V.

Dr. Snowden knew how close V and Emily were, so maybe this was V's opportunity to learn more. Dr. Bryson had spent some time with V as well, and he seemed eager to engage V in theoretical discussions.

When they came to a storage-container room, Levaran paused. She raised a hand for everyone to stop, then motioned with two fingers forward.

Edev shimmered out of view and flew forward.

Dr. Snowden could feel it too. His nanobots were tingling, which probably meant that a Time Warden was around. Their energy signatures had a temporal component to them, which is something he was more aware of now. He stood next to Levaran. "How many?"

Levaran narrowed her eyes. "I'm . . . not sure. I can detect something, but not its location. Edev can't see it either."

Dan exhaled slowly as he looked around. "You think this thing has stealth?"

"Predators don't have that. This is either a new creature or a new type of Time Warden that Evaran and I haven't seen before. We should proceed with caution."

The krall took the right side of the group while V took the rear with Kri'tokhaar. Dr. Snowden went to the left side, and Levaran took the lead, with Edev flying around.

Dr. Snowden did not like storage rooms. It seemed every one they had encountered on the ship contained a nasty surprise. The dim lighting and light mist on the floor added to the foreboding atmosphere, but it was the eerie silence that unnerved him.

Dan's eyes darted around when they were at the room's halfway point. "I have a . . . weird sensation."

"Like a tingling?" asked Dr. Snowden.

Dr. Bryson nodded. "Getting it too. Feels weird."

"Same here," said Sarah.

Dr. Snowden rubbed his chin. "It's probably not temporal awareness. My guess is you're stressed and the nanobots are boosting your body to compensate."

"Huh," said Dan. He snapped his head to the side. "I thought I saw something."

Levaran raised her hand to pause the group and took a few steps toward the area Dan was inspecting. "Let's check." She raised her right arm and fired a repulsion blast.

Dr. Snowden's heartbeat ramped up when the blast unveiled a large spherical body that had multiple tentacles.

It was a Time Warden, but unlike any he had seen so far. Small holes on the sphere opened up, and smaller Time Wardens with just three tentacles and a small orb in the middle crawled out.

"The hell is that?" said Dan with widened eyes.

Levaran motioned forward. "Move!"

As the group surged forward to the exit, another Time Warden similar to the first one appeared in their path.

Dr. Snowden peered back and saw that yet another had come out of stealth behind them where they first entered the room. "It's a trap!"

"Then we're going through them!" said Levaran. "Follow me!"

Dr. Snowden ushered Dan, Sarah, and Dr. Bryson forward while watching the rear with the others.

The clickety-clackety noise of the smaller Time Wardens filled the room.

His mouth went dry as he saw the smaller Time Wardens shooting a line at the ceiling and pulling themselves up and then sailing around. They were taking positions high up on the storage containers. He pointed near the ceiling behind them. "The small ones can grapple!" A quick sweep around showed that the smaller ones were coming on the ground as well.

V grabbed Dr. Snowden's arm. "We must go."

Dr. Snowden nodded and spun around. He and V hustled up to the others.

Edev hovered behind them and shot a mix of repulsion and stun beams as she dodged fire from the smaller ones.

Levaran ran headlong into the Time Warden in their path. It wrapped its tentacles around her, tangling her up. The smaller ones jumped on her and began to attack.

The krall raised its shield and charged into the side of the Time Warden, knocking it and Levaran over.

V began to pull the smaller ones off Levaran as Dan, Sarah, and Dr. Bryson sidestepped the fight and tried to slip past.

Kri'tokhaar activated a shield and began firing a small weapon. His energy beams were knocking back the smaller ones, and the ones he focused the beam on for a little longer evaporated.

Sarah and Dr. Bryson screamed as two smaller ones jumped on them and pricked them.

Dan was a blur as he pulled them off and smashed them into the ground.

Sarah fell to her knees and squinted as she doubled over.

Dr. Bryson fell forward and struggled to get up.

Levaran had been able to regain control of the Time Warden that had wrapped her up, and with a strike from her energy gauntlet, she smashed the central orb, causing yellow goo to run out.

When the goo evaporated, the Time Warden stopped moving. The smaller ones approached in large numbers.

Levaran pointed forward. "Into the hallway!"

V picked up the remains of a Time Warden and tossed it behind him, knocking out several of the smaller ones. Dan picked up Sarah while Dr. Snowden steadied Dr. Bryson. The krall had taken up the rear with Kri'tokhaar and Edev, and between their shielding and weapon fire, they were able to keep a buffer.

As they entered the hallway, Dr. Snowden froze. It was a Time Warden predator. They had been corralled.

Kri'tokhaar rushed to a door console and, using his claw print, sealed the door to the storage room.

Levaran waved for everyone to step back as she positioned herself front and center to face the Time Warden. She wobbled for a moment, and raised a hand. "Hear me, Time Warden."

Dr. Snowden's eyes widened. Whatever the paralyzing toxin was, being stabbed so many times had an impact even on Levaran. He could see her straining to just stand up.

"You have already been heard and judged," said the predator. It rushed forward and knocked Levaran away.

The krall growled and pushed the predator back using her shield.

Edev fired, but her repulsion beam could not move the predator, and the stun beams had no effect on the shielding.

V rushed forward and grabbed one of the predator's tentacles.

The predator tried to stab V with its top tentacles but could not penetrate V's shielding.

V was able to grab another top tentacle.

The predator lifted V and began to squeeze. It staggered around while using its remaining two tentacles to keep the krall and Kri'tokhaar at bay.

Dr. Snowden saw an opportunity. With the others keeping the tentacles busy, the core body was vulnerable. Peering back, he observed that Levaran was kneeling and trembling. Her face showed pain, and when she tried to stand and fell back, a chill shot up his spine.

The krall kept a bit away from the predator and provided cover against its energy beams.

Kri'tokhaar popped out behind the shield and took pot shots, but the predator's shield held.

Levaran gestured forward. In an anguished voice, she said, "Dr. Snowden. The rod."

Dr. Snowden exhaled raggedly and laid down Dr. Bryson. He extended the rod from his PSD and approached the predator with his shield out. When he was getting close, the krall, Edev, and Kri'tokhaar joined him and spread out to draw the predator's attention.

The predator spun around and shot out a scanning beam.

Dr. Snowden peered back and saw that Levaran had activated her shielding and had Dan and the others behind her.

V ripped out a tentacle, but was still tied up. He grabbed one of the predator's bottom tentacles, causing it to falter.

Time seemed to slow down as Dr. Snowden's nanobots went into overdrive. He could see the elliptical body dipping toward him. His eyes searched, and although he was not sure how, he thought he detected a weakened spot in the shielding. He surged forward.

The remaining top tentacle moved to grab him, but Kri'tokhaar jumped forward and got rolled up by it.

Dr. Snowden stepped to the side and, with a grunt, plunged the rod deep into the predator's body. When he yanked it out, the end was covered in a yellow goo that then evaporated.

The predator crumpled lifelessly to the ground.

"You did it!" said Edev.

Dr. Snowden exhaled as he helped Kri'tokhaar up. These predators were no joke. He nodded at Edev. "Yeah, barely." He glanced at Kri'tokhaar. "Impeccable timing."

Kri'tokhaar rubbed his sides. "It was worth the bruising."

V had untangled himself and joined Dr. Snowden and Kri'tokhaar. "Analysis. That was a tough fight."

"I'm with ya," said Dr. Snowden. He gestured at the predator while looking at Kri'tokhaar. "That's an apex predator if I ever saw one."

Kri'tokhaar nodded. "Their shielding is quite advanced. Your weapon is more formidable than it appears."

Dr. Snowden snorted. "Well, wouldn't have gotten it in there if it wasn't for teamwork." He patted the krall and then hustled over to Levaran and the others. Sarah and Dr. Bryson were seated against the wall, struggling to breathe.

"Levaran said they're going to be okay," said Dan.

Dr. Bryson grimaced. "Feel like I've been stung by a large wasp. Hurts to move."

"It's your nanobots fighting it, I'm guessing," said Dr. Snowden.

Levaran stood and nodded. "The smaller ones don't have a lot of the toxin."

"Paralyze by a thousand cuts approach," said Dr. Bryson, wincing.

Dr. Snowden laid a hand on Levaran's arm. "You okay? You took a ridiculous amount of those attacks."

Levaran nodded. "Better me than the others. I suspect with that much, they would have been completely paralyzed now, if not dead. Evaran has contacted me, and I will need to update him. Then we have to move. The Time Wardens know where we are now."

Dr. Snowden nodded as Levaran interacted with her ARI. He helped Dr. Bryson up.

The krall went over to Sarah and laid down next to her. She nuzzled Sarah and let Sarah use her to stand up.

Levaran returned. "Evaran has Emily in the medical lab and has cleared docking bay 3. He's on his way now."

Kri'tokhaar gestured down the hallway. "We're near the service tunnels I mentioned before that run through several system control centers. The connecting corridors were built with my species in mind. It would be cramped for the Time Wardens, and even the krall."

Levaran nodded. "Lead on."

The walk to the side corridors took around ten minutes. When they got there, Dr. Snowden could hear the sound of a Time Warden predator off in the distance. Not only did he now know what to listen for, he could feel them. It was like being able to differentiate tastes. Although he knew it was actually an energy signature and his nanobots knew how to interpret them, he always associated a color and taste with them. The predators had a metallic taste and the color purple.

Kri'tokhaar wasted no time in getting the corridor open.

Levaran went first, followed by the krall and Edev. Dan, while supporting Sarah, went next. Dr. Bryson was supported by V and went after them.

Kri'tokhaar gestured in.

Dr. Snowden nodded and stepped into the corridor.

Kri'tokhaar followed him in and sealed the door. He interacted with a side console and, after a moment, turned toward Dr. Snowden. "The local security drones are active. Let the Time Wardens play with that."

"It woulda been nice to have had their help back there," said Dr. Snowden.

Kri'tokhaar nodded. "Unfortunately, the global security system, while intact, wouldn't initiate security measures unless locally activated. It's part of the protocol to ensure that someone doesn't hijack the global system and cause mayhem. I checked back there when I sealed the door, and the local security system was down."

"Makes sense. You think the drones could take a Time Warden?"

"I do, if they have enough numbers. They can deal with shielding, and are adaptive."

Dr. Snowden examined the area around him. "Wow, you weren't kidding about tight corridors." There was barely enough room for two Krotovore to walk side by side, and the height was just shy of eight feet. Although he was not claustrophobic, being packed in with the others and the threat of the Time Wardens made his nanobots tingle. The smell was odd to him and reminded him of moldy bread. Maybe that was a soothing smell to the Krotovore.

After fifteen minutes of walking, they reached a small circular room large enough for everyone to fan out.

The sides of the room were coated in a material that allowed a holographic projection of a workstation to appear, and Kri'tokhaar headed over to interact with it. "According to this station, the life-sign detectors are down." He shook his head. "A lot of systems were already down, and now it's cascading through the tertiary systems. I suspect those systems won't even make it to the sun. Not that it would matter, since the ship is headed there."

Levaran surveyed the area. "Interesting setup."

"We have several per ship section," said Kri'tokhaar. "They all share the same functionality, and only those of certain clearance can enter them. I can enter any of them due to my status."

Dr. Bryson twisted his back around a bit. "I like it. I wish I could study it without getting stung or chased."

Levaran raised a finger. "Knowledge pollution is a concern. If you were to study it, go back to Earth, and be tortured for information, it could damage the timeline."

Dr. Bryson's eyes widened. "I was just kidding. I mean . . . I know I'll need to be quiet about this. INRA and all."

Dr. Snowden eyed Dr. Bryson. "And that is . . ."

"International Nonhuman Response Agency. They'd snatch us up in a heartbeat."

"Huh," said Dr. Snowden. "We don't have that on our Earth."

"You do," said Levaran. "You just don't know about it."

"Wait, you mean they know about Daedroulds, Outsiders, and all that?"

Dr. Bryson nodded. "In our universe, nonhumans are hunted. Not sure how they are verified or what those terms you said are. I don't agree with it, a lot of us don't, but it's there in the open."

"The one in your universe," said Levaran, pointing at Dr. Snowden, "is held in check by powerful interests. I suspect when I visit the Earth here, my adventures may be a bit different from what your Evaran experienced."

"Sounds like it," said Dr. Snowden. He had met nonhumans such as the Greek god Hermes and the ancient vampire Lord Vygon. He wondered what their status was in this universe.

"Done," said Kri'tokhaar. "I've released docking bay 6's doors and sealed the entrance to the interior. I don't know if it will stop the Time Wardens from punching through, but it should hold them up some. I've also activated the local security drones outside the door."

Dan exhaled. "Finally. It sounds like we're getting close to getting out of here."

Kri'tokhaar faced Dan. "I just hope that you don't think ill of all Krotovore."

"I think I speak for Dr. Bryson and Sarah," said Dan, looking between the two, who nodded, "in saying we appreciate all the help you've given."

Kri'tokhaar swept his six eyes across them. "I wished I could have done more."

Dan slapped Kri'tokhaar's shelled back. "We're thankful."

Levaran gestured forward. "Evaran has contacted me and has landed the Torvatta in the docking bay."

"There should only be one more control center before the docking bay, but it's clear from here on out," said Kri'tokhaar.

Dr. Snowden smiled. "Let's go!"

Levaran and the others headed into the corridor.

As Dr. Snowden followed them, the door behind him slid shut. He turned and saw that Kri'tokhaar was still in the room. The group paused and turned to face the door.

"Kri'tokhaar, what are you doing?" asked Dr. Snowden as he peered through the window on the top half of the door.

"You all should go now. I'm going to make sure this ship never hurts anyone again," said Kri'tokhaar, broadcasting into the corridor.

Dr. Snowden clenched his jaw for a moment. "There's no need for this. We can get you back to your planet and your people."

"You could, but there's nothing there for me except shame. I can't do anything there, but I can do something here. I know the ship is headed to the sun, but I will self-destruct the ship after you have left."

"Oh, c'mon, man," said Dan. "Things aren't that bad."

"For a Krotovore, the shame is worse than death. Go. Your ship's presence seems to have attracted a lot of activity this way. I can slow them down, but you must hurry."

"You could travel with me if you wished," said Levaran.

"I . . . appreciate the offer, and it is enticing. However, I've thought about this for a while, and after seeing what we did to these humans and others, I must do this. I simply cannot live with this."

Dr. Snowden pounded the door with his fist. "Damn it!"

"Go!" said Kri'tokhaar.

Dr. Snowden's eyes watered as Dan laid a hand on his shoulder. He had started to really like Kri'tokhaar and wanted to talk with him more. His earlier sense about Kri'tokhaar seemed to be correct, but he did not think it would go this far. He wiped his eyes and exhaled from his mouth.

"Let's go," said Levaran.

Dr. Snowden took a final look at Kri'tokhaar.

Kri'tokhaar put his hands over his four eyes and slowly closed his two big ones.

Dr. Snowden dipped his head as his eyes searched the ground. With a sigh, he wheeled around to follow the others.

After ten minutes, they had passed the empty control center and reached docking bay 6.

Although Dr. Snowden was glad to see the Torvatta along with Evaran and check up on Emily, Kri'tokhaar's decision to stay behind ate at him. By showing Kri'tokhaar what he thought was the best of humanity, he had deepened Kri'tokhaar's resolve. Even when trying to do what he thought Evaran would do, it did not work out as he had planned.

Evaran walked out of the Torvatta as V and Edev led everyone except Levaran and Dr. Snowden inside. He faced Levaran. "Where is Kri'tokhaar?"

"He opted to stay behind, and secure our escape," said Levaran.

"There is no need for that. We should go get him," said Evaran.

Dr. Snowden grimaced.

Evaran observed Dr. Snowden for a moment. "You seem troubled."

Dr. Snowden sighed. "Kri'tokhaar doesn't want to come. He intends to blow up the ship."

"I see," said Evaran. He rubbed his chin. "I suspect, to Kri'tokhaar, this last act is one of redemption."

"I know," said Dr. Snowden, swallowing hard. "It just feels . . . like a senseless death to me is all, but I understand his reasoning." He cleared his throat. "And I'll respect it, even if I don't like it. I seem to be doing that a lot lately." He gestured at the Torvatta. "How's Emily?"

Evaran nodded. "She will be out of her paralyzed state soon. We need to leave now, though."

Dr. Snowden nodded as he followed Evaran and Levaran into the Torvatta's shielding. The fight noises outside the door caught his attention for a brief moment. With a final look around, he shook his head and entered the Torvatta.

19

Emily awoke to noises outside the slab shielding. She tested moving her arm by reaching back and feeling her wound. Her fingers touched healed skin, and with one motion, she grabbed the towel over her buttocks and flipped around. Her first point of order was to pull up her lower armor.

After securing it in place, she sat up and cracked her neck while doing a final check to make sure everything was covered. Twisting from side to side caused her back to pop. A grin formed on her face as she pressed the button at the top of the slab.

The shielding dissipated, causing Evaran, Dr. Snowden, and V to look over at her.

She swung her legs to the side and then slid off the slab. The first thing she noticed other than Evaran and the others was that there were two other shielded slabs. Since she could not see Dr. Bryson, Dan, Sarah, or Levaran, she figured two of them were injured and being attended to.

The second thing she noticed caused her eyes to light up. It was the krall, which laid off to the side with a content look. She did not see Kri'tokhaar anywhere after a quick glance around, and the others were heading her way.

"Looks like someone had a good nap," said Dr. Snowden, tapping her arm when he arrived next to her.

Emily snorted. "I couldn't do much else."

"Analysis. You look well."

"Thanks, V," she said.

"It is good to see you are up," said Evaran.

She lurched forward and embraced Evaran in a bear hug. "Thanks for . . . taking care of me."

"You are welcome," said Evaran. "For the record, I was not uncomfortable."

Dr. Snowden wrinkled his eyebrows as his eyes searched Emily.

Emily ran a hand over the back of her neck. "I'm . . . glad."

"Not quite following here," said Dr. Snowden, raising a finger.

"Not important," she said, scratching her cheek. She pointed to the krall. "I see you found her. Where's Kri'tokhaar?"

Dr. Snowden ran a hand through one of his gray tufts as he sighed. "He decided to stay behind."

"Why?"

"Guilt, I think," said Dr. Snowden. "He said he couldn't live with the shame of what his species did while he stood by."

"I sensed that about him. I don't know if he was a typical Krotovore, but I had hoped maybe to interact with him some once he was on board."

"We all got to know him better," said Dr. Snowden. "*And* he helped us all the way to the docking bay. He made sure that the Time Wardens were occupied for our escape."

She shook her head. "I'm just glad you're safe." She gestured at the shielded slabs. "So who got hurt?"

"Dr. Bryson and Sarah. They were attacked by a new type of Time Warden. Dan is with Sarah, and Levaran is applying some gel to their wounds. Edev is helping her."

"Oh," she said as she cocked her head. "So . . . what was the new Time Warden?"

V shot up a projection from his head, showing the Time Warden with smaller ones crawling out.

She rubbed her arms. "Yeah . . . that one gives me the creeps."

"Edev was a machine keeping them off our tail. After getting away and sealing them in a room, we had to fight a Time Warden predator," said Dr. Snowden.

"Analysis. I would like the enhancement to shoot from my arms like Edev. Also, for the record, Dr. Snowden delivered the killing blow."

Emily jerked her head back as she eyed Dr. Snowden. "You did?"

He snorted. "I had some help. V kept it occupied while Kri'tokhaar, Edev, the krall, and I approached it. Kri'tokhaar took a hit from one of the tentacles trying to knock me away, and I took the opening to jab it."

"Where was Levaran?"

"She was hurt," said Evaran. "Based on what she showed me, she took enough toxin to kill a human about five times over. It would appear that the Time Wardens decided to overdose and kill instead of paralyze after my and Emily's incident."

Emily's eyes widened. "Wow. She really is strong."

Evaran nodded. "Much more so than I. Although not knocked out, her movement was severely limited."

"We had her back," said V.

Emily chuckled and extended her hand toward the krall, who rose and sauntered over to her. When the krall arrived, she nuzzled Emily's hand.

Evaran tilted his head. "Intriguing. I did not need to introduce you as a friend to the krall."

"Maybe . . . ," said Dr. Snowden, rubbing his chin," since Sarah and the krall sort of bonded, she senses Emily is somehow . . . similar."

"Perhaps," said Evaran. "Although I doubt she can sense three-Ls, she may have sensed the similarity in body chemistry."

Emily knelt and rubbed her thumbs along the krall's face. The krall's eyes blinked slowly as she nuzzled the side of Emily's face.

"The krall protected Sarah during our Time Warden fight," said Dr. Snowden. He narrowed his eyes. "I still can't believe you and Evaran took one down. Those things are tough."

"Yeah, but I was paralyzed shortly after the fight began."

"Analysis. You delivered the killing blow, from what Evaran has shown me."

Emily bobbed her head. "I got that off before going down."

"You did admirably," said Evaran. "Bear in mind, if you did not have your nanobots and training, you would have gone down instantly."

"I coulda done better," she said.

Dr. Snowden smirked. "I'm betting you found a new opponent for your holo room training."

She nodded. "By training against the toughest, you become better. I want to look into some suit upgrades too. That predator went right through my body armor."

"We will," said Evaran. "Your armor can stop most smaller Time Warden attacks already. However, I was not expecting predators or the new one Dr. Snowden and the others encountered. We will make adjustments prior to going to the timeplex."

Emily focused on Evaran. "You said it was different than the anchor stations."

"I did, and judging by the activity level of the Time Wardens at this point in this universe, I suspect it is probably much larger and more advanced. We will deal with it after getting Dan and the others home and then retrieving Levaran's Torvatta."

She nodded and eyed Dr. Snowden. "Hungry?"

Dr. Snowden chuckled. "Actually, I am. Tired too, but I want to stay awake until Dan and the others come out." He extended an arm out to the medical lab entrance. "After you."

"How gentlemanly of you," she said, raising her head a bit.

V swiveled his head between Dr. Snowden and Emily.

Emily laughed as she slapped V on the back. "C'mon." She shot Evaran a look.

"You three go ahead. I need to go over some things in the research lab."

She nodded and exited the room with Dr. Snowden, V, and the krall in tow. When she got to the conference room, she eyed the krall. "You know . . . I don't know what she eats."

"Analysis. She has meat desires like Dr. Snowden, per the Krotovore logs, except she prefers it uncooked."

Emily chuckled as she went to the replicator station. On the larger station, she replicated a plate with some raw meat and a large bowl of water. She placed them on the ground and waved her finger between the krall and the plate and bowl.

The krall dipped her head and sniffed around the meat.

Emily patted her on the head.

The krall raised her head a bit, then dove into the meat and took large gulps of water.

"Whoa," said Dr. Snowden. "I think she was famished."

"I think so," said Emily. She got two plates with a burger and fries and some soda and headed toward the conference table. "I got us both something to eat, unless your diet has changed."

"No, no, you're fine," said Dr. Snowden, eyeing the plate she put before him.

She took her seat and started on her burger as V sat next to her. While she was glad to be off the Krotovore ship, the loss of Kri'tokhaar bothered her. Maybe if she had gone with them, Kri'tokhaar would have stuck around. Maybe not, but she would never know. That opportunity was now gone. Although she did not want to admit it to Dr. Snowden, the thought of talking with Dan and Sarah caused butterflies in her stomach. She realized, after she had left with Evaran, that maybe they thought she did not want to be around them.

Dr. Snowden tapped the table with his finger as he eyed her.

Emily smiled. "I'm just taking a cue from you. Thinking."

He nodded as he continued with his burger.

She half smiled at V and Dr. Snowden as she returned to her plate.

Emily surveyed her bedroom. After finishing her late dinner, she wanted to relax a bit. Evaran had joined them when they had finished and said that Levaran was going to show Dan and the others to their temporary rooms. Although she wanted to talk with them, she understood that they were probably exhausted and tempted by the thought of sleeping in a safe environment.

She removed her suit and took a quick shower. Once she was out and had on a light nightgown, she positioned herself on the couch in the main area of her living quarters.

A soft beep echoed above her.

She had not been expecting anyone. "Who is it?"

"Sarah. I heard you might still be up."

Emily jumped off the couch and headed to the door. After opening it, she saw that Sarah had gotten cleaned up and wore jeans, comfortable shoes, and a light shirt, with her hair pulled back in a ponytail. Emily nodded, stood to the side, and gestured for Sarah to come in.

Sarah smiled. "I hope I'm not bothering you."

"Not at all," said Emily. "I was just contemplating if I wanted to do some stretching before I went to bed."

Sarah entered and followed Emily to the main area. After taking a seat in a chair perpendicular to Emily on the couch, she said, "These rooms are amazing."

"Yeah," said Emily. "I love them." She wrinkled her eyebrows. "Where's Dan and Dr. Bryson?"

Sarah pointed up. "Dan went to the roof to talk with Albert. James said he wanted to pass out, and Levaran wanted to catch up with Evaran. V and Edev are in the holo room."

"Makes sense," said Emily. She studied Sarah. The resemblance was uncanny. It struck her that even Sarah's clothing choice was similar to something that she would have picked out. She chuckled. "I feel like I'm a carbon copy of you, just a bit younger."

"Yeah, but you're a lot tougher, smarter, and prettier," said Sarah.

It was not lost on Emily that Sarah's response was very motherly. "I wish I had the opportunity to know my version of you. But . . . I was the cause of her death." She pulled her lips in.

Sarah smiled. "If she was anything like me, she would have gladly given her life if it meant her child could live."

Emily fidgeted with her hands. "I know you aren't my birth mother, but it's hard not to think, in some way, you are, especially given what I know of how . . . everything works."

"I would be honored to have you as a my parallel-universe daughter."

They both laughed.

"That sounds weird, doesn't it?" asked Sarah.

"Weird is no stranger here. I actually met a pure nanobot version of myself before."

Sarah's eyes widened. "Was it just like you, or something different?"

"She was me before . . . my experience on the prison planet. We had different outlooks on life."

"Oh," said Sarah. Her eyes softened. "Albert filled us in a bit on that. It sounds like you had a very rough time there."

Emily nodded. "Yeah . . . but it made me stronger."

Sarah chuckled "That's definitely a Dan trait. Now, if you play sports and study history, that's me."

"Actually . . . I do both. I'm a history major, or was . . . until all this."

Sarah wrinkled her eyebrows. "That's fascinating. You don't happen to have any video of your version of me or Dan, do you? My Dan recorded every moment he could, especially the holidays."

Emily's eyes lit up. "I brought some with me when we started traveling with Evaran."

Sarah nodded.

"If you want to see them, I can alter the room to show them. I know you're probably tired."

"I'm up for checking some of them out. I'm guessing we'll be here at least for the next day or so."

"Okay," said Emily. "I feel like we need popcorn."

"Extra butter?" asked Sarah.

Emily smiled. She and her father used to watch the old videos, and he always wanted popcorn with extra butter. Maybe he got that from Sarah. She hopped up, and when she was at the replicator, she noticed that Sarah had jumped over to the couch. Her eyes misted as she wondered if this is what it would have been like growing up and knowing her mom—movie nights with popcorn and soda. Her nostrils flared as she exhaled. With a tray holding two sodas and a bucket of popcorn, she headed back to a smiling Sarah, the couch, and late-night videos.

Dr. Snowden leaned out over the guardrail and gazed at the sun in the distance. Although it was peaceful since the Torvatta was stealthed and a few light-years from the Krotovore ship, he knew how chaotic the universe could be. He ran a hand through one of his gray tufts.

Going to bed like Emily was probably the smart thing to do, but his mind kept going over the events that led up to Kri'tokhaar staying behind. He wondered what he would have done had he been in the same situation. The initial thought was that he would try to make things better, and re-form. Given what he knew of Krotovore, that would be a hard pill to swallow. He jumped when a voice rang out behind him.

"Watching the stars?" asked Dan, joining Dr. Snowden by the guardrail.

Dr. Snowden smirked. "As always. I'm not sure if your Albert had a telescope, but Mom used get on me about sneaking out to use it in the backyard."

Dan chuckled. "It was the same with our Albert, except that I helped Dad cover for him."

"Amazing," said Dr. Snowden, glancing at Dan. "It was the same with the Dan I knew."

Dan narrowed his eyes. "I know parallel universes are supposed to have . . . duplicates, but it blows my mind how eerily similar they are. I'm not sure at this point if I could tell the difference, honestly."

"Same here. I know Emily is looking forward to spending some time with you and Sarah."

Dan tossed his head back. "Sarah went to visit Emily and see if she was up. V said you were up here, so I came."

"Let me guess," said Dr. Snowden, gesturing outward, "James probably went to bed."

Dan laughed. "Just like college. Every time our Albert and him came to visit, he always passed out early."

"Yeah," said Dr. Snowden with a chuckle. "He has a good reason to this time. This whole thing has just been . . . a surprise. Not just about you and the others, but . . . other things as well."

"Like what?"

Dr. Snowden sighed. "I'm not sure what I can and can't say, but if you travel with Levaran, I'm sure she'll tell you. Just be prepared to have your mind blown. I have to pinch myself half the time to make sure I'm not dreaming."

"That crazy, huh?"

"Yeah."

"Well . . . hell. It is what it is. Whatever comes up, I'll deal with it."

Dr. Snowden nodded. "Our Dan was always the anchor of the family. Everyone looked up to him as the person with the answers, the rock that never broke." His eyes misted. "That first year after he was gone was painful."

"I'm sure you stepped up."

"I tried," said Dr. Snowden, frowning. "Emily was a mess. All the cousins went their ways, and well, holidays were just me and Emily, and Chinese takeout."

"Damn," said Dan, shaking his head. "In this universe, I still have the big get-together, but with you gone, it was different. Karen came the first few years."

"I'm surprised that she wasn't here on the ship with you and the others."

"What do you mean?" asked Dan.

Dr. Snowden pulled his lips in and swayed his head. "I can't really get into it, but it sounds like she woulda been chosen, assuming she was James's wife like in our universe."

"James's wife? She was yours. Well, our Albert's. Unless the Krotovore can raise the dead, that wouldn't have happened."

Dr. Snowden jerked his head back. "Come again?"

"Karen killed herself. She simply couldn't live without you."

"Oh . . . ," said Dr. Snowden. He swallowed hard as he imagined how Dr. Bryson in his universe would have reacted to Karen's death. "In our universe, I hooked Karen up with James."

Dan snorted. "This is kind of weird comparing and contrasting parallel lives."

"Yeah it is, but you know . . . at least we're here to do that."

"Right on," said Dan. He swept his head around. "This kind of reminds me of being in the backyard with my Albert."

Dr. Snowden chuckled. "Yeah, all that's missing is Dad whispering and Mom screaming at everyone when she found out."

They shared a laugh.

"I forgot how much I missed talking to our Albert," said Dan as his eyes watered. "Life is . . . just not the same."

Dr. Snowden nodded as he drew his lips down. "At least you have Sarah. For me, Emily is around. Sometimes when I talk with her, it's like I'm talking to our Dan again."

Dan half smiled. "She's tough. Definitely got a spine of steel."

"And defiant at times. However, she also has a lot of our Sarah's traits. Compassionate, kind, and wanting to help others. Mix that with the capability to physically enforce it, and you have a tough combo."

Dan gulped. "She has the best of our traits. What year was she in college?"

"Sophomore."

"Huh. I'm guessing with this aging thing, she's put a hold on college since she travels."

Dr. Snowden nodded. "This is her home."

"That means it's yours too," said Dan.

Dr. Snowden wrinkled his eyebrows.

Dan extended a hand out. "I'm just saying that as close as you two are, her leaving after college would be hard for you. At least here, you get to spend more time with her."

Dr. Snowden pursed his lips for a moment, then nodded. "She's all I got left."

"I hear ya," said Dan. He turned around and examined the roof. "I wish pizza could be delivered up here."

Dr. Snowden cleared his throat as he walked to the center of the roof and, using the raised console, summoned two chairs, a small table, and a cardboard plate with a pizza on it. A paper towel roll sat to the side of the box.

Dan's eyes widened. "Are you shitting me?" He took a whiff and studied the pizza. "Double pepperoni, light sauce, onions, and garlic crust?"

"Yep," said Dr. Snowden with a smile. "I had it saved in my favorites."

Dan pointed at Dr. Snowden before taking a seat and grabbing a slice and a paper towel to hold under it. His eyes closed as he took a bite and then chewed slowly. After he swallowed, he said, "This is awesome."

"If James were up here, he would grab two slices in one go," said Dr. Snowden.

They both chuckled.

Dr. Snowden took a seat and eased back as he grabbed a slice with a paper towel.

Dan sighed. "This . . . just seems like such a great adventure."

"That's the ironic thing," said Dr. Snowden. "Our Dan was the adventurer. I knew he would love this and be the first one to sign up. Instead it was me and Emily that went on it. I'm guessing you're similar to our Dan in regard to the adventuring."

Dan nodded. "You know it. You really think Levaran will let us travel with her?"

"Count on it. That's the whole reason we're here."

"So we'll get one of them suits and that magic pen thing you got?"

"Personal support device, or PSD," said Dr. Snowden. "And yeah, you would get all of that, a place to stay, any food and drink item you can imagine, a room that can create any environment, and, of course, to travel everywhere."

Dan's eyes widened. "That's the adventure of a lifetime."

Dr. Snowden furrowed his eyebrows. "It has a lot of positives, but it also has some negatives. Coming to grips with your nanobots will be a bit easier, I think."

"Sarah would come if I went, and I suspect James would too."

Dr. Snowden chuckled. "James is a lock. Evaran made us wait three months, so not sure if Levaran will do the same for you."

"Huh," said Dan. He scrunched his face. "I'm guessing we're headed back to Earth now."

Dr. Snowden nodded. "From what Evaran said, the krall gets dropped off, then you three are next. After that, we get Levaran's ship, then have to deal with the Time Warden timeplex, wherever that is."

"I wish we could help in some way."

Dr. Snowden gazed off into the stars. "In time, I'm sure you can. Starting off with something like that, though, would be too intense is my guess."

Dan followed Dr. Snowden's gaze. "Yeah, I'm with ya. It makes me wonder if we will do the same things you've done, or if it'll be different."

"Based on what I've seen so far, I suspect it will be different."

Dan chuckled. "Who knows, maybe we'll go to a parallel universe and I'll be where you are, talking to another version of you."

"It could happen," said Dr. Snowden. He did not think it would due to the plane form situation, but he figured Dan would understand that in time.

Dan swatted Dr. Snowden's arm. "I'm just glad it was you who was there when we came out of that simulation thing. It's made this . . . a lot easier to digest. It's going to take a while, but I think we're going to be okay."

Dr. Snowden smiled as his chest tightened. Although he knew that he would go back to their own universe, the thought of traveling with parallel Dan, Sarah, and Dr. Bryson as crew members was appealing. He knew Emily would definitely be on board with it. He sighed as he looked out at the stars again. Reality as he knew it was not only strange, it was downright bizarre.

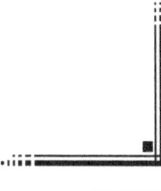

20

Dr. Snowden stood in the command area, observing Evaran and the others outside saying goodbye to the krall. He had said his goodbye already but knew that for Dan, Sarah, and Dr. Bryson, this was their first opportunity to be on an alien planet.

The previous night with Dan had lifted his spirits. After a good night's rest, Dr. Snowden had enjoyed breakfast with everyone around. It made things feel festive, although he knew that they had a much tougher goal ahead of them.

A smile formed on his face as he watched Sarah and Emily hug the krall. He had learned that the krall had stayed the night in Emily's room, as had Sarah. A chuckle escaped his lips as he imagined trying to explain that sleepover to anyone else. Sarah spending time with Emily probably did Emily good. He had not talked to her about her thoughts on it but figured he would after everyone else was dropped off.

He smirked seeing Dr. Bryson looking around outside. It must be like a wonderland to him. Dan was scanning around as well. Dr. Snowden figured it was more for security reasons than wonderment. After the Krotovore ship, he could still sense some apprehension from Dan and the others. He recalled how he felt after their rescue. It took a while to come to grips with everything.

"Analysis. You are deep in thought," said V.

Dr. Snowden nodded. He thought V would have gone outside like Edev, but V was content to pat the krall on her way out. "I was just thinking about my experience relative to theirs. They've taken the first step." He glanced at V. "I didn't get to talk with you much since we got back. What's your take on all of this?"

V's lights glowed a bit. "It has been interesting. I spent most of my time helping Edev. She was frustrated that she could not help as much as she wanted."

"I thought she did fine. I mean, that whole spinning and shooting thing. Sure, an additional body could have helped, but honestly, those Time Wardens were tough."

V nodded. "She has expressed a desire for a body. Her thought was that it may have been more helpful in that situation. I showed her U4's design, and she liked it."

"Oh," said Dr. Snowden with wide eyes. "That'll be interesting."

"Query. For what reason?"

"You know," said Dr. Snowden, gesturing toward Evaran and the others.

V studied them for a moment, then swiveled his head toward Dr. Snowden. "Analysis. You believe Evaran will be sentimental."

"Maybe," said Dr. Snowden. He shook his head. "Okay, I get your point. Still, I think it would intrigue him at least."

"I do have an observation."

Dr. Snowden shrugged. "Okay. Let's hear it."

V paused for a moment, then swiveled his head toward Dr. Snowden. "Kri'tokhaar decided to stay behind. This appeared to bother you, even though a parallel version of Kri'tokhaar was part of the crew that abducted you in our universe."

Dr. Snowden swallowed hard. "I'll admit . . . I wanted to hate him." He sighed. "But . . . I was just angry at the situation back then. It's the same reason I'm not angry at Evaran. That event occurred because it was part of something bigger. Kri'tokhaar was an actor, and as I found out, one whose moral code was against what happened, but he gave his life to make sure it didn't occur again. I respect that. I didn't like the decision, but it is what it is. Besides, hate takes a lot of energy."

"I see," said V. He tilted his head. "So you are not bothered that Evaran put you and Emily in danger?"

Dr. Snowden shook his head. "He didn't really. When he places those emergency beacons, he does it knowing that he will rescue us. It's that whole . . . time loop thing."

"Analysis. It appears you are part of a future event yet to occur that deals with the Hoxscarus. This may be a time loop inside a time loop."

Dr. Snowden rubbed his temples. "That makes my head hurt."

"I apologize," said V.

Dr. Snowden chuckled. "You're good." He peeked out the window and saw that the others were headed back in. "Well, looks like it's time to visit Earth."

"Acknowledged."

Dr. Snowden sat down, and when the others filtered in and took their seats, he looked around. Levaran was to his left along with Dr. Bryson. Dan and Sarah sat with Emily, while Edev floated next to V.

Evaran sat in the command chair, interacting with his chair console. "V, take us back in time, then portal us to Earth. Engage stealth mode prior to entering the portal."

"Acknowledged."

As the Torvatta rose, Dr. Bryson exhaled from his nose. "Albert . . . that was . . . amazing. An alien planet."

Dr. Snowden nodded. "To the planet, you were the alien."

Dr. Bryson eyed Dr. Snowden. "Good point. I'm just glad we could breathe out there."

"The krall was happy," said Levaran. She raised a finger. "She appeared to have bonded with Sarah and Emily."

"Yeah, I noticed that," said Dr. Snowden.

Sarah wrinkled her eyebrows. "I felt like . . . she knew me."

"Well, we can't take her in," said Dan, eying Sarah. "Imagine what the neighbors would say."

Everyone chuckled as the Torvatta reached space.

Dr. Bryson's breath staggered when the outside faded away, and eased back in. The Torvatta opened a portal.

"Torvatta stealth mode engaged," said V.

Dr. Bryson sat back in his chair as the Torvatta flew through the portal and exited it above Earth. He faced Dr. Snowden and Emily. "This travel ability is . . . incredible. This must be routine for you two."

Dr. Snowden nodded. "You get used to it."

Levaran gestured to the conference room. "Dan, Sarah, and Dr. Bryson, I have some things to cover with you before we drop you off at your respective points. Please follow me. Edev, come."

Dr. Snowden watched as Levaran led them to the conference room. Once they were inside, he said, "The whole keep-it-quiet and any-questions talk, huh?"

Evaran nodded. "Levaran has my experience with you and Emily to compare against."

Emily wrinkled her eyebrows. "They doing the three-month thing too?"

"I do not know," said Evaran. "It could be longer or shorter. Whatever it is, we can visit them once we are done with the Time Wardens." He examined Emily for a moment. "Did you enjoy your time with Sarah?"

"Oh, yeah," she said. "I could see elements of myself in her, and I'm sure she could see parts of her in me."

Dr. Snowden chuckled. "This Dan is every bit the Dan I knew. He may not have memories of Emily, but his personality is a match."

She swallowed hard. "I . . . look forward to talking with him when this is all done."

"And you will," said Evaran. "Dan has brought it to my attention that we are to attend a cookout at some point."

"Yeah . . . those are fun," said Dr. Snowden. "Looking forward to it."

After thirty minutes of light chat, Levaran exited the room with the others in tow.

The Torvatta had landed in Dr. Bryson's backyard.

Dr. Snowden joined Evaran and Emily as they headed over to meet Levaran and the others at the Torvatta exit. It was time to say goodbye to them for now and begin the next step.

Dr. Bryson extended a hand to Dr. Snowden. "As always, it's been interesting. Although I think this ranks right up there with absolutely crazy. However . . . it was good to see you, even if you are a parallel version."

Dr. Snowden returned the handshake. "I'll see you again here soon."

Emily hugged Dr. Bryson. "Be safe."

"I'll try to," said Dr. Bryson. He shook everyone else's hand.

Dan gestured at Dr. Bryson. "You should come down and visit us. We have a lot to talk about."

"Absolutely," said Dr. Bryson. He laid a hand on V's shoulder. "I enjoyed our conversations. You're truly unique."

V's lights glowed a bit brighter. "I enjoyed them as well."

Dr. Bryson high-fived Edev. "And I hope to have more conversations with you."

"Likewise," said Edev as her lights glowed brighter.

Dr. Bryson nodded at Evaran and Levaran. "Time to go." He turned halfway around and waved as he exited the Torvatta.

"V, take us to Dan and Sarah's house," said Evaran.

"Acknowledged," said V as he headed to the command area.

"I guess this is goodbye for now," said Dan, focusing on Dr. Snowden and Emily. "I fully expect you to join us for our cookout when you can."

"You can bet on it," said Dr. Snowden. He shook with one hand while leaning in to hug and slap Dan on the back with the other hand. "We're not that easy to get rid of."

"No . . . you're not," said Dan with a smile. He faced Emily. "I didn't get to spend much time with you, but I'm looking forward to it."

Emily's eyes misted as she smiled and hugged Dan. "I am too."

"To think that me and Sarah could have a daughter like you makes me proud," said Dan.

Emily smiled as she swallowed hard.

Sarah hugged Emily. "I really enjoyed last night."

Emily shuddered against Sarah.

Sarah stepped back and wiped a tear from Emily's face. With a cracked voice, she said, "You know you're always welcome in our home."

Emily nodded as she gripped Dr. Snowden's arm.

Sarah hugged Dr. Snowden. "Albert . . . the same goes for you."

"What about outside of it?" asked Dr. Snowden with a smile.

Sarah stepped back and swatted Dr. Snowden's arm. "That's exactly what I would expect you to say."

Dr. Snowden chuckled.

V had returned to the group. "We are in the backyard of Dan and Sarah's house."

Dan and Sarah shook hands with Evaran.

"I appreciate you helping Levaran and, by extension, us," said Dan, facing Evaran.

"It was my privilege," said Evaran.

"We got your back," said V. He raised a hand in the air.

Dan and Sarah laughed as they high-fived V.

"Right on," said Dan.

They hugged Levaran and high-fived Edev's claw.

"Look forward to seeing you all again," said Sarah. She latched on to Dan's arm.

Dan did a two-finger salute to the group, and then he and Sarah exited the Torvatta.

Dr. Snowden's throat constricted as he watched them leave. In the short amount of time he had been with them, they had grown on him. He knew they were not the versions he knew, but he found it hard to find much of a difference. The tightness of Emily's grip did not surprise him. She was probably going through a hurricane of emotions. Hanging out with Dan was like old times, and he was looking forward to seeing them again.

"It is time to get Levaran's Torvatta," said Evaran, raising a finger.

Dr. Snowden nodded as he cleared his throat. "Let's do it." He hugged Emily as the others headed to the command area. "We'll see them again."

Emily half smiled. "I know. Maybe we can stay a while when we do."

Dr. Snowden tapped her hand. "You can count on it."

⸻

After going through the portal to leave the timeline, Emily watched as the Torvatta approached Levaran's Torvatta. Although she had tried to be strong when Dan and the others had left, her emotions had been all over the place. Sarah staying the night had been fun, and they had roped the krall into staying over as well with some raw meat Emily replicated. The krall seemed to enjoy the attention she got. Although Emily did not get to spend much time with Dan, she was hoping to make up for it at the cookout.

Levaran's Torvatta had changed significantly from the shell she remembered. The black mesh side panels, side door, and back end thruster panels were now visible. A light-yellow glow emanated from the shielding around it. It occurred to her that the actual development of the Torvatta was not hard; it was the gathering of the re-formation energy that powered it and having the environment to support that. She noticed Levaran had scooted to the edge of her seat.

"Careful. You might fly out of your chair," said Dr. Snowden, patting Levaran's arm.

"I'm okay," said Levaran. "I can already feel my Torvatta. It's . . . a unique experience, one I thought would never be available to me."

Emily swiveled her head toward Evaran. "Did you feel that about this one?"

Evaran nodded. "I did."

"Well, it looks great. Like an exact replica," said Dr. Snowden.

"It should be," said Evaran. "V, align with the ramp, and we can cross over."

"Acknowledged."

After V had parked the Torvatta next to Levaran's Torvatta, everyone headed over to check it out.

Emily's first impression when she walked in was the smell. It reminded her of a new car smell mixed with the sterile smell she was used to. The layout was slightly different. The six dimensional doors were the same as in Evaran's Torvatta, but the elevator was essentially another door to the right of the conference room.

Gone was the entrance area with ramps and a walkway. The whole room was the command area, with Levaran's command chair in the middle, a large seating area to the right comprised of several rows of seats, and a front console to the left of the command chair. The front half of the ship was transparent, except for the dimly lit and glowing lines that showed the shape of the ship.

"I like it," said Emily. She cracked a smile as she watched Edev zoom around.

Levaran smiled. "I do too."

"So . . . why is this layout different?" asked Dr. Snowden.

"It appears it conforms to the plane form's preference," said Levaran. "In this case, I like open spaces."

Emily half smiled. "Makes sense." She strolled around and ran her hands across the U-shaped seating area. The seats seemed softer, and the cushions seemed larger. Compared to Evaran's Torvatta, these were much more plush. She poked around the command chair and noticed it was a bit bigger than what she was used to. Edev's console was larger as well. The large open front that constituted about forty percent of the layout stood out to her. It would definitely make looking around outside a lot easier. On Evaran's Torvatta, she sometimes felt like she was floating.

"Now who's thinking?" said Dr. Snowden, slightly bumping into her.

"I really like this layout."

"Me too," said Dr. Snowden.

"Me three," said V.

Everyone chuckled.

Levaran walked over to the dimensional rooms and peeked her head in each one. "I will need to do a survey of the ship and make sure everything is as it should be."

"When you are ready, we can stealth and head to the coordinates for the Time Warden timeplex," said Evaran.

Levaran faced Evaran, and then they nodded in sync.

Evaran gestured toward the Torvatta entrance. "Come, we shall leave Levaran and Edev to their Torvatta."

Emily figured this was a bonding moment for them. It must be special for Levaran to have another plane form aboard for the first time. Emily followed Evaran along with the others back to Evaran's Torvatta.

She spent the next few hours training with V while Dr. Snowden went to the planar cartography lab. Evaran had gone to the research lab and said he was going to look into some new data he got from the Krotovore ship. Her thoughts were still a bit scattered, and V let her know it when her guard went down. After their session, she got cleaned up and headed to the conference room where everyone was.

Evaran sat at the head of the table, with Levaran to his immediate left, followed by Edev. Dr. Snowden and V sat to Evaran's right. She grabbed a drink and sat next to Edev.

"I am glad we are all here," said Evaran. "Levaran has finished her inspection, and everything appears to be as it should be."

Levaran nodded.

"Our next step is to scout out the Time Warden timeplex. I do not know if it is similar to the one I encountered, but based on the incidents we have had with them, it may be much larger," said Evaran. He tapped at the table console. "This is a visual of the one I encountered."

Emily studied the odd-shaped octagonal object that appeared above the table. Each panel had a solid border, with the internal sides shooting a beam at a circle in the middle that reminded her of a portal. There were some large entrances to the object that were scattered around.

"To give you a sense of the size of this, I am bringing up Earth's moon," said Evaran.

She raised her eyebrows as she saw that the timeplex was about a quarter larger than the moon.

Evaran pointed to one of the portals in the panels. "Those are rifts, kept anchored by their stations. This allows them to travel to fixed points. From there, they spread out, searching for other rifts and those who have traveled through them."

"So . . . where is it?" asked Dr. Snowden.

"It is approximately two hundred million years after the creation of the timeline. It is at the earliest point in time that a rift can go. There is not much in the way of what you know as galaxies. From there, they can operate with relative impunity in the future. The timeplex must be destroyed."

Emily wrinkled her eyebrows. "With two Torvattas, we could just smash it up, right? Like the anchor station?"

Levaran shook her head. "From what I experienced in our sync, those shields are much tougher."

"How was it destroyed in our universe?" asked Emily.

Evaran drew his lips flat. "I disrupted the timeplex's connection outside the timeline. The resulting explosion removed them from the timeline. However, this does not mean that the Time Wardens already scattered in the future from that point have been removed. The ones I did encounter have been, though."

Levaran sighed. "I have my work cut out for me here."

"With our aid, hopefully we can do this more efficiently," said Evaran.

Emily bobbed her head. "How did you disrupt the timeplex connection in our universe? Sorry to ask so many questions."

"You are fine," said Evaran. "I went in with HA4, and together, we fought the Time Wardens to the control chamber. I took the command claw off the Time Warden commander and used it to destroy the magnetic shielding that held the connection in place. The connection is pure timeline energy and is what fuels the portals. There are buffers that dilute it. Once the shielding was gone, it interacted with matter in a pure state and not a diluted one. The resulting explosion took care of everything else."

Emily nodded. She remembered that V had said Evaran lost HA4 in that event. "Well, we're not losing V."

V's lights glowed a bit brighter.

Evaran half smiled. "I believe I have an idea that will make this go a bit smoother." He tapped at the table console, causing a large Time Warden with specialized segmented tentacles to appear. "I used brute force before, and although successful, I lost HA4. We will use guile for this approach. This is a Time Warden maintenance drone. It is rather large and can house all four of us. We just need to find one. They may be a bit different here, but we will find one with a similar role."

"Like wearing a Time Warden skin," said Dr. Snowden.

"It should get us where we need to go without too much suspicion," said Levaran. "V and Edev can secure the exit point when the time comes for us to leave."

"Right," said Evaran. "We will scan around while in stealth mode and find a suitable maintenance drone. Once we have that, we can pick an entry point and go from there."

"That sounds pretty straightforward," said Dr. Snowden.

"Perhaps, but there are still some unknowns. There is the possibility of new Time Warden types that I have not encountered before, such as the one you and Levaran faced. The timeplex could be a different shape, or have different technology. It may not even be where it was relative to our universe."

"Couldn't we have gotten that information from one of the Time Wardens we fought?" asked Emily.

Evaran shook his head. "Their information is tied to their form. When they exit the timeline, that information is purged."

"Oh," said Emily. "Whatever it takes, we can do it."

Levaran smiled. "You humans are quite resilient. I like your spirit and look forward to seeing if Dan and the others wish to travel with me."

"I'm sure they will," said Dr. Snowden. "At least James will."

"Dan will too, and Sarah by extension. He's an adventurer, and this is right up his alley," said Emily.

"Yep," said Dr. Snowden.

"Then let us go," said Evaran.

Emily's heartbeat had increased at the thought of taking on the Time Wardens again, but with this group, it would be easier. Evaran's plan eased her mind a bit, but the thought of just one predator taking her down gnawed at her. What if she encountered a pack of them? Hopefully Evaran had a counter for that. She exhaled as she stood and then exited the room with the others.

21

The stealthed Torvatta exited through the portal from outside the universe and back into the space outside the timeline, then into the timeline itself.

Dr. Snowden's eyes widened when he saw the Time Warden timeplex. He was not sure what he was seeing, but it differed substantially from the projection that Evaran had shown before. Instead of one octagonal object, there was a large one with multiple smaller spherical ones floating outside it. It reminded him somewhat of an atom model. Large ships, similar to the one he had seen before when meeting the matter mages, cruised between the spheres. "That . . . is much bigger than I thought."

Evaran nodded. "V, approach and begin standard scans."

"Acknowledged."

Dr. Snowden checked the front right side of the command area, where a holographic image of Levaran, in her command chair on her Torvatta, sat facing them. He noticed her talking but could not hear anything. Maybe she was telling Edev the same thing Evaran told V.

Levaran focused on Evaran. "This is much different than what you encountered."

"It would appear so. The large one is similar. I am guessing the smaller ones are replicas that are being built up. Although they are spherical, I suspect that is just the base form. The pattern should be the same in each one, though."

Levaran interacted with her chair console. "We'll take the far side and verify."

Evaran and Levaran locked gazes for a moment, then nodded at each other.

"The Time Wardens really screwed with the timeline," said Emily.

"They are much more powerful here," said Evaran.

She wrinkled her eyebrows. "Is the plan the same? Destroy this . . . timeline connection thing, and get out?"

"It is. As long as we are back in the Torvatta when it blows up, we should be okay. The resulting devastation should also take out these smaller ones."

"A lot of death," said Dr. Snowden.

Evaran raised a finger. "Think of it as a relocation. Letting the Time Wardens run unchecked would be disastrous for the timeline, and for Levaran."

"I understand," said Dr. Snowden. "So . . . we're two hundred million years after the creation of the timeline if I recall, but where are we exactly?"

"Analysis. We are approximately one point five billion light-years away from where Earth would be."

Dr. Snowden raised his eyes. "That's quite far away."

Evaran nodded. "It is when the rifts formed along with other stellar phenomena. As for distances, the rifts do not respect that, so they could be anywhere."

Dr. Snowden sighed. "I'm glad you already took care of this in our universe."

"Yes, but at a cost," said Evaran, looking down.

Dr. Snowden glanced at V. "Do you have memories from HA4?"

"Analysis. I do not have any personal memories of HA4. However, I do have HA4's memory of leaving the Torvatta for that mission."

Dr. Snowden pursed his lips. "So when you leave the Torvatta, it always has an up-to-date history of what you've been through, then syncs with whatever new experience you had when you get back."

"That is correct," said V.

"Fascinating," said Dr. Snowden. "I take it it only stores the factual part, like writing an entry in a book."

"It is a visual history, so it is more of an observation for me than an experience."

"Like watching a video clip. That's hard to fathom," said Dr. Snowden.

V nodded.

Evaran cleared his throat. "V will be flying the Torvatta, and Edev will fly Levaran's. They can block off the entry point as needed. We will need that when we escape."

"Analysis. The planar beam generator can be used if necessary."

"Sounds like a plan," said Dr. Snowden. "Let's hope we can pull it off," he said, glancing at Emily, "flawlessly."

She snorted. "We better not be detected then."

He pointed at the smaller octagon as they approached it. "Look at the size of that thing. Even the small ones are large." Judging by the panel count, he figured it was about seventy-five percent the size of the one Evaran had encountered previously. Detailed labels popped out on the screen showing various statistics about the portals and the material used to encase them.

It was the small specks walking around the panels on the outside that attracted his eye. They appeared to be individual Time Wardens, but these were larger than the defender types he had seen before.

Evaran sat forward as he interacted with his chair console. A smaller window appeared off to the side showing the Time Warden. "It is a maintenance drone, the type we are looking for. We can get one once our scans are done and hopefully avoid any battle."

Dr. Snowden gulped. "Speaking of battle . . . our repulsion and stun beams were useless against the predators. We have the rods, but that requires us to get close. Are we going to have any advantage at all other than the Time Wardens being distracted?"

"I have been thinking of that," said Evaran. "We just need the individual shielding to drop so that your stun beams can then incapacitate them. To that end, I am going to add two new beams to your PSDs as well as to my utility handle." He raised a finger. "The first is a mist beam. It will generate a cloud around a target that not only interferes with any electronics, but also can be hit by the stun beam to dissipate the charge in an area of effect. This is highly effective against regenerating shields and creatures who have a weak point that is hard to get at." He raised another finger. "The second beam is the targeting for shooting sticky globules. It might not hold the bigger ones, but it would be effective against the smaller ones."

Emily smirked. "Debuff beams. Slow their movement and blind them, and then shock the hell out of them if needed."

Evaran nodded. "One note on the mist beam. By itself, it is not damaging to living matter, other than to obscure their vision."

"We could always revert to close quarters if need be," said Dr. Snowden.

"You are correct, but I am hoping we will not need either," said Evaran.

"What about our suits?" asked Emily.

He nodded. "That will take some time. I need to think further on that."

"Sure," said Emily.

He smiled at them. "I am trusting that you will use these new beams responsibly outside this situation."

Dr. Snowden felt a warm glow wash over him. He raised his head a bit. "We won't let you down."

"You can count on us," said Emily.

V pivoted around.

Evaran smiled. "Yes, V, I will add this to the list of enhancements to your outer container after this is all done."

Everyone chuckled.

Dr. Snowden understood the new beams intuitively. They were not lethal by themselves, but could be depending on the situation. The sticky beam could hold something while the environment crumbled around it. He realized that the mist beam may have made previous encounters a bit easier. The grapple beam was something he wanted to be added, but he figured he would take what he could get.

He focused on the screen as the Torvatta entered through one of the smaller sphere openings. Inside was pitch-black except for a glowing item in the middle. As they approached it, he could see it was a spherical floating facility of some type. The busy surface was packed with towers and structures he could not make heads or tails of.

They could see the faint outline of beams shooting out from the facility to the portals lining the interior sides. Smaller structures near the portals absorbed the beams, then transmitted them through other beams into the portal.

Dr. Snowden pointed at the smaller structures near the portal. "Those look like anchor stations."

Evaran tapped at his chair console to zoom in on the smaller station. "They are. The sheer amount of them indicates the Time Wardens have been at this for a very long time. If Levaran had not been captured, I suspect they would already be destroyed."

Levaran's projection lit up. "I'm seeing the same thing over here. I'm headed to the main structure."

"As are we," said Evaran. "V, take us in."

"Acknowledged."

Dr. Snowden had noticed Levaran watching the discussion between him and the others. It made him think that she wished she had that with her now. It probably reinforced what Evaran had shown her about what traveling with others could be like. As the Torvatta exited the small structure and headed to the larger central one, he could see that the activity from where they had just come from had picked up. He tilted his head. "Are you sure they can't detect us?"

"They cannot. However, they probably detected something moving through their opening via their sensor net. They would not know it was us," said Evaran.

Dr. Snowden bobbed his head as he refocused on the looming central structure. As the Torvatta cruised toward it, his thoughts wandered to the potential fighting that would take place once they were inside. He had hoped the situation could be resolved by maybe the Torvatta pulsing its shields and disrupting a beam, or even ramming into whatever device was keeping the time vortex open.

Emily was confident in her physical abilities, whereas he was not. He was sure he could contribute, but the Time Warden predator fight shook him a bit. They had fought one while Evaran and Emily fought one, and it took everything to take it down. Even with new gadgets and tactics, he had his doubts.

After thirty minutes, the Torvatta approached the large central octagonal structure. It had panels like the smaller ones as well as openings. What stood out was that some of the panels had a tower on them. When the Torvatta ran a scan, it showed the towers to be defensive in nature. Some had communication streams highlighted, whereas others pointed at the smaller structures and shot a light beam at them.

Dr. Snowden marveled at the fact that he could see the beams at all. From past experience, he knew that if viewed from the outside, they would be invisible, and the Torvatta just colored it for the screen.

Emily pointed at the opening as they crossed through it. "There's a lot more activity here."

Dr. Snowden studied the maintenance Time Wardens scurrying about. He saw another type that was a bit smaller. After gesturing at it, he said, "It looks like there is a new type of Time Warden there too."

"I know of this type," said Evaran. "It is specific to these structures and is a like a soldier. They can propel themselves around and are meant to be used inside the structure's open space."

Dr. Snowden bobbed his head. "I guess they'll investigate the blip from when we passed in then."

"They are already headed that way," said Evaran. He tapped at his chair console. "Observe."

Dr. Snowden studied the small panels that popped up on the front screen. It showed packs of Time Warden soldiers headed toward them. Some had already passed and were near the entrance. A shiver went up his spine. They were deep in enemy territory. He knew they were safe inside the Torvatta, but the fact that the Time Wardens marched through the Krotovore ship with no fear added to his perception of their power. He wondered if the Slivyn could have destroyed one.

As the Torvatta approached the center of the structure, Emily's eyes widened. "What is that?"

Dr. Snowden studied the octagonal object. It had large buildings on each face. In the center of each face was an opening that led deeper inside. It reminded him of an eight-sided die with holes drilled on each side.

"It is the timeplex's control facility," said Evaran. "Each face has a buffer behind it, and it runs all the way to the center. The center itself is protected by a strong spherical layer, at least in our universe it was."

"How the heck are we supposed to get in there?" asked Dr. Snowden.

Evaran half smiled. "The tunnels are several hundred miles long. Landing pads should be at the end of them. Based on what I know from our universe, they should be about five miles out from the control facility center, known as the chamber. We will head in to one of the openings and go from there. Due to the size of this one and the unusual readings I am getting, it may be more difficult. We will see."

Dr. Snowden fidgeted with his fingers as the Torvatta continued scanning around. When they were inside one of the holes in the face, he observed that large pipes lined the sides. There were various outcroppings and landing pads, and Time Wardens were everywhere. He rubbed the goose bumps on his arm. If ominous was what the Time Wardens were going for in their aesthetic, they nailed it. He gulped and continued his survey.

After four hours, Emily felt her stomach growl. They had gone to the end of one of the tunnels and already exited. Levaran had docked and was coming on board, and Emily was looking forward to getting something to eat while they went over the next step.

Her mind had wandered over the different situations in which she could use the new beams. It dawned on her why Evaran did not add lethal means to a weapon. While the Torvatta might inhibit it, she figured there were ways around that. However, it was clear that a certain type of thinking was required when nonlethal means were your only option. It reminded her of her talk with Evaran in their previous adventure, when he told her that violence was not always the answer, and Levaran's talk with her earlier.

Emily headed to the conference room with Evaran and the others. After grabbing a steak salad and some iced tea, she sat next to Dr. Snowden, who had grabbed something to eat as well and sat to Evaran's right. V, in orb mode, had taken a position in the seat to Evaran's immediate left. Only Levaran and Edev had to come.

After ten minutes, Levaran and Edev joined the group and took seats next to V.

"We can begin," said Evaran. He tapped at the table console. "Per the scans from both Torvattas, we have found an entry point. It is a landing pad at the end of the tunnel as I suspected. The landing pad should lead directly toward the control chamber. There are information centers along the way. We will access one and grab whatever data we can."

"So did we get scans of the interior from the landing pad to the control chamber?" asked Dr. Snowden.

Evaran shook his head. "The spherical layer I mentioned before prevented that. We will need to determine the best path once we are there."

Emily's eyes raised. "So we don't actually have a specific route?"

"We do not. However, I have gone through a similar structure before, and they seem to follow the same pattern here, just larger."

Levaran smiled at Emily. "Don't worry. As long as we remain undetected, we should be okay."

"I guess the information center would be a good test. I figure that will be protected heavily," said Emily.

"Surprisingly, they usually are not. Then again, the hall-ways are patrolled," said Evaran.

"Oh," said Emily. "Well, what if the Time Wardens attack our landing spot?"

Levaran gestured at V and Edev. "They will be in control of the Torvattas and can stuff the entrance. If needed, the planar beam generator can be used."

"Analysis. We will hold them back if required."

"Most assuredly!" said Edev.

Everyone chuckled.

Emily half smiled. "As long as we're prepared."

"No problem at all," said Evaran. He gestured at Emily while looking at Levaran. "Curiosity is a defining trait of humans."

"It's admirable," said Levaran.

Emily smirked. "Well, since I'm on a roll, what do we do when we get to the control chamber?"

Evaran changed the projection.

Emily studied the cylindrical pure-black beam that shot from the ceiling to the floor in the center of the large room that the projection showed. A shield with a thin porous metallic backing surrounded it with a variety of large segmented arms connected to the backing. The room was crawling with Time Wardens. Some interacted with the forest of pillars in the room, while others roamed around.

"This is the recording prior to when I shut down the one in our universe," said Evaran. "We just need to get to the command interface on the other side of the room and activate the self-destruct. We will need to override the self-destruct timer in order to give ourselves time to leave."

Dr. Snowden shook a finger. "I seem to recall that in order to interface with the Time Warden systems, we needed a claw thing."

"You are correct," said Evaran. "I will climb out of our drone, and we will try the one from our universe on the command interface."

"Try?" asked Dr. Snowden with widened eyes.

"If it does not work, there will be a Time Warden commander there we can take it from."

"Oh, yeah. Not a problem," said Dr. Snowden, shaking his head.

Emily swatted Dr. Snowden's arm. "Don't worry, we can take it if we need it."

"As always," said Dr. Snowden with a sigh. "Let's hope it doesn't come to that. By far, that seems like the point where if things go bad, it'll really go bad."

"I understand your concern. However," said Evaran, gesturing at Levaran, "they have not met Levaran in this form. Her strength should be able to handle a commander."

Levaran cracked her neck. "If we need a distraction, then V and Edev can cause that. The doors will seal, and then we face whatever is left in the chamber."

"Well, then I guess it's drone capturing time," said Dr. Snowden.

Evaran nodded. "I will need to upgrade your PSDs with the new enhancements while V and Edev find a suitable drone nearby." He tapped at the table console, causing the projection to vanish.

Emily studied the ground as she followed Evaran to the research lab. If everything went as planned, this should be over fairly quickly. If not, then it would be the toughest fight she had been in. The fact that there was so much fighting reminded her how chaotic the universe was. At least Evaran and Levaran were trying to make it more peaceful, though at the cost of using the one thing they wanted to avoid. The irony was not lost on her.

Thirty minutes later, Levaran had gone back to her Torvatta while Evaran and the others sat in the command area of their Torvatta.

Emily noticed that her upgraded PSD did not feel any heavier. The beams were just additional selections. The Torvatta was created using dimensional mechanics, so it made her wonder how it worked for the PSDs. Probably something much lower level since the changes were made quickly.

Her attention focused on the maintenance drone that had been located outside the main sphere. It occurred to her that the ones they fought when helping retrieve Levaran were also maintenance drones, but maybe they were specialized to that type of facility. She watched as Levaran's Torvatta bumped up against the drone, which swung its tentacles around.

Levaran was on the edge of a ramp that extended from the roof. She jabbed the drone with her utility handle, which had a rod formed.

The yellow goo from the drone formed small globules in space and then evaporated without a trace. Its metallic body then began to drift.

Emily smiled at the size discrepancy of the drone versus Levaran's Torvatta. The drone dwarfed the Torvatta, and as both Torvattas sandwiched it, the main sphere of the drone collapsed onto the roof of Evaran's Torvatta. She noticed that the tentacles extended out a bit past the shielding.

Evaran pointed up. "Time to reconfigure its internals." He stood and headed toward the elevator with Emily and Dr. Snowden in tow.

When they got to the roof, Evaran pulled up a console and then began to interact with it. Levaran's Torvatta was upside down and on top of the drone. She jumped from her Torvatta to Evaran's, making sure to flip as the gravity on Evaran's Torvatta took hold.

Emily smiled at Levaran. "That went pretty well."

"Indeed. I had to extend the rod a bit more than expected," said Levaran, eying Evaran.

Evaran half smiled. "These drones are a bit larger than what I remember. Nonetheless, all we needed was the main drone body inside our shields so we can make the interior palatable for travel. Our stealth should give us some cover to do so."

"I have to see this," said Dr. Snowden, peering over Evaran's shoulder at the console.

Evaran turned his head, causing Dr. Snowden to back away a bit.

Emily shook her head.

"Just curious," said Dr. Snowden with a grin.

"We can use holo-room-like capability on this. Observe," said Evaran, tapping at the console. A portion of the drone's side disappeared.

The maintenance drone's internals reminded Emily of steel blocks with multicolored spaghetti splashed all around it.

With a swipe of Evaran's hand, the interior hollowed out, leaving a large, empty space. He walked up to it and began to point and twist his hands. A flooring appeared about the middle of the drone and, on top of it, a slightly curved couch with one chair in front. A console wrapped around the front. Underneath the flooring, a mass of wires, circuits, crystals, and oddly shaped blocks materialized. Large screens covered the top front half with smaller ones right above the front console.

"Whoa," said Dr. Snowden. "That's impressive."

Emily peered around inside after Evaran had finished configuring the drone interior. "Well, at least we will go in comfort, sorta."

"I will pilot it, and everyone else will take the couch," said Evaran. "Any communication will go through a filter, and we should be able to mimic a standard response and communicate if need be using the native Time Warden protocols. There is no offensive or defensive capability, it is purely for getting us in and out."

"How are we going to get inside it once you close it up?" asked Emily.

"I will add a side door with a small ramp. We will need to be careful to open it away from any Time Warden's line of sight," said Evaran. "If you need to use the bathroom or anything else, do so now. V, take us to the landing pad."

"Acknowledged."

22

After two hours, they had reached the landing pad at the end of one of the tunnels five miles from the control chamber. Evaran sat in the front of the maintenance drone, while Levaran sat between Emily and a fidgeting Dr. Snowden.

It was a tight fit, and the strength of Levaran's legs against Dr. Snowden's surprised him. He had never really touched Evaran other than shaking his hand or clasping his shoulder, but Levaran's leg felt like a coil full of muscle. Other than a hug, he had never been this close for an extended period of time. He caught Emily grinning a few times when he moved around.

The inside of the drone was dimly lit by all the consoles and screens.

He had his helmet down, so he was aware of the metallic smell along with something sweet punctuating it. He ran a hand along the back of his neck as the drone lurched off the top of the Torvatta and onto the empty landing pad. The screens showed a full view around the drone, giving him an excellent chance to study where they were.

The landing pad they were on looked like someone had grabbed a rectangular piece of metal and jabbed it into the metallic paneled wall at the end of the tunnel. A smaller tunnel stood out ahead of them. The only illumination came from small embedded lights along the sides.

There was a mist present, but he figured maybe it was steam or something.

"We are off," said Evaran.

The inside of the drone shuddered as it moved.

"Bumpy ride," said Emily.

"It will bob as we go, but I have added some shock absorbers to help smooth it out," said Evaran.

Dr. Snowden moved around on the couch as they approached the entrance. It resembled a gaping mouth, but he knew that was his mind playing tricks on him.

"Relax," said Levaran, laying a hand on his arm. "We will know here shortly if there's a problem."

Dr. Snowden gulped. "I guess better early than later."

Levaran nodded.

As they entered the smaller tunnel, he noted that it had a ribbed pattern.

Metallic beams with elaborate designs formed an arc with a mesh-like pattern between them. The lighting had an orange tint to it, causing the hallway to look like there was a fire somewhere in the distance.

The small flying drones caught his attention. Unlike the other Time Wardens he had seen up to this point, these had a smaller body split into several parts, with tentacles hanging down. Each end of the body had a tentacle that resembled a scorpion stinger. He figured that whatever the light-blue glow was on the underside was what kept it in the air, similar to what V had. The Time Warden reminded him of a metallic wasp without the wings.

When the first Time Warden soldier crossed their path, one of the interior screens lit up.

Although Dr. Snowden saw unusual symbols, he knew what they meant. It was an issued challenge.

"Just a routine ping," said Evaran. He tapped at the console, and the other Time Warden continued on. "I gave it a routine reply. It appears to have been accepted."

"How do you know what answer it was looking for? I thought the data was purged on death?" asked Dr. Snowden.

Evaran turned his head halfway around. "From the data I mined at the facility in our universe. I was not sure if it would work here, but it appears it has."

Dr. Snowden's eyes widened. "You weren't sure?"

Evaran turned back around. "There was a high probability it would work. If V were here, he could give you an exact percentage, but I would say it was in the nineties."

"Oh," said Dr. Snowden. He continued to study the screens as they strutted along the corridor.

Several other Time Warden soldiers passed by and issued the same ping.

When they came to a four-way cross, they paused for a moment.

"There should be access stations with information dotted throughout. Not all will be occupied. They are usually off to the sides, so we will try the left side," said Evaran.

Dr. Snowden watched the front screen as the drone turned and headed left. The lighting seemed to be a bit more reddish in color, and he noticed that there were small open holes near the ceiling.

Emily pointed at one of the holes. "I remember those. We saw them in the facility that held Levaran."

Levaran nodded. "Quick access tunnels. Soldiers can crawl through them to an area as needed. They also have maintenance controls in there, and although we could access that, being caught inside wouldn't be good. Not a lot of room to maneuver."

"Gotcha," said Emily.

After twenty minutes of crawling around in the drone, they came upon an enclosed side room with an arched doorway. Evaran piloted the drone into the room.

Dr. Snowden noted that the room had ribbed walls like the tunnels outside, except that between each one was a screen embedded into the wall. Below them were several circular ports.

When Evaran placed the drone's claw into one of the ports, he leaned back a bit as he studied the flow of information that appeared on the interior screens. Levaran handed Evaran her UIC, and along with Evaran's, they lit up when placed on the console.

Dr. Snowden understood that they were downloading data on the Time Wardens. His skin crawled when another maintenance drone joined them in the enclosure.

The routine ping came through, and Evaran sent back an answer. After a tense moment, the all clear was given by Evaran.

Dr. Snowden realized that the exterior screen was showing the same statistics and metrics as it had before. It stood in contrast to the stream of data flying over the interior screens. He gestured forward. "Find anything interesting?"

"I have," said Evaran. He spun around in his chair. "There are approximately eight thousand Time Wardens in this timeplex. In our universe, there were four hundred. That is a significant increase. It also appears that they are evolving. There are several new Time Warden types I have not seen before, and it looks like there are some organic hybrids they are testing."

"Abominations," said Levaran. "That would give them a foothold that doesn't require the external requirements of a Time Warden suit."

Evaran nodded. "This would greatly increase the reproductive aspect and their numbers. Being native to the universe has many advantages that they currently cannot enjoy. The biggest being that they cease to exist in the timeline when exposed to it."

"How close are they to becoming semiorganic?" asked Emily.

"Still a bit away, based on what I am seeing," said Evaran. "However, they have time on their side and, due to the time period they are in, no enemies. Although they would be a power player wherever they go, the universe is large, and filled with powerful races and beings. Since Levaran would interact with rifts more than others, she would encounter them on a more frequent basis."

Levaran half smiled. "Anchor stations would be easy to clear, but if they had planets full of these organic hybrids, that might be a bit more difficult to deal with."

"Couldn't you go back to the point when the planet was being populated and stop it?" asked Dr. Snowden.

Levaran shook her head. "The Time Wardens are time aware. If I were to do that while the timeplex was active, they would just take the rift nearest to that point and then fight me. However, I might be able to do that to some planets. Depends on the web of connections the Time Wardens have weaved."

"Oh," said Dr. Snowden.

Evaran spun back around to the front. He tilted his head while studying one of the screens. "Intriguing. We are now downloading the list of species and beings they have encountered, along with their threat assessment. There are some here I have not heard of before."

"I assume the highest threats are the ones they lost to," said Dr. Snowden.

Evaran nodded. "The top ones include the Geneers, a machine race that wiped them out in the far future. There is also mention of several beings who have given them trouble." He rubbed his chin. "That could bear further investigation on my part in our universe."

Levaran eyed Evaran. "You're thinking of immortals."

"I am," said Evaran. "The Time Wardens would be no match for one, depending on what form it took."

"Are these the same immortals from that other plane system? I forgot its name," said Emily.

"You are referring to Druuzgortatares, the plane system of the immortals. That is what I was thinking of. Inside this plane, they would have a plane form similar to me and Levaran. An immortal can only be expelled."

"Like the Hadryn, right?" asked Dr. Snowden. He recalled that the overlord had been more than a match for Evaran.

Evaran nodded. "They share similar traits. Immortals are quite devious. However, not all are bad." He narrowed his eyes. "The Time Wardens have not expanded much into the Milky Way, it seems. The rift endings are contested there."

Emily snorted. "I'm sure the Kreagan Star Empire wouldn't let them expand if it found any."

"Probably not," said Evaran. "However, there are two other end points at different times. Intriguing. I do not believe these exist in our universe, but worth checking out at some point."

Levaran grinned. "It's high priority on my list to check out."

Dr. Snowden noted that Levaran was spoiling for a fight with the Time Wardens. Where Evaran was cautious, Levaran was more gung ho. Of course the strength disparity might be a contributing factor. "I assume Emily and I can check out the data when we're back on the Torvatta?"

"Of course," said Evaran. "It would be a good primer on what exists. You can compare it to what I gathered from our universe."

"Excellent," said Dr. Snowden as his eyes lit up. He imagined days in the holo room conjuring up locations and the species and beings that the Time Wardens had run into. It was one of the highlights, learning about these types of things at a high level.

After another ten minutes, Evaran pulled off the UICs. He handed Levaran's UIC back to her. "That took a bit longer than I expected, but we have the full data dump. We should move from here, as I suspect the security system has detected this."

Evaran detached the drone's arm from the circular port and maneuvered the drone out of the side room. They headed back the way they had come, and when they arrived at the four-way intersection that they had encountered before, they took a left toward the control chamber.

Dr. Snowden's mind wandered as they continued on. He saw several packs of soldiers hustling past them. The sense that the facility was under a higher alert pervaded him. Maybe getting the data was something they could have done afterward. Then again, if they had to fight in the control chamber, they might not have had the time. It seemed this was a calculation that Evaran had made. According to the distance metric displayed on the screens, they still had about four miles to go. He hoped it would be without incident.

Emily cracked her back as the drone lumbered along. Although she was trying to appear strong, the thought of fighting another Time Warden predator without having trained for it ate at her. Training as hard as she had, only to be taken out so easily was not something she could simply forget. Levaran would have probably knocked a predator all around, but even she had limits when stung multiple times.

"Somebody's mind is somewhere else," said Dr. Snowden with a smile.

"Just focusing on the control chamber and when we get there," she said.

"We are almost there," said Evaran.

Emily nodded. It had taken them about two hours to go four miles. She knew this was the safer route, but the anxiety of getting inside the control chamber was beginning to build. While she was getting used to having some unknowns, the Time Wardens were an unknown that could punish with severity. There was not much on their way in, other than Time Warden soldiers and a few of the flying drones. Looking at her PSD, she saw it was around 11:45 p.m. Although she knew she should be tired, her adrenaline and nanobots were fueling her.

They arrived at the large arched doorway into the control chamber.

She scooted to the edge of the couch. The elaborate gold markings on the border were punctuated by metallic vines. Scanners near the top had a continuous set of beams sweeping the entrance. A new type of Time Warden stood at each side of the door.

They stood out to her because unlike the others, these had defined legs like a quadruped and also a body on top. Two towers stood on their backs, with a plethora of thick tentacles swirling around. The sturdier legs gave the appearance that they could support more weight than just the tentacles she had seen on the others. They could probably move faster too.

"And . . . what type are those?" asked Dr. Snowden.

"According to the data we retrieved, they are Time Warden guards. Highly specialized for defense and stationed at critical points," said Evaran.

Emily nodded. "They look tough."

"Perhaps physically, but they do not have paralyzing toxins. They rely on their shielding and also brute force. Although they can shoot energy beams, I suspect they are meant to tear their victims up," said Evaran.

"Oh, that's great," said Dr. Snowden, smirking.

The scanners shot a beam over the drone they were in.

Emily tensed up.

Levaran laid a hand on Emily's leg and smiled. "Relax. Those beams will register us as a regular maintenance drone."

Emily half smiled and nodded. "I'm cool. I was just thinking if we have to fight those guards, what the best approach would be. I haven't trained against them yet."

"Understandable," said Levaran. "Your mist and stun beam combo should take out their shields. Then use the sticky beam to tie them up, or shoot another mist and stun beam combo to disable them."

"Two combo shots or one combo and a sticky. Got it," said Emily.

"Yeah . . . If it comes down to it, I'll follow suit. Going toe to toe with that thing in close quarters is a no go for me," said Dr. Snowden.

Emily's eyes widened as they passed through the arched doorway.

The massive room they were in had pillars that stood equidistant throughout, with large spaces between them. In the middle of the room was a purple beam that shot from the ceiling straight through to the floor. Large, circular, raised edges marked where a semitransparent shielding covered the beam. Various small tubes ran off the shielding and to the walls.

The light emitted made her squint.

"That's the connection?" asked Dr. Snowden, raising his hand over his eyes.

Evaran tapped at the console, causing the screens to dim. "You are correct. The center is pure timeline energy. The magnetic shielding around it keeps it contained, and the tubes running off split it into various buffers, which allows them to dilute it enough to be of use to them." He pointed at the far wall. "The command interface is there."

Emily wrinkled her eyebrows as she pointed at the large sphere embedded above the command interface. "What is that?"

"The Time Warden commander," said Levaran. "It is interfaced into every system. If we need to get a command claw from it, we will need to have it come out."

"Let's hope it doesn't come to that," said Dr. Snowden.

Evaran nodded. "I concur. I am going to head in that direction and interface with a few maintenance nodes to appear as if we are doing a routine check."

"Sounds good," said Emily. She watched with rapture as soldiers passed between the other two doorways in the room. There were other maintenance drones milling about and guards at each doorway. It surprised her that the room was not heavily secured, but she figured not many would make it this far. With that thought in mind, she said, "The Hoxscarus could rip through this place."

"They could," said Levaran, raising a finger, "but I sent them away. They were not meant to be involved in the plane outside their ascension."

"They were, though," said Dr. Snowden. "We saw it with the matter mages here, and in our universe when we met one."

Evaran turned his head to the side. "It seems I told them to do some of it, although as Levaran mentioned, I would be against it and limit it if I could. However, that knowledge they gain from me is from a future event that I am involved in and is part of the time loop. Those should be the only instances we see them, unless we go outside the plane."

"I understand, although I'm with Emily on this one. The Hoxscarus would make this place Swiss cheese," said Dr. Snowden.

"We are with the Hoxscarus, in some regard," said Levaran, raising her head a bit.

Emily grinned at Dr. Snowden.

When they worked their way around near the command interface, they paused. In front of the circular command port was a guard.

Evaran rubbed his chin. "Hmm, this could be tricky." He tapped at the console.

The drone ducked off to a side room that had an open entrance. Once it was inside the room, Evaran moved it over to the farthest spot out of the line of sight of any Time Warden.

"I will need to go out there with the command interface claw. Emily, we will need your camouflage," said Evaran.

Emily nodded. "How do we want to do this?"

"You can ride my back."

"Got it."

Dr. Snowden shook his head. "This is nuts."

"We can do it," said Emily, squeezing Dr. Snowden's arm.

"Well, as a side note, we should probably think about adding camouflage to my and Evaran's suits. Then you don't need back riding."

"It has moved up in priority on my list of things to do," said Evaran.

Dr. Snowden nodded.

Emily activated her camouflage, and when Evaran and she were outside, she hopped onto his back.

They crept along the wall out of the side room and headed toward the command interface.

Emily thought she saw the guard wave a tentacle in their direction, but it went back to looking forward. Since they were coming in from the side, she understood that they were only outside the guard's line of sight unless it decided to turn their way or wave a tentacle toward them and scan.

Her camouflage had turned out to be more useful than she had imagined. Maybe there was some enhancement that could give it a larger field. V already had stealth, and like Dr. Snowden, she agreed that he and Evaran could use it. Evaran had the ability to change his clothing appearance, so she did not think it would be a stretch to mirror the environment. She understood Dr. Snowden's concern, but moments like this fired her up. Going with Evaran while deep in enemy territory was not something she gave a second thought to.

When they arrived at the command interface, Evaran inserted the command claw into the circular port.

She checked on the guard.

It still stood stationary.

She had wondered if it could smell them, but since they were in suits, maybe not. Her heart fluttered a few times when the guard swung its tentacles around. She figured that was maybe part of some rotation.

At one point, the tentacle was only a few feet away, but aimed up high.

She wondered if maybe the sensors had detected a command claw being used. Her lips drew flat when Evaran shook his head. He pulled out the command claw, and together, they began to creep away.

When they got back to the side room, another maintenance drone was there.

Evaran stuck to the wall while facing it and walked sideways. At one point, the maintenance drone began to turn, but focused on their drone when it waved a tentacle at it.

Emily figured Levaran had initiated some type of communication with it.

Once the other drone had left, they crawled back into their drone.

Evaran sighed. "The configuration is different. It would not activate."

"I guess then it's time for plan B," said Emily.

"Which is . . . get it off the commander embedded in the wall, right?" asked Dr. Snowden.

Evaran nodded. "We will need a distraction to clear this room. It should then seal the doors. They will expect an attack from the outside." He placed his UIC on the console and interacted with his ARI.

A projection of V and Edev appeared in split-screen mode on the front screen.

"We need a distraction," said Evaran.

"Acknowledged," said V.

"You got it!" said Edev.

After a few moments, the lights in the room changed color, and soldiers scurried out. Every other Time Warden except for the guard and the commander stayed in the room as the three doorways sealed shut.

Evaran interacted with the console. After a minute, he said, "I have secured the door access controls to the control chamber for now. This means the guards and soldiers outside will not be able to get in. They will try, so we will need to hurry."

"So it's just us, one guard, the commander, and a ticking clock then," said Emily. "We can do that."

Evaran nodded.

"So . . . how are we going to get the claw off the commander then?"

Levaran smiled. "I have an idea."

23

Dr. Snowden gulped as he shuffled along behind Emily. She was sandwiched between him and Evaran, and although they moved slower, the camouflage was working. This just strengthened Dr. Snowden's resolve to get camouflage on his suit. The Time Warden guard was much bigger up close than he expected. A trickle of sweat ran down the side of his face.

It took them a bit, but they reached a spot by the command interface.

He was not sure he was fully on board with the plan, given the unknown nature of the commander. Per Evaran, this one was bigger and had eight arms instead of six.

Evaran surveyed the surrounding area and then tapped at his ARI.

Levaran rushed out of the side room and to the entrance they had initially used. The Time Warden guard rose up and began to move toward her. She raised her hand. "Hear me, Time Warden commander."

The commander began to move, and after a moment, its massive body fell forward out of the wall with four legs holding it up.

Evaran and the others had moved out of the way as the commander reached down and inserted one of its tentacles into the command interface.

"You have been heard, and judged," said the commander in a deep digital voice.

"Excellent," said Levaran. She tilted her head and aimed forward.

Evaran had extended his utility handle into a sharp blade. With one downward slice, he cut off the commander's tentacle and separated the command claw.

As the commander began to spin around, it was yanked back by Levaran's grappling beam.

The guard spun around and charged Evaran.

As it got close, Dr. Snowden fired a mist beam and Emily fired a stun beam.

The guard paused for a moment, allowing Evaran to rush forward and pierce the body. Yellow goo oozed out of the puncture wound, and the guard fell to the side.

"I need some time with this claw, but time is of the essence. Help Levaran!" said Evaran.

Emily and Dr. Snowden hustled off to the side.

Dr. Snowden saw that Levaran had grappled one of the commander's tentacles and slammed the commander into the wall.

The commander pulled itself forward and grabbed Levaran with two tentacles.

Emily glanced at Dr. Snowden while pointing at one of the rear tentacles holding up the commander. "Sticky that!"

She rushed forward with her PSD extended in a blade similar to what Evaran had.

Dr. Snowden took aim and fired several rounds of the sticky globules at the base. Although he missed a few times, it did not take long to cover the commander's splayed-out claw in gooey white muck.

As the commander tried to move, it slowly began to break the hold. Emily charged forward and sliced the splayed-out claw from the rest of the tentacle.

The commander emitted a shrieking noise and dropped Levaran as it turned toward Emily.

Dr. Snowden rushed forward with his shield raised, and when he got to Emily, they stood together and were pushed back by the commander's energy beams.

Levaran cut two tentacles that served as the commander's legs in half.

The commander tilted toward Levaran. It pulled in its remaining tentacles and rested its spherical body on the ground. After a moment, it straightened out its tentacles horizontally and began to spin as it moved around. When the tentacles hit Levaran, she went flying back and crashed into one of the pillars in the room.

Dr. Snowden and Emily were knocked off their feet at a high velocity. They slammed into the wall and then fell forward to the ground.

Dr. Snowden tried to get up, but his body was not responding. Although his nanobots were at full tilt, he could not feel his legs or arms. His head was turned in such a way that he could see Emily, and she was out. He screamed her name a few times, but she did not respond. His nanobots ramped up to a level he had never felt before, but his body still did not respond. He shouted Evaran's name several times.

Evaran paused what he was doing and rushed over. After scanning with his ring, he said, "You both have sustained massive internal injury. You are dying." He faced Dr. Snowden. "I am unsure how you are still conscious, but there is only one thing that can be done. You would not make it to the Torvatta in time." He ran off to help Levaran, who was struggling to get back up.

Dr. Snowden could see what was going on, and the thought that he might die had never seemed possible. Although he could only feel a cold sensation and his nanobots, a sense of panic began to swell up in him. His chest had tightened, and it became difficult to breathe. It was like the cold, dark hands of death were climbing up inside his body.

He could move his head, and when he saw Emily, his eyes misted. Thoughts of them celebrating her various birthdays sprang into his mind. He clenched his jaw. This could not be the end. There was a future event, but maybe time could be rewritten and them out of it. He gritted his teeth as he watched Evaran.

Evaran was a blur as he shot a grappling beam at the ceiling. After reaching the top, he fell and jammed his blade deep into the commander's body.

The commander shrieked nonstop as it tried to shake Evaran, but it began to slow down.

Levaran ran under the commander's tentacles and extended a rod into the side.

A deep gash formed on the commander's side as it stopped spinning.

She grabbed the two sides of the gash.

Rip!

She reached in and pulled herself inside, tossing out chunks until a yellow goo began to ooze out of the gash.

The commander stopped moving.

Levaran jumped out of the commander's body as it rolled to the side. She joined Evaran in rushing over to Dr. Snowden and Emily.

"They are dying," said Evaran. He clenched his jaw as he looked down and away. "I know it is not my place to ask . . ."

Levaran shook her head. "You don't need to. I owe you and both of them already."

Dr. Snowden had no idea what they were talking about, but he could feel his nanobots winding down. The panic that had begun earlier was consuming him. He tried to talk, but nothing came out. Tears ran down his face as his head trembled.

Levaran knelt on the ground and placed a hand on both Dr. Snowden and Emily. She closed her eyes. A yellow glow emanated from her hands and surged into both of them.

Dr. Snowden's eyes popped open. It was like a fire had been lit in every part of his body. He understood why he could not move before, everything had been smashed. How he remained conscious was a mystery to him. As his internals reorganized, he screamed.

Emily gasped and then screamed along with him.

Although he did not know what was going on, he could feel everything healing. He thought he saw a yellow glow shoot out from his mouth when he screamed. The fire in him had subsided, and a warm glow began to spread. He coughed, spitting blood, and began to move. As he propped up on his right elbow, he began to breathe faster. Something was off. It was like the feeling he had when his nanobots were going full strength, but this was something beyond that. After a moment, he hopped up and noticed Emily had as well.

Evaran nodded at Levaran. "Thank you."

"The pleasure was mine," said Levaran.

Evaran placed a hand on Dr. Snowden's and Emily's shoulders. "I will let Levaran explain what happened. I need to get the command claw functioning. The doors are close to opening." He hugged Emily, then Dr. Snowden, and headed back to the command interface.

"What . . . what happened?" asked Emily.

"Yeah . . . I'd like to know too," said Dr. Snowden.

Levaran smiled. "I have given you the remainder of my re-formation energy. You are fully healed, and then some. The unusual effect you're feeling will wear off soon, but for now, you possess advanced strength and speed and . . . a heightened regeneration factor."

Dr. Snowden's eyes misted. "We . . . we were dying."

"We were?" asked Emily with widened eyes.

"You both were, but now you're not," said Levaran.

Emily frowned as her eyes watered. She rushed forward and hugged Levaran.

Dr. Snowden joined them.

Levaran put her arms around them. "You are both worthy, and I was glad to offer any help I could."

They stood for a minute crying in Levaran's embrace.

It dawned on Dr. Snowden how close they had come to dying. Traveling with Evaran had given him the impression that anything could be overcome. Apparently there were limits. His mind reeled at the thought that without Levaran, they would have died. Levaran's calmness as she held them soothed his nerves.

Emily stepped back and wiped her eyes. "Are there any repercussions? Are you going to be okay?"

"I will not be as strong," said Levaran, glancing toward Evaran. "However, maybe strength is not the answer to every problem."

"It helped in this situation," said Dr. Snowden.

"Perhaps, but Evaran was able to do it with a strength level even lower than my current weakened state."

Dr. Snowden and Emily nodded.

Levaran gestured toward Evaran. "Take a moment, then join us." She headed toward Evaran.

Dr. Snowden trembled as he hugged Emily.

She laid her head on his shoulder. "I . . . can't believe we almost died."

"Me either," he said. He exhaled from his mouth. "Seems like every adventure gets crazier."

She stepped back and swallowed hard. "But we somehow survive, and get stronger."

He met her gaze and nodded. "That we do." He motioned toward Levaran and Evaran, who were discussing things. "Let's go."

Emily gripped his arm as they walked over.

When they got there, Evaran extended his arms out. Dr. Snowden and Emily both hugged him again.

Dr. Snowden gulped as he realized that Evaran had to ask Levaran to give a part of herself to them. He was not sure of the protocol on it, but there appeared to be one. It seemed like a big sacrifice. Something he would ask about later.

As they all stepped back, Evaran smiled. "I am glad you two are safe now. However," he said, pointing at the command interface with the commander claw still in it, "I have configured the self-destruct on the timeline energy shielding, but not set the timer yet. When the timer hits zero and the shielding is gone, the timeline energy will surge forward unobstructed. We have a problem, though. The sequence can only be delayed for up to twenty minutes. That was not the case in our universe. Heading out of here in the maintenance drone would take too long."

Emily nodded. "Then we fight our way out. I feel like . . . I could run on the walls."

"The effect will only last inside you for a few hours. There is a price your body has paid for it, but we can discuss that later," said Evaran.

Dr. Snowden's eyebrows rose. He was not sure what the price would be, but like Emily, he felt like a car revving its engine.

"Are we ready?" asked Evaran.

"Let's do it!" said Emily.

Evaran reached into the command claw and fidgeted around. After a moment, the doors to the room opened. He pulled out the claw, hooked it onto his belt, and then gestured forward. "Go!"

Evaran and Levaran took the lead and rushed headfirst into the guards and soldiers spilling into the room.

Dr. Snowden fired mist beams to the sides while Emily shot her stun beams. The mass stun effect halted the advance on the right and left sides.

Evaran and Levaran engaged the two guards ahead of them.

Emily ran alongside Evaran and jabbed the guard, causing its yellow goo to come out. Dr. Snowden did the same for the one Levaran was fighting. Evaran nodded at everyone, and they exited the room.

As they ran down the tunnel, they overpowered small packs of soldiers and shot down the drones that flew in.

Dr. Snowden noted that there was a growing army behind them. He could not only see them, but he could feel them, and hear them, to the degree that he knew how many there were. The small packs of soldiers were no match for them. He could see Levaran's weakened state when she punched one and it did not fly back as far as he had calculated it would. It still got jabbed, though.

Emily was a tornado. She had one end of her PSD extended as a blade, the other a rod.

He imagined the Time Wardens they ran into were shocked to be sliced up so fast.

She was smiling while she did it, as if it was redemption for having almost died and for the previous encounter with a predator.

Although he opted to go for range usually, he found that he too could determine the path a Time Warden would take in combat. He wondered if this was how Evaran and Levaran saw things. Dodging tentacles while shooting at drones was like second nature with whatever was inside him.

In one fight, he shot a sticky globule at several drones, sliced off two tentacles from one solider, then jabbed another, and batted one away like a baseball. And it was done without breaking a sweat. No wonder Evaran and Levaran were confident.

When they got to the entrance, both Torvattas were stacked on top of each other and blocking the way. Evaran's was on the bottom, and it swiveled around, exposing the entrance.

They rushed on board and assembled in the command area.

Emily surveyed the landing pad as Time Warden ships began to arrive. They fired on the Torvattas to no avail. The energy Levaran had dumped into her was still surging throughout her body. She realized she should be sleeping, but half of her wanted to go back in and fight the Time Wardens. If this was how Evaran and Levaran felt all the time, it was no wonder they did not fear much.

V and Edev had greeted them upon their entry. V had rushed over to hug her and Dr. Snowden. She wondered if V had been monitoring everything. Both V and Edev were now at the front console.

"So . . . we just sit here and wait?" asked Dr. Snowden.

Evaran nodded while in his command chair. "That is correct. The explosion will incinerate everything around us and toss both Torvattas out of the timeline. However, we can go back in, whereas the Time Wardens will be where they should be."

"What if when we come back in, the Time Wardens sneak in?" asked Emily.

"They would not have their suits and would end up evaporating back out," said Evaran.

The landing pad shuddered as a wave of energy swept the Torvatta down the tunnel.

"It begins," said Evaran.

Emily gulped as she saw that they were surfing the explosion out. The Torvatta showed a screen behind them, but it was just an orange glow. To the sides, she could see everything become part of the explosion.

It did not take long before they were tossed out into space. A moment later, after the smaller structures had been destroyed, the Torvattas were pulled back in.

Emily saw that they were headed to an irregularly shaped patch of space. The Torvatta had outlined it with a green border. She pointed at it. "That's the timeline exit?"

"It is," said Evaran.

She took a measured breath. "I don't mean to change the subject, but you said earlier that there was a price our bodies paid for Levaran helping us . . ."

Evaran gestured at Levaran.

"You've lost approximately thirty percent of your nano-bots. My re-formation energy used them to help re-form your body," said Levaran.

Dr. Snowden furrowed his eyebrows. "Are the nanobots still the same, or different now?"

"They have transformed," said Levaran. "I'm unsure what impact that will have on you, but Evaran will study it and let you know."

Dr. Snowden chuckled. "Well, sure beats dying."

Emily nodded. "Was that the fire we felt? The nanobots being transformed?"

"I don't know what the sensation would be, since a plane form would not give away their re-formation energy before the plane form is settled."

Dr. Snowden swallowed hard. "But . . . you did . . . for us."

"You saved me when I was going to die. I have not for-gotten that I am only here due to you three coming to my aid," said Levaran, looking down. "I have a second chance, and I'm beyond grateful for that. Losing some strength in order to help those who helped me is an acceptable trade."

Emily smiled at Levaran. "That commander was a hell of a fight."

"It was, and although I suspect I could've taken it in time, it would've been hard, if not impossible, while trying to figure out how to stop the facility."

Dr. Snowden nodded. "Well, I think I have a taste of just a glimmer of your power. It's intoxicating, scary, and feels good at the same time."

"I didn't know if your forms would accept it," said Levaran. "Your nanobots are what I infused to do the work. They acted as a buffer so that your internals were not liquefied."

"Oh," said Emily with widened eyes. "I'm glad that didn't happen."

"You will be fine, and," said Levaran, gesturing at Evaran, "if there are any complications, I'm sure he will be able to help you."

"We can train and assess any changes," said V, glancing at Emily.

Dr. Snowden raised a finger. "I think . . . I'm going to join you."

"Analysis. Your presence would be appreciated."

Dr. Snowden chuckled. "I'm sure it would be. After all of this, I need some training."

V's lights glowed a bit brighter.

Emily narrowed her eyes at Levaran. "So . . . where are you headed now? I mean . . . after we exit the timeline?"

"I will go meet with Dan and the others. From their perspective, it would've been about three months. You three should come a day later, and we can have that cookout event Dan mentioned," said Levaran.

"Sounds like a plan to me," said Dr. Snowden, suppressing a yawn.

Emily noticed that it was pitch-black outside the Torvatta. "Looks like we're outside the timeline now."

"Analysis. Your assessment is correct," said V.

Levaran stood. "I will return to my Torvatta. Get some rest, and I will see you all here shortly."

Dr. Snowden and Emily hugged Levaran.

V and Edev joined them, causing them all to laugh.

After they separated, Levaran and Evaran touched hands, palms forward. They nodded at each other, and then Levaran and Edev headed to the elevator.

After Levaran and Edev had departed, Evaran gestured at Dr. Snowden and Emily. "You two should get some rest. It has been a while since you slept, and after these events, it would be good to recharge."

Dr. Snowden shook his arms out. "I still have this energy in me. My body feels tired, but my mind is on fire."

"It will pass," said Evaran. "When it does, you will feel the full effects of exhaustion. I suggest whatever you decide to do, you do it in your quarters."

Emily sighed. "I feel like I want to train, but . . . maybe I'll just take it slow." She cocked her head toward Evaran. "So you don't know what impact this new type of nanobot will have?"

Evaran shook his head. "I do not. There has never been a merging of this type before that I am aware of, and I have been around for a long time."

"New territory," said Dr. Snowden. "This must be exciting for you too."

Evaran dipped his head. "I am just glad you are safe. I think our next trip after all of this will be to Earth. We can take a break there, and you can take some time to assess if you wish to continue traveling with me."

Dr. Snowden snorted. "No question here on that."

"Here either," said Emily.

"You almost died. That is not something to take lightly. I suspect the infusion of re-formation energy is clouding that aspect from you at the moment," said Evaran. "There was nothing I could do to prevent your death from occurring. If Levaran were not around . . ."

"But she was," said Dr. Snowden.

Emily could see that it bothered Evaran that he was powerless to save them. Despite all his knowledge, strength, and power, he had to ask for help to save them. She could see how that would be disconcerting. With a wagging finger, she said, "You can't get rid of us that easy."

Evaran smiled. "That was not my intent. However, I understand that a near-death experience can change someone's views. I think some time on Earth back in our universe will be helpful."

Dr. Snowden shrugged. "Works for me, but it still won't change my opinion."

"Same," said Emily.

Evaran nodded.

"To our quarters then," said Dr. Snowden.

Emily watched as Dr. Snowden nodded at everyone and headed to the living quarters. "I guess I'll go too. I'm not ready to sleep yet, but I'm sure I will be once this thing wears off." She eyed V. "If you're interested, maybe those massage techniques you claim to know will help."

"Analysis. The claim is valid. I am knowledgeable in many techniques."

She stood and slapped V on the back, causing him to stumble forward a bit. "I have some time to kill. Prove it."

"Acknowledged."

She squeezed Evaran's shoulder as she passed him. Evaran would probably chew on the events throughout the night. She would too at some point, but for now, a bath, a massage, and sleep were in order.

24

Dr. Snowden cracked his neck as he followed Evaran out of the Torvatta. They had landed at Dan and Sarah's house approximately three months and one day after Dan and the others' abduction. It was eleven in the morning, and the sun was out, with a calm breeze blowing. His body was sore. He knew it had been damaged, and it felt like it still had some adjusting to do.

Going to sleep the previous night had been hard, so he had spent the time going over the data Evaran had collected about the Time Wardens. It surprised him how spread out they were, not only across space, but time. With over 700 anchor stations, that would have been about 350 rifts. Given how rare they were, it indicated that they had been at it for a while.

The organic hybrids that the Time Wardens had tried to create were disturbing. Some were humanoid, but most were a mash-up of an insect and a reptile, with a few birdlike parts tossed in. All had some type of mechanical aspect to them.

The data was very detailed, and he tried to stay awake. When the energy had worn off, he slumped to the ground off his chair and slept there for a while. His hurting back woke him, and after crawling into bed, he slept the rest of the night.

It was when he woke up in a cold sweat that he realized how close to death he had come the previous day. The clawing darkness as it had crept through him left an impression he would not soon forget. Possessing the re-formation energy of Levaran had subdued all thoughts of the event, but now that it was gone, the full impact of it weighed on his mind. The fact that Evaran could not save them, and that that could have been it, did not escape him. He wondered if Emily was having the same thoughts.

He was excited about going to the cookout and seeing everyone. That would be just the thing to take his mind off the near-death encounter. When he exited the Torvatta, the smell of grilled burgers and hot dogs led his nose to where Dan was cooking with a beer in his hand. Sarah had rushed over and hugged Emily. Dr. Bryson was headed toward him, and Evaran walked over to Levaran. Edev and V had flown out and entered scout mode.

Sarah hugged Dr. Snowden, then gestured toward the grill. "Come on, food's ready."

Dr. Bryson hugged Emily and shook Dr. Snowden's hand. "Figured you'd come after all the hard work was done."

Dr. Snowden chuckled. A lump formed in his throat as he slowly swept his gaze across the scene before him. It could have been any day in his universe. Unfortunately, he knew that life was not always fair, but he guessed if you mashed enough parallel universes together, it could be. To go from possibly dying, to embracing the exuberance of life in front of him made him catch his breath.

"You okay?" asked Dr. Bryson.

Dr. Snowden nodded. "I am now." He watched Emily head over to the grill with Sarah.

Dr. Bryson's eyes narrowed. "Some bad stuff happened, didn't it? I know that look."

"We almost died," said Dr. Snowden.

Dr. Bryson studied Dr. Snowden for a moment. "That's part of the package of traveling with Evaran, isn't it?"

"If Levaran hadn't come with us, I would be dead right now."

Dr. Bryson's eyes widened. "Oh . . . that bad, huh?"

"Yeah . . . I'm just . . . happy to be alive," said Dr. Snowden, pulling in his lips.

"Okay . . . it was really bad, I can see."

"Broken bones, barely conscious, internal bleeding. Emily was completely out, and a Time Warden the size of a building spinning around with huge tentacles. Yeah . . . bad."

Dr. Bryson laid a hand on Dr. Snowden's shoulder. "But you're here. Now. In the present. Whatever happened, it's in the past."

"Mr. Philosopher over here. We took care of the hard stuff with the Time Wardens so you won't have to," said Dr. Snowden, slapping Dr. Bryson's chest with the back of his hand.

Dr. Bryson shook his head as they both laughed and headed over to the grill.

Dr. Snowden noted that Evaran and Levaran stood off to the side a bit with their hands clasped behind their backs. They were talking back and forth and glancing at the group. Sarah and Emily had a plate of food and sat in lounge chairs, and Dan was waving him and Dr. Bryson over.

His throat tightened. This was one thing he had not thought about missing until it was smack dab in his face. He shook Dan's hand and grabbed a plate.

Dr. Bryson followed suit.

Dr. Snowden took a bite out of his burger. His eyes closed as he savored the taste of it. While replicated burgers always tasted the same, his taste buds preferred the real thing. Maybe it was the variance in flavor, or how it was prepared. The smell of the food being cooked was also something he did not experience with replicated burgers. Perhaps he would look into making his own burgers when back on the Torvatta. Maybe even a holo room simulation for cookouts.

When everyone was seated and digging in, Levaran raised a finger. "So everyone knows, Dan, Sarah, and Dr. Bryson have agreed to travel with me. We leave after this event."

"So looking forward to it," said Dr. Bryson.

The group laughed.

"We are too," said Dan as Sarah leaned over and squeezed his forearm. "I know it won't always be easy, but that's a challenge. Besides, with these nanobots in us, we'll have a long life, and this'll be one hell of an adventure."

Dr. Snowden wondered if this was how he and Emily appeared to Evaran when they first asked. He gestured at Dan. "The nanobots will surprise you at times, but they're worth it."

Dan nodded at Dr. Snowden.

"I can't wait to use the holo room," said Sarah.

Emily shook a finger at Levaran. "Speaking of which . . . can we transfer my simulations to your Torvatta?"

"Already done," said Levaran. "I also have the same survival suits, with some minor tweaks, and their PSDs. We'll have a crash course on them after we leave."

"Before all that," said Dan as he pressed a button on a remote, "we should relax and enjoy the day."

Music played from the speakers outside the house.

Dr. Snowden shook his head. He knew Dan was a big fan of music, and it was something that he took with him everywhere. One thing that did not escape his attention was that they were not at the Florida house as he thought they would be. They were instead at the house with the four-acre backyard that he had grown up in. He had not noticed it before, but then again, he just saw them walk into a big backyard earlier. Dan had not sold their parents' house, but instead chose to live there.

Over the next five hours, they enjoyed laughter, food, drink, and good conversations. Emily had spent most of her time with Dan and Sarah. V and Edev had flown around and engaged in various conversations while in stealth mode. Evaran and Levaran had been cornered at times by Dan and the others, but for the most part, they kept to themselves.

Dr. Snowden wondered what they had discussed. As Dan, Sarah, and Emily cleaned up the place, Dr. Bryson came over.

"So . . . this is it," said Dr. Bryson. "I saw the planar cartography lab you talked about. It's just . . . amazing. I can't wait to spend my time in there."

Dr. Snowden nodded. "And you will too. It's been the cause of me losing track of time before."

"Any tips or anything I should know about?" asked Dr. Bryson.

Dr. Snowden rubbed his chin for a moment. Thoughts of things he wished he had known prior to some adventures crossed his mind, but he decided that it would be better for Dr. Bryson and the others to learn it as they go. "Don't skip training in the holo room."

"That's it?" asked Dr. Bryson.

"Things are different here, and you may go places or do things we haven't."

Dr. Bryson nodded. "Right, of course."

"Oh . . . and if you go to a planet called Roeth, don't get attached to time refugees. Other than that, you'll be fine," said Dr. Snowden. He wondered how much their adventures would differ. Maybe if they met again at some point in the future, they could exchange stories.

"No attachments to time refugees, whatever that is. Got it," said Dr. Bryson.

After thirty minutes, everyone assembled outside Levaran's stealthed Torvatta.

Levaran gestured at the Torvatta entrance. "It's time to go." She focused on Evaran. "You should head back to your universe after we leave in case the timeline changes. However, your presence here was greatly appreciated."

Evaran nodded.

"Will we see you again?" asked Emily.

"Anything is possible," said Levaran. "Although multiple plane forms are rare, they generally should travel independently so as to have unique experiences and not cross each other's timeline changes, and that protocol will be observed. However, that doesn't mean we can't have companions."

Emily nodded.

Dr. Bryson shook Dr. Snowden's and Evaran's hands. With V, he shook a claw, and Emily hugged him. He flashed two thumbs up, and with a goofy smile, he said, "And so it begins."

The group laughed as he entered the Torvatta.

Dan laid a hand on Dr. Snowden's shoulder. "I know you weren't our Albert, and I would have loved to spend more time with you. I feel like . . . this is a second chance at life."

"Enjoy it for all that it is," said Dr. Snowden. They hugged, and Dan moved to Emily.

"I hope that if we have a daughter, she is every bit like you," said Dan.

Emily's eyes misted as they hugged.

"Same goes for me," said Sarah as she joined them.

Dr. Snowden waved a finger at V and Edev. "I know what you two are thinking."

Dan laughed as he waved Edev and V over. They joined in the hugging.

Dr. Snowden shook his head.

Sarah hugged him and said, "As Dan said, I know you aren't our Albert, but you coulda fooled me. I'm better for having known you."

He nodded as Sarah pulled back. "I just hope you all stay safe."

"We will," said Dan. He shook Evaran's hand, as did Sarah. With a final look around, he gave a two-finger salute, and they entered the Torvatta.

Emily gripped Dr. Snowden's arm.

He could see she was sad, and he was to, but he also knew the excitement about something that was game changing. He hoped they did not have to go through all the wild life-and-death situations he and Emily had.

Levaran walked over to Dr. Snowden and Emily. "You two will always have a part of me in you. I don't know how that will manifest, but I'm going to miss you both."

Dr. Snowden's chest tightened. In a cracked voice, he said, "We owe you our lives."

"It is I who owes all of you my second chance. I won't forget that. Ever," said Levaran.

"Well, now you have your own crew," said Emily, sniffling. "I think you're going to enjoy that experience."

Levaran nodded as they group hugged. She turned toward Evaran, and they touched hands, palms forward with arms raised. After a moment of looking at each other, they nodded in sync. With one final wave at Dr. Snowden and Emily, she began to walk up the ramp.

"Umm . . . I'm still here," said Edev.

Everyone chuckled.

Edev flew around and high-fived each of them. She paused at V. "Thank you for helping me."

"Analysis. It was my pleasure."

Dr. Snowden chuckled. "You're going to be an interesting companion to the others."

"Thanks!" said Edev as she flew in past Levaran.

Levaran shook her head and waved again before entering the Torvatta.

After a moment, their Torvatta took to the sky.

Emily had wanted to talk a bit with Dr. Snowden, Evaran, and V, but Evaran had insisted they leave immediately per Levaran. The near-death experience still shook her a bit, but the cookout had been a perfect counter for that. At least she got in some good talking time with Dan. The fact that her training meant so little against the Time Warden commander chewed on her mind, even while talking with Dan and the others.

First the predator, then the commander. The Time Wardens were tough, but her new game plan was to step up her training and find ways to beat all of them. Never again would she embarrass herself in front of Evaran, in any form. A part of her yearned for the life she saw at the cookout. The other wanted total destruction of anyone who would threaten her or her friends.

They were now back in their own universe. The Torvatta was stealthed and hovering above Earth. They assembled on the roof.

She was beginning to consider the roof as their post-adventure analysis. It was a good spot to do it since they were usually in space and stealthed, and it was calm and free of distractions. On top of that, they could summon things now. Typically, though, they all leaned on the guardrail. V had joined them in orb mode, and they were all to the right of Evaran.

"Well . . . that was one heck of a trip to find about your origin," said Dr. Snowden.

Emily chuckled. "The Evaran origin." She expected a half smile or a grin from Evaran, but was instead met with taut lips.

Evaran raised his head a bit to look out into the stars.

"Evaran?" she asked. She knew that look. He was struggling with something.

Evaran sighed. "Levaran saved you both. I am eternally grateful to her for that action." He turned toward them. "Plane forms cannot see their own energy signature. I realized after she gave you her excess re-formation energy that hers had changed." He extended his hand, and his ring projected a striped bar. The individual segments varied, as did the colors.

Emily remembered that every living thing had an aura-like energy signature, and the various segments she was seeing corresponded to the identification of energies present.

"Wouldn't it have changed anyways when the excess energy had left after her re-formation stage?" asked Dr. Snowden.

"It would have. In essence, her re-formation stage was shortened. I have seen that signature before," said Evaran. He clenched his jaw for a moment. "It . . . took some time, but I was able to match it, along with four other related signatures."

Emily narrowed her eyes. "And . . . where did you find the match?"

"In the main rift crystal that we found on the Purifiers planet."

"What!" said Dr. Snowden.

"Are you saying the female Evaran that was tortured and killed by the overlord is going to be Levaran?" asked Emily.

Evaran drew his lips flat. "I am sure of it. Our past . . . is her future. She is going to meet the overlord, and then fall in battle. She will not be killed right away. She will be tortured until she is dead, and her energy will be absorbed into the rift crystal."

"Wait a minute," said Emily. "I thought the overlord gained the re-formation ability from you."

Evaran nodded. "He did. It is apparent now that while the overlord may have killed Levaran, he only got some of her energy. The rift crystal absorbed the majority of it. I suspect she disabled her ability to re-form as a precaution."

Emily shook her head.

"So when she ran into the overlord, she probably realized she was going to die, probably from your sync with her," said Dr. Snowden. He rubbed his temples. "You said there were other signatures?"

Evaran sighed. "In the crystal, there were other signatures absorbed around the same time. I checked their patterns." He swiped his finger, causing four other patterns to appear next to Levaran's. He pointed at the first one. "This is Dr. Bryson's." He pointed at the second one. "This one is Dan's.

Their time aboard Levaran's Torvatta would have altered their energy signature, as this Torvatta has yours. Given the changes I saw in yours, I was able to extrapolate a formula onto theirs, and when applied, it matches. Their energy would have been able to be absorbed by the rift crystal."

"Oh, no," said Dr. Snowden with a grimace. "Let me guess, the other two are Sarah and Edev."

Evaran shook his head. "I am afraid not. Based on my analysis of the patterns, it is two teenagers. Twins. A male and a female. They are related to Sarah and Dan."

Emily gasped. "Their kids. The Purifier event must have happened much later then." She swallowed hard. "What about Edev and Sarah?"

"Edev, like V, is special. V's energy would not be able to be absorbed by the rift crystal since Syrilus is a part of him, and she is raw planar energy. It is most likely that Edev's inner container was destroyed," said Evaran. "My working hypothesis on Sarah is that she died sometime prior to that event."

"That would mean no nanobot version of her," said Emily.

"Possible. They could have gotten someone else, but the fact that the overlord won would lead me to believe that did not happen. Levaran would have assaulted the Purifiers' pocket universe with Dan, Edev, and the twins. They would have gone willingly with her to her death."

"That's just . . . just horrible. They didn't want her to die alone," said Dr. Snowden. He sighed. "I remember you said a while back when we were fighting the Purifiers that their pocket universe got kicked out of a universe. You think it's related?"

Evaran nodded. "I do. I think Levaran, knowing she would be defeated and absorbed by the plane, played her last card. In the brief moment when she had enhanced abilities, she destroyed her Torvatta and sent the pocket universe to the place she knew the overlord would be killed. Our universe."

"She knew that we would defeat him," said Emily.

Evaran nodded. "She also knew that she had to die in order to complete the time loop."

Emily cocked her head to the side. "She could have re-formed in her Torvatta, right?"

"Yes. However, she knew it was part of our past. It was a sacrifice she was willing to make. That is part of the danger of knowing your future."

Dr. Snowden sighed as he leaned back against the guard-rail. He ran a hand over his mouth. "We can change things, right? I mean . . . she saved our lives! By saving us, it made her weaker. We . . . we can't let her go out like that!"

Evaran looked down. "It has already happened, and is part of our past now." He sighed as he gazed out. "I do not know what became of my other plane forms. My main form is gone. Syrilus is gone. The Hoxscarus have gone. I am alone."

Emily's eyes reddened as she moved to the side and laid a hand on Evaran's right shoulder. "No, you're not."

Dr. Snowden put his hand on Evaran's other shoulder. In a choked voice, he said, "Yeah, what she said."

V flew behind Evaran and placed his claws on Emily's and Dr. Snowden's hands. "And what he said."

Everyone chuckled.

Dr. Snowden wiped his eyes. "We're not going anywhere."

"Even death cannot seem to claim you," said Evaran. He nodded. "I am glad to have you three with me. Unfortunately—"

"Analysis. Everything is as it should be," said V.

Evaran smiled. "What he said."

EPILOGUE

After a good night's rest, Dr. Snowden had enjoyed breakfast with Emily. He was now in the command area, with everyone in their respective locations. Looking out through the transparent front half of the ship, he could see that they were at Dan's grave site. A date-and-time panel that hovered on the inside wall showed February 4, 2012, at 1:00 p.m., just ten minutes after he and Emily had arrived in the past to visit it. He knew they would leave at 2:00 p.m., have a late lunch, and then get abducted by the Krotovore a few hours after that, around 6:00 p.m.

His lips drew down when he saw himself and Emily standing by the grave. He remembered being there. The sniffling he heard coming from Emily verified that she did too. Their earlier versions had spent a good hour talking to the grave, so he knew they had time to place the emergency Krotovore beacon on the car.

"V, take us to their car," said Evaran.

"Acknowledged."

The Torvatta landed in the parking lot in an empty slot next to their car.

Evaran stood and held up a small device. "Time for me to place this." He exited the Torvatta.

Dr. Snowden watched as Evaran placed the beacon on the inside fender of a rear tire. The memory of Evaran pulling something off the side of the car when he had dropped them off after their abduction flashed through his mind. He did not make much of it before, but now he knew it was Evaran who had to do it.

Emily pointed at Evaran. "Look."

Evaran paused as he put his hand in the air and scanned the sky. After a minute, he returned and took his seat in the command chair. "It is done."

"What was all the hand-raising stuff?" asked Dr. Snowden.

"I thought . . . I sensed something. Apparently I was mistaken. Nonetheless, this time loop is completed."

"But it's part of a bigger one that involves some future event with the Hoxscarus, right?" asked Dr. Snowden.

"That is correct. It is nested in a larger one, it would seem."

Emily sighed. "It's hard to believe all that has happened to me and Uncle Albert started right here and now."

Dr. Snowden smiled. "At least we know now." He rubbed his hands together. "Any chance we can stop by our house? I mean . . . I know we have to go to a time after we began traveling."

Evaran nodded. "I think it would be good to spend some time on Earth and immerse yourself back into your normal routine prior to traveling with me. It would be a good reminder of your past. Everything is as it should be. V, take us to their house at the designated time."

"Acknowledged."

NOTE FROM
THE AUTHOR

I hope you enjoyed the fifth book in the Evaran Chronicles! Two of the most asked questions up to this point have been who is Evaran and where did he come from. This book is the definitive answer to both questions. The cosmological framework in which Evaran exists is complex, but I wanted to shine a spotlight on the highlights of it in this book. I also wanted to introduce the Time Wardens, one of the bigger threats to Evaran inside a plane. You have not seen the last of them yet! This book wraps up the first series arc, but there are more coming! If you liked the book, and have the time and inclination, a review would go a long way in helping out this indie author. If you do submit a review, I'll put in a word to Evaran should you find yourself stuck in a Time Warden siphon tank! Want to be notified about new book releases? If so, you can sign up below.

www.AdairHart.com/MailingList.aspx

I will only send you email about new book releases, major updates, and the occasional newsletter, usually once a month. I dislike getting spammed too, so I will use this sparingly to keep you in the loop.

ABOUT
THE AUTHOR

I have been dreaming about fictional worlds since I was a kid. I devoured anything related to fantasy and science fiction. I developed a setting over the last twenty years and struggled to find a medium I could express it in. Several years ago I discovered I enjoyed writing. It is a passion of mine now, and exploring my setting with it has been an awesome journey.

I work in the information technology field and have my bachelor's and master's degrees in it. It has helped me to shape some of the concepts I write about. I also enjoy keeping up on futurology and science in general.

I live in central Ohio and enjoy walking, reading, gaming, learning, listening to music, and trying to keep up on my never-ending list of TV shows and movies to watch. If you want to contact me, you can do so on my website at

www.AdairHart.com

YOU CAN ALSO REACH ME ON

Facebook............................fb.com/AdairHart
Goodreads.....www.goodreads.com/AdairHart
Email..............Adair.Hart.Author@gmail.com

DEDICATION

To my grandparents, who continue to inspire me.
Their impact on my life is immeasurable, and I am
thankful I had the chance to learn from them and
grow into who I am now.

ACKNOWLEDGMENTS

This was a great journey for me, but I wouldn't be here without the help of others. I would like to thank, in no particular order,

My awesome editor, Laura Petrella. Once again, she puts me on the right path, and I know that with her looking over my shoulder, everything will be okay. Her work ethic is impressive as always, and I enjoy our communication. This is my sixth book with her, and I am thrilled she is on this journey with me.

My cover artist, Tom Edwards (tomedwardsconcepts@ gmail.com), for another great cover. His ability to transform my mockups into art is a testament to his skill.

My family and friends who helped encourage me along the way.

My proofreaders, Graham, from Fading Street Publishing, and Alexa for providing a fantastic service. They were prompt, efficient, professional, and very easy to work with.

My formatter and interior designer, Colleen Sheehan (www.wdrbookdesign.com/), for making my interior pop.

She has been with me for the whole series, and it is always a joy to work with her.

My beta readers, Montzalee Wittman, Dennis Michaels, and Scott Ellenwood, for taking the time to help me make this book the best it could be.

BOOKS

You can see all books in the Evaran Chronicles series at

www.AdairHart.com/Books/Books.aspx